ADRIFT

BRIDGET E. BAKER

 Created with Vellum

For Jocelyn and Jesse

The only thing better than a sibling is a twin

PROLOGUE

When I was eight, my favorite cartoon featured a red-haired, arrow-slinging main character. Her best friend was a dashing black horse that she rode without even using a saddle. The wild-haired hoyden's defining feature was her in-your-face bravery. I wanted, badly, to be just like her. I wanted to spit in the face of fate when it outlined the life I would have as an orphan, when it tossed me into the home of an aunt who wanted nothing to do with me.

So when Aunt Trina told me I was lying about my dreams being real, when she told me to stop talking about Terra, I channeled my inner cartoon heroine. I insisted that I *wasn't* lying, and when she slapped me for my insubordination, instead of curling into a ball to protect my squishy parts like I had learned to do, I tried to kick her.

After all, a Scottish princess wouldn't have curled up to mitigate the damage—she'd have fought back. She'd have done something to dissuade her oppressor from any future torment.

I'm no Scottish princess, as it turns out.

My kick had the opposite effect that I intended. I took

the worst beating of my life that day, and it was the last time I faced something head on. I've tucked tail and run every day since.

And you know what? Running gets a bad rap. I think the media pushes a false narrative. Books and movies and even religious texts all teach the same thing: if you don't stand and fight against the evil of the world, you're making a huge mistake. . . and you're a coward.

The message is inspiring, sure.

It probably also feeds the delusion of a heroic inner self we all long to possess, the hope that deep down we're the person who will confront injustice and triumph. Like I did, we all secretly believe we're brave Scottish princesses who will take on the world.

But most people aren't like that.

I'm guessing that most of the writers sitting behind their keyboards, churning out these inspiring stories, would do the very same thing as me when faced with identical circumstances. Otherwise, they'd all be killed for their idiocy and we wouldn't have any inspiring stories at all.

Because sometimes, kicking someone three times your size just makes you an epic moron. Sometimes, poking a bear gets you mauled. I probably know that truth better than anyone.

Bottom line: running is a legitimate option that more people should consider.

I wish I'd insisted upon it. When Jesse encouraged me to stand tall, I should have thrown a bag over his head and dragged him onto the Greyhound bus, kicking and scream-ing. I didn't, and now he's dead. Or at least, Earth Jesse is gone. I ripped Terran Jesse out of the ether and slammed him onto Earth, but I'm not sure how well that worked.

Which is why, from now on, I'm not standing tall. I'm not standing at all. I'm running and hiding and crouching and sneaking away quietly from every single thing that comes at me—just like I learned at the age of eight.

Hey, maybe that tired old cliché really is true. Maybe you really *do* learn everything you need to know in kindergarten.

ERRA

I'm lying on my back, staring at the bluest sky I've ever seen.

Actually, that's a strange thought. I don't recall seeing any sky, other than this one, in the entirety of my life. I'm not sure how I know that the vast expanse of deep blue above me even *is* a sky. Or that the color I'm staring at *is* blue.

Something hisses behind me and I shove myself up into a seated position.

I promptly scramble backward like an awkward crab, covering the back of my jeans and the palms of my hands in sooty black ash. No longer distracted by the sky, I peer at my surroundings in horror. A sandy, barren wasteland stretches away from me for 180 degrees, and an enormous charcoal mountain looms directly ahead.

The hissing and spitting sound that first drew my attention recurs, but I'm facing the right way to see the cause this time. Lava erupts down the side of the mountain—*the volcano*—and oozes downward, streaming steadily toward me.

Where the heck am I?

Who am I? What's my name? I should have a name. I drop my face in my hands, probably smearing soot on my face, and the action seems familiar. As soon as I focus on the familiarity of the movement, any understanding evaporates. Why can't I recall who I am? Why don't I have any idea what I was doing yesterday, or where I was, or what brought me to this miserable point? I'm acutely aware that I *should* know these things—but I have no idea how to find answers.

I must have done something pretty bad to have been dumped here, wherever this is. It doesn't look like a place anyone would want to be. It's certainly not hospitable. I glance around for any kind of supplies or identification I might have brought with me and find nothing. Which means not only did I wind up here—I've done it with either no preparation or no support system in place. It feels like it might be a punishment.

Am I a bad person? I don't *feel* like a bad person, but wouldn't bad people think they were alright?

I force myself to my feet and begin to move away from the active volcano. I've heard—*where?*— that volcanoes that are currently erupting are erratic. Sometimes they hiss and spark. Sometimes they overflow much more quickly. That thought motivates me enough that I break into a jog. It doesn't take me long to realize something about myself.

I don't like to jog.

In fact, I don't think I'm in great physical shape.

Since I don't seem to be in any imminent danger, I slow to a walk, dragging the miserably dry, ashy air into my lungs. At first I moved away from the volcano, but there appears to be nothing in front of it other than sand dunes as far as I can see. Walking off into nothingness is even more nerve-wracking than standing near a live volcano.

At least the volcano's a landmark.

I shift directions to circle it instead, careful to give it a wide berth. I quickly realize as I make progress that, bizarrely, there's *another* volcano directly to the left of it. At least this one isn't spewing lava like the first, but why are there two? Where in the world am I?

Am I in purgatory? I have to consider the possibility.

It's hot. Check.

It's never-ending. Check.

I'm suffering. Check.

Technically, I'm not in agonizing pain, but maybe that's coming next. Goodie.

I keep walking, for a really, really long time. Then I walk more. The sun starts to set. My stomach growls with hunger. Turns out, it's not only jogging I don't like. It's also walking for long distances. And being hungry. Beyond the second volcano is. . . another friggin' volcano, even smaller than the second one. It's also black, the color of the igneous rock into which lava cools. Okay, how do I know any of this and still have no idea who or where I am?

When I move in closer to investigate, I discover a smooth pathway between the second and third volcanoes. It's flat, wide enough for about three people to stand shoulder to shoulder, and I'm gripped with a desperate desire to discover where it leads. With the sun setting, I better investigate now, or I'll have to wait for tomorrow. The prospect of lying down on a vast expanse of sand or a bed of black ash for the night isn't appealing. I start trotting down the path that I hope leads to someone or something friendly before I have time to second-guess myself. Even if whoever or whatever made this path doesn't welcome me, perhaps they can tell me who I am and what I'm doing here before they send me packing.

Small details pop out at me as I move away from the sand dunes, even in the dimmer light. Pebbles, not ash or loamy soil, line the walkway. Someone clearly carved the sides of the volcanoes to allow this path to continue. When

I look around, I see nothing but tall, sloping walls that reach up to the top of the volcanoes, and an empty path ahead of and behind me. But someone must have made it.

"Hello?" I call out. "Hello! Is anyone there?"

Once I start, I can't seem to stop myself from talking. The words pour out. "Where am I? Who made this pathway? Where does it lead? How did I get here?"

The spear misses my shoulder by less than an inch, slamming into the thick, porous rock at the base of the larger volcano hard enough to punch through the crust of rock and sink into the loamy soil beneath. I drop into a crouch and leap toward the wall on the same side from which the spear came, hoping they can't see me as well if I'm directly beneath them.

"I mean you no harm!"

Who's throwing spears? And from *where*? And why? I'm in between two volcanoes. The only place anyone could even be that I wouldn't have noticed is the rim of one of the volcanoes. . . so I look up. It hadn't occurred to me that there might be people standing on the top of a *volcano* for heaven's sake.

But there are. Dozens of people stand in a long line on the top of the third volcano, the smallest one.

I stand slowly, my arms raised and my palms clearly empty. "I don't know who you are or where I am. I'm not armed and I mean you no harm, I swear." I wonder whether they can understand me.

No one says a word, but at least they don't throw any more spears. I can't really see their faces, between the waning light and the angle—they're all kinds of backlit.

I consider grabbing the spear they tossed me, but that doesn't feel like something I'd do—and I doubt I could throw a pebble that would reach them where they are, much less a hefty wooden spear. And that's assuming I could even dislodge it.

I'm still contemplating what more I might say, or why they're standing up there staring at me, when lava erupts from the second volcano and spews toward me, large blobs of it flying right at me. I see it coming, but I'm not fast enough to avoid it. A large blob slaps into my leg, melting through my jeans and plowing onward. The agony as it melts my skin and muscle is beyond anything I can imagine —I *writhe*.

Fire. Flame. Unquenchable heat. My entire world narrows to that one place, the size of a pancake, that is melting through to my bone. And then the heat just. . . disappears. My leg gives out anyway, and I collapse on the ground. The now-cool black stone drops out of my leg wound and onto the ground, and I'm unable to look away from the smoking flesh of my ruined thigh. Something inside me snaps and the pain shuts off.

It's not gone, but it's contained. I'm not sure how or why, but I've locked it down. I'm still stuck on my knees, in between two volcanoes, with hostiles hovering above me. I can't fixate on the blob of lava or become insensible from my injury. For all I know, another attack is coming any moment. I need to stand up and get away. I need to hobble back the way I came. Endless sand is better than attacks and lava.

But even if the pulsing, incapacitating pain is gone, my leg doesn't work, no matter how much I try to force it to stiffen so I can shove to my feet. The pain was horrifying, but this. . . what I feel now is abject terror.

Something new clicks: I'll probably never walk again.

And I may be about to die.

In the middle of I don't know where, attacked by I don't know whom, for no reason I can comprehend. Maybe it's a mercy that I don't know. Maybe I really am a bad person. And at least, if I can die, this will end. I won't be stuck here forever, in a never-ending purgatory of confusion, boredom, and pain.

But even if I don't know who I am, or why I'm here, or where I am. . . I know I don't want to die.

The image of a dark-haired male smiling swims through my memory. The same man, but as a boy, laughing, his head back, his eyes narrowed. And then again, as a young child, handing me something, with a look of affection on his face. I don't know who he is, but suddenly, I just know.

I'm not evil. I don't deserve this—none of it. I shouldn't be here. And I need to get back to him, somehow. He needs me, and I need him. Because if I'm here, he's alone.

Someone loves me. That's all I needed to know to *fight*.

I crawl toward the spear, dragging my leg behind me. The stabbing pain radiates up my thigh with the jarring movement, but I freeze long enough to lock the agony away again. I can't let it stop me, or I'll die slowly here in the middle of some kind of nightmarish pathway to nowhere.

The second my hand closes around the base of the spear, the people above me start shouting. At first I can't quite understand them. I might be going into shock, or maybe my ears are taking a break while my body deals with the trauma. Either way, a moment later, their gibberish begins to make sense.

"—can't ignore it. What if she's Wind Called? Or if those "

"We're so far up—"

"You've been hiding too long. They can do—"

"I think she's listening to us." I blink at the backlight and try to make out the speaker who's paying attention to me. "Now I'm sure of it. She's looking right at me—she knows we're discussing her."

"I can hear you," I say, my brain somehow spitting out the same language they're using. "I mean you no harm."

"Who are you?" The same woman calls. Based on the timbre of her voice, she's older. She might be a grandma, but her voice is still hard. She clearly holds no sympathy in her heart for me.

"I don't remember. I was hoping you might tell me—"

"She shouldn't be here. We need to eliminate her."

My plan to grab the spear seems more pathetic than ever, since I'm still a few yards away. I grit my teeth and try to force myself to my feet again, imagining my bad leg is merely in a cast.

Bizarrely, it works. Flashes of light and blinky spots flicker in front of my eyes, but I shove to my feet anyway. "I'm not a threat, and I'm not an enemy. I'm not sure what this 'wind' called thing is, but I'm not that either."

"You said you don't know who you are." The older woman's voice sounds even flintier than before.

"I guess you're right, but if I don't *know* I'm 'wind called,' how could I pose a threat?"

The gathered people, whom I've come to realize are mostly women, murmur amongst themselves. After a moment, the older woman straightens again. "Why did you come to Volcano City, if you aren't Fire Called?"

"Volcano City?" There's a city somewhere? It must be where the path leads.

Before anyone replies, someone else crests the ridge of the volcano, someone much larger, with a broad, heavily muscled chest. I can't make out his features between the dim light and the fact that what light exists comes from behind him, but his arrival startles the women and they shift away from him.

That can't be a good sign.

"I told you to execute her."

"The lava didn't harm her," a figure I mistakenly took for a female says.

"What about the spear?"

The slender man's voice drops lower. "I missed."

The burly man grunts and grabs the younger one, yanking him backward. "You're worthless, Jackson. Report to Kent and tell him how miserably you failed at dispatching one lone traveler."

"In his defense, the lava spew did injure her leg." The woman points. "She can barely stand."

"I'm not a threat," I shout. "There's no need to execute anyone." My hands tremble, but I still them with a substantial effort. I'm not sure how much longer I can stand upright, but seeming competent feels important to my survival. "Do you have a healer? That's all I really need right now."

"I have to do everything myself." The disgust is plain in the man's voice. He clenches his fists and roars, and the mountain next to me rumbles.

I'm beginning to grasp that, somehow, these people of Volcano City. . . *control* the lava.

But thankfully, nothing happens, in spite of the rumbling. I finally exhale and shake my head. I need to calm down. People don't control volcanoes.

Maybe this is all a bizarre nightmare. Hopefully I'll wake up soon and remember who I am, and this will be hilarious.

A wave of heat rolls over me a split second before a huge cracking sound yanks my head toward the larger of the mountains. The same one that shot out blobs of lava before.

This time, nothing flies out.

Probably because inconsistent blobs like the last time might not kill me.

But the wave of lava that pours over the side and hurtles toward me—nothing can save me from this. The heat pouring off it—I may as well climb into an oven.

Idly, I wonder whether burning alive is quick, and how

badly it will hurt. Maybe it'll overwhelm my nerves. There are probably worse ways to die, but I can't think of a single one. I clench my fists, much as the burly man did, and I squeeze my eyes shut.

I can almost sense the magma as it flows toward me in a sheet of instant destruction. Justice and fear and anger and sorrow evaporate in the sweltering waves of instant death rolling toward me. And in that split second, I embrace it. Something deep inside me revels in it—the primordial force of it all. It's out of my control, what happens now. With my ravaged leg, I can't even try to outrun it. A single step would be a miracle.

I'm caught like a spitted rabbit.

So I open my eyes to face it with as much bravery as I can muster.

But in a reflex, in the moment before it incinerates my feet, I throw my hands outward, and some kind of inexplicable force flies out of me, sucking the heat into myself, and hurling it back toward the rock as something else.

What I watch makes no sense.

The lava was rolling toward me, and less than a foot away, somehow it instantly cools in place.

"Girl, what did you do?"

The man starts down the volcano toward me, and I remember the spear. I turn to see that it has been incinerated—the place where it stuck has disappeared under cooled lava that would have killed me if whatever happened hadn't happened.

The muscled man's running down the side of the smaller volcano now, and something gleams in his hand. Other men pour over the side of the volcano at the same time.

I can't catch a break today.

Do I deserve any of this? I reach, desperately, for any kind of memory, any kind of awareness of who I am and what I want. . . the waves of torment that crash over me suddenly eclipse my leg and the fear of death. I'm overcome with a tearing, ripping, screaming, *shredding* feeling of utter loss. The memory of that horror is right there—and I claw at it with everything I am.

What did I lose? I can't remember.

Why can't I remember anything?

The men rushing me are armed. Tears stream down my cheeks, and I'm not even sure why I'm crying. Am I that sad to die? Or is it something else? A profound belief that something terrible brought me here in the first place settles in my chest.

Was my trip here a suicide mission? That feels right in a strange way, like it's something I might do.

But when the large man gets closer, a long, gleaming sword clasped in his meaty hand, the same primal force inside of me reacts. I throw my hands wide again, and this time flames burst from my hands and shoot outward toward the sword-carrying maniac.

I expect him to shout or dodge or anything a normal person might do. Instead he freezes, his sword arm upraised, and the flames I expelled blink out around him, as if. . . as if he's somehow able to control fire.

"You're Fire Called," he says. "Why didn't you say so?"

"I didn't know."

He closes the space between us, but his sword is gone. Where did it go?

I blink once. Then again.

The world's going spotty. Something is definitely wrong.

My leg collapses and the world around me blessedly disappears, too.

❧ 2 ☙

EARTH

A string of curse words tumbles out of my mouth the second I wake.

The door to John's guest bedroom flies open. "Alora?"

I throw the blankets back to expose the melted mess of my leg. I'm still wearing the clothing I had on in that horrid place, which confirms my fear: it wasn't a dream.

Shining white bone gleams up at me in the center of seared flesh and charred skin.

Oh, the smell.

"What happened? It smells like barbecue."

I gag.

His eyes drop from my face to the rest of my body and his jaw drops. The choking sound he makes isn't very helpful, but it's almost comical. "Are you laughing?"

Tears roll down my face, and I'm not sure whether they're from pain or absurdity. "I'm not sure, but I think laughing is better than sobbing, maybe."

"How did this happen?" John races to my side and shoves the sheets and blankets away, blanching when he sees my injury.

"Clearly I miscalculated, thinking I'd be able to dream now. I got shuttled and dumped into some ghastly place called Volcano City."

John's hands freeze and when his eyes meet mine, they're wide and horrified. "No."

"Yes." Another wave of incapacitating pain rolls over me and I clamp down on my own tongue to keep from screaming like a ninny on a slasher film. I close my eyes and try to find the place inside myself that I found in volcano world—the place where I blocked the waves of agony that washed over me. I can't find it—so I try to distract myself instead. "I don't know how to explain the lousy place I went. There's sand, everywhere, and then these three black mountains that—"

"Three?"

I swallow. "What?"

"Three mountains?" He clears his throat. "Or is there a ring of them that circles the city?"

"I'm not an eagle," I practically shout. "I can't tell you how any of it looks from the air. I hiked around three of them for a while, and then one erupted and practically melted me into slag."

"You need a healer. Immediately." He straightens. "At least it appears that whatever burned you cauterized most of the blood vessels." He cringes.

"What aren't you telling me?"

"Nothing."

"Something. You asked me about the volcanoes, and instead of looking surprised, you looked pained."

"It's just that—between the burn and the mountains." He shrugs. "It sounds a little like the descriptions I've heard people give of Erra."

"Erra?" The word sounds familiar, but pain seems to be warping my ability to think, too. "What's that?" A moan escapes. Why can't I find that no-pain place here? It's too hard to focus.

"It's a prison world like Terra, but created to contain elementals instead of telekinetics."

"No, no, no. Surely—"

"They must be linked. When you unraveled Terra. . . "

"I got sucked into bloody frigging lava land."

"Actually, the volcanoes are a defensive—"

I clutch at the fabric of my pants that hadn't burned away around the wound and realize it had melted to the skin of my leg. "You need to call 911. I think I'm going into shock."

He pulls out his phone, but he's shaking his head. "We should call my dad's Healers—"

"No," I say. "No way." Another wave of pain crashes over me, and I sink back against the pillows.

"You need help this second."

"I need to figure out how I turned off the pain when I was on Erra." I grit my teeth. "That's what I need."

John frowns. "You did what?"

"When this first happened, I completely collapsed, but then I shut off any feeling from the injury so that I could still function. I just need to remember how I did that."

John's brow furrows. "Don't you think that might have something to do with you being the Warden? You don't know you're in charge of the whole thing, but the injury took place *there*. I almost wonder whether, if you knew, you could heal yourself on Erra, before you ever returned."

Which is a pointless consideration since I *don't* know who I am there, but it's an interesting thought.

"But my dad's in the family room right now," John says. "Since he knows you're here, we may as well make use of his resources."

"Absolutely not," I say.

"Why not? I don't get it. You brought him back, and he

wants to help. He's your biggest supporter, Alora. You passed out moments after you brought all those souls here, and I had to carry you into this room. What should I have done? Incinerated him?" His eyes dart down to my leg. "I'm sorry, but you need healing right this very second."

"Not one of his people," I insist.

"You can't go into a hospital like that. I may not be a doctor, but I know they can't repair *that*. If you rely on modern medicine, you'll never walk without a prosthetic again."

I had the same thought, back on Erra, when I didn't know who I was. "Who else can we call?" I can't be indebted to *Devlin*. I won't.

"I have a childhood friend who's a Healer we could call, but Alora, it's risky. He's with Isis."

Everything is risky. "For me, going to sleep is risky. Call him." I grit my teeth and pray under my breath that this random friend lives close. Otherwise, walking may be the last of my worries. I could go into multi-system organ failure and die.

His friend picks up right away, thankfully. "Oliver. I've got a 911. Like, it's bad."

He pauses.

"It's a two-person job. It would likely incapacitate you alone. Is there anyone you can trust? I'm calling in a major favor."

John's quiet again. I try to listen, but I can't focus long enough to do more than register that there's noise coming from the phone microphone. I lose time as waves of pain roll over me—John's standing in one place, and then in a blink, in another. Spots cover my vision, and I shake my head until they dissipate.

Finally, he hangs up.

"He's coming?" My voice is way too quiet, but I can't seem to make it louder.

John nods. "Should I wake Jesse? I'm sure he'd like to be in here with you."

That sounds too much like asking if Jesse wants to be here for my last minutes. I'm not about to die and abandon him, not for something this stupid. I shake my head and close my eyes. "If he's sleeping, let him." I inhale through my nose. I need to think about something else. "Did he know who you were?" I force my eyes back open, careful not to look at the open wound.

John shakes his head. "I told him I'm a friend of yours, and he calmed down."

Then the very last thing Jesse needs is to be woken so that he can stress over a new place, new people, and an injured sister. My heart breaks just a little bit thinking of how lost and confused he'll feel, and all the memories that are gone, but there will be time to process that later.

Right now, I need to stay awake and alert until John's friend comes.

It's the longest twenty minutes of my life. When I hear a tap at the door, I offer up a prayer of thanks to anyone who might be listening. "You'd better have your dad hide before you answer, if this guy's with Isis."

He nods and leaves. I hear murmurs and low voices, and then a tall man with a mop of curly hair flying every which way shoots through the door. Oliver's eyes widen when he sees my leg, just like John's did. He swears under his breath, but it's nothing I didn't say myself upon waking.

"I told you to bring someone with you."

"He's on his way," Oliver says. "But I don't think she should wait."

"No," John says. "But you'd have to take the entire injury on you until—who's coming?"

"Kevin." Oliver crosses the room in three steps and crouches near the bed. "When I Heal someone, I take roughly a quarter of the injury myself. If I wait, she's enduring the full damage." He looks up at John. "As a Healer, I won't wait. She's suffered enough."

John's brows draw together. If I wasn't in such miserable condition I might feel bad for him—he's a good person. He wants to spare me and Oliver any and all pain. "Maybe it's better this way, actually. The less Kevin knows, the better."

Oliver's lips tighten. "What am I missing? Obviously I don't need to know how this happened, but how is Healing someone dangerous for me? I'm a Healer—dealing with terrible injury is what I do."

John shakes his head. "The less you know, the better, trust me."

Oliver's hands drop gently to the edge of the wound, and I hiss involuntarily.

"I'm sorry," he says, "but it'll soon be over." An icy chill washes through me and then a pulling, tugging sensation I remember well. And then between one blink and the next, my leg is whole again, the smooth skin perfect where before, it was gone.

Magic.

My life used to be relatively normal, other than some odd dreams.

Now I'm being roasted by lava, Healed by people I don't know, and I'm throwing flames from my fingers. I could have used that trick a decade ago, actually. I bet Aunt Trina would have backed off double quick if I could've set her hair on fire.

Oliver doesn't cry out or even moan, but he does inhale sharply. And then he stands up slowly and with great effort and struggles backward toward John. "Last night, someone brought the Terrans all slamming back into our bodies here on Earth."

John nods. "I'm aware."

"You are."

"My dad informed me."

"They say it was a woman who just. . . collapsed the prison, like it was a video game or something. I don't remember a lot of details, but I saw a woman's face just before the world imploded."

John steps toward the door.

"She had very unique hazel eyes, high cheekbones, and a beauty spot just here." He brushes the spot just under the outside edge of his left eye. The exact spot where I have two dark brown, slightly imperfect moles.

"The less you know. . . " John tosses his head at the door.

"I just Healed the Warden, didn't I?"

John shrugs. "What if you did?"

Oliver swallows, his Adam's apple working in his throat. He runs one hand through his mop of curls. "I guess nothing."

"You're likely to hear more about this Warden in the coming days," John says. "I'd greatly appreciate it if you didn't mention any bizarre impressions or any guesses you may have for who or where she is."

Oliver spins toward me then. "Are you really Isis reborn? A lot of people are saying you are."

I have no idea how to respond to his bizarre question. I pull the sheets back over my leg, shifting so that the edge of my destroyed jeans doesn't stick and pull so badly, well aware that it's sticking because of the residue of my melted innards.

And this man just saved my life.

"I'm not Isis or anyone else." I meet his eyes. "I'm sorry if that disappoints you, but I'm just me."

"The prison was collapsing, for the record," John says. "She didn't have a choice."

"I believe you." Oliver breathes in slowly, and then he half-bows. "It was an honor meeting you. Thanks for saving our lives. I swear I won't divulge where I've been. I should leave right away, though, or Kevin will likely arrive before I can stop him. He's much, much more curious than I am."

"Gotcha," John says. "I'll—"

"Alora?" Jesse's standing in the doorway, rubbing his eyes. "Are you alright? I feel like I dreamt you were screaming."

Oliver spins and stumbles, probably forgetting about the injury he took from me until he tweaked it. "Who's this?"

"Actually." I slide out from under the blankets and stand slowly, but my leg doesn't even twinge. "Since you're here. I know you're injured already, so I hate to ask this of you, but I don't think there will be anything for you to do. Would you mind delving my brother for me? Jesse has made a long. . . journey lately. I just want to make sure he's alright."

To his credit, Oliver raises his eyebrows, but doesn't argue or object. "Alright."

He steps closer to Jesse, who doesn't seem concerned about a Healer checking him out. It's certainly something he experienced in Terra, so perhaps that's why. He crouches down so that Oliver can easily reach his head.

I circle so I can watch Oliver's face.

Before Oliver's hands touch my brother's head, John coughs. "Are we sure this is wise?"

I nod. "I need to know whether I harmed him."

Oliver's hands tremble, either because he's nervous or because he's in pain. I'm not sure which is worse. "You brought him here from Terra, but some part of the trip went wrong?"

That's the simplest explanation, even if it's not exactly the full one. "I did."

His hands lower the last few inches and make contact with my older brother's head. Oliver closes his eyes. It should be quick—then he can tell me that Jesse's fine, and I'll be able to rest much easier. Oliver holds on much longer than normal, and his brows draw together. He glances my way, his hands tight against Jesse's hair. "You brought him back just like this?"

I swallow. "Yes."

"How long ago?"

"Last night." A worm of unease wiggles its way down my spine.

"You must have done something wrong." He releases Jesse. "He's—I don't know how to describe it. It's like he has a hole. . . in, well, I'm not sure how to describe it."

He doesn't meet my eyes. Or Jesse's. He's staring at the floor.

My eyes lock with the dark, deep blue of my brother's. He looks unconcerned, but I'm sure I'm not nearly as calm. "Try harder to explain."

"He came back like everyone else?" He shakes his head. "You must have made some kind of mistake. Can you go back and fix it?"

The words are a dagger to my heart. More painfully shocking than a glob of lava landing on my thigh. "Are you sure? Maybe you delved him wrong." I examine Jesse from head to toe, and he looks fine, the same as always.

Oliver stumbles toward the door. "I can't help him. It's like. . . there's a leech attached to him, draining his energy. Or like he's spilling blood—but like, not real blood, soul-energy blood." He shudders. "I know that doesn't make sense, but I don't know how else to explain it." He looks me dead in the eye, his expression dire. "Whatever you did, undo it. Fast."

The trouble is, if I hadn't done what I did, Jesse wouldn't be here at all. I have no idea where that leaves us.

But I'm worried this isn't a problem I can solve by running away.

John bundles his friend off once it becomes clear there's nothing further he can do for either of us. Any guilt I'd have felt about his hobbling gait evaporated at his declaration that Jesse's not well. Maybe that's wretchedly ungrateful, but it's honest.

"What did you do?" My brother's voice is soft, but his eyes are full of admonishment.

"What do you remember?" I point at my bed.

He perches like a bird on the edge. "I was Wasting. And you were going to confront Devlin. . . Kahn was with us."

John steps into the doorway, leaning against the frame with a sigh. "Kahn."

Jesse's eyes widen and he glances back at John. "Who's that?"

"He's a friend," I say. "And you're on Earth, now."

My big brother frowns. "Earth."

"Terra was never real." I sigh. "It's a lot to take in, even for me, and I've been dreaming of Terra while living on Earth my entire life. Basically, you've always existed in both places, and you've been my brother in both places, but you didn't realize they both existed."

"And now I'm only here?" He blinks. "On Earth."

"The women sacrificed their power on Earth to create a spirit prison of sorts, which we called Terra."

"How can I understand what you're saying right now?" Jesse asks slowly. "You're not speaking Terran."

I switch to Terran without much thought. "John speaks English, and I spoke to you that way to see what you'd comprehend. The fact that you can speak English tells me that *my* Jesse, *Earth* Jesse is in there somewhere. When you were here, you spoke English."

"But I'm here now." His brows draw together.

I explain, as quickly as I can, what happened. Devlin, who happens to be John's father, killed Jesse on Earth to Wake me. He's one of the Followers of Amun, who wanted me, as the Warden, to collapse Terra. Devlin insisted it was the only way I could save the people who were trapped in the telekinetic prison world. He said they'd been slowly dying as it destabilized for more than a decade—since my birth, in fact.

"But why you?" Jesse asks. "Why can you Lift when all the other women can't? Why were you able to bring people back to Earth?"

"She's the Warden," a deep voice behind John says.

My head whips around, but Jesse's faster, leaping to his feet in a battle ready position. He casts around frantically for a weapon.

"I'm not your enemy here," Devlin says. "I wasn't actually your enemy anywhere."

"Forgive me for questioning you," Jesse says, his hands clenching, "but Alora says you killed me."

Devlin sighs. "I didn't know what else to do. We had tried every single thing I could think of, and in the balance of you versus the entire world, I still believe that I did the right thing. I'd do it again if it came to it."

Which is exactly what I'm worried about. I Lift Devlin

and let him dangle in the air. He puts up no resistance whatsoever.

"So you can Lift here, too?" Jesse asks.

I nod.

A lamp rises off the bedside table and floats across the room to bash Devlin in the head. He grimaces, but otherwise doesn't fight or complain.

"Looks like I can as well," Jesse says, his eyes still lit up. "Even better than I could on Terra."

"Easy, tiger," I say. "Let's be minimal until we figure out what exactly is wrong with you."

Jesse rolls his eyes. "I feel healthy—I think I'd know if I were actually leaking blood from my soul."

I'm glad he's not worried, but Oliver's words still ring in my ears. "How about, just for now, you let me handle the wham, bam, and slam?"

Jesse lifts one eyebrow. "What does that even mean? Did you slip into another language, one I don't know?"

John laughs. "He may not remember his interactions here, but he's picking up the snark again pretty quickly."

"Snark." Jesse rolls the word around slowly as he says it, as though he's evaluating it for meaning. "Sarcasm?"

"You speak English," Devlin says roughly, clearly just processing what that means.

I drop him to the ground and don't bother suppressing my smile as he crumples to the ground. "I haven't decided what to do with you yet, so maybe don't remind me how you killed my brother for a while."

He rubs his throat slowly.

"What do we do next?" Jesse says. "Who knows we're here?"

I glance at John.

He shakes his head. "I shut off my dad's cell so they can't track him, but if they pull data they'll see this is the last place he came."

"Which means they will trace us here as soon as things settle down enough for them to come looking." Fantastic.

"They know it's my son's house," Devlin says. "They'd have come out to check on him eventually. You're lucky they didn't come while your little friend was here. That would have gotten him killed outright."

"I'd have kept him safe," I say.

"I'm sure you would have," Devlin says, "but you'd be stuck dragging around another person. Is that really what you want? To accumulate a following of people whom you don't trust to leave your sight?"

"In addition to *you*, you mean?" I have a feeling I might need a Healer a lot more in the future, especially with Erra being what it is. I can't help thinking about what will happen tonight when I'm forced to go back.

Devlin frowns. "Why was he here? Just to check on Jesse?" He shakes his head. "You had to know he wouldn't be quite right. It seems like an unnecessary risk to bring someone from Isis to confirm something you already knew."

John widens his eyes at me, clearly asking what we should do with his father. He's too smart to keep around—he picks up on little things and extrapolates. "It was a mistake—"

Devlin shoves up to his feet again. "You need me. There are too many things you don't know—and Amun isn't your enemy."

"I don't know who I am—how can I know who my enemies really are?"

He sighs heavily. "You were dropped into another of the prison worlds, weren't you?"

"How could you possibly know that?" I plant a hand on my hip.

"It's logical," he says. "Think about it. There are four prisons, each of them holding a group of people based on their abilities. You broke the first, but the Warden should have the key to each."

I'm sick to death of people telling me what I should and shouldn't do and have and be. "There's no way--"

"I bet John called that boy to Heal you—let me guess. You're not accepted there either."

I swallow. How does he figure all this out? Or maybe it's only so confusing to me because I know so little of Amun and Isis and the prison worlds in general.

"You're the Warden. Did you think it was a coincidence that you could unravel the prison of Terra and use the power from that miraculous and massive spell to save your dead brother?"

"Dad," John says. "Enough. You're not helping."

"Actually," I say, "as much as I hate to admit it, what he's saying is true. I don't know who I am. I don't know who my enemies really are. I've got a father who abandoned me and a mother I assume died years ago, since she Wasted on Terra. And a whole superpowered cult of followers who are very likely gunning to take me out." I fall back onto the edge of the rumpled bed. "And when I close my eyes for too long, I'm dumped into a barren volcanic wasteland, which is full of spear- and fire-throwing lunatics who mostly also want me dead."

"The Fire Called." Devlin's eyes widen and he meets John's gaze.

"There are no coincidences," John says.

Devlin shakes his head.

"What does that mean?" Jesse asks.

"I'm Fire Called," John says.

Jesse beams. "Finally, a break. You can keep her safe."

"I don't remember anything about my Earth life while I'm there," John says. "Which means I have no idea how I'll react to Alora's presence."

My big brother blinks. "This whole thing is confusing, and really hard to believe."

"Tell me about it." I need some time to think—but we need to get out of here pronto. "John, can you keep your dad under control while I take a shower, or should I truss him up?"

Devlin rolls his eyes. "Eventually you'll see that I'm on your side. I don't need to be trussed *or* controlled."

I leap from the bed and stalk toward him. "Is that so? Well, with friends like you, I really don't need enemies, do I?"

"I'm still terribly sorry about how badly I hurt you," he says. "And if there were any other way—I'm sorry." He shoves his hands in the pockets of his very rumpled slacks. "But now that you're here, and so is Jesse, and you've dismantled Terra, you ought to consider that the resources I command are at your disposal."

"I heard you're only in charge of the telekinetic branch," I say, "which means you have a boss."

Devlin rolls his eyes. "I have three partners, and the four of us constitute the Regents of Amun."

"Why not call yourselves kings?" I shrug. "I mean, who would that offend? Isis?"

"Regents rule on behalf of a king or queen who is currently unable." Devlin crosses his arms. "If you'll trust me long enough to learn a little something, I can show you a lot of fascinating and illuminating records."

"I'm pretty good at Googling," I say.

Devlin laughs. "You'll get a truckload of confusing stories, most of them the bastardized versions of stories that Isis spread after Amun-Ra was put to sleep. You always need to consider the source when you're doing your research."

"We're back to Isis and Amun again?" I roll my eyes. "Do you really think that ancient Egyptian gods are at the center of all this? Do you really think some Big Bad is trying to come back and take over the world?"

"I do," Devin says. "I believe exactly that, except I don't think he's a 'big bad' as you say. I think he's the one who will restore order and save us from ourselves."

"I'm going to shower," I say. "Roast him if he moves."

John's expression is flat, but he doesn't stop me.

When I come out, entirely Healed and finally, blessedly clean, I think about the bizarre world I'm living in right now. When I sleep, I pop into a world even stranger and more hostile than Terra ever was. Some old Egyptian gods that have apparently been in a time-out for thousands of years are possibly returning, and I'm connected to all of it somehow.

That's the strangest part.

I know *myself* at a baseline. What could any of this have to do with me without my knowing about it?

"We need to leave quickly," John says. "The question is —do we take him with us?" He's holding two bags, and he drops them by the door.

"Don't take this the wrong way," I say. "But I don't want your dad around for a second longer than is strictly necessary."

"You need me." The smug smile on Devlin's face infuriates me.

"If what you're saying is true and there are ancient gods at work, then how could a man who's only a few decades older than I am possibly help?"

"The records at our headquarters—"

I Bind Devlin in place in the armchair, securing his wrists, his ankles, and his waist a little tighter than necessary. "Musty scrolls? Scribbles carved into metal plates?" I step toward him, and I won't lie to myself—it feels really good to be the one in control after so many years of running and hiding. "After all this time, why should I trust anything you show me? The world's chock full of scholars, and all of them can tell me their thoughts on Egyptology. I've spent a decent amount of time researching things— I've even been to see a few artifacts when they rotated through the Houston Museum of Natural Science."

"You're still studying the records left behind *after* the prison was constructed, and history is written by—"

"By the winners—I know."

He shakes his head. "By the people who are *Awake* to write it. When he awakens, you'll understand, but it may be too late by then."

Oh, please. "Let's go." John picks up the bags and Jesse and I walk toward the door to the garage.

"You may not trust me, but what if you found out there was someone who you could talk to who was around when that prison was constructed? What if I could put you in contact with a person who will have the direct answers you need? He might even be able to tell you who you really are and why you can dismantle the prison."

"May. What if. Might." I clench my fists. "I'm sick of people teasing and tempting and taunting me with hypothetical, conditional things. What I know is that I don't trust you, not for a moment."

"His name is Mehen, in Egyptian. Legend holds that he was a 'serpent' god who wrapped himself around Ra to keep him safe from attacks by Apophis, Amun-Ra's greatest opponent."

"I thought that was Isis?" I cock one eyebrow.

"Isis and Apophis worked together," Devlin says. "And if you study the records, you'll see that Mehen is mentioned over and over."

I've seen the name—Devlin's not lying about there being a Mehen affiliated with Ra—but what does that prove? I could pick any name I wanted from the Egyptian pantheon and make any claim I could concoct. "Well, that information changes everything." I spin on my heel. "Why don't you have him call me, and then I promise that I'll put in a good word for you with Isis when we get together for brunch next week, okay?"

"I'm not—"

It takes every bit of my self-control not to Bind a gag in his mouth or better yet, choke him. "My life isn't a joke." I step closer still, until I'm staring down at him. I wish he looked terrified, but he only looks sad. "How about this? You have Mehen call me when he wakes up, and if he can tell me anything helpful about this terrifying Amun, then I'll get him a signed headshot from Hathor or maybe Seth. Deal?"

"I know it sounds insane. Believe me, I get it. But that's what convinced me. It's the reason for mummies all over the world. It's the reason I was willing to kill your brother. The perfectly preserved body of Mehen—breathing, alive, in some kind of preserved state, it's what made a true believer out of me."

"He's. . . just lying there? Alive, but unmoving?" I put a hand on my hip.

"The Followers of Amun have a number of. . . mummies, for lack of a better word, but they aren't mummies, not really. Mummies are the carefully preserved and wrapped remains of dead humans." He pauses. "These are all alive."

In spite of myself, I want to know more. "There are hundreds, no, thousands of people alive in hospitals all over the place on ventilators and whatnot—what makes these people special?"

"We've been clipping their nails and trimming their hair for years—and no one feeds them, and they don't drink anything either. There has been no medical intervention whatsoever for any of them at any point, and yet, they're alive, and perfectly healthy looking."

Oh, come on. "You expect me to believe—"

"I don't expect you to believe me without evidence," he says. "I didn't believe it until I saw it for myself. The Followers of Amun were tasked to care for Ra's lieutenants when he disappeared, and we've done it for all these years. But we've done nothing to keep them alive—Ra does that himself. I swore an oath never to share any information about them with anyone—they'll kill me if they discover I violated that oath."

"Why did you?"

"Because each lieutenant was marked, and Mehen's tomb says he was telekinetic."

Which is why Devlin thinks he'll be awake now. Because I dismantled Terra. "He was stuck there for thousands of years?"

"Which means he's likely to know why you're the Warden. He could tell you who you really are."

"You said that he has something to do with mummies."

"We believe that the practice of wrapping the deceased pharaohs in Egypt initially sprang from a desire to keep the existence of these lieutenants secret and therefore safe."

This gets more and more ridiculous. "I'm sure it had nothing to do with preserving the bodies of the dead."

He frowns. "I don't mean the embalming. I mean the wrapping of the corpses in so many layers of fabric so that no one would realize that some of them *weren't* dead."

"It's not like there's a way for me to really verify this without simply surrendering to you," I say. "I'm not friends with anyone from the Smithsonian, and internet searches aren't very reliable."

Devlin laughs. "The Smithsonian."

"Where do you have them, then?"

"They've always been privately maintained," Devlin says. "The historians of our day, the ones not affiliated with the Followers of Amun, know nothing. That's why meeting one of Ra's commanders is the only way you'll get answers."

"I could contact the Followers of Isis," I say, without much conviction. Nothing I've heard has inspired much confidence. And thanks to our meeting with Oliver, they may already know I'm alive and where I'm located.

"I'd make doubly sure I knew which contingent I was reaching out to before I did anything like that."

"What does that mean?" John asks.

"They're split, as you likely already know, and I imagine the divide has only deepened after the events of the past few days." Devlin grunts, and I realize he can't do much else.

He hasn't made a move against me since that night—since I Awoke. It pains me to show him any sort of kindness, but I release him. "I think you'd better explain. Quickly."

"All of the Followers of Isis favor the ongoing existence of Terra. They want the prison to stay and they'll surely want the portions that you have collapsed to be rebuilt, but their position on the Warden is not uniform. Half of the Followers of Isis think you're some kind of safecracker Amun-Ra has managed to liberate. They believe you're essentially a demon sent to free him from prison. They're obviously the contingent that wants you dead."

"And the other half?"

"They'll protect your life with everything they've got at their disposal, because they believe you're Isis herself— which means they believe that the reason you can dismantle the prison is that *you created it in the first place*."

My jaw drops. "That's absurd."

"I don't understand much more than you do," Devlin admits, "but I think if you'll trust me, I can get you some answers. I owe you that, at least."

No matter how tempting his offer, no matter how badly

I want to know the truth of who I am and why I can do the bizarre things I can do. . .

"I'm sorry." I clear my throat. "Actually, I'm not sorry. I won't go back with you, not even with all the answers I desperately want dangled in front of my face like a big, fat carrot. I just don't trust you."

Neither Jesse nor John argues with me when I Bind him back in place and walk out the door.

I hope they're right to place that kind of faith in my judgment, because I'm not at all sure of my judgment where Devlin is concerned.

❧ 4 ❧

EARTH

"You need a new car," I complain, the second John frees me.

"I offered to ride in the trunk," Jesse says. "You should have let me. That didn't look comfortable."

"I would have been fine for five or ten minutes," I say. "But how long was I stuck in there?" I massage my neck grumpily.

"I went as fast as I could," John says.

Jesse's almost green. His first time in a car, and he was stuck in a sports car with John racing to reach our destination quickly.

"I know you wanted to be the one in there, with Jesse sick, and with Oliver recognizing your face, but. . . " John offers me his hand to help me climb out of his tiny trunk. "I spent the entire drive worried that you were melting in there."

That reminds me to mop my forehead with my sleeve. "Not my first Houston summer," I mutter. "At least now that it's late September, it's cooled down some from July and August highs." It's above eighty degrees even now, but the breeze on my neck makes a huge difference.

"Grandma has an old farm truck she keeps here. We'll use it from now on." John's tone couldn't be more apologetic. It's not his fault we have one more person than he was prepared to transport, but I'd rather not repeat the ride we just made anytime soon.

I blink and glance around at my surroundings now that my eyes have adjusted to the bright light of late morning. "Where are we, exactly?"

"A rural Houston suburb called Fulshear."

"You're sure you trust your grandmother?" Jesse tilts his head, and I try to see the enormous barn from his point of view. He and I were always city dwellers on Earth, but since he's accustomed to Terra, this must be an even sharper departure from the norm.

"There aren't many people in this world I do trust," John says. "But Grandma Jean is one of them."

"Is it safe to stay here?" Jesse scrunches his nose, and I'm reminded that he has spent his entire life living in a castle. Surrounded by servants. "It looks like it would be full of rodents."

I laugh. "We've stayed in way rougher places than this, J," I say. "Trust me on that one."

"It's actually much nicer inside than it looks. We've let the outside go on purpose," John says. "Most people don't bother looking past a shabby exterior."

"I can see why." Jesse's shoulders slump.

I hope it's because of the clumps of weeds sprouting through the bumpy pavement of the driveway, or the rust patches that decorate the corrugated metal siding of the enormous sky blue barn. Because if his soul really is leaking energy, that's a much tougher problem to solve than helping him grow accustomed to the lack of glamour in our Earth life.

"Let me park the car in the shed and then we'll all go inside." John ducks back into his red sports car and revs the engine, zipping a little too fast across the potholes and craters and around the corner to a shed. But I don't even have a driver's license, so I'm not about to criticize his driving. At least his ostentatious sports car is out of sight in the ramshackle outbuilding.

"You really trust this guy?" Jesse asks softly.

I didn't realize until just now that it's our first moment alone since I tore him away from Terra and brought him here.

"I do," I say. "Completely, actually. Our interests may not always align, but I believe he'll respect my wishes enough to let me know when they don't. I think, in spite of his father, in his heart, he's a good person."

"I didn't think you'd be able to save me," Jesse says, his eyes wide. "No one stops the Wasting."

I swallow. "I'm not sure that I have, J."

"Is that what you call me here?"

My heart breaks then. I saved him, for now, but not all of him. A sob wracks my body—I'm involuntarily mourning the brother who's gone. The one person who truly understood me, who knew me—everything about me. Nothing will ever bring him back—Devlin took that from me. Even if he won't acknowledge what he has cost me, it's right there, a mirage stretching before me. The life I should have had, would have had, if he hadn't stolen it.

Jesse's arms wrap around me, more muscular than Earth Jesse's were, but also, the same. My heart expands, the cracks and fissures healing just a bit. "I'm sorry I don't remember. I'm sorry I'm leaking soul energy. And I'm sorry you've had to do everything alone. I would do it all for you, if I could."

"I know," I say. "I know you would."

"I'm not sure I'd have been able to save you if our situations were reversed." His cheek presses against my hair. "I know I haven't known you that long yet, but I knew about you all along, and I loved my memory of you, even when you were with the Healers. If you died right now—" He chokes. "I might curl up and die too."

I know just how he feels. "But you're discounting the rage," I say. "It overwhelmed the sorrow." It still does, sometimes.

"I know that I'm not quite right," he says. "I know I'm not really *him*, not here, and I know we're busy and you have a lot to do, but when you have time, I want you to tell me everything. If you tell me all the things you wish I remembered, I'll do my best to remember them."

It's exactly what Jesse would have said, in exactly the way he would have said it. Maybe the memories don't matter so much as the soul. The kid who pulled me down the hill on my skateboard with his bike, the kid who picked the blueberries out of my muffins, and the kid who tossed M&Ms in the air and caught them in his mouth—that kid may be gone, but the parts that really mattered—they're the same. Which means we'll make new memories that will matter just as much.

If we have enough time to make them.

"Do you two need a minute?" John asks. "I can head inside and you can join me whenever."

Sweat's trickling down my back. I let Jesse go and step back. "We're fine. We can have our moment inside just as well—please tell me it's air conditioned."

John laughs. "It's Houston. I wouldn't even consider a place without an AC."

"It *is* hot here," Jesse says.

"Yeah, if I really am Isis, I did a better job on the climate in Terra, right?" I shake my head. "I think I took all the extra heat and jammed it into Erra instead."

John unlocks the front door. "From what I hear, it's just the domain of the Fire Called that is so unbearably hot, and it's better inside Volcano City than out. The

Wind, Ice, and Earth Called all have much nicer home bases."

"They have four different nations?"

John bobs his head. "It's a lot bigger than Terra was. The number of Fire Called alone is close to the number of Lifters and Healers who lived on Terra—two hundred to three hundred thousand, according to Amun's estimates, spread between two different settlements. I live in Volcano City, but only because my mother defected. I wish she hadn't. I hear the Followers of Isis are much nicer—more Zen and less flamey. Their settlement's called the River of Flame, and it's supposedly circled by a lava fed river."

"Your mom defected?" My eyebrows shoot upward. "Like a Russian spy, or something? Are you serious?"

"I only know what Mom told me here on Earth. Apparently on Erra, she had a change of faith or something and decided she needed to join the group that was more proactive." John opens the door and steps inside. Jesse and I follow quickly on his heels. The cool air is like a balm on my skin, and I'm momentarily distracted by the comfortable interior of the ratty old barn.

"It's beautiful inside," Jesse says.

John smiles. "Grandma Jean loves camouflage. She says it's nature's best idea."

That explains why the outside doesn't match the inside. The ceilings are high—huge, dark-stained oak beams meet in the center with wooden paneling between each that has been whitewashed. Enormous iron light fixtures dangle above a spacious great room and a wide, wood-floored dining room. The furniture matches the rustic formal decor perfectly—rough grains and rich hues in every direction, and they all blend a variety of textures. Chunky, knit ivory blankets. A dark, reclaimed wood entertainment center with intentional knots and seams. Large, loose linen window coverings in sky blue filtering the morning light. And pristine white marble countertops in the kitchen.

"How did your brilliant grandma feel about your mom's defection?" I ask.

John drops the two bags he brought next to the large leather sofa. "They never really talked to me about what happened on Erra. Nothing they think here impacts their decisions—I only know grandma didn't go with Mom because Dad mentioned it."

"The people are split into followers of Isis and Amun on Erra, too?" Jesse asks.

"I can't speak to all the prison worlds, but from what I understand, the initial philosophical division that necessitated the creation of the prison continued thereafter. No one really knows whether the people dumped into the worlds initially retained their memories. There was a lot of speculation on that in my Erran history classes."

"You had classes?" Jesse looks excited at the idea.

"Some people study religious doctrine or philosophy. If you're Awake and your parents have joined either Isis or Amun, you study their belief set."

Lately, it feels like I'm constantly drowning in new knowledge. I suppose that's the point of taking those classes in the first place. "You said the Fire Called are more calm and less angry in the Isis settlement?" Too bad I didn't appear there. Maybe I wouldn't have been roasted right off.

John drops onto the corner of a dark brown sofa. "Fire called have hot tempers, naturally. On Earth, we slap them with labels like 'anger issues' or 'impulse control deficiencies.' But Amun embraces those impulses and wages war constantly. They feel the only way to bring peace is to subjugate the other disciplines so that they have one leader. The Isis segment, I hear, believes it's their job to overcome those impulses so they can live peacefully."

"Do they peacefully coexist with the other elements, then?" Jesse asks.

John laughs. "I don't think so, but I suppose it's possible. I wish I had any recollection of my time there—I'm sure I could answer these questions better than I'm able to now, based only upon what the female dreamers have shared. Honestly, I didn't pay the best attention at the time. I didn't see how the ins and outs of a world I never saw would matter in my life."

Spoken like someone who always had access to answers. "If the Fire Called are hot-heads, what about the Wind, or Ice, or Earth?"

John smiles. "If I could go back to my place, I'd whip out my old Erran textbook for you. A lady named Cassie Mi wrote it, and she was thorough. Basically the Wind called are tempestuous, changing their minds and tempers quickly and unpredictably. They're not necessarily happy or sad, angry or patient. . . they're capricious. Their moods and plans and desires change often."

I've known people like that. "And those Called to Earth?"

"They're not quick to make any decisions. They want things to be safe, predictable, and planned. And they love growing things--gardens, trees, orchards. They're the kind of people that 'need to hike or be outside.' They often leave their corporate jobs to join some kind of commune on Earth."

I laugh. "And Ice?"

"That one's easy. They're condescending, cool under pressure, and they know better than everyone else."

"Careful, your bias is showing," I say. "Even if you don't dream of Erra, it's clear you hate them."

"I've met a lot of other elementals who are Awake, and the Ice ones are always the most annoying, hands down, but they're also the most likely to become surgeons or ER doctors. I don't hate them, exactly. I just don't understand them. They're cool under pressure. They don't get ruffled easily. They're smart, usually to the point of being intellectual bullies, but if you do manage to upset them, they burn as hot as the Fire Called."

"It's hard for me to process that every single person on Earth is trapped in one of these prisons. The structure must have grown in size dramatically over the years." Trust Jesse to point out things I haven't even considered.

John says, "I was taught that since the prison pulls its power from all the women it houses, robbing them of their abilities, it's self-sustaining."

"Which begs the question of why it's unraveling." And what I could possibly do about it.

"How many people are we talking, here?" Jesse asks.

Another good question. I try to imagine anything beyond Volcano City, and come up blank.

"The Earth Called settlements boast close to thirty million by Amun's latest projections. Ice is almost as big. Wind's the smallest, other than Fire, with only a million people, I think."

I blink. "There were only three hundred thousand people on Terra, but there are more than *sixty million* on Erra?" Ferrying those people to safety taxed me to the limit. I'm not even sure I can save everyone from Erra, if it comes to that.

"If you think Erra is big, wait until you reach Rra. The majority of people on Earth are Reapers—shifters who consume plant life. Think, were-rabbits, were-mice, were-squirrels, or were-fish. There are also a few million Renders, of course, to keep populations reasonable. Rra is absolutely massive. I imagine most of the energy of the creation of Terra went into fashioning Rra alone."

I can't even begin to imagine Earth as a place where

everyone can shift into animal or marine life. The entire world would be a foreign place.

"What?"

"I've known about Terra my entire life, but sometimes I still struggle with the thought that there are—were—four linked prisons—and that somehow everyone assumes that I was involved in some aspect of creating it. Maybe it freaks me out so much because it means the world around me, the place I've always known, is a big fat lie."

"It's not like everyone is powerful enough to completely transform," John says. "If that helps."

"I don't understand most of what you just said," Jesse says.

We walk through the things he doesn't get—having missed the conversations about most of it, including what I know of the prison worlds, Terra, Erra, Rra, and Ā.

"The shifters, apparently, can't all shift," I say. "That's what I was curious about."

"It's like any of the other powers," John says. "Let's say the most powerful Renders—those who tear the flesh of other animals—are the alphas. They can control the others, even influencing their thoughts and desires. But then there are less powerful alphas, and omegas who can only calm others, and there are the regular shifters. Lots of people can't quite manage to shift into their animal forms. Maybe they can take on fangs or a tail, or even ears, but they remain mostly human."

"You're saying that, like some people on Terra might only have been able to Lift a pebble, there are people who can literally only give themselves. . . a rabbit tail?" The corner of Jesse's mouth quirks up. "I'm glad I was born on Terra, and not on Rra."

"To be clear, you were born on Terra *because* of the powers you had, not the other way around."

Jesse frowns. "Right. I was born on Terra—which was

itself a prison—because I had telekinetic powers here, on Earth." He blinks. "It's hard to remember that the only world I remember is the fake one."

"I just can't wrap my head around the idea that I might have *created* this whole bizarre thing," I say. "It's like a governor on a kids' four wheeler, or something, right? The whole thing was set up to eliminate our powers on Earth before Amun developed a workaround, and minimize them on Terra, right?"

"So you believed Dad?" John's eyes are earnest.

I shrug. "About my involvement being likely? It makes sense. I wish it didn't, but why would I hold the key to any of it if I didn't have something to do with it at some point?"

"Or maybe your ancestors did," Jesse says.

"Sure," I say. "Maybe so."

"Here's what bothers me," John says. "If you were born as a newborn, then why would there be people who are basically preserved mummies? Who are *they* and why weren't they swept into Terra?"

"I assumed they were snatched in there when it was first created," Jesse says. "If they're constantly asleep here on Earth, it seems like a sort of hibernation, for lack of a better word. Do bears and whatnot hibernate on Earth?" Jesse's forehead wrinkles as his eyes widen.

He knows nothing about Earth—it makes me sad every time I think about it. "They do, yeah."

"You get what I'm saying then. It could be that these guys, if Devlin is being truthful, had their essence trapped in Terra, or Erra, or Rra, whatever, but as those prisons collapse, their energy returns to their awaiting bodies."

"Ready to serve whomever left them in some kind of stasis on Earth," I say.

"Presumably Ra," John says.

"I won't sleep very well tonight," I admit, "knowing that

one of Ra's goonies is likely awake and walking around doing whatever wicked thing he was tasked to do."

"So we're assuming Ra is evil?" John asks.

"He was shut in a prison," Jesse says.

"But he wasn't killed." John shifts on the sofa, stretching out his legs.

"Maybe they couldn't kill him." My thought isn't a comforting one. "Or perhaps it's crumbling because he's served his time."

"Wishful thinking," Jesse says.

"Probably," I say. "How often do people who claim to be gods turn out to be the good guy?"

"What if he *is* a god?" John asks.

No one knows what to say to that. The idea of a god being stuck in a prison isn't reassuring either. I doubt he'll be pleased with anyone affiliated with the entire project if or when he escapes.

And certainly not the woman holding the key.

Although. I am the one letting him out, sort of. Maybe I shouldn't be. I wish I knew anything about what's going on for sure.

"What's our next step?" I ask.

"This is small," John says, "but I need to retrieve the contacts from my phone so that I can make a list we can use with our new burners."

"At some point, I'll have to figure out whether to trust Isis or Amun," I say. "I mean, they don't believe the same things, but both of them have more information than me."

"I vote for Amun," Jesse says.

My eyes widen. "You do?"

"Half of Isis wants to kill you." Jesse sits in a large suede armchair. "And the other half thinks you're Isis reborn. If that turns out not to be true, they may switch goals."

"I have to agree with him," John says. "I'm really wishing I hadn't contacted my friend Oliver."

"You think I should trust your dad?" I sink into the other side of the dark, shiny leather sofa in the great room.

"I think we don't have a better option," John says. "Although I'd never trust him entirely, in this case, I think Dad wants you alive. I believe that Amun's main goal is to free all the people stuck in Erra. And then Rra and Ā, of course."

"But is that what I *should* be doing?" I shake my head. "I need more information."

"Then we use them to get it." John sits next to me. "And then you do what *you* think needs to be done."

"Do you believe there's really a zombie guy who has been frozen in time for thousands of years?" I lean back and close my eyes. "Every time I think I've figured out most of the weird things that exist in this world, something new and even more unbelievable shows up."

"To be fair, he's a mummy, not a zombie." When I open my eyes, John's smiling. "I know it's not a huge distinction, but I've always thought mummies made more sense than zombies."

I glance at my watch. "It's already lunchtime."

"You're hungry?" John stands up and walks toward the kitchen.

I shake my head. "I mean, I should probably eat, but my point was that before too long. . . "

"You'll have to go back to sleep." John's brow furrows.

"And you don't want to," Jesse says.

I describe a few things from last night, like the confusion, and the walking. . . and the wanting to die.

"I don't blame you," Jesse says. "Erra sounds terrible."

"At least on Terra, I was born there. I had a family and a place. People knew who I was—I knew who I was. But on Erra, I was just dumped there. I don't know what I can do, or even my own name. Plus I don't know a single person."

"But John's there, right?" Jesse frowns.

"It's bizarre she was dropped outside the exact Fire Called location where I am—unfortunately, I won't know her there." John crosses his arms. "I wish there was some way to pass a message. . . to myself."

"I could carve or burn one into my arm again," I say.

"That only worked because Jesse was there and he was in danger," John says. "Don't you think?"

I sigh. "I'm not sure what else to do. We should try to figure out whether Erra has been unraveling too, like Terra was. Maybe we have years yet before I need to do anything at all, other than survive." Jesse may not have years to wait if he's 'leaking' like Oliver said.

He's probably buying himself time to think, but John busies himself making us lunch in the kitchen. He drops bowls on the counter and waves us over.

"What is this?" I ask.

"Orange chicken and fried rice," he says. "It's not gourmet, but it's not bad. We keep the freezer stocked with basic frozen meals. Grandma Jean and I aren't here much— it's more of a safe house—so there's no fresh stuff of any kind."

"Smells great," Jesse says.

While we both shovel food, John pulls up his laptop and starts clacking away at the keys.

"You're not going to do anything that will let anyone know we're here, right?" I ask.

Jesse glances from John to me and back again. "What could he be telling anyone with that little box?"

"It's a computer." Another wave of sadness overcomes me. Jesse should be explaining this to me. "He's using it as a data interface and some people can track information on there, and things like location too, from a thing called the internet."

"Not many people are as tech savvy as me," John says. "Jesse was close, before." He swallows. "But you still weren't quite at my level. No one will find us because of me."

"I was good at using the box?"

"You were," I say. "In fact, you handled pretty much everything that had to do with computers. We even shared an email account."

"Do you need to check that?" John asks.

I shrug. "Doubtful."

"If you do, now's the time. After this, we ought to shut it down. It's one more thing they'll use to trace us."

I nod, and he swivels the machine in my direction. I log in to our joint account, profoundly sad at the thought that Jesse couldn't even do this himself, not anymore.

Amid the piles of promotional messages and spam, I do have one email that I don't expect.

From Henry.

I do my best to keep my hand steady and my face calm as I click on it.

Alora:

I don't know whether you'll get this message. I'm not even sure what to say. I just want you to know that I'm sorry. I liked you from the very first day we met, and I had no idea who you were or anything about you. I just liked you. And then when you were in trouble—when they fired you, I wanted to help. I guess I wanted to be the knight in shining armor who got to save the girl who was way better than him but didn't know it.

Only, when you really needed me—when you were in true danger, I let you down.

I'm sorry that when it came down to it, I wasn't who you needed me to be. I swear, if you give me another chance, I'll do better. I'm not delusional. I know you're not into me like I was with you, but I also figure things might be hard for you. And I want to tell you that whatever you need, I'll do it.

Anyhow, I don't expect to hear from you, but if you ever need to reach me, no one knows about this email. Plus, I went ahead and bought a burner phone. I'll include the number at the bottom. I'll keep it with me, just in case there's ever something I can do, some way for me to make it up to you.

With regrets,

Henry

"Is something wrong?" Jesse asks. "You look really sad."

I swallow, and relax my face. "No, I just missed the Gap's semi-annual sale." I snap my fingers. "Bad timing."

John's looking at me funny. Not buying that, I guess.

"I got an email from Henry," I say. "And the thing is, he says all the right things."

"Wait, Henry. . . the same one from Terra?" Jesse asks. "Was he part of the Unit?"

"He got bumped when I beat him in the Ascension, yeah." I nod. "Same Henry. Only, I also worked with him."

"And you went on a date or two with him," John says.

"You did?" Jesse's eyes widen. "On Earth, you mean? Because on Terra, I swear, the only person you ever looked at dreamily was Kahn."

John grunts.

This is getting awkward super fast. "It's not like I have to do anything. In the email he gives me an email address and phone number. Maybe we write them down just in case, and then I delete it."

"It could be a trap," John says. "When was it sent?"

I check the time stamp. "Early this morning."

John shrugs. "He's with Isis. I'm sure they're using anyone they can to find you. Henry would be their biggest lead."

I hate the thought that he might have sent me that heartfelt message. . . to lure me out of hiding. So that Isis could bag and tag me. But I can't rule out the possibility. I write his number and email down on a notepad John slides over to me anyway, but I doubt I'll ever have the guts to use them. The thought that I may never see

Henry again—my only real friend other than Jesse—is surprisingly sad.

"The rest of the messages are just a bunch of spam," I say. "We didn't use email for much." I try not to get bummed out by the fact that we have no family or friends to whom we ought to send a final goodbye, but before I can pass the laptop back to John, the email bings.

It's from the Greater Houston Sleep Lab.

"What?" John asks.

My face has frozen in place. One of the last things Jesse did before he died was set up a time for me to be evaluated by a sleep lab. That was when we still thought that maybe Terra wasn't real. It was back when I had hope of a happy future—a time when we wouldn't be hunted.

A single tear streaks down my cheek. "The sleep lab—" I can't force any more words out.

"The sleep lab?" One of John's eyebrows rises. "You made an appointment to go to one?"

I nod. "Jesse made it for me. We were hoping that we could figure out how to reset my dreams, you know, so I'd have a normal one." My laugh comes out more like a sob.

Jesse scoots his barstool closer and wraps an arm around my shoulders. "I'm sorry."

"I know."

"Maybe you *should* go to a sleep lab," John says.

"Um, I doubt they'll be able to help me much," I say. "Seeing as Erra is very, very real."

"That's exactly why they might be able to help you." John presses his palms flat against the counter. "Think about it. What if you're in Erra when you're, I don't know, in REM? They have machines and stuff that can kick you in and out of that, I think. Maybe?"

It might be worth a try. I glance at the body of the email. "Unfortunately, my appointment is in three and half weeks."

John smiles. "No, Alice Walker's appointment is in three and a half weeks."

I don't understand.

"I just explained that I'm better than most anyone at computer stuff." His grin turns predatory. "I didn't explain that dear old dad didn't really have to bankroll my company quite as much as I might have given him credit for."

"Huh?"

"I'm also a hacker known as the Jackal."

"What?" I'm not sure whether I like him more or less right now.

He shrugs. "What can I say? I went a bit. . . off course when my mom died."

"So you're saying you can get me an appointment sooner?"

"That's exactly what I'm saying."

And that's how we wind up in his grandma's old Chevy truck, bouncing down the road just after dinner—headed for the West Side Sleep Lab.

It's not nearly as depressingly sterile and clinical as I expected it to be, but it looks a lot less impressive as well. "It's not in a hospital?" I stare at the small sign above a door that leads into a strip mall shopfront. "Is this legit?"

John laughs. "Did you expect dozens of doctors and nurses to be running it?"

I hate the feeling of heat rising in my cheeks. "Maybe."

"People usually come for restless leg syndrome and sleep apnea," John says. "It's not really 'fate of the world' stuff, typically."

I swallow. Which means they're totally not equipped for someone like me.

"If you don't want to do this, you don't have to," Jesse says. "We can just drive back to the barn."

For some reason, calling that place 'the barn' makes me laugh. If I had any idea a few weeks ago that my life was going to take this turn. . . I'd have hitchhiked to somewhere new, like for reals. Something between a chortle and a chuckle escapes me, and then I'm bawling.

"Hey, what's wrong?" Jesse grabs my upper arms lightly and ducks down so I'm forced to look at him. "John said this isn't a big deal. What am I missing?"

I inhale as big a breath as I can—that usually helps me get control when life feels like too much. "No, it's usually not." I look down at my shoes. "You don't remember this, but the reason we set this up in the first place is that you thought I was crazy. You thought Terra was all in my head, and you didn't want to run from the social worker who was chasing us anymore." I risk a glance at my brother.

Jesse winces. "I'm sorry I doubted you. I'm sorry I wasn't there to support you when things were hard. But you can't let my failings weaken you."

I shake my head. "You don't even know. I was never the strong one. You are."

"I don't agree with that at all. You've always been there for me on Terra, and I'm guessing if I remembered it, I'd be able to tell you about a bunch of times you've taken care of me here as well. Most importantly, the world needs you right now. If Erra's crumbling, you're the only person who can save the lives of the sixty or seventy million people trapped there."

I nod. I should feel motivated and inspired. Instead, I'm full of dread. If someone gave me an out, a way to never go back to Erra, I'd take it. "What if I'm not the person who will save the world? What if I don't care about all those people?"

"We need each other," Jesse says.

I shake my head again. "No, I need you. I don't really care about anyone else."

"Rude," John says. "I mean, at least wait until I'm out of earshot."

I can't help laughing at that. "Fine. I care about both of you, but the rest of the world can burn."

"You don't mean that," Jesse says. "I've seen you fight fiercely for what's right. For justice."

I was a different person on Terra. I cared more—which means he doesn't remember the *real* me. "Mostly, here on Earth, I've seen people hurt one another. I'm not entirely sure I'd be doing anyone a disservice by letting the whole thing collapse."

"But you won't do that." Jesse's resolve never wavers. I have no idea why he's got so much faith in me, but it's probably what I need to hear.

I grit my teeth and push past them both and through the doors. Only to be mired in mounds of paperwork I'm not really capable of filling out. John leaps in to help, thankfully, because I can't even recall my fake name, much less what he said to write down about being cash pay. Once we've finally leapt through every hoop and checklist they can push at us, we're finally taken back to a hallway with four doors opening off of it.

"This is where you'll need to tell your, er, your friends goodbye," a man wearing white from head to toe says. He forces a smile that doesn't relax me much.

"Uh, they'll be staying with me," I say.

He frowns and shuffles his feet, his thick white rubber soled sneakers squeaking on the polished tile floor. "That's not allowed."

My heart begins to race.

John murmurs something to him, and I'm pretty sure he passes him a wad of cash. I don't even care—I'm beyond feeling bad about someone with money shelling it out on my behalf.

I do care that the awkward attendant waves us all into the room. "I guess I'll have some cots brought in?" His voice hitches upward at the end.

John nods.

This time, his smile is real. Now I'm positive John paid him off. "Alright, well, let me walk you through what we'll be doing here." He points at the bed, and I sit down obediently. "I've got a few diodes I'll need to apply that will keep track of your vitals, and a few more monitors I'll be using to measure things like your brain activity and the movement of your legs and arms, etcetera."

Sounds comfortable. "Okay."

"None of it should bother you much. We do this literally every night." He points. "There's an en suite bathroom right there, and you're welcome to eat snacks, or watch TV, or do whatever you'd like until you fall asleep. Keeping as close to your typical nighttime routine helps you fall asleep in a strange place."

He has no idea what I consider strange. This bizarrely clinical room is practically a warm security blanket compared to a bunch of places I've slept. Then again, as happy I am that Jesse and John will be close, I'm not used to falling asleep with two guys in close proximity. "What if I can't go to sleep?"

"We prefer for you to fall asleep on your own." He compresses his lips and sighs. "But if you can't, we have some medications we can provide." His voice drops until it's quite low. "They can interfere with our readings, so we really prefer to avoid using them if at all possible."

"Noted," I say.

"I'll be just down the hall and around the corner. If you need anything, you can poke your head out the door and shout, and I'll hear you."

He takes a few moments to hook me up, and he's right. Other than the nuisance of having round stickies on my head and some wires that jumble up if I'm not careful, it's not so bad. He wheels two cots in, which he's barely able to jam into the small room. Jesse takes the one at the foot of my bed, and John takes the one to my left, leaving me a clear shot to the bathroom.

I tell Jesse stories from our childhood for an hour or two, but for all my anxiety over not being able to sleep, I'm good and tired by nine-thirty. After I yawn the second time, John says, "Are you ready to try lights out? It's been a long day, and we didn't exactly get a lot of sleep last night, what with the Terran collapse."

It seems like much more than twenty-four hours since I was screaming at Devlin and slamming him against a wall. Since I was carving a message into my arm and collapsing Terra into Earth.

It has been a long day, and my time on Erra was hardly restful. Hopefully tonight will be better.

"Sure," I say. "I think I might be able to go to sleep."

Jesse's the first one to drift off, judging by the familiar sound of his even breathing. That small comfort is enough for me, and I finally relax too. My last thought before I drift off is that I should have practiced throwing a spear. . .

5

ERRA

Once again, when I open my eyes, I'm staring up at the sky above me. Unlike the last time I opened my eyes, my view of the sky is marred by at least a dozen scowling faces. I close my eyes and reopen them, but nothing changes.

That sucks.

I groan. "Who are all of you, and what do you want?"

Something sharp pokes my ribs. "We ask the questions, girl."

"How did you Heal yourself?" one man shouts.

"How can you Call fire? You're a woman!"

"Where did you come from?" The woman who levels that question at me is scowling, but her hair is pulled into a full bun and her face is lined with creases. It's hard to be afraid of such a grandmotherly-looking woman.

"Who sent you?" The man who asks that pokes me again, and it hurts. "Are you a Follower of Isis? Do you hail from the River of Flame?"

I turn sharply toward the Flame River guy and realize he's poking me with the sharpened end of a wooden spear. "I'm not from there!" Or at least, I don't think I am. The name sounds ridiculous and totally unfamiliar. I push myself all the way up into a seated position. The frowning man right in front of me is tall, broad-shouldered, and has hair cut into a wide strip down the center of his head. The sides are shaved smooth.

A mohawk.

The bizarre word pops into my head and rolls around there like it belongs.

Does it?

Who am I? And where are these strange words without context and disconnected memories coming from? Why can't I remember anything before yesterday? Was it yesterday? I'm not even sure how much time passed while I was unconscious. I shake my head, hoping to dislodge some of the answers these people are seeking, as much for me as to make them happy.

"Answer us," the mohawk man growls. "Are you a defector?"

"A what?" I'm so lost.

"I'm losing my patience." He holds out one hand and a flame dances over it.

"If this is patience, I'd hate to see urgency." My voice is raspy, uneven. I swallow, and then I lift my empty palm and turn it upward. I concentrate on heat, on fire, on power, and on protection. In a flash, an answering flame dances over my hand.

"He must be a man," the woman says. "No woman can be Fire Called."

"That's no man." The mohawk man grunts. "She's a woman alright."

A stocky man next to the older woman stares pointedly at my chest.

I drop the flame and cross my arms over the front of my body. "Look, I don't remember who I am, and I have no idea how I got here. When I try and think back to where I came from. . . there's nothing." I shake my head. "I just don't remember."

"No way," a man behind me says.

"She's lying," another man says.

"Maybe it's a trick," a woman a few feet behind the mohawk man says. "Maybe someone else sent her to make fools of us. This feels like a River of Flame trap." She glances around as if she expects to see a man jump out from behind a rock and attack them. Not a very trusting group—and clearly they have enemies on all sides.

Which makes me glance around. I'm no longer on a narrow path between two smallish blackened mountains. I'm now in the center of some kind of town. Buildings line the road I'm sitting in the middle of—and the largest building of all looms behind the mohawk man. It has giant white columns, but behind it, I see the blackened mountains. "Where am I?"

That earns me another poke. "You'll get nothing from us until you confess who you are and why you're here."

I rack my brain for information, but come up blank. I have no idea where I came from, why I can make fire dance on my palm, or why anyone would dump me in the middle of this. . . whatever this is. Camp? I think they called it Volcano City.

"I'm done waiting," the mohawk man says. "You either tell us by the count of ten, or we stop wasting our time and eliminate you."

He reaches behind him, waving his hand for something. Someone hands him a bow and an arrow. He nocks the arrow in the bow and swings it toward me. The end of the arrow is made of a clear black glass, and it looks both sharp and deadly. I don't doubt that he'll hit me exactly where he intends to at this nearly point blank range, and that the arrowhead is capable of piercing my heart. But if that wasn't enough, he wiggles two of his fingers and the end of the arrowhead bursts into flames.

Perfect.

"One," he says.

Who am I? A name. A hometown. Anything. What can I tell them? I close my eyes and think hard.

"Two."

Flashes of someone with dark hair.

"Three."

Someone slapping me across the face and shouting at me.

"Four."

The same dark-haired boy, sitting on the ground, his face contorted, a pool of blood spreading out around him.

"Five."

An all-consuming rage rises inside of me.

"Six."

Who are these people? How dare they treat me as if I'm the one in the wrong? For the first time, something feels *right*. The world is unjust. I've been wronged. Livid anger makes my hands tremble.

"Seven. You're running out of time, girl. Tell me something. Anything."

The dark-haired boy screaming with fury, "Stop right now!" Even as a memory, his shout shatters something inside of me.

"Eight." Mohawk man shakes his head, his eyes full of disgust. They remind me of someone else. Someone I hate.

My memory is of a blond man this time, a man who makes my heart expand. "It was too late to save Jesse." His face is grim. My heart shatters into a million pieces.

"Nine."

A corpse. The dead body of the boy with dark hair.

Jesse.

I may not know my name, but I know his.

At that thought, my fury takes form. My target is my tormentors, surrounding me like a bunch of cowardly vultures. I'M DONE BEING A VICTIM. I'M DONE ACCEPTING AND PROCESSING AND ALLOWING.

"Ten!" I leap to my feet, all of the ferocity with which I reject the flashes I've seen rising up inside of me. The injustice. The helplessness. The feelings of horror, of terror, and of despair all pile up on top of me until something explodes, like an inferno, like a cataclysmic conflagration. It erupts from my fingertips, from the top of my head, from my heart, from my face, torn out of me like the scream of utter desperation when I saw the corpse of the dark-haired boy.

And the world around me burns.

And burns.

And burns.

Until all that remains is ash and cinder and smoke.

Finally, I draw a ragged breath. And I smile. It felt good to *burn*. When I look down at myself, I'm shocked to see that, although my clothing has been reduced to soot, my flesh is unharmed. How? I blink my eyes to clear the bright light spots from them and realize that the people around me are also wearing nothing but ash in place of their clothing.

But they're alive.

"The Inferno," the mohawk man says softly.

"The Inferno," dozens of voices repeat.

And then they drop into low bows all around me.

Um. What the. . . ?

They stay like that, prostrate, until a man walks down the steps of the large, columned building behind us. His snowy robes are pristine, his short ivory hair combed perfectly, but the forearms that are exposed are roped with muscle. When he smiles at me, he exposes two beautiful white rows of perfect teeth. "The Inferno." He inclines his head. "Which means she must be General Katika's stolen daughter."

The mohawk man splutters. "He never—" At the slight shift of the robed man's hand, he cuts off.

"His line is the only one that has ever manifested that particular talent, Robert. I think you'll agree with me that even among the Followers of Isis, no other Fire Called have ever recorded that particular talent in any family line. Only in the one."

The mohawk man, Robert, nods and bows again.

"But I hardly think you should be bowing to her." The white-all-over man's smile is mocking.

The people around me rise up slowly, and I realize that, although they're covered somewhat by ash, it's not a very good concealer of the human form. It's too easily brushed aside.

"Surely now that you can see I am indeed Fire Called, I'm entitled to a shower and some new clothing?" I hate the desperate note in my voice.

"We still require your name," the white-robed man says calmly.

Perhaps I should give him the only name I remember, even though I know it's not mine. At least it's something.

Before I can open my mouth to say I'm Jesse, he speaks again. "Perhaps you could simply nod if we suggest the correct one?" He lifts one eyebrow.

"Uh, okay."

"Does the name Laney sound at all familiar?"

None of the people circled around me seem to be surprised by that name.

"It does?" If my voice wobbles, well. I'm not sure whether that's the correct answer. Who is this Laney?

"That wasn't so hard. Why don't you come with me, Laney? We have some things to catch up on, of course, and we definitely want to provide you with that shower."

"You can't possibly mean to welcome her." A man robed in bright red stands at the top of the steps. His eyes flash, and his robes are shoved up above his elbows. "She can't train. She's a woman. And that makes her a liability we cannot tolerate. It would put the whole of Volcano City at risk."

"I'll train her, Marcus, since the prospect seems so far beneath you—even though you're the Warrior tasked specifically with education of the newly Fire Called." Another man, this one in a blue robe, steps into view next to the man in red. His hair is dark, almost black, and his eyes stand out startlingly. A shimmery golden-green. They practically shine above the sharp cheekbones of his face.

"Will you really, John?" the white-robed man asks. "What could you possibly hope to gain from that?"

The laughter that comes from all around surprises me. I had no idea so many people had gathered. Why is it funny that he'll train me?

"It's a complete waste of time," Marcus says. "I doubt she can learn any measure of control at her age, not to mention the fact that she's a woman."

"Which is precisely why we have no idea what to expect. Her abilities are unprecedented." John raises his eyebrows, clearly addressing more than just this surly Marcus person. "Isn't our motto, Raze the World? Don't we always need more soldiers? Especially those with unique or significant talents?"

Marcus rolls his eyes. "Her mother has seen to it that we won't be going to war again anytime soon."

My mother? Or is he talking about someone else now? I hate that they're talking about me as if I'm not even here.

"My mother?" I ask.

The man in blue jogs down the steps, past the white-robed man, and stops at my side. Thankfully, he keeps his eyes trained on my face. I have no idea how well the ash is keeping me covered, but I'm not optimistic. "Where have you *been* all these years?"

His breath warms my face, and his kindness warms my heart. I wish I knew how to answer him, but I have to settle for shaking my head.

"We have time," he whispers. "There's no rush. I'm sure it's been a traumatic few hours. You're finally released, or you escaped, whichever it was, and now that you're back to your own lands and your own people, you're attacked, you're injured, and then you're threatened." He shakes his head. "I'm sorry I couldn't do anything before now. Unfortunately, I'm the youngest member in the Circle of Warriors, so no one really tells me anything. I didn't even know there was someone in the pass until after—and now I'm rambling. It doesn't matter."

The circle of what? "Uh, that's okay."

He gestures behind me. "We better get you cleaned up and into some new clothes."

No one needs to tell me twice. I follow him quickly as he elbows a path through the gathered crowd.

Except there's one woman who doesn't move out of the way when we reach her. She's standing in the center of the street, her feet wide, her pants blowing in the gentle wind. Her shirt and pants are both made of fabric of the deepest black, but her hair is so light yellow that it's nearly white. The only signs of age she shows are small crows' feet near the corner of each eye, and slight lines around her mouth.

John inclines his head. "Marietta. We were headed your direction."

She purses her lips. "Were you?" She doesn't look at me —her eyes remain trained on John.

"I assumed you'd want me to bring her straight to you." He tosses his head my way, probably pointing out my lack of proper clothing. It's certainly one of the only things I can think about right now.

"And what exactly do you expect me to do with her?"

John stammers. "Do? How—what—" He coughs. "I expected you to—"

"Never mind all that." She pivots on her heel and walks straight toward me. "I hear she was able to invoke the Inferno."

John grunts.

"It has been generations since my husband's family possessed that power." She stops right in front of me, her slate-grey eyes boring into mine. "You're saying. . . ?" She lifts both eyebrows and meets John's eyes.

He nods.

"What is he saying? Neither of you are saying anything."

"You're my daughter, Laney." She reaches out and wraps bony arms around my back and squeezes me tightly.

6

ERRA

I feel much better after I've scrubbed the ashes off my body. I examine my fingers and toes, now that the soot is gone, and my legs. My stomach. Then once I'm dry and dressed, I poke at my face in the reflecting glass. Thick, relatively shiny light brown hair. A little curl on the ends. Bounces when I shake my head side to side. High cheekbones and a wide face, with hazel eyes. My teeth are large—almost too large. My nose is fairly nondescript. I have two freckles that would make a diagonal line under my left eye if they were connected.

I look like most anyone. Nothing special, that's for sure.

I'm young at least. Nothing on me sags yet, so there's that. But I'm not sure how this woman could possibly know that I'm her lost daughter Laney. I put on the black pair of pants and a simple black cotton shirt left for me by. . . well, I suppose by my mother. It's not like I can argue with her about being her daughter when I don't know my own name.

I square my shoulders.

Then I go out to interrogate my mom.

She's sitting on a plain wooden bench near the window, but when I walk out the bathroom door, she stands immediately, her hands at her side like she's a solider. I wonder again how I know that soldiers stand with their hands at their sides, or how I even know what a soldier is at all. I certainly haven't seen any armies here. Yet, I do know.

"Laney." The word sounds strange on her lips, as if she's not accustomed to saying it. Or as if it's not quite right for me.

"Mom?" Nope. That sounds even more wrong. "Mrs." Uh. I clear my throat. "I'm not sure what your last name is. Er, what our last name is."

"You don't feel comfortable calling me 'mom'?" The corner of her mouth twitches.

"I'm not trying to hurt your feelings," I say. "But the thing is, I don't really remember anything." I pause. "Unless."

"Yes?"

"Do I have a brother? With dark hair, maybe? Much darker than mine?"

Her mouth dangles open.

"Is that a yes?"

"I have no idea whether you do or not."

I blink. "You have no idea?" Wouldn't she know whether she'd had another child? Or. Oh, no. Is she unsure how to answer because he's. . . dead?

"I have no idea. . . because you're not my daughter. You're not Laney Katika."

It's like the entire world is in some kind of perpetual freefall. Didn't she just say that I was? "I'm not."

"No." She sinks back to the edge of the bench, her hands balled in her lap. "Not even close."

"I don't understand."

"No," she says. "I don't suppose you do." She points at the plain wooden chair across from her. "Maybe I can explain some of this."

Some is better than none, which is what I understand at

present. "Alright." I perch on the edge of my seat too. If she's not comfortable in her own home, I'm certainly not going to settle in.

"Where to start." She taps her lip.

"Why does everyone think I'm Laney?"

"Yes, that's as good a place as any. What do you know about the Fire Called?"

I shrug. "Nothing?"

"What do you know about Erra?"

I shake my head.

She looks upward as if she's pleading for divine help. That makes two of us, lady. "Look, Erra has four groups. Ice Called." She spits, but nothing I can see actually leaves her mouth. I'm guessing it's more of a habit than anything else. "Wind Called. Earth Called. And of course, Fire Called."

Of course. The volcano people. Why not?

"We're the smallest group."

"The Wind Called are small, too." I freeze. Where did that information come from?

"So you do know some things." She narrows her eyes at me.

"I—I'm not sure—"

She waves her hand through the air. "It's fine. You've clearly endured some kind of trauma. Probably you'll remember everything with enough time. But for now, you may as well know the basics. Wind is the second smallest group, which is good. The strongest of the Wind Called can fly, and they can become quite a nuisance."

"Alright."

"Luckily we don't fight them often. They live on mountaintops, using land we don't want in any case. It's the Earth Called that annoy us heartily and the Ice Called whom we despise."

"Despise?"

"We've been at war with them since the beginning."

That's not promising.

"There are far, far more of them than there are of us," my non-mom says. "But luckily most of them are weak, their power not only unimpressive, but unsustainable."

"Oh?"

"And almost all of our men can light a spark. Almost a quarter of them can sustain it. And the strongest among us can burn a city down to cinders."

Fabulous. Wait. Only the men? "Why can't the women?"

My non-mom squirms. "As far as I know, you're the first female who has ever been Fire Called."

That can't be good. The first of anything is a bad place to be. "Maybe it's an accident," I say.

She frowns.

"I can't keep thinking of you as my 'non-mom.'" I lean toward her. "What's your real name?" I think they said. Marion? Melissa?

"Marietta," she says. "But for now, until we think this through, you need to think of me as 'Mom.'"

A banging at the door nearly shocks me right off the edge of the seat. I catch myself in time, bracing my hands against the bench surface and forcing myself up to standing. Marietta's already halfway across the room. She swings the door open when she reaches it without hesitation. Her narrow shoulders are squared, and her head's held high. If she were my mom, I'd be proud of her. "What do you want, Elbion?"

Elbion? What a ridiculous name. It's the white-robed guy again. Peachy.

"I've come to deliver the Circle of Warrior's edict."

Her shoulders don't dip a bit. Her stance doesn't shift. "Deliver it, then."

Elbion smiles, as though he's won something, or perhaps as though he's delivering some kind of blow to his enemy. "We find her to be an aberration."

That doesn't sound good.

"What are you going to do about it?" Marietta shifts enough that I can see her face, and the line of her mouth is grim. "John offered to train her, so the decision can't have been unanimous."

"John won't contradict all of us, not on this. He doesn't even know her." Elbion's smile spreads. He's definitely gloating about something.

"What's the edict?" Marietta's words are clipped, and she's tense, but she's not surrendering, not yet. I know she's not my mom, but part of me wishes she were. This woman may not be Fire Called, but she's fiery. She's a warrior where it matters.

"As you're the only thing standing between us and future victory, we offer you this chance to spare your aberrant daughter. You may choose the noble defeat of death, or you can watch as it overtakes her instead."

Marietta's hand tightens on the edge of the door until her knuckles whiten, and then she slams it in Elbion's delighted face. She stares at the back of the closed door for a moment. And then another.

I take a few steps in her direction. It's not very reassuring that she's confessed that I'm not really her daughter, because it sure sounded like the elderly Elbion just told her that either she's dying. . . or I am. "Noble defeat of death? What are they talking about?"

Marietta spins around, one hand pressed to her heart. Her face is white, completely drained of all color. "Either you die or I do."

That sucks. The now familiar, inexplicable fury rises in my chest. Why does everyone want to kill me? I don't even know who I am, but I'm beginning to doubt that I'm a villain. I'm worried I'm something far worse: a perpetual victim. "I'd like to see them *try* to kill me." My palms heat at the thought of danger, and I ache to Call fire.

Marietta's bony hand wraps around my wrist. "Let me finish explaining."

"Do it, then."

She releases me, but when she crosses the spartan room and sits back on the bench, she may as well have been dragging me along. I follow her, as desperate for information as I've ever been for anything.

Instead of talking, her eyes dart out the window. She must be sitting here instead of on the plush couch because of the view it affords of the street outside. It didn't warn us of Elbion's approach, but probably only because I was distracting her. Presumably, we're now on some kind of timetable. I'm assuming it's Marietta who will decide which of us they'll be eliminating.

She closes her eyes, as if she's recalling something particularly distasteful. "My daughter Laney was perfect in every single way."

Oh, oh, no.

Her eyes open and rest on mine. "She had the smallest hands, but each finger was perfectly shaped. The immaculate curve of her brow brought tears to my eyes. When she smiled." She looks out the window again and wipes away an errant tear. "One morning, when I went to pick her up. . . " She closes her eyes and inhales and exhales slowly several times. "She suffocated on her blanket."

"I'm so sorry," I say. "That's awful."

"It wrecked me," she says simply. "To my very core."

Why does the Warrior Circle or whatever think I'm her? I want to ask, but it feels like something she needs to share at her own pace.

"The Fire Called warriors capable of burning an entire building to the ground vote on representatives for the Circle of Warriors."

Okay.

"And that circle, in turn, chooses a General."

"Elbion?" I may hate the guy, but even I can tell that he's in charge.

She shakes her head. "Not exactly, no."

Now I'm confused again. "He seems to be running things."

"He's the Senior Warrior, which means he's sort of their default mouthpeice, but it's the General they choose who leads them when they go to battle."

"He's not the general?"

She shakes her head. "And even the General doesn't rule the people or even determine when they go to war."

I'm so confused.

"We believe in balance among all things. Water quenches fire. Wind dries up rain. We eat crops, and in turn, when we die, our ashes nourish those same crops."

I can't help scrunching my nose at that thought.

"Just as a fire cannot quench itself, a warrior cannot determine when war is necessary. Even among the Followers of Amun, we believe that we need someone who can step away from the battlefield, someone less controlled by their passions and base urges to make those decisions. Leadership of an entire people requires patience, dedication, intelligence, and insight. These are skills that are exemplified by women, not men."

I agree with her there.

"That is why one of the only things we have in common with our Fire Called compatriots in the River of Flame settlement is that the chosen General's *wife* becomes the Head of the Circle and makes all decisions pertaining to daily life and when to go to war."

But. . .

"The Head is only accountable to one entity: the Circle of Warriors, and only if their edict on a particular topic is unanimous. Even by a unanimous vote, they cannot overturn her decisions regarding war."

But that Circle just issued an edict to Marietta. The wheels inside my head turn and click . . . "Wait, *you're* the Head of the Circle?"

"My husband was elected General. He died in a duel with the Captain of the Ice Called," she says. "But his death did not relieve me of my obligation as Head of the Circle. They can elect a new General only upon my death, with the Senior Warrior handling most of his duties until a new General may be selected. Although, in the Circle's defense, most Heads commit suicide after the death of their warrior spouse."

That's messed up.

And clearly Marietta hasn't followed the behavior expected of her. I wonder how long her husband has been dead.

Clearly none of this sits very well with Elbion. They think I'm Marietta's daughter, so they're using me to force her out of command. I imagine that eliminating the weird *woman* who's Fire Called is a bonus. "Why don't they like you?"

She smiles. "My husband was an unparalleled warrior. More than half the Generals in the history of Volcano City hail from his family line—and they had a unique power granted them by Isis herself, something called the Inferno."

"An explosion of fire?" I guess.

She nods. "They tell me you did it, on a limited scale, perhaps, but the idea is the same. It will incinerate anything and everything in its direct line. . . except the Fire Called. You can see how that would be advantageous in battle. He could protect his people while decimating all others. It's also the reason we poured so many resources into developing a city surrounded by volcanoes. If we were ever threatened, and anyone in residence had this ability, they could use it to encourage the volcanoes— leveling any armies that threatened. When a General who can Call the Inferno commands, no one can stand against us."

That thought makes me more than a little ill, honestly.

"The point is that my husband, bloodthirsty though he naturally was, wasn't the only member of the Circle of Warriors whose desire for bloodshed had waned. After losing his sons, he wanted to stay home and live in peace."

"Why didn't he keep his sons home?" I guess it doesn't sound super brave, but as General, surely he could have assigned them to safe positions.

Her eyes are sad. "They all died before he was voted in as General. All we had left for many lonely months was Laney, and at the time, we felt truly bereft. We didn't yet know the meaning of the word."

That resonates with me for some reason. The idea that I might feel sorrow, but not yet fully comprehend how bad things could become.

"When Laney suffocated, something inside my husband broke. He was a good man, a strong man, but I think all the wars and destruction, they were something he was prepared to withstand. He wasn't made to handle the meaningless tragedy of daily life. I think that's what focused him in on what we were doing wrong—he wanted something good to come from her death, so he lied in order to take control— to be elected as General."

Lied about what?

"He told the men that Laney had been stolen by Ice to overcome their reticence to commit to a war to end all wars."

Oh.

"We had been at peace for almost a year, but he knew that we'd go to war again soon enough. He didn't want just another battle in a long string of pointless attacks. No, he wanted to marshal every single warrior we had. He wanted to end it all—to finish Ice's resistance against us for good."

"Didn't you say Ice is much bigger than the Fire Called?"

"We're three hundred and forty-one thousand strong between our two settlements," she says. "Whereas there are millions of them among their dozens of settlements. They reproduce like rabbits." She scowls.

Okay, that's bizarre. "But you thought you could win anyway?"

"You don't understand. As an offensive, Fire can't be beaten. It consumes—it's really all it does. Ice is a terrible defense, because what will it do in the face of flame? It melts, like everything else."

"But water puts out the fire. Seems effective enough."

"The Ice Called have outposts on icebergs floating in the ocean. They make numerous crafts out of ice and sail the seas, but they mostly live on land," she says. "You can see that it's problematic. If we cut off their access to water. . ." She shrugs. "Boom."

I don't want to think about that. Would her husband really have condoned the slaughter of men, women, and children? And not only that, would he have *lied* to bring that to pass?

"I understand your disgust. Unfortunately, all we felt at the time was the rage of loss. Our anger at the Ice Called was embedded deeply, from birth really. That's my one excuse."

"Wait, you changed your position?"

Marietta nods. "My husband's ruse worked. Our grief became the impetus for a war like we'd never seen before or since. Even Isis joined us, in their fury at the theft of a child. In the war that followed, we lost almost a hundred thousand soldiers, but the Ice Called." She bows her head. "I'll never forget the magnitude of their losses."

"You were there?"

"As Head, I'm required to be on the front lines of the

battle—or at least, the front line in the staging location. It was enough. I saw the battlefields. Finally, the Ice Called proposed a solution. They offered one-on-one combat between our leaders."

"If Fire's stronger, how did your husband lose?"

"I've been over that in my mind more times than you can possibly imagine." Her nostrils flare. "Any way I look at it, I come back to the same answer. He must have lost on purpose."

"What?"

"In all the carnage, our desire for revenge for the loss of our sons withered. We saw nothing but unending tragedy on those battlefields. But the desires of our friends and his fellow warriors only grew as more and more of their own fell." The profound sadness on her face cuts me like a knife. "I really do think he sacrificed himself to save our people. To prevent the death. To end the wars. He met my eye just before he died and he smiled. He whispered the words, 'you can stop it.'"

Stop what?

"He must have intended for me to do exactly what I have done. He must have wanted me to maintain my position, and to block every single petition for war that the Circle of Warriors has proposed, just as I have done. They can oppose my actions, but they can't initiate a war without my consent."

"That's why they want you dead." My voice is flat, because I realize now that I may have survived the spear, the lava, and the attack by the warriors upon waking.

But I'm about to die anyway.

It's either that, or the hideous war she's describing restarts and countless lives are lost. The war her husband sacrificed himself to halt.

"They think you're my Laney, somehow captured by Ice, and returned now that you inexplicably pose a danger to them. Some of them are probably already saying it's a sign—that the Inferno has returned. That we will succeed where we previously failed. Or perhaps they even believe that you escaped for exactly this purpose. I'm not sure, but I understand why they believe it." She stands up and begins pacing. "Only I know the truth—that you're not Laney. We have no idea who you really are or why you're here." She stops and stares directly in my eyes. "I'd like you to tell me the truth now, please. What do you really want?"

I wish I knew. "I woke up beside an active volcano, with no memory of what brought me there or what my purpose is. I can't even recall my own name."

She waits. She knows there's more than that.

"The only thing I've been able to remember is that I have a brother named Jesse." Please recognize the name. Please.

She shows no signs of recognition whatsoever.

"I believe he's dead."

"You killed him?"

I jump to my feet, my hands fisted at my sides to keep me from burning her to the ground. "Never."

"So you have enemies too, and likely a score to settle."

"I have a rage I don't understand that surges upward from deep inside me." So much for convincing her I would carry on her vision of peace if she had any selflessness left in her.

"You'd go to war with Ice, then?"

I stumble back. "I don't even know them."

"What if you discovered that they killed your brother?"

My palms heat.

"I see." She sits down, but this time, she sinks onto the large green sofa in the center of the room. "I know you're not our daughter, but I think my husband would have liked you. He never thought it was fair that women aren't Fire

Called. He was a good man. Fair. Brave. Magnanimous. With a wonderful vision of the future."

She's lost everyone who matters to her. Her husband, her sons, her daughter. I recognize the thing about her I couldn't place before—a profound exhaustion. "I know it's hard," I say, "to hold the line against them, but you're doing the right thing." I sit down next to her and place a hand over hers. "I don't even blame you. In fact, part of me will be relieved when it becomes official. Truth be told, I've felt like I was doomed, or at the very least, living on borrowed time, since the very moment I walked down the path between those volcanoes."

"What an idiotic waste of resources, don't you think?" Her smile is crooked.

"The volcanoes?"

She nods. "No one has attacked us here in centuries. It takes the dedicated resources of dozens of men to keep them all active, and we've done it for what? To show everyone around us that we're dangerous?" She snorts. "As if anyone on Erra doesn't already know." She leans backward on the sofa. "At least you know the pain of loss, even if you're not sure what form it took. At least you feel the costs of anger and rage."

"I don't understand."

She sits up straight and reaches for something in her boot. At the flash of silver, I realize what she's grabbed. It's a long, black-handled dagger, the hilt formed in the shape of a dark, frozen flame.

Adrenaline pulses through my body, but I know in that moment that I won't fight her. The same image comes to me again and again—the dark-haired boy's corpse. If he's gone, if he's dead, maybe I should stop fighting. If that's the only memory I can dig up, then maybe I really am like a wounded animal. I can't help these people, I can't help anyone.

I couldn't help my brother.

I probably deserve to die.

When Marietta lifts the dagger in the air, I look at her sad, sad eyes. "I don't blame you, you know. Hold the line against those warriors."

Her hand pauses where it's lifted, extended to its furthest reach above us. "If I were to tell them to kill you instead of me, I would be proclaiming to the world that you aren't my daughter. I'd have to explain how I *know* you aren't, and that would reveal that my husband's election as General was predicated on a lie. The result would be the same as if I died. Don't you see? I haven't had a choice, not since the second you walked down that path, *Laney*. Some may look at you as a savior, as a miraculous weapon in our time of need, but just as many will see you as a pure, unadulterated threat to their power. You'd better figure out why you're here and how you plan to protect yourself, because I can only spare you this once."

Marietta's smiling when she plunges the dagger into her own heart.

7

EARTH

Air, I need air. I inhale a ragged breath, and then another. Only then do I open my eyes. And sit up abruptly. Thank goodness I'm back on Earth.

"Alora? Are you awake? And you're not burned or sliced or diced?" John's face is familiar, and yet also foreign, as I recall how he looked as a warrior in robes on Erra. Which reminds me that he's part of the Circle of Warriors that forced that poor woman to kill herself.

John won't contradict all of us, not on this.

"I'm fine." But my fingers grip the blanket too tightly and my breathing's shallow.

"You look distressed." He sits on the edge of the bed, only a few inches away from me. "What happened?"

I scoot away from him, hating how his eyes widen in alarm. He deserves some kind of explanation, at least. "I met you there."

I've seen people die before—thousands on Terra, and even a few on Earth. Some of those—many of them on Terra—I killed myself, but this was different somehow. In almost eighteen years, only one other person has been willing to die to spare me: Jesse.

And now Marietta, a woman I didn't even know.

Although, arguably, it's possible that she died to preserve the good memory of her husband and herself more than she did to protect me. Either way, she clearly hoped that the world wouldn't descend into complete chaos after she went.

"Alora, say something."

I glance at the foot of the bed where Jesse's still asleep. "What time is it?"

"Nearly six a.m."

I will never understand how the time passes from place to place. It makes no sense how it can be a few hours there and more than eight here. Or a full day there and only an hour here, depending on the night. I suppose, seeing as I am somehow connected to a prison realm that contains millions and millions of people, somehow muffling their powers, this isn't really the most inconceivable part of my life.

"Did I do something awful there?" He tries to take my hand, and I flinch. He hops off the bed and slides back onto his cot. "You know I don't control my actions there, right? I don't even know what they are." He exhales heavily. "I am so sorry if I hurt you. I would never—" He throws his hands up in the air. "I hate this."

"You didn't hurt me." I pat the spot next to me.

His mouth and eyes relax. "Thank goodness. You had me worried."

"In fact, you stood up for me." I look up into his eyes, and I realize that he's really the only person other than Jesse that I trust. He's had my back, even when the enemy was his father. He's never harangued me, or guilted me, or told me what to do. When I asked him to call in a favor with Oliver, he just did it. When I told him to leave his dad behind, he walked away without complaint. And on Erra, without knowing who I was, he stepped forward and offered to train me.

I've never really felt safe around anyone other than my brother—but I might be starting to feel safe around John.

A slight movement near my lap draws my attention. His hand covers mine slowly, like I'm a horse he's afraid will spook. "I barely slept last night. I was too worried that you'd hate me when you woke up. So when you shuddered earlier. . . when I tried to touch you—"

I turn my hand over so that his palm touches mine, and our fingers slowly interlace, as if he's savoring every second of the new contact. "Even if you had been awful, I wouldn't hate you. You should know that."

"If I hurt you, I'd hate myself."

"You're a good person, John, and I don't think your dad was right about us not being the same in both places, or at least, not exactly right. Someone might encounter different circumstances on Earth and Erra. Someone might even be taught different things, but I think the core of who they are stays the same." I glance at Jesse. He doesn't understand computers or even know what a video game is. He's never eaten an M&M. He has no idea how many times he beat me at chess when we were kids, but his instincts haven't changed. The part that matters to me is still safe, still here with me. I squeeze John's hand. "I feel lucky that you're Fire Called."

"So you're alright over there? You're safe?"

"Well, I didn't say that. In fact, you basically forced this woman, the Head of the Warrior Circle or something like that, to choose whether to kill herself or me."

He winces. "Really?"

I shrug. "I figured I was a goner, actually, but she stabbed herself to death right before I woke up. The people there were nothing short of jubilant about her suicide, which was disturbing in and of itself. They claimed her body and left me there—in her house, alone, to mourn, maybe? I don't know what they expect me to do—I'm not sure they cared. But you did promise that you'd come back to train me, so I suppose I'll find out their plans for me soon enough."

"They haven't said anything?"

I shrug. "When they threatened me before, I managed to incinerate their clothing and everything around us in a bizarre blast. It was something they called the 'Inferno.'"

John's eyes widen. "I shouldn't be surprised. You're the strongest Lifter ever recorded, according to Dad. Of course you'd be able to do something that legend says hasn't been done in more than a century on Erra."

"Not that it'll do me any good. What everyone cares about—restoring Terra and trapping all the Lifters back over there." I shake my head. "I still have no idea how to do that, even if I decide it's the right call."

John's face is barely six inches from mine. His mouth's so close that he could whisper and I'd hear him like a loud-speaker. "You're a good person, Alora, and you're strong. We'll figure things out, and you'll make the right decision. I may not know much, and I'm certainly no help in choosing whether to trust Amun or Isis, but I'll trust you until the day I die."

"I'd really rather you didn't die anytime soon." My eyes drop to his mouth.

His breath hitches and he leans forward, slowly, too slowly. His lips are almost on mine when the door to the outside hall opens.

The same tech who hooked me up to all the diodes last night walks through. "Well, that was an interesting night."

John leaps from the bed so quickly that his momentum carries him too far. His shin bumps into the cot, knocking it into the side wall with a clatter. Jesse sits up with a small shout.

"Everything's fine," I say, as much to myself as to either of them.

But Jesse's pale. Too pale. Like someone who has lost too much blood. I try to stand, but the wires attached to me become all tangled in the process.

"Easy there," the tech says. "Let me get you disconnected before you start doing calisthenics."

Hilarious. "My brother—can you check him first?"

"I'm not actually a physician," he says.

"Thanks for that, Greg," I say. "But can you just look him over? Make sure nothing is wrong?"

"My name is Scott," he says, "and I suppose I can try, but I'm not sure what exactly you're hoping I'll find."

Jesse steps out of bed, still fully dressed in John's jeans and t-shirt. "Ignore her. I sustained an injury not long ago, and she tends to fret about it still. I feel fine."

That's what I'm worried about. *Fine* is what people say when they're not doing well, but they're putting on a brave face. For now, I don't push the issue. It's not like Scott can do anything, as he already pointed out. I stare at the ceiling and wait patiently while he peels off the monitors and leads and whatnot. Something he said when he first entered finally registers in my brain. "You said it was an interesting night. What does that mean?"

Scott grunts. "You didn't enter REM sleep once all night."

"What does that mean?"

Scott freezes. "Did you skip all the material you were supposed to read before you registered?" He narrows his eyes accusatorially.

"You got us," John says. "We've been so busy, we figured it wasn't that important."

"It's my entire job," Scott says, "to diagnose whether you're falling into the right sleep patterns. It's the whole reason you're here." He sure seems grumpy for a guy who's paid to explain this stuff to us.

"Maybe you could give us the short version, and when we get home, we'll read the materials." John draws an x over his heart. "Scout's honor."

"You don't look much like a boy scout," Scott says.

"He's a team leader," I say. "Loves the scouts."

"They're called troops." Scott rolls his eyes, but doesn't argue further, thankfully. "Basically there's REM sleep, which stands for rapid eye movement, and there's non-REM sleep. You have three cycles of non-REM sleep, and once you've passed through all of them, you enter REM. That's the time when all your dreams happen—rapid brain activity. Without REM, it's hard for you to learn new things. Also, your body makes a lot of proteins you need for good health during REM, so without it. . . "

"Got it," I say. "REM, good. No REM, bad."

He huffs. "It's not only REM we monitor, of course. Deep sleep in the non-REM stage is also critical. You only experienced a few moments of that, and they came quickly at the beginning. You spent almost the entire night in what we call light sleep, which is stage two. Your heart rate slowed, and your body temperature dropped, but you barely reached deep sleep at all, and I'm guessing without hitting REM even once, you had no dreams."

Huh. This actually might be helpful. "Yeah, no, I never have real dreams. That's why we set this up."

"Now that we have your baseline and we know your issues, we have methods to induce both deep sleep and REM. A lot of sleep study participants who experience REM for the first time report vivid dreams, and even the revisiting of old memories they had all but forgotten."

I can hardly believe my ears. "Memories I've forgotten?" Like who my real parents are? And then I connect the dots on something else. "Wait, when do I come back?"

"I tentatively scheduled you for tonight. People often like to space these appointments out, but when someone isn't reaching REM at all, we find that a few nights in a row might actually improve their sense of rest and peace in the morning, rather than stressing them out."

"Sure," I say. "That's totally fine. But is there any chance that we can also schedule a time for my brother?" I glance at Jesse. "He's had some issues lately, too. He could really use some good REM sleep—maybe he'd even remember some things he's forgotten." I widen my eyes pointedly at him.

Scott frowns. "I'm afraid we're booked up at least a month out right now, and we don't simply accept anyone who comes knocking. We operate by physician referral, because you need someone to read your chart and order the tests and treatments that are indicated."

I can't believe he shut me down that fast. If there's any chance that Jesse could regain some of his memories on Earth, well, I'd try most anything. "Isn't there something—"

"Come now, Alora." John winks at me before he turns back to Scott. "That's totally fine. We understand entirely and we thank you for your time. We'd love to return again tonight."

I practically storm out, irritated that he thinks winking at me will make up for how he totally cut me off. Where was he with his bribes when I needed him? The second the door closes, I spin on him. "Didn't you hear what he said? REM is how you regain lost memories."

John laughs. "You're *so* Fire Called. You have patience of, like, negative four. I have no idea how I never saw that until now."

I throw my hands onto my hips. "What does that have to do with anything? Look, what I'm saying is—"

He presses a finger to my lips, and I strongly consider

biting it. "Alora. Their back end is a mess. There's no sense badgering poor Scott, who doesn't have the authority to give you what you want anyway. I'll simply fake some doctor's orders and schedule Jesse tonight right alongside you. I'll include notes that he's changed sleep centers and copy your results so they give him the REM-inducing treatment as well."

Oh. "Well, that's not a bad idea." I should've known. "I'm sorry. I guess I'm so used to no one ever fighting for us that I just assumed."

"Can I just say that, while I don't remember knowing you for very long, I'm happy you're on our side." Jesse's smile is exactly the same as always.

"Do you really feel alright?" I peer up at his face, thankful that the color has mostly returned.

He rolls his eyes this time. I must be a really irritating person. "Of course I do. I'm fine."

"Alright." I let it go, for now.

"You did keep your friend Oliver's phone number though, right?" I ask. "Because there's no telling when Jesse might not be okay, and I have no idea who else we could call."

We all climb into the truck, with me in the center of the bench seat, and John slides the key into the ignition. It may not be the fanciest truck, but the starter works and the whole thing roars to life just fine. "We should stop for some supplies on the way back to the barn," John says. "And yes, I was able to extract all my contacts, so you don't need to worry about that."

"What are his politics?" I ask.

"Are you asking whether he wants you dead, or whether he thinks you're the rebirth of an Egyptian goddess?" John smirks.

"Basically. Although, even the 'good' one sounds insane."

"I didn't ask him straight out, but think how respectful he became after asking about Isis. He made a point of telling me that he'd be happy to help again, anytime you might need him, and he swore he'd keep our meeting a secret."

"It could be a ruse, to induce you to lead him to Alora," Jesse says.

A ruse? To induce me? Terran Jesse's language is a lot stiffer than my Jesse's ever was. I guess that's a small price to pay. "It could be," I say, "but I didn't get that vibe from him."

"His parents are zealots," John says, "and they're fairly well connected within Isis, as far as that sort of thing goes. But they're Healers, so they're low on the power grid. When we were kids, he did something really, really stupid. He needed money, and he was a little lazy, and he agreed to transport some stuff for some bad people."

"What?" Oliver as a drug mule doesn't quite compute.

"Why did he need money?" Jesse frowns.

"It's a long story, but basically Oliver's girlfriend was a bit of a mess. She knew all the wrong people and had a few bad habits. He was terrified she'd get into trouble if he didn't come up with the money to pay off some of her debts. So he took the jobs she found for him to earn the money, which worked for a while. Until he got caught."

"He went to jail?" Geez. He was wearing loafers, for heaven's sake. I would not have guessed he was an ex-con in a hundred years. Not that I know any other ex-cons. Or not that I know whether I know any others. . .

"He didn't go to jail," John says. "I told you I'm a hacker."

"Wow, I didn't realize. . ."

He shrugs. "Among other things, I've hacked several government sites and removed any evidence of certain crimes."

"I'm not certain what all of that means, but if you made this man's problems disappear so that he would be indebted to you, and then called in that debt to save Alora, I have a newfound respect for you," Jesse says.

I'm not quite sure what I think. "We may need him," I say. "So I suppose it's good to have a back door into Isis, especially the part of Isis that doesn't despise me."

John pulls into a Kroger parking lot and kills the engine. "Let's go grab supplies—whatever you think of that we might need. Definitely things like fruit, water bottles, bread. And any snacks you like."

"M&Ms," I say. "For sure."

Jesse frowns. "What are M&Ms?"

"Oh, you're going to love them," I say. "They were your favorite."

"Then we'll get all the kinds," John says. "You can try each one. Actually, it might be kind of fun to try all my favorite things again. I could pretend it's my first time."

"Yeah, not much about our situation is great, but that would be kind of amazing." The cart return is nearly empty, but I grab the second to last one and shove it through the doors absently.

I'm shocked when we walk through the door. It's like a scene out of a movie.

"What's going on?" John asks slowly.

I scan all the aisles I can see, and they're nearly all bare. "Where's the produce?" We move quickly, darting around the other shoppers, most of whom have very little in their carts. Several of them shoot me aggressive, nervous looks.

A bag of oranges, two bell peppers, and a pile of onions are all that's left. John snags the bell peppers and some spotty brown bananas I didn't notice.

"Did the world end and no one told us?" I ask.

John's eyes widen. "How could we have been so dumb?"

I shake my head. "What?"

"You dumped a lot of people from Terra back onto Earth, many of whom hadn't Awoken."

Oh no. "And they suddenly have powers. They can Lift things, and they recall a whole other world, and they don't know why or what's going on."

"I've been so worried about keeping you under wraps that I didn't even think about how the collapse of Terra would affect the rest of the world." We throw a few more oddball finds into the cart, like tortillas and mayonnaise, and race to the checkout. There are three bags of M&Ms left when we reach the register, and I grab all of them. John goes to pay with his card, but I stop him.

"They can track that, right?"

He groans. "I don't have that much cash left." He has just enough to cover our oddball finds, though, thankfully. "I think Grandma Jean has some at the barn. I hope."

"Have you called her at all?" I ask.

He shakes his head. "She's Isis too, and you said not to reach out to anyone at all."

"I'm beginning to think we need information more than anything else," I say.

"You might be right."

I watch the world around us more closely on our trip home. There are dozens of people waiting in line at gas stations, some of them holding gas cans. Many of the restaurants we pass are closed—big signs posted in the front windows. What does everyone think is going on?

"We need to find a television," I say.

The moment we reach the barn, we grab our meager supplies and head inside. John turns on the television, but it takes a bit to find a channel with news programming.

"—many things that we never would have believed." A man with a puffy helmet of hair bobs his head.

A woman with a cute blonde bob half smiles. "I completely agree, Stan." She shakes her head. "It's hard to know what to believe. This time yesterday, bizarre videos were beginning to flood social media and websites all over the world. All legitimate media outlets discounted them as some kind of bizarre hack. It was as though the newest and greatest fad was some kind of science fiction video, but now I think we're all wondering."

The helmet hair guy lifts both eyebrows. "What if they're real?"

"Exactly."

"I think we should cut to some clips, and let viewers decide for themselves. One of the first videos posted, which now has more than one hundred million views on YouTube, is a little girl who loves cookies."

"That's right, Stan. Her mother's in the process of telling her she will *not* grab the Oreos from the top of the fridge and the father, as I understand it, is videotaping the whole thing. She always sits down on the floor and screams, and he wanted to document it for posterity, presumably to get a good laugh later in her life, when she's at an age where tantrums are no longer acceptable."

"But she doesn't throw a fit," Stan says.

"Not at all." The woman bobs her head, and the feed cuts to a somewhat grainy video of a small, chubby cheeked kid, maybe three or four years old.

"I want a cookie!" She stomps her foot.

Her mother smiles fondly and puts one hand on her hip. "You didn't eat your dinner. I told you that if you didn't finish those peas, you wouldn't get any Oreos. You can always go back and—"

"No!" The girl stomps her foot again and then reaches up, as far as her arms will go, almost as if she thinks she might be able to reach the top of the fridge, and then, clear as day, the Oreo package flies off the top of the fridge and down toward her outstretched hands.

She's so shocked that she drops her prize, cream-filled cookie sandwiches spilling out everywhere.

"But that's not even the tip of the iceberg." Stan's face suddenly fills the screen again. "Accounts and videos like this have been popping up in more and more places. Here are a few, but if you log in to your social media, I'm sure you'll find dozens more of your own."

There's a clip of a teenager dropping his iPad off the roof of his house. . . and the tablet floating right back up to him. When he throws a thumbs up at the camera, his eyes are spilling golden-brown light.

Then a woman is raking the leaves in her yard, and a ten-year-old kid runs and jumps in the pile. The mother starts to fuss, when the kid's eyes light up and leaves lift up in the air.

Another shows a tall, thin man who's juggling, and then one by one, he stops touching the bean bags with his hands at all, his eyes light up with a grayish glow as they spin around and around. He crosses his arms and stares at the camera. "Now tell me there's no such thing as magic."

The screen cuts back to the broadcasters again. "Someone or something has been shutting a lot of these posts down," the woman says, "but not fast enough. There's either some new kind of software that allows for impressive photo editing, or something very strange is happening."

"Theories abound," Stan says, "from aliens, to mutations, to a technological conspiracy, but one thing is certain."

"True, and it's this." The woman leans toward the camera. "If you don't have to go out of the house today, we recommend staying home. The President has said he will be making a statement first thing tomorrow morning, and we'll wait for guidance from him."

John shuts off the television. "Clearly Isis and Amun haven't gotten things under control."

"I thought they were present at every level of government," I say.

"But they can't control the internet," he says. "And right now, the two groups are decidedly at odds. Which means the Isis representatives will be fighting the Amun ones, and that makes for a very scattered approach to how to handle this kind of thing."

"At least no one is mentioning Alora," Jesse says.

That hadn't even occurred to me. "Oh no," I say. "What if they do?"

"I might need to make another run to the store," John says.

"For what?"

"Not something they'll be out of, I imagine," he says.

"Which is?"

"Hair dye and a lot of makeup."

I wish he was kidding, but he's not.

❀ 8 ❀

EARTH

I look really, really strange with black hair.

"I like it," Jesse says. "Your eyes really stand out."

"I was hoping my eyes would stand out more." I roll my eyes. "Or it could be the impact of me wearing eyeliner and mascara for the first time in my life."

"Sure, that too," Jesse says.

"What are we going to do?" I drop my face into my hands. "How am I supposed to trust anyone? And if I don't trust anyone, how can I even figure out what I should or shouldn't do?"

"Whether you should try to collapse Erra or reinforce it, you mean?" Jesse asks.

Try. He's right. Even if I knew what to do, I don't know whether I can do it. It's like I'm feeling around in the dark.

John opens the bathroom door and steps into the doorway, his hair mussed from being freshly washed. "What move feels right to you, in your gut?" He looks almost unbearably sexy, leaning against the bathroom doorframe like that, his eyes focused on me. "I like the dark hair, by the way. It really puts the focus on your eyes."

"That's what I said," Jesse says.

"I don't care how I look," I practically wail. "I don't know what to *do*."

"You need training, at a baseline," John says. "I can't help with mastering telekinetic powers, but I can help if you're able to access fire at all."

I lift one hand, palm up, and focus on—

"Whoa, pyro. Let's go outside before we attempt any kind of torching and incinerating, okay?" John's holding both hands out toward me like he's worried I'll burn us all to the ground.

"Not a bad idea." I can't help my smile.

"Yeah, the first time I Called fire, I burned my family home to the ground, so maybe we move outside, away from anything that matters to any of us."

"I'm so sorry," I say. "That's terrible."

"It wasn't a good day," he says. "In any case, I'm not at all sure you'll be Awake to fire like you are to your telekinetic abilities, since the prison for that is still up. Either way, prudence is usually the best modus operandi. I think last time you tried, right after waking up, nothing happened, right?"

I shrug. "I haven't really put forth much effort."

"That's fair," he says. "But either way, you'll need someone to help identify exactly what you can do and train you to use your telekinetic powers. It's only a matter of time before you need to protect yourself."

He's trying to focus me in on this one thing. . . so I stop freaking out about what to do with the prisons—and essentially everyone else in the world. I see what he's doing, but I still appreciate it. We're out the door and halfway down the path that leads between the barndominium and the shed when I realize Jesse's coming along. "Um, I'd prefer you not get incinerated," I say. "Maybe you can wait inside. Watch some television, or read a book. Might catch you up on some Earth stuff."

Jesse stops walking, but his brow furrows. "Really? I figure that, with powers being stronger here on Earth, I'd need to train some, too."

I hadn't thought of that. It makes sense, but if his soul's leaking energy, I'm also worried that any training will only speed the process. "I'm not sure—"

"If you're going to wrap me up and stick me on a shelf, I may as well be dead," Jesse says. "You said that I died trying to save you. I don't think it's only the Terran side of me that wants to learn to do whatever I can to help."

No, it's not. Earth Jesse would have been right here, arguing with me, probably a lot more vehemently. "Fine," I say. "You can come, but for now, just watch."

His smile lifts my spirits, even if it doesn't ease my growing anxiety. He may not want to sit on a shelf, but I'd prefer Jesse on a shelf, wrapped in bubble wrap, to no Jesse at all. If I have to do it. . . even knowing it's a double standard and that I'd hate him for doing the same to me, I will.

In the end, my concerns are a total waste. "How can I not Call fire?" I moan. "I already Woke."

"To your telepathic abilities," John says. "Clearly it requires a new breakthrough for any power that's still trapped in an existing prison."

I swear under my breath.

"Maybe that's a good thing," Jesse says. "You wouldn't want any more humans running around with newfound powers. It means the prison walls of Erra are still solid."

As solid as they were, at least, which isn't saying much. If Devlin's to be believed, and if John's mom really *did* Waste on Erra and *then* die on Earth. . . which feels like a huge *if*, then the walls have been coming down for a long time. "But the only defense I've got on Earth is this one." I Lift a huge, round hay bale and toss it a dozen feet away.

"Hey now." John looks around frantically, checking to make sure no one might have seen that.

"We're in the middle of nowhere," I say.

"It might seem that way to a city girl, but there are neighbors out here," he says. "Not a lot, but a few." He points to a tiny house that's so far away I can barely see it.

"How much property does your granny have?" I ask.

"Grandma Jean owns four hundred acres," he says. "I used to think it was ridiculous to have a half dozen abandoned farms scattered around the United States, but I'm beginning to think she's brilliant."

"Maybe we should be calling her," I say.

John's face shifts into an expression I can't read.

"Wait, did you already call her?"

"I checked in with her via text, only to let her know I'm here and not to come."

"When?"

"While we were watching that news report. I didn't say anything about you—just that I came here to wait things out."

I suppose that's not a betrayal, but I wish he'd told me when he did it. "Maybe we should loop her in more extensively."

"She hates Devlin," John says, "but I'm worried she may be part of the 'eliminate the Warden' camp."

My pulse accelerates. "Why do you say that?"

"Remember, my dad dragged me out of Isis pretty spectacularly a while back." He kicks a clod of dirt in the empty pasture. "She hasn't exactly been very forthcoming since then, but she did mention once that the prison was all that stood between us and a world teeming with monsters. She told me that if Dad ever did anything to change that, she'd kill him herself."

"Not promising," Jesse says.

"If confessing to grandma is out," I say, "that only leaves your dad, who assures me he's on my side, and—"

"What about *our* dad?" Jesse says. "All you said earlier

was that he's with Isis, and that here on Earth he abandoned us, but I'm sure he had a reason. I know you didn't know him like I did, but there was nothing in the world as important to him as his family."

"I might have a slightly different perspective on that," I say. "And you would too, if you had your Earth memories intact."

Jesse frowns. "But I'd also have my Terran ones, and even if he was imperfect or distracted from what matters here, the part of him that I know has rejoined the Earth part of him, yes?" He looks at John, as if John would know.

"We'd have to interact with someone who has been rejoined to know for sure," John says.

"Like Oliver?" Jesse says.

"Or Kahn." The suggestion just shoots out—I have no idea why. I know he's got to be pretty far up in the Isis power structure, since they let him interrogate me last time. And he knows my dad, for sure.

"I'm not sure that reaching out to him is a brilliant plan." John jams his hands into his pockets.

Something about his reaction makes me even more determined to look into the possibility. I know they don't get along, but in all our interactions, on both Earth and Terra, Kahn has been honest. Or at least, I believe he has. I hope it's not the strange pull I feel around him impacting my judgment. "Maybe I should call him."

"You can't," John says. "We destroyed your phone, remember?"

"I didn't save his number in my phone," I say. "It's in my bag—he wrote it down for me."

"You can't really mean to call him, just like that," John says. "If you freed him before you brought everyone else from Terra back over, or if he noticed that you saved Jesse before the world imploded, he'd have reported it. Even if he didn't, people would have noticed that you knew one another well on Terra. Either way, they'll be watching him."

He's probably right about that, but my disappointment at the thought of *not calling him* is acute. It's not rational, the faith I have that Kahn wants to help and protect me, but it's there all the same. I'm not certain that rationality is my strongest suit at this point. Not much that's been happening in my life makes logical sense. John did ask earlier what my gut said—but around Kahn, I'm not sure I can trust my gut. It's clearly been monkeyed with by someone or something I don't yet comprehend.

"Fine, then call Oliver. If you think he's on our side, and I know it's a gamble, but everyone we call, everyone we trust, they're all a risk, right? Let's call him."

John stares at me for a moment. "Are you sure?"

"I think so. I can't just hide out here, hoping no one finds us, and hoping I don't die on Erra."

"We do have the sleep study tonight," Jesse says. "Maybe it'll jog some memories loose. Something our parents said when you were small, or something else that might help us know what you should do."

"Or maybe an angel will fly down from heaven and sing me a prophetic song that tells me what to do, step by step."

The hurt look in Jesse's eye guts me.

"I'm sorry, J. I don't mean it like that. It's just that I've been hoping most of my life for good things to happen, and they never do. What I really want, more than anything in the world, is to run away and hide. You, me, and John. I wish I could just let the world burn or whatever's going to happen, and wash my hands of it. I don't owe anyone a thing. But the problem is that. . . "

"My soul's leaking." Jesse's voice is flat, but he sees right to the heart of it. Like always.

"I have no idea what we may need to do to fix that, but that's not the only issue. No matter where we go, I have no way to stay away from Erra. I have to sleep, even if it's not very good sleep, and when I do, I'm stuck there."

"You might unravel the prison without even meaning to, if you do nothing," John says.

"I either figure out how to reinforce it, or I figure out what will happen when I pull it apart like I did with Terra. Either way, I need answers before I can formulate a plan." I'm sick of being the last one to know. The one with the keys to the prison cells should be in the know, not in the dark.

John holds up his new cell phone. "So. . . I should call Oliver?"

I gulp. "Yeah, call him."

Jesse walks over next to me while John manually presses the numbers to call one at a time. My brother doesn't say anything, he just stands close. I'm not in danger, but he can sense that I'm nervous, that this matters to me. "When he presses buttons on that little gadget, someone else can hear what he says on the other end?"

Poor Jesse. His whole world is entirely different. Everyone else on Earth had their memories here to rely upon, but he's like a stranger in a very foreign land. "Yes, that's right. Assuming the person on the other end has a phone as well, the name for the gadget, their phone has a number assigned to it. John ditched his old phone, so Oliver's phone won't recognize that it's him calling. Often people won't answer phone calls from unknown numbers, but sometimes they do. Especially if they're hoping someone might call. . . "

Oliver has answered and John's talking. "Right. Can't talk long. If you're willing, we'll pick you up. I'll text you the address before I shut down this phone."

Silence.

"Do you think you can get away clean?"

Another pause.

"I guess since they don't know you came to see me, you're a low-level connection."

Ah, because they may have recognized that Jesse was working for John, which puts me on his radar. There really are too many crossovers between Amun and Isis. If they suspect I'm with John, they'll be tracking anyone he might call, and known associates, including Oliver. . . or worse, John's grandmother.

"Obviously I never told anyone what I did for you—did you?"

Silence again.

"Right, I'll text you, but I'll ask her first." Instead of hanging up, John turns toward me instead. "Do you know someone named Martin?"

My heart contracts. "Is he a Healer?"

John nods.

Tears spring to my eyes. I'd given up on ever seeing my Troupe family again.

"I'll take that as a yes. Which brings me to the more relevant question. Would you trust him to keep your existence secret?"

"Yes," I say without a second thought. I'd trust them with everything.

"Apparently they're being treated pretty roughly by Isis —Martin and a few others weren't Awake on Earth, but they've been located thanks to their close geographic proximity, Dallas, Oliver says. Your father Duncan's knowledge of their relationship to you, which you shared with him on Terra, hasn't helped them."

Martin's more of a father to me than Duncan ever was. I'm assuming that 'treated roughly' is code for torture, and that noncompliance will make things worse—and I don't want to think about what's worse than torture. Especially since the abuse is because of their connection to me. "We have to help them."

"You can't help anyone right now," John says bluntly. His face softens when he notices my dismay. "I don't have time for diplomacy, Alora. We can't keep this call live much longer or they'll be able to trace me if they're trying, even with my precautions."

"Fine, then what can you do?"

"Oliver says if he had help from someone. . . higher up, he might be able to get them out."

"You want to know whether he can reach out to Kahn."

John's nostrils flare. I can tell how much he hates the idea, but he's a good person. He didn't have to tell me about Martin, or mention that with Kahn's help, they might be able to free him. He did anyway.

"Do it," I say. "Or I can call him."

"It'll be way safer for Oliver if Kahn reaches out to him," John says. "Or at least, much less suspicious."

"Tell Oliver to wait for word from Kahn, and then hang up," I say.

John looks ill, but he does it. Then he hands the phone to me. "Should I use one of the other ones instead?" I ask. "So that they can't tie the two of them to the same phone?"

John shakes his head. "I've got the incoming data blocked on this one anyway. It's being rerouted—you know what? Don't worry about it. Trust me. This one's fine."

I jog back to the barn to grab the piece of paper Kahn gave me. I thought about tearing it up a few times, but now I'm glad I never did. My heart's not racing at the thought of talking to him—I'm just worried about Martin and Rosalinde, Thomas, Roland, Betty, and Abraham.

Even so, my hand trembles when I press the numbers. What if things are different now? What if, now that I've collapsed Terra, Kahn hates me? What if, by calling him, Martin and the others are killed instead? There are too many unknowns. I can't focus on all the things that could happen right now. If I don't do everything I can, I'll never be able to live with it. I press talk.

Half of me hopes it goes to voicemail.

The other half is desperate to hear his voice.

"Hello?" It's just as deep as I remember.

My heart hammers so heavily in my chest that I worry I'll pass out. "Hi," I say.

A sharp intake of air. "I think you have the wrong number."

"Oh," I say. "This isn't Domino's pizza?"

He tries to suppress it, but his low chuckle still sends chills up my spine. "No, but you should be glad of that. If you wait ten minutes, Jimmy John's on Eldridge will be open. That's much tastier." It's one-eleven p.m. Nothing opens at one-twenty-one in the afternoon. Clearly he's sending me a message.

"Got it."

I hang up.

"What did he say?" John's eyes are intent.

"He said to call the Jimmy John's on Eldridge in ten minutes."

"Smart," he says. "He can act like he's hungry and get away from whoever's bugging him."

"He's a bright guy," I say.

John cocks one eyebrow, but doesn't argue with me. I need to find out what their history is, but it probably shouldn't be my top priority right this second.

"I realized when he answered that I hadn't worked out with you what to ask. Should I mention that Martin and Rosalinde and Thomas are my friends, obviously, and tell him that Oliver will help him get them out?"

"That should be enough," John says. "If he betrays Oliver, he won't get your location. I trust Oliver to keep that information safe. As a Healer, he's not nearly as susceptible to mind control as anyone else."

"Whoa," Jesse says. "*Mind control?*"

John nods. "It's the province of an alpha Render. Reapers can't do things like that, and neither can your usual shifter, but the alphas. . . have special powers. I think it's so that they can keep the animal instincts of the pack in check."

"Fantastic," Jesse says. "Things weren't quite weird enough before."

"Kahn could probably be forced to reveal what he knows," John says, "but I doubt they could make Oliver say much at all."

"Which means Martin can't likely be forced either, or any of my other friends."

"Wait, your entire group of friends are Healers?" Jesse asks.

"Bingo," John says, "which is the only reason they haven't already cracked like eggs. They're stuck using old school tech, like some combination of drugs and psychotherapy on them."

"What kills me is that they don't know anything." I shudder. "This is all my fault. If they hadn't helped me on Terra—"

"Then they'd all be dead, because you'd never have been able to bring the souls back to Earth if you'd been caught as a child and killed. Stop beating yourself up, right now." John wraps an arm around my shoulders. "You're doing the best you can, and so are the rest of us. Sometimes fate's a real beast, but it doesn't help to dwell on it, or blame yourself for things you can't control."

"What I ought to do," I say, "is have Oliver figure out where they're keeping them." I flex my fingers and tighten them into fists. "Then I can go get them myself."

"Alora." John releases my shoulders and swivels me around until we're staring right at one another. "I know you want to do something. I know it's not in your nature to let other people suffer in your place. That's admirable. But consider what is at risk. If the wrong group within Isis finds you. . . they'll kill you. And then we're all doomed. Me, because I'm stuck in Erra, and the millions upon millions stuck on Rra."

He's right, of course. I'm just sick of doing nothing but sitting around. I must glance at the clock a dozen times in thirty seconds.

"What are you looking at?" Jesse asks.

I waste a few minutes explaining how we use clocks to tell time.

"That's so much more sensible than relying on the sun," Jesse says. "Do you know how often I had to blink for minutes at a time from the retinal burn?"

Ah, Jesse. He may not remember our past, but he's just as funny now, and he's still the light in my life. Soul bleed or not, I'll do whatever it takes to keep him by my side.

"It's time." John hands me the phone.

I focus on holding my hands steady when I press talk. "Jimmy John's Eldridge," a girl says.

"Yes, I was hoping to speak to a customer," I say. "I think he might be hanging around near the phone? He's tall, blond, and broad-shouldered, with a strong jaw?"

"Um, I don't see anyone like that." The girl laughs. "But if I do, I won't be passing him off to another woman on the phone."

Did I misunderstand him? Was he actually blowing me off? Maybe he didn't know it was me.

I lower the phone, my heart in my throat, about to hit end when I hear a squeak from the microphone. "Wait. You have got to be kidding me."

"Yes?"

"Your guy just walked in the door, and he's way hotter than you said. Like, wow."

"Can I talk to him?"

"Alora?" His voice is a slice of flourless chocolate ganache. . . for my ears.

I can barely breathe, but I manage to say, "Yes."

"You're alive." He exhales. "Thank goodness."

"I'm alive, and I need your help."

"Anything." His deep voice is confident, unhesitating. "Tell me what to do."

"Isis has taken my friends." I hate how small my voice sounds—how helpless I feel. A small part of me shouts that I should confront Isis—show them what I can do. Eliminate any resistance and free my friends myself. But how many would die? And would Jesse be safe if I fail? No, I can't. I *want* to be that person, but I'm not. I never have been. Also, there's the issue of the risk I'd be taking with the only person who can ferry people from Erra to Earth if the prison does fail.

"Martin," he says. "Right?"

"Yes, he was my adoptive father on Terra."

"I remember," he says. "He's going to be hard to reach."

"Do you know who else they have?"

He grunts. "A few, I think. Maybe someone named Rose? And a kid named Tom."

I close my eyes. "Anyone else?"

"I'm not totally sure, Alora. I'm not exactly their favorite person right now."

"Why not?"

He laughs. "We need to talk."

I *yearn* to talk to him, which kind of pisses me off. I shake all over like a dog evacuating a river. "I agree that we do, but I don't think I can risk them connecting you to me until you've done whatever you can. You don't have to be alone in this. John has a friend named Oliver Braetyllo who'll help you."

"The Healer?" Kahn pauses. "Wait. John *Rochester* has a friend who can help me?"

"I need you to focus." I really need to figure out what the deal is with these two. "Can you reach out to Oliver? If you two can get my friends out, Oliver knows how to find me."

"I'll do it," he says, "but our only hope is to move right now, before the top brass has worked out a game plan. Before they've gotten desperate."

"Fine with me. Wait, do you mean, *right now*, right now? As in, you'll leave from here to go free them?" I hope so—I really want them out. The sooner the better.

"They're distracted by the power struggle in the US government and trying to contain the rumors of telekinetics."

I bet they are. The idea actually makes me happy. Good luck containing this, jerks. "What do you need from me?"

"Nothing, except a promise that if I get them out, you'll be there to take us in." His voice drops an octave. "I really need to see you, Alora."

My heart lurches dangerously. I need to see him, too, even if I simultaneously hate that I do. Even if I have no intention of giving in to whatever this thing is between us. "I'll be here."

"Stay safe, then. I'm coming for you." He hangs up.

❧ *9* ❧

EARTH

"I think you have a story to tell me." I hand John his phone again and cross my arms over my chest.

He sighs, but he doesn't try to argue with me. "You might want to sit down for this one."

"Oh, I like story time," Jesse says.

John shakes his head. "You won't like this one."

I sit on the edge of the huge, leather sofa. Jesse sits down right next to me.

"You should eat something," John says.

"I'll eat when you're done." I point at the huge armchair across from the sofa.

He ignores me and starts to pace back and forth in front of the enormous television, which is thankfully off. "My mom's family was Fire Called, as you know. Well. So was Kahn's dad."

My jaw drops. "Wait, what?"

"It's actually quite uncommon for anyone who knows about Terra, or Erra, or whatever—the active followers of Amun and Isis—to marry outside of their particular strength."

"Really?" I scratch my head. "But your mom couldn't have been Fire Called herself."

"No, but her father was Woken by some overeager Followers of Amun when she was only seven years old. She was injured in that attack. Her family has been strongly Fire Called for generations, and Kahn's dad is her first cousin."

"Whoa," Jesse says. "So you're related to Kahn?"

"Second cousins." John's expression is sour.

"And you still hate each other?"

"I'm getting there." He drops into the chair, finally. "Mom's cousin, Lionel, who is also Kahn's dad, well, his dad was Fire Called, but powers follow the mother."

"Okay," I say.

"And his mother's parents were both from Lifter lines."

"I don't see—"

John stands up again. "Just listen, alright?"

I sit back on the sofa. Clearly this is a sensitive issue, so as hard as it is for me, I resolve to keep my questions to myself until he's done.

"Kahn and I were best friends," John says. "My mom and his dad were close. They grew up together after Kahn's grandpa died. Even as adults, they stayed very close. I think that's why we lived next door to each other. Mom loved Lionel and Margaret, Kahn's parents. When Dad was on business trips, or when he was busy dealing with Isis stuff, we ate dinner at their house almost every night."

I open my mouth, but I remember to shut it again.

"Then Dad found that prophecy and left Isis." John sits again, but he's looking at his feet. "He was given an ultimatum. Wake me up, or they'd assume he was either a traitor or not fully dedicated. So he did it."

It might just be me, but the room feels hot, even with the sounds of the air conditioner blowing. I tug the hem of my shirt out to encourage some airflow. But even waiting what feels like a long time, John's not saying anything else.

"Did Waking you somehow upset Kahn?"

"He's Awake on Earth. Did he tell you that?"

I shrug. "I mean, I assumed."

"Well, my dad told Amun to do what they had to do to me. They sent a few guys out, following 'standard protocols.'" He glances at Jesse and then turns to me again. "You can imagine how that went, probably."

I close my eyes, trying not to relive the night they shot Jesse in the foot and attempted to rape me, which Woke Jesse. I really don't want to think about the moment they finally killed him, which Woke me.

"I'm only talking about this because you asked me to." John's kneeling in front of me. "I'm so sorry—it's why I never mentioned it before. I knew it would hurt you."

I shake my head. "Keep going. I need to know."

"They didn't expect me to be quite as strong as I was. When they Woke me, I flamed them good." John's hands squeeze the couch cushions on either side of me. "It set my house on fire."

He did mention something about that—I can't even imagine.

"My dad wasn't home—one of Amun's terms. He couldn't interfere." The muscles of his jaw work. "I was actually relieved that my mom had already left my dad at that point. I had no idea that she was going to—" His Adam's apple usually isn't very prominent, but I see it now, shifting up and down as he swallows. "That meant I was alone in the house. I didn't bother trying to figure out how to stop the flames. I think I wanted it to burn. I wanted to hurt my dad the way he had hurt me. I wanted to ruin something that mattered to him."

I can understand that.

"To this day, I'm not sure whether I'd have been able to

snuff the flames." John's eyes are unfocused, staring past me at something that happened a long time ago. "I didn't even try."

I put my hand on his arm. "It's okay. It was just a house."

His eyes snap to mine. "That's the thing. My house was empty, but when the fire jumped to the house next door, by then, it was too late. I couldn't suppress the flames, not then. It was too big and I had no idea what I was doing. I did try, but I couldn't stop it."

Oh, no.

"Kahn's house burning Woke him. He was so strong, he basically blew the wall off the side of his house and jumped to safety. By the time he reached the curb and realized his parents hadn't escaped, it was too late to go back."

I close my eyes. Kahn blames John for killing his parents. I knew he was an orphan, but. . . what a tragedy. They'd have Wasted afterward on Terra, just like Kahn said. What a misery all around.

"Stop beating yourself up, right now." I throw his own words back at him. "You did the best you could, and you still are. Sometimes fate's a real beast, and it doesn't help to dwell on it."

When he looks up into my eyes, his own golden green eyes haunted and ashamed, I do the only thing I can think of to take that pain away. I press my lips against his.

His hands grip my thighs, claiming me. His mouth slants across mine immediately, hungrily.

A shiver climbs upward from my belly to my throat, and the second he pulls back even a hair, I pant against his mouth. "You're a good person, John. One of the best."

"Is this usual behavior, on Earth?" Jesse's mouth is twisted, but his eyes sparkle. "Kissing someone like this, in front of other people in the family room?"

I laugh then, and John does too, his forehead leaning

against mine. "Nope," he says, "but it should be." He kisses me again, but this time it's light. Playful. "And I mean to repeat it as often as Alora will allow it."

With nothing else to do, after we eat lunch, we turn the television back on.

"If you're tuning in right now, we're sharing a special broadcast. The President decided not to wait for the morning to make his statement. They've discovered the cause of the strange happenings around the world, and it appears the culprit is right here, on domestic soil."

My eighth grade school photo was an especially unflattering one, what with my thrift store shirt and the haircut I gave myself, but I certainly never expected to see it staring back at me on a sixty-inch monitor blaring the national news. "This is an old photo, of course, but we have a digital rendering of what we believe she would look like today."

An image that strongly resembles the Terran version of me flashes across the screen next. My hair is light brown, which might help me, and my eyes are fiery and full of confidence.

"She could be going by the name Alice Walker or the name Alora Benson. You should assume, if you see her, that she is armed and extremely dangerous. Even if you consider yourself to be a military grade weapons expert, and even if you're armed to the teeth, you are to stand down and call this hotline. It is absolutely imperative that we recover her immediately."

"Looks like Isis has taken control of the US government," John says.

"Why do you say that?" I ask.

"Because my dad was having you surveilled. He'd have actual photos to share."

"That's not very reassuring," Jesse says. "And your dad would be able to discover the whereabouts of this barn too, wouldn't he?"

John shakes his head, but the discomfort in his eyes isn't very reassuring. "Grandma Jean would."

"And she's with Isis," I say. "As soon as anyone there realizes for sure that we're connected. . . ." A terrible thought hits me. "Wait. Did Henry know you? Because you met that night in La Centerra, after our date."

"I knew an Isis family owned the Perry's chains," John says. "When I heard you were going on a date with one of them, I looked into him, but I doubt he knows who I am or that I had a startup around the corner. I'm an elemental remember? And even on Earth, I'd switched to Amun. We moved in pretty different circles."

"That's a relief."

"What are they saying to explain how you caused people to have bizarre telekinetic episodes?" John asks.

We focus on the television broadcast again, although they're mostly obsessed with the importance of identifying me and immediately notifying the government when someone does. Ugh.

But finally, the broadcast restarts.

"A child prodigy has developed a new technology that is rendering people temporarily able to move things with their minds. Yes, you heard that correctly. If you or anyone you know has suddenly become able to shift objects with the power of your mind, even if it's only something as small as a pencil, it's urgent that you call the following number immediately. You'll need to be treated for this side effect immediately. The reaction is the result of your body's response to an experimental pulse that is traveling through electronics—which means it could affect literally anyone at all. The government has thrown all its resources into halting this disturbing attack as quickly as possible and studying the impact. But we can't help you if we don't know you're affected."

"I'm a child prodigy now?" I snort. "And my science

experiment gives select people the power of telekinesis, but not others?"

"Look," Jesse says.

"Anyone found possessing these skills will receive immediate compensation from a fund the US Congress has taken emergency measures to establish. Make sure you call right away, not only to be treated for any possible complications, but also to gain access to your share of that compensation pool."

"Brilliant move," John says. "Isis will gain immediate access to anyone who isn't aligned with Amun."

"Are we sure it's Isis?" I tilt my head. "Your dad is smart. He knows that *you* know he has surveillance photos of me from more recent times. He knows I don't trust him. What better way to drive me to him than to pretend that Isis is in control, while he's the one pulling the strings?"

John shakes his head. "Wow, they really underestimated you, didn't they?"

Jesse's beaming. "A child prodigy who is also unbelievably paranoid. A dangerous combination for sure."

I slap my forehead. "Where did you tell Oliver we'd meet him?"

"A feed store," John says. "I figured that's the last place anyone would hunt for you, plus it has a lot of paved space and outbuildings." He's pretty creative. I'll give him that.

"Good idea. At what time?"

"Six-forty-five. It closes at seven. You both have to report to the sleep lab by nine at the latest, or they'll cancel your appointments."

"I'm not sure we should really go," Jesse says. "Not now that everyone will be looking for you."

"No one will expect her to show up at a sleep lab," John says. "Even if they manage to hack your email address, which you did a decent job of hiding by the way, they would go to the wrong place. There are hundreds of sleep labs in the greater Houston area. They'd never obsessively check each one, precisely because they'd expect you to lie low."

"I agree that learning about how I access Erra and finding any memories I might not recall is urgent," I say. "But we can't risk being taken by Isis—or Amun—so I think we'll need to sort of play it by ear. There was only the one guy there the last time we went."

"Scott," John says. "He didn't seem very competent."

"But he saw my face clearly," I say. "Their age-progressed photo isn't great, but there are decent odds he'll recall the name I used—Alice Walker—and he'll be calling that number right now."

John swears under his breath. "Fine."

He clacks away on his keyboard. "I'll book you at another lab, under a different name, and we'll tell them you forgot your ID. I don't even recall the last guy asking for it. It's a little further away, but it's not far from the feed store."

"If he did report her," Jesse says, "they'll be checking all the area sleep labs tonight."

John curses again.

"How do you feel on Earth about . . . borrowing people?" Jesse asks.

"It's called kidnapping, and we frown on it," I say.

"That's too bad," he says.

I roll my eyes. "Why is that too bad?"

"Because Jesse and I could certainly nab a sleep lab employee and their equipment in the truck and bring them back here instead," John says. "And although kidnapping is widely considered to be wrong, I think there's something to be said for weighing the greater good against a lesser evil."

It's a slippery slope. I don't like it at all.

"Maybe instead of kidnapping someone, you make them explain what you need to do and just steal their equipment?"

John and Jesse look at each other and speak at the same time. "Sure," Jesse says. "Okay," John says.

I'm immediately suspicious. "You're not planning on doing that, are you?"

John shrugs. At least Jesse has the decency to look guilty. "We won't be harming anyone, not in the long run."

"Unless they freak out and try to escape," I say.

"You'll Bind them in place," John says. "They won't be able to injure themselves or anyone else."

"All night?" I sigh. "This plan is flawed."

"We literally just conceived it. We'll work out the issues," John says.

We argue in circles for more than an hour, but they never relent. Finally I get sick of it and tell them to go.

"You keep this phone on you," John says. "I don't like the idea of leaving you here."

"What choice do you have?" I ask.

John clenches his fist. "None at all."

"Please keep Jesse safe." I glance at my brother. I hate the idea of him being away from me more than I hate the thought of being alone. Because out of the three of us, he seems like the weakest. The most vulnerable.

"I'll be fine, Alora. I need to help."

"Alright, then do it. Just hurry so we aren't late to that feed store."

"Steinhauser's," John says. "It's an odd enough name that I bet you remember it."

While they're gone, I practice Lifting things. As easy as it was on Terra—with the strength I had there—it's even simpler here. I Lift an enormous steel tractor like it's a shoe. I set it down gently, and pick up some of the attachments that are practically hidden in the tall grass next to it. One of them looks like a rototiller. One is. . . to drag the pasture, maybe? I have no idea what the big metal box is for. Eventually, I get bored, so I work on more complicated things, like Lifting the water from the pond. I start with small batches, but by the end, I Lift each and every drop and everything contained within it. I had no idea quite how much vegetation grows in a pond.

The fish hate me, basically.

I don't blame them. Being forced to acknowledge your own mortality is uncomfortable, I imagine, but they don't have the capacity to understand what's going on. Eventually they're jumping and flopping and generally thrashing around in all parts of the pond, so I decide to call it quits.

I ought to practice my agility. Without a course of any kind, I have to improvise. I start by Binding odd farm equipment in the air, and racing around on top of it. I leap from one thing to the next.

I stumble when my toe catches on the edge of a wheelbarrow, and I'm forced to Bind air to keep from plunging to the ground and landing on my head. The impact wrenches my shoulder painfully. But it reminds me that I can Bind air. I release all the various tools and pile them into a heap. Then I practice Binding air and sensing where it's located.

Once I tire of that, I work on expanding my senses.

I feel for the grass. The bushes. The trees. The birds.

Each and every one feels just a little different. Each and every one pulses, somehow—at least, the living things do. Even the inanimate objects have an energy signature. I close my eyes and spin in a circle. Then, keeping my eyes closed, I reach outward, sensing for everything around me. The wheelbarrow's only a few feet to my left, turned sideways. I right it without thinking.

There's a bird watching me from a live oak at the edge of the pasture. A lizard's hiding not far from me, around the back corner of a half-rotted fence post. A wasp—no, a yellow jacket—buzzes a few feet from my head. I bat him sideways and he veers toward me. I slap him away easily, opening my eyes with wonder.

The world is a place I never before knew.

How could all of this have been around me all this time and I never bothered to even *feel for* it? Sometimes we're so focused on the things in front of our eyes that we ignore our other senses. The squirrel races along the lowest branch of a pecan tree. A family of mice freeze as if they can sense me reaching out for them on the rafters of the outbuilding where John's BMW is parked.

All of this has always been here.

It's me who has changed.

The rev of an engine in the driveway calls my attention forward, but it's not John's grandmother's truck. It's a huge white delivery truck. The engine is much louder, the rear cargo space tremendous. I brace myself to fight, until I extend my senses to the cab.

Jesse and John are both inside, along with a heavy, older woman—they likely traded the truck for this because the equipment wouldn't quite fit in the other vehicle. After all, what's grand theft auto when you're already stealing some very expensive medical equipment and kidnapping the person who knows how to run it?

John pulls the truck right up in front of the barn and shuts it off. He opens the door, revealing the shrieking voice of our newest team member.

"—told you already," she says, her voice shrill. "I don't know how to interpret any of the readings. I'm useless without a doctor to read the findings."

I'm sure she's terrified already, so I doubt that seeing the villainous mastermind from the news is going to reassure her. I wait for John and Jesse to go inside the barn, leaving the door hanging open, before I walk toward the truck. I Lift the back latch open and then Lift the contents from the back and float them inside the front door of the barn, the light from my eyes illuminating the ground in front of me.

I follow the huge machines and computer equipment inside, a few steps behind.

John and Jesse are arguing with the woman in the hallway that leads to the bedrooms when she turns toward me.

Her jaw drops open and the loudest scream I've ever heard emerges from her mouth.

I can see that they're trying to quiet her, but their pleas have no effect whatsoever. Finally, John tackles her and covers her mouth with his hand as they tumble toward the ground. "It's not what you think," he says.

Her eyes are so wide that I can practically see all the way around her eyeballs.

"She's not a terrorist, and she's not a prodigy," John says. "She's not a scientist at all."

"It's a vast government conspiracy," Jesse says, "perpetuated by either the Followers of Amun, or the Followers of Isis, two groups that have been around since the days of Egyptian supremacy."

We maybe should have told him the truth of Earth's history in a slightly less stilted way. I set the equipment down wherever it will fit. "I assume we're going to set this up in one of the bedrooms?"

John nods.

"Are you planning on letting her go so she can tell me where to put it?" I lift one eyebrow.

"Will you keep quiet if I uncover your mouth?" John shakes her a bit as he asks the question.

She whimpers.

"Is that a yes?" Jesse asks.

John rolls over her with an irritated huff. Thankfully, she doesn't moan any more.

"It's nearly six," I say. "How far away is this feed place?"

John looks at his watch. "Sorry it took us so long. She wasn't exactly very helpful."

"I will escape," she says, "and I'll call that number and report her."

"That would be a big mistake." I walk toward her. "My brother might not have explained things very well, but he wasn't kidding. What you're seeing on the news right now are the results of a prison break, of sorts. There was a wall in place that kept the citizens of Earth safe." I Lift a chair and spin it around in front of her like a top.

She gasps and begins to shake.

"I'm not trying to scare you, and I won't lie to you like the people on television have. It's partly my fault that all the people around the world have discovered they have telekinetic abilities. I clearly possess them, too, but when they call that number, the government isn't going to compensate them, and there's no way to cure it. It's an ability they've always had. The reason we need your help is that I'm the Warden—the only person who is capable of either releasing, or preserving the wall that keeps every person on Earth from accessing their special powers."

She gulps. "What about me? Do I have magical powers I can't use?"

Jesse laughs.

"You do," I say. "It's crazy to think about, but if you're not telekinetic, that means you have some affinity to an animal form, or you have the ability to manipulate the elements in some way."

"Everyone tells me I have a green thumb," she says. "I love my garden. It's the only place I'm happy."

"What's your name?" I ask.

"Beth."

"I know that things are scary right now, Beth." I crouch next to her. "I'm the poster child of things going wrong. In fact, I fought with my brother and my friend John about this whole mad plan—I begged them not to bring you here. But they insisted that we would keep you safe and you'd be unharmed, and they saw something I didn't quite accept yet. They recognized that I need answers—things I may only learn in my dreams, from my past memories. The news was wrong when it said that I'm a terrorist, but they're looking for me for a reason." I stand up. "I'm the only one who might be able to stop them from running every aspect of America."

Beth sits up.

"I would hate to have to restrain you. I would feel terrible about making this experience more miserable than it has to be, but I really do need your help, and I don't think we can risk you contacting anyone about my whereabouts."

"You're going to kill me, aren't you?" Her lower lip trembles.

I shake my head. "No, I won't do that, no matter how you react."

"Well," Jesse says, "provided you don't try to attack or kill Alora, we won't."

I glare at him. "We won't kill you, even if you try to kill me."

"I'm not promising that either," John says.

"Oh, come on!" I rub my forehead. "Look. I'm not sure how to convince you that what I'm saying is true, but—"

Beth mutters something under her breath, and I realize it's not English. Maybe this is my solution. "What language was that?" I ask.

"I was born in the Netherlands," she says. "I moved here when I was fourteen."

"Ah." I crouch down next to her again. "One of the bizarre things about being the Warden, about being the one person who can dismantle the various prisons, seems to be that I can understand the languages of everyone held within them. It makes sense, if you think about it. I can't very well manage people with whom I can't communicate."

"You're saying that you speak Dutch?"

I shrug. "I never have before, no. But if you speak to me in Dutch, I'll understand you, and I'll be able to respond in kind."

She stares at me for a moment. "The news didn't say anything about that."

"I doubt any of them know I can do it."

"It's the reason I believed her wild stories when we were kids," Jesse says.

My eyes fly to his. Has he remembered?

He shakes his head slightly, and I remember that I told him about that—this morning. Dang. "What about it?" I ask. "Care to test my claim?"

She rubs her hands together briskly, and then straightens her shoulders. "Was jij erbij?"

I blink for a second. She's asked whether I was there. 'Were you there?' is literally what that means. I think. "Waarbij?" I blink.

"Aardbei!" Beth says.

"Strawberry?" I'm so confused. "You're asking me whether I was there? At. . . a strawberry field?"

Beth laughs. "If you learned Dutch, literally anywhere on Earth, you'd have heard that phrase sometime. It's a common rhyme we teach children. Everyone says it. Where and strawberry rhyme, see?" She switches to Dutch. "Waarbij? Aardbei."

"So. . . you. . . don't believe that I speak it?"

She stands up and brushes off her pants. "Actually, I do believe you. You couldn't have known I'd speak Dutch, and you understood me and replied appropriately for someone who comprehends the literal words but knows nothing of the culture."

"So you'll help me?"

"I really hope I'm not wrong, but yes. I'll help you. And I'll be praying that God helps us all."

❧ 10 ❧

EARTH

"It's time to go," John says. "And no matter how much you've bonded, or how politely she's helped us set up the equipment, I strongly recommend you Bind Beth."

I turn her way, worried about how she'll react.

She drops into a chair. "Go ahead," she says. "I understand why you need to do it."

Just when I think I have people figured out, someone goes and surprises me. "Thank you," I say. "I wish I didn't have to do this."

"It's hard to trust anyone when the whole world is out to get you."

Exactly.

"It's alright," she says, "but maybe hurry back?"

"I will." I Bind her hands and feet, and then I Bind the chair in place for good measure.

As we climb into the truck, Jesse asks, "Do we know how long the Bindings will last on Earth, with you gone?"

I shrug. "No, but I'm not worried. I believe her."

"I'm sure it'll hold," John says. "With your massive

power, I imagine, even from a more substantial distance they'll be fine."

"Why are we heading to the feed store so early?" I glance at my watch. "We have half an hour. Is it that far away?"

John shakes his head. "We need to return this truck before its owner realizes we stole it."

I don't know anything at all about the geography here, but it looks like we're headed somewhere decidedly not rural. "Whoa," I say. "How did you take it? I assumed its owner was bonked on the head and already reporting it's loss."

"We didn't want to do anything that would draw attention to us," John says. "Jesse Lifted the keys from the delivery driver as he was headed into a diner. We're hoping he won't have contacted anyone by the time we get back."

"We were only gone an hour and some change," Jesse says. "Right?"

"Yep," John says.

"We went to a market for food," Jesse says. "And then we have been to sleep labs, but what are all these other storefronts? Do people not make anything in their own homesteads anymore?"

Ten minutes and a rather boring discussion about economics of scale later, and. . . "Um, are those police lights?" I point.

John swears. "I figured that with as much going on today as there is, they'd be slower to respond."

"Or they're on high alert, since Isis knows I'm probably still close by. If I were them, I'd have all the police units working double duty right now."

After a bit of back and forth, John decides to ditch the van in a nearby neighborhood, leaving me and Jesse to hike across an empty field while he retrieves the truck. Luckily, no one so much as glances our way—probably thanks to my black hair and sunglasses and Jesse's open and friendly demeanor. I don't mention to him that, on Earth, smiling at everyone indiscriminately usually means you're a pervert or a little dopey. Why burst his bubble of happiness?

"Need a ride?" John waves at us from the road.

Even with our scenic detour, we're only on track to be five minutes late to Steinhausers. My eyes scan the road obsessively, searching for police officers or anyone who might notice my face, my knee bouncing persistently for the entire drive.

"We're nearly there." John drops his hand over my knee. "It's going to be alright, Alora, I swear."

"Oh, it is?" I hold up my index finger. "Martin could be dead." I hold up my middle finger. "Kahn and Oliver could have been caught trying to save him." I hold up my ring finger. "They could all be under interrogation right now." I waggle all my fingers, on both hands. "Or this could be a trap. Oliver could have betrayed you. Or they could have been followed. There are a million ways this goes wrong, and only one way it goes right."

"You're adorable when you're freaking out." John brushes a kiss against my mouth while we idle at a stoplight.

Part of me wants to slap him for acting like I'm being ridiculous, but most of me just wants to kiss him back. I sigh against his mouth. "I hope you're right."

"Everything's a gamble right now. Every single move. All we can do is our best, right?"

It helps—his confidence, his surety that we'll be okay. And then I see the sign: Steinhauser's. My heart accelerates, even as my eyes scan for any sign of Oliver, or Martin, or Kahn.

"Guys?" Jesse points around the back of the storefront, to what looks like a loading area. John swings into the very far edge of the front parking lot, allowing us a view of the back and front simultaneously.

Which is why I can see perfectly when a teenager driving a forklift miscalculates as he's rolling up a ramp, and the entire thing tilts sideways. I want to Lift him to safety, but I can't, not out in the open, not with the entire world searching for me. I'm stuck watching, gape-mouthed, as the entire thing tumbles three feet to the concrete below, crushing the kid underneath like a beetle under a steel-toed boot. I can't suppress the involuntary cry I make at the sight.

Before I have time to formulate any kind of plan, someone small darts in next to it, and tugs and tugs and tugs the boy out from under the forklift. Where did that person come from? I squint, but can't make out any details, not from this angle.

But I hear someone else shouting at the Good Samaritan. "Rosie, not here. You can't."

My breath catches in my throat, and I shove Jesse out the door so I can escape. I'm sprinting across the parking lot and around the corner without another thought. "Rosalinde?"

Her hands are above the boy, her eyes shining, and then she slumps. *My* Rosalinde, Healing people. I can hardly believe my eyes.

I'm not the only woman with powers.

I should have processed this when I was watching the video of the little girl on TV, but that felt almost fake somehow. I'm accustomed to assuming things on television aren't real. But this happened right in front of my very own eyes. And it means that Rosalinde may have saved the boy, but now she's injured herself—not to the same extent, but judging from the accident, still pretty badly.

Martin reaches her before I do—putting his hands on her as his eyes light up, too. He looks exactly the same as he always did on Terra—other than the Earth-appropriate clothing. His hair's even a little too long here, just like it always was with the troupe.

"Martin," I say.

He turns toward my voice with wonder in his eyes. "Alora! It is you."

Rosalinde and Martin both stand up and walk toward me.

"You got out!" I open my arms wide.

They step toward me without hesitating and Martin wraps me and Rosalinde both in a bear hug.

"We did." Oliver steps out from behind two huge semi-truck trailers full of hay, and I realize that's where they were hiding.

"How many of you are there?" I look around, but I don't see anyone else.

Thomas and Roland hop down from the trailer, both of them beaming at me. "Four of us, and Oliver," Thomas says. "Your friend Kahn was brilliant, by the way."

"Where is Kahn?" I spin in a circle.

The teenager who rolled the small forklift is climbing to his feet. "Whoa, dude. I can't believe that thing didn't crush me."

So, he's clearly not the smartest, but at least he's unlikely to report that we did anything dodgy. "I'm so glad you're okay," Rosalinde says.

"Thanks for dragging me out from under there," the kid says, running a hand through his tousled hair. "I think I must have been pretty dazed."

Rosalinde smiles at him, and I realize she's distracting him so he won't look at me. Smart girl.

I walk quickly toward the truck, wondering where exactly we're planning to put everyone. I guess I kind of assumed they'd have some sort of transportation of their own. "Where's Kahn?" Jesse asks. "I was looking forward to seeing him."

Oliver answers from right behind me. "We ran into a snag," he says. "And he had to fall back to deal with it."

I spin around, less concerned about being spotted than I am about what exactly that means. "A *snag*?"

"The thing is, to break them out, Kahn had to attack the guards," Oliver says. "But he had to make sure people didn't realize it was him doing it."

"Okay," I say. "Did it not work?"

"It did, actually," Oliver says, "and I reported to Heal the injured guards, just as he planned I would."

"Then what?"

"He hit all the guards with a tranq," Oliver says, "which was another stroke of brilliance. He's quite the tactical planner, that guy. But it meant we had less than twenty minutes to get them loose and then clear out of there."

"Could you drag this out any more?" John glances around. "We need to leave ASAP. Spit it out, Oliver. What went wrong?"

"Everything went according to plan," Oliver says, "until we got close to here."

"I noticed an Isis operative in a car behind us," Kahn says quietly from behind me.

Everyone jumps, and we turn around. He's standing on the top of the ledge from which the teenager fell, light streaming across the planes of his face. His eyes are clear and bright, and his mouth is as full as I remember.

He's bigger somehow, bigger than I remember him being on Earth, more like Terran Kahn. Broader shoulders, dark golden skin. I should be asking about our plans, or encouraging him to get everyone loaded up to go, but I can't seem to do anything other than stare at him. My mouth is dry, and my eyelids flutter.

"I thought I should report from a different direction,"

Kahn says, "now that I've lost them. But we really ought to leave right away. Being out in the open's a bad idea right now."

The same joy I've felt every time I see him swells in my chest, and a familiar golden halo of light surrounds Kahn's face, as though his diamond-cut features needed an extra boost of any kind. It usually pisses me off, but right now, I'm too full of relief that he's alright.

"Where to?" John asks me.

"I trust them," I say. "Let's take them straight back."

John gestures toward the truck.

"I doubt we'll all fit in that," Kahn says, "and we should probably split up and take different routes to wherever we're going if possible. If you'll send me the address, anyone who can't fit in your truck can ride with me."

"I'm delighted to see you," Jesse says, "but I'm not leaving Alora."

Kahn almost drops his keys. He steps a little too close to the ledge, not paying attention to anything but Jesse's face. "How are you—Is that really you?"

"I'll explain later," I say. "I swear."

Kahn's eyes drop to mine and a thrill zings up my spine. Like before, on the phone, his voice drops to a timbre I'm beginning to think is reserved just for me. "We have a lot of things to discuss."

John rattles the address off for Kahn, whose head snaps up. He taps it quickly into his phone.

John practically glares at Kahn. "Please tell me that's not your normal cell phone."

"Of course it is," Kahn says. "Why? Are you implying they can track me with this little old thing?" He rolls his eyes and turns around.

"He's such an insufferable jerk," John says.

"Kahn?" Jesse asks. "Really?"

"Let's just go," I say.

I pretend not to be counting down the moments on the drive home, but I doubt Jesse or John buys my faux calm. The anxiety is obvious in my tapping fingers, my furrowed brow, and my frenetic scanning of the roads. "Everything's alright," John says.

"It's just that, in my life, things rarely go well."

"Breaking your innocent friends out of prison so you can hide in a nondescript barn, where you've kidnapped a sleep study tech to try and shock you into REM sleep for the first time in your life—this is your version of 'things going well' in your life?" John's eyes are serious, but his tone is light and playful.

"Actually, as pathetic as that sounds, yes. Things are going almost unbelievably well for me right now."

"Geez." John tightens his hands reflexively on the steering wheel. "Well, I hope we can change your usual pattern, then. I have every hope that over the next few days, you'll reach new heights of good fortune."

Jesse chuckles. "We can dream."

"Well, you can," I say. "Not me."

John hangs a right, and pulls out in front of a white 4Runner that flashes its lights. I turn around and realize it's Kahn. We're less than two miles from the barn, and they're here, right when and where they should be. Maybe things are looking up for me, finally. Heaven knows I'm due. Jesse bumps me with his shoulder and I lean on him. If it took a lifetime of lousy for me to save up enough good luck to save him, I'm okay with it.

We reach the barn and get both vehicles tucked into the outbuilding, hidden from view of the road. Before I can go inside, Kahn reaches for my arm.

John blocks him.

The two men lock eyes.

A tiny flame springs to life in front of John, and Kahn's eyes light up.

"Whoa, whoa, whoa," I say. "We're all friends here, remember?"

Oliver clucks. "I'm gonna go inside and look for something to eat. I'm starving, and no restaurants are open today, thanks to the collapse of Terra."

"I'll join you," Jesse says. "I learned how to make a TV dinner this morning."

"Huh," Oliver says. "I'm not sure whether that's sad or kind of awesome."

"If you're asking me, I'll go with awesome," Jesse says. "It had something called macaroni with cheese as a side dish, and while it wasn't very large, I can't stop thinking about it. It was salty, and creamy, and soft all at the same time."

"I'll follow you," Martin says. "In fact, I bet we all will." He tosses his head, and Rosalinde, Thomas, and Roland all duck through the door.

"You two don't like each other," I say. "And I get it. John told me why."

"Did he?" Kahn lifts one eyebrow. "That's surprising. I wonder whether he told you the truth."

"Stop," I say. "Just stop. I don't care whether you're best friends. I don't care whether you want to make macrame necklaces together or braid each other's back hair."

"I don't have back hair," John says.

"That must mean that Nair really works," Kahn says.

John balls up one hand into a fist, like he's going to punch him.

I reach my hands out without thinking, pressing one against each man's chest. John's pec muscles are broad and well defined. I could probably hold my hand against his pectorals all day.

But when my hand touches Kahn, a shock rocks through both of us. I practically tumble back against John from the reverb. "What was that?" I whisper the question.

Kahn shakes his head, and his consonants are clipped. "I need to talk to you."

"Pass," John says.

But I'm about done having someone speak for me, or over me, or about me. "Actually, we do need a minute." I step away from John and turn to look pointedly at the front door, silently commanding him to go inside.

He hesitates a second or two, and he swallows slowly, but when I don't relent, he spins on his heel and does it.

Kahn steps away from the house and toward the back pasture, where the sun is rapidly setting on the horizon.

I don't have the energy to argue with anyone else, so I follow him as he walks away from the barn. I pause for a moment and feel for my Bindings on Beth inside, releasing them. Then I jog to catch up with Kahn. I'm not a small person, but he's enormous. It's almost uncomfortable for me to keep up with the pace set by his natural stride length.

The barn's almost out of view, occluded by a large pecan tree and a live oak, when he finally stops. He spins toward me so fast that I startle. "You're alive."

I nod.

"And you saved Jesse?"

"I'm not sure, if I'm being honest," I say. "I'm surprised Oliver didn't tell you about it."

He frowns. "What does that mean?"

"Oliver Healed me yesterday. He did tell you that?"

Kahn steps closer, looking me over head to toe, his eyes distressed. "Healed you from what?"

"I had a little run-in on Erra. Some lava ate half of my thigh."

Kahn's eyes drop and he stares intently at my thigh, as though it might give out at any moment.

"I'm fine now, in case you haven't developed x-ray vision," I say. "He Healed me. It's what Healers do."

When he looks up, his eyes are practically shining, but

not because he's Lifting. They're watery, almost, and I realize he's relieved. He was worried. . . for me. For my well-being.

"Hey." I touch his arm, delighted when nothing bizarre jolts me this time. "I'm fine. And look! I can touch you without being shocked."

His laugh is rough, like pebbles grinding together under pressure. "Were you funny on Terra? I don't remember that."

"Earth me is funnier, a little less reverent, and a little more willing to compromise."

He steps closer still, not stopping until only inches separate us. For the first time in months, the Houston heat doesn't even bother me. "I like every version of you I've ever met."

My heart soars as I make sense of the words, and something strange pools inside my belly. My arms itch to circle his neck and my lips practically buzz from an overwhelming desire to kiss him. His head lowers toward mine slowly, so slowly, his eyes never wavering, intent on mine even in the quickly fading light. Standing next to him in the dark feels more intimate, somehow, even than the alcove on Terra felt.

The pounding of my heart in my ears brings me back to myself when he's only a hair away.

It's like ripping off a Band-Aid, like claws on a chalkboard, like stepping in an icy puddle, but I stumble away from him. "No," I say. "No."

"No?" He looks dazed. "Why?"

"Is that why you walked out here?" I ask. "You didn't want to talk, you wanted to kiss me?"

His fingers brush against his mouth absently, like he's forgotten his own name. I know that feeling, and it's not good. I have no idea what power is pushing us together so forcefully, but when I'm in control of my senses, I hate it.

"I'm dating John." I'm not really sure whether that's true, but I need it to be. "I can't kiss you. If that's all you wanted, then we should head back."

He shakes his head. "No, that's not it. I brought you out here to confess something. I lied to Oliver, and I lied to the rest of them, but I can't lie to you."

Lied? My anxiety redoubles. "About what?"

"I couldn't have saved them," he says. His voice drops to a whisper. "Not alone, anyway."

"What did you do?" I grind out the words. Rage bubbles deep inside of me, and I'm sorely tempted to see exactly what I can do here on Earth against another Lifter.

"Nothing that will harm you, I swear it. If I had a way to reach out to you and ask your permission, I would have. I knew the people you asked me to save mattered to you. I knew you wanted them removed from harm's way, and if they hadn't been extricated when they were. . . " He shrugs. "I'm not sure there would have been much left."

"I'm grateful you saved them, but what haven't you told me?"

"I needed help," he says simply. "Your father, Duncan, helped me. I wasn't shaking an Isis tail. I was circling back to lose *him*."

"What?" I don't understand.

"I told him I'd lead him to you if he helped us escape, but I didn't tell Oliver or the others about my deal."

"When will he be here?"

Kahn shakes his head. "He won't. I circled back to talk to him—and instead of planning our approach and what he might say to you, I knocked him out. I ditched my cell phone and the tracker he left on my car, and then I rejoined the rest of you."

"What do you need to confess to me, then?"

"I wasn't sure it would work," he says. "I put you at risk

without your permission, and I probably pissed Duncan off royally."

"But ultimately, your plan worked, and you're the only one who's likely to suffer any adverse impacts?"

He thinks for a moment. "I suppose so."

"I'd have approved it, if you'd run it past me."

His exhalation of air amuses me.

"I'm surprised you didn't tell the others."

"I figured I owe your dad this much—that I should plead his case with you personally, without input from the others."

"What does that mean, his case?" My hackles rise.

"He's leading the contingent within Isis that believes you're the only one who can save us. He insists that only you can restore Terra and prevent the collapse of Erra, Rra, and Ā."

"At least my own father isn't trying to kill me."

"The bad news is that, while he struggled to generate support for you, the other faction within Isis secured control of the American federal government."

I groan. "So it wasn't Devlin."

Kahn frowns. "As far as I know, he's still missing."

"I'm sure he's reported back by now."

"Wait, he was with you?"

"I have a lot to catch everyone up on," I say. "We should head back so I can share everything just once, but first tell me why you said you'd plead my dad's case? I still don't get that."

"He wants to protect you," he says. "He wants to propose that you rejoin with him and fight by his side, as you did in Terra. He wants to share all their knowledge and resources, and our agreement wasn't that I'd hand you over to him. It was only that I'd get him an audience with you. I'd still like to provide that, if you're amenable."

"I'll think about it," I say, "but do me a favor."

"Anything," he says.

"Don't mention this to anyone else."

His eyes widen. "Really?"

"Jesse's already suggesting that we contact him. I can't handle any more pressure when I'm deciding. It's really hard for me to tell him no."

"I can't believe he's really here." Kahn leans against the pasture fence. "No one has ever stopped the Wasting—because they've already died by the time it starts—but he seems the same. How *did* you do that?"

"I don't know how to describe it, exactly. What do you remember from our last night on Terra?"

"Not much," he says. "While you were talking with Devlin outside the main gate, Jesse collapsed. Things kind of started to flicker after that? I don't know if that makes sense."

"It does, yeah. I think you were starting to see the framework of Terra, which was already fraying."

"Then you kind of. . . disappeared, but somehow I could still see you, like you were at the end of a tunnel. So I *jumped* into the tunnel with you." He shrugs. "The next thing I knew, I woke up in my bed on Earth, except I remembered my life in both places."

I swear.

"What?"

"I was hoping you'd remember more than that, like what happened after you followed me."

"Wait, are you saying that I have something to do with any of this?" He straightens. "Is that why I'm so drawn to you?"

I wish I knew. "All I can say is that I had to gather every single soul on Terra and pull them back home to Earth. The only way I could even do that was by, kind of, slurping up the energy of the entire prison structure and using that to fuel the trip home. But when we got close to Earth, the people I transported all sort of zoomed away from me, like fireflies shooting off on their own. Except for one soul—one single, solitary soul didn't need me to drag them back to Earth. Kahn, you made the trip on your own."

"How can that even be possible?" He tilts his head sideways.

"Maybe you were a tagalong? Or a stowaway? As to *how* you knew to do it, I don't know."

"I was close enough to see you, so maybe that's how I could follow. Or maybe it's something about the connection between us. I wish I remembered what I did."

Without even meaning to, I realize I'm leaning toward him. A single step, and I'd shift into his personal space. I could lean my face against his chest. His arms could wrap around me, and I wouldn't feel quite so alone.

No, bad Alora. I straighten my shoulders and back up a pace.

"But how did you get Jesse back? Was that the same thing? You just gathered his light and dragged him along, and now that his Terran body is here, everything's fine?"

I stumble forward and lean against the fence a few feet from him, unwilling to look him in the eye, even as the sun drops below the horizon and the light dies. "I'm not sure. That day, when I could finally *see* that Terra wasn't really quite what it appeared to be, when I saw the skeleton of it for the first time, I took the filaments that made up Jesse in Terra, and I sort of ripped them out, like tearing a page out of a magazine. The slow unraveling of those filaments *is* the Wasting, obviously. I think that when your body dies on Earth, your energy signature that's stuck in Terra sort of just, dissipates." I gulp. "It was way harder to bring him back to Earth than it was to bring anyone else. I wasn't sure I'd be able to do it near the end."

"You didn't think that might mean that you *shouldn't* do

it?" Kahn's tone is surprisingly nonjudgmental, in spite of his words.

"He was the first person I brought back," I say. "So I didn't have a comparison point yet, except for you, flying along next to me. But to be honest, I wouldn't have cared. Should and shouldn't weren't concepts I weighed and considered in that moment—I would have tried to do it with everything in me, even if God himself stared me in the face and ordered me to let him go."

"But. . . he's fine?" He quirks one eyebrow upward.

"He looks fine," I say, "but Oliver delved him and said it felt like he had, I don't know, like a little rip in his soul or something."

"What does that even mean?"

I shrug. "He said he's *leaking*."

"Oliver's young," Kahn says. "Not to disparage John's friend, but I doubt he knows much. Maybe get a second opinion."

It's totally dark by the time we head back to the barn, but with our Lifter senses, neither of us trips over anything or even stumbles. Even if we did, we have a house full of Healers, now. Thinking about Martin and Thomas, Roland and Rosalinde, safely here with me, fills me with joy. Or maybe I'm just high from the bizarre buzz I always feel when I'm around Kahn. It's like a fizzy happiness I can't quite explain or make sense of, and I'm not sure there's much either of us can do to stop it.

As if his thoughts are migrating the same way, Kahn asks, "Are you really dating John?" He stops in the circle of light made by the too-dim porch light. The way he forms the words, as though they've been ripped out of him, pains me.

I nod.

He flinches. "I was hoping you were lying to keep me at arm's length."

That's a little closer to the truth than I'm comfortable admitting. "Well, I'm not. I don't know what this thing is with us, but I didn't choose it, and neither did you. I've had things shoved at me my entire life, and I'm sick of it."

"Are you sure you're not shying away from me *because* of it?" His face is so unbearably beautiful that I have trouble looking right at him.

"Of course I am."

"So, if we didn't have this weird pull, you might have liked me."

I cross my arms and look to the side. I can't stare into his eyes for another second. "I probably would have." Because I have eyeballs, hormones, and a functioning heartbeat.

"Which means that you're being manipulated in another way." His voice drops even lower. "In a way that's making us both miserable."

I should contradict him. I should insist that I'm happy with John, and that I don't *long* to brush my fingertips across his jaw, or flatten my hand against the curve of his waist. But I can't quite force out a lie of that magnitude, not when he's looking at me as though I'm the sun, moon, and stars. Not when his eyes are keeping me from floating away from the Earth forever.

"What if it's not a manipulation at all?" His head drops until it's barely above mine, his breath warming my temple and my neck.

I suppress a shudder, and pretend that my knees aren't so weak I could crumple at any second. "We could go back and forth on that forever," I whisper. "We might never know the truth." I make the mistake of looking at his face, at his ravenous eyes, at his devilish mouth.

The side of that full, mischievous mouth curves upward, exposing teeth I remember. Teeth I may never be able to forget. "I'm game."

No! No, Alora, no. This isn't normal, and it's not right. "Gah." I push past him and shove through the door like a rabbit slipping a snare.

"Oh, good," John says. "I was beginning to worry Kahn had shoved you into a hole and we'd never see you again."

"No holes," I say. "And no shoving."

"Beth's ready to hook us up," Jesse says. "Hopefully we both have a very restful night's sleep ahead of us."

"I'd really like Martin to delve you first," I say.

Jesse winces.

I glance around the room until I find Martin.

His face crumples.

"You already tried."

"I'm sorry. Should I have waited?" The closest thing I've ever had to a loving father glues his eyes to the toes of his boots, unable to meet my gaze.

"What happened?"

I already know the answer before he says it. "There's something wrong, Alora. I can't really describe it, since I've never encountered anything like it. He's there, but he's also. . . fading, albeit slowly. I can't find anything that would cause him to. . . unravel like he is, so I can't do anything to stop it."

Fading.

Unraveling.

As in, my brother is disappearing slowly. As in, he's here now, but he won't be for much longer. He's still Wasting, only this time it's on Earth. People don't Waste on Earth. It's not a thing that happens. Not unless someone breaks the rules. Not unless someone does something she shouldn't.

Jesse's going to disappear. Again.

My heart constricts in my chest, and I struggle to breathe, but freaking out won't help anyone. Not me and certainly not Jesse. As much as I want to bolt, as much as

I'd like to try to outrun this problem, I can't. You can't run from a problem you don't understand. Escaping won't fix a tear in the fabric of someone's soul.

What I need is answers. Surely if I can tear down a prison made by a goddess, I can find some spirit caulk. I need to find someone who has answers, or dig them out of my own head.

"Let's get hooked up," I say. "Apparently there's no time to waste."

ERRA

A tapping sound wakes me, and I'm momentarily disoriented. Where am I? A barn? A house? I look around—at the spare wooden furnishings, the light and airy curtains, the fertile farmland rolling on and on outside my window.

Several mountains of varying sizes frame the horizon off in the distance, a few of them smoking.

I'm still not quite sure where I am, so I stand up and stretch. The persistent tapping is coming from the front door, but I have no idea whether to answer. Do I want to see the person demanding my attention? Or should I hide? I'm wearing plain black pants and a black shirt, and the wood floor is smooth and cold against my bare feet.

"Laney," a deep voice says.

I walk toward the door. I've heard the voice before, and I recognize the name—but it's not my own. I'm sure of it.

When I see the bloodstain on the floor in front of the window, I remember what happened. I'm not Laney, daughter of Marietta Katika, but everyone thinks I am. She chose to *die* rather than reveal the truth: that she and her husband lied years and years ago in order to start an epic war. I wonder whether, in the great universal scales, Marietta's refusal to go *back* to war offsets the great slaughter they caused.

My life might also factor into their heavenly ledger. If it hadn't been for the lie they told so many years ago, I might have been killed yesterday instead of her.

How my life might tilt the scales, I'm still not quite sure.

I thought the Fire Called people might mourn the death of their leader of quite a few years, but I was wrong. They started bonfires the second the sun set and danced around them until very late. No one seemed to remember I was even here, which was just fine with me. I watched them dance and chant until quite late, and then I finally went to sleep myself.

Unfortunately, it seems someone has finally recalled my existence.

"Who is it?" I ask, my voice noticeably wobbly.

"John," the deep voice says. "I've come to train you."

The sun has barely risen outside. Judging by the lack of any other sound, birdsong aside, I'm guessing it's pretty early and that not many others are awake. I open the door. "I'm embarrassed to say that you woke me. I haven't had time to change clothes, let alone bathe."

"Believe me, you won't want to bother with that before we train." His smile is kind. "It's hot and frustrating and you'll work up quite a sweat."

"If you say so."

His eyes dip to the bloodstain and he flinches. "Are you planning to stay here?" he asks. "Perhaps the happy memories outweigh the bad?"

I shake my head. "I don't remember living here at all."

"When we return, you're welcome to stay in my household," he says.

I shuffle a bit, nervous to turn him down, but unwilling to live with a man I don't know.

"I have dozens of servants," he says. "I'm not proposing anything indecent, I assure you. But if my mother had—" He cuts off abruptly. "There's no pressure from me either way. I'm sure I can find you other accommodations where you'd have more privacy. They might not be quite as fine as this, but they'll be free of ghosts."

I'm afraid nowhere is really free of ghosts for me. The same dark-haired face flits through my mind, this time smiling, and then disappears again. I wish I knew who he was, or, I suppose I really wish I knew who *I* was. I know he was my brother, but I'm not sure what that means, or who we are. "I don't have any shoes. I borrowed some clothing, but couldn't find footwear that fits."

John frowns. "You'll need boots, that's for sure." He looks past me. "Do you mind?"

I shift backward and he clomps past me, clearly not uncomfortable invading a dead woman's space. "I wonder if you'll fit your mother's shoes." He rummages around in a closet and stands up with a pair of dark brown lace-up boots.

They're much too large, but I lace them up as tightly as I can. "I might be a bit stumbly," I say, "but I don't think they'll fall off."

"More importantly, the lava rocks won't cut your feet," he says. "No one can figure out how you healed that awful burn before, but unless you can repeat that trick, you'll want to be more careful in the future."

"Careful?" It's not like I threw a spear or hurled lava at myself. "Are you saying I wasn't purposely attacked?"

"We aren't exactly friendly to outsiders," he says. "I am sorry about your—well, your welcome was lacking. If I had known what was going on, I'd have put a stop to it."

I don't know him, but for some reason, I believe him.

He seems uncommonly kind for the Fire Called, and he stood up for me, offering to train me when everyone else laughed at the very idea.

He walks toward the door.

"Why can't women Call fire?"

His hand freezes on the knob. "I'm not sure." He shrugs. "They never have."

"Do they Call earth or wind or water?"

He turns around. "You really know nothing about Erra?"

Maybe I shouldn't have asked such pointed questions. I can't assume that someone's kindness means they're safe. I have no idea who or what might cause me problems. Even people who aren't threatening me sometimes stab themselves without warning. The image of Marietta plunging the knife into her own heart flashes through my mind, and I shudder.

"Are you alright?"

"I'm fine," I say. He's offering to teach me, to prepare me, to make me more able to defend myself. I can hardly afford to turn that down. "Let's go."

He opens the door, but as I walk after him, he whispers, "I've never heard of any woman being Called to any of the elements."

"I find that strange," I say. "Don't you?"

"I'd never thought about it until this moment," he says. "But now that you mention it." He turns in the opposite direction from the large central building where I first saw him, the one with the imposing columns. Instead, we head down the main street in the opposite direction. The houses we pass seem to shrink as we walk. "I do, yes. It's bizarre that the women can't do something that the men can."

A little boy jogs out of a door in front of him. He's holding a big blue ball. He bounces it as he crosses the street. "Women have children—men can't do that."

"That's true," he says. "I've always thought that was odd

as well. Why does that burden fall only to them? Why can't we share the responsibility?"

Before the boy can even reach the front door of the house he's aiming for, another child shoots out the front. He snatches the ball, and both boys squeal. "Maybe it's a blessing." Certainly the joy of those children is a blessing. Joy in any form should be appreciated.

"Can it be both?" John's watching them, just as I am.

I suppose it can. We pass the boys, but another door to my right opens, and another child darts past—this one female. Clearly there's some kind of game about to take place—planned or not. I watch as the girl joins the two boys, her smile just as big, her energy just as infectious.

They're passing the ball back and forth, and shifting in a circle, chanting something strange. One of the boys misses the ball and it bounces behind him, rolling into a field. The first boy I saw scowls and throws his hands up into the air. Sparks fly from his hands and all three children startle.

Nothing catches fire, but it makes me think.

"Why do I have to train?"

We're passing beyond the last of the houses now, and up ahead, both sides of the road are framed by fields and fields of crops with houses only every few hundred feet. He stops and turns to face me. "Where did you come from, Laney? Where were you kept all these years?"

I shake my head. I don't want to lie to him, but I'm afraid of telling anyone the absolute truth.

"Fire Called must be trained or they can't control their powers. They're a danger to themselves and others. Did you notice the little boy who grew angry back there?"

I swallow.

"He probably experienced his first spark in the last week or two, and if he's not trained properly, instead of sparks when he's mad. . . he could explode."

Explode? I have no idea what to say to that.

"That might not be the right word. For someone as strong as you, an explosion is possible. But for most Fire Called, if they don't train, if they don't learn to channel and control their powers, those sparks will grow, occurring even without warning or provocation. He could set his house on fire. Depending on the season, he could burn down entire fields of crops. His own clothing could catch fire—he could badly injure himself."

"So it's a safety issue," I say.

He bobs his head. "And also, you're not very formidable until you harness that potential you have resting inside of you." He presses his hand against the pulse point of my wrist.

My pulse pounds erratically. He stepped closer to grab me, and now that he's a breath away, I'm far too conscious of the sweep of his hair across his brow, the angle of his lips, and the strength in his fingers. His warmth against my body feels. . . strange and also. . . wonderful. I clear my throat, and he drops his hand.

"I'm sorry. I don't know what came over me."

I didn't want him to let go. My eyelids flutter a little when I say, "It's alright."

"From the moment I saw you, I felt. . ."

He stepped in to defend me immediately. "You felt?" My eyebrows rise.

"It might sound ridiculous." He coughs. "It does to me, even, but it felt like I'd known you for far more than a few moments. When I touched your arm." He shrugs. "Like we had a past already."

My heart leaps into my throat. I long for a past, but the most I can hope for with anyone is some kind of future.

"We'd better hurry." He sets off at a brisk pace again, toward the black mountains up ahead. "We have a lot to do."

"Can't we start here?"

He doesn't slow, just shakes his head. "We're not allowed to train inside the ring."

"What's the ring?"

"I forget how much you don't know," he says. "The ring is the dozen volcanoes that surround the heart of Volcano City. They protect the fertile soil where the Fire Called in this region make their home."

I glance around as he says that, counting systematically to verify that he's right. Sure enough, there are twelve volcanoes, varying in height and width, surrounding the farmland and homes we've been trekking past. "Why can't we train inside the ring?"

"People dislike losing homes and crops." John smirks. "Can you blame them?"

Not really, but I can wish it wasn't such a stupid distance. My feet hurt. Also, as the volcanoes loom closer, a tight feeling starts in my chest.

"You're lagging." John turns to look at me over his shoulder and stops. "Are you alright?"

"I'm fine," I say. "The boots are just rubbing a blister, that's all."

"You're white as fresh snow," he says.

"The last time I walked through two volcanoes, it didn't end well."

He steps closer, stopping near enough that I can feel his breath on my face. "The last time you didn't have me with you. Nothing bad will happen to you while I'm close."

"You're so sure you can keep me safe?"

John holds out one hand. A flame sprouts from it, dancing merrily in the air. He tosses it up in the air, and almost instantly, another flame appears to replace it. He catches the one he tossed with his other hand, and then tosses it again. A second later, he's tossing four or five flames in a tall circle.

When he snaps, they all disappear.

"I didn't realize how much juggling would intimidate any would-be adversaries."

His laugh booms across the remaining crops and bounces back from the nearby volcanic rock. "Maybe this will impress you more." He throws his palms outward, and flames billow from them, blowing hot and hard across the air, only a few feet above the crops, crashing into the side of the mountain ahead.

I stumble back a step, the blazing heat from his display searing the exposed skin of my face and arms.

The flames blink out.

"I thought you couldn't Call fire inside the ring."

His grin is lopsided. "You can't train someone inside the ring. The Circle of Warriors can do whatever they want."

"That was more impressive than the juggling." My voice is small.

"I may not be the most vicious member in the Circle. I may not be the most devious. I may not even be the most intimidating, physically, but I have more control than any of them, and more firepower than all of them. That's why none of them argued when I said I'd train you."

"Why did you defend me?" I force my feet to move toward the volcano, somewhat less anxiously with John at my side.

"Because I know what it's like not to have someone to protect you."

"You do?"

He nods. "Most Fire Called are born with two parents. After a child is born, there's usually a naming, an occurrence wherein Mother Erra shines her favor on a couple, naming the child they're to care for together, but I was not blessed in that way."

"You had no father at all?"

He shakes his head. "It's rare, but it happens. In a world

where only men are Called, the fatherless among us have a more difficult path to walk."

"Thank you," I say.

"For what?"

"Not everyone who has endured something difficult themselves steps in to defend someone else."

"I suppose not," he says. "Fire Called aren't really known for our empathy—in fact, it's considered more of a liability, but I've always thought that was a major problem within our culture."

"You're more than just a pretty face." My cheeks heat when I realize what I've just said.

The smile that curves his lips upward only intensifies his beauty. "A *pretty* face?"

I tilt my chin upward. "I stand behind my statement."

"Do you?" He shakes his head. "If you were a man, I'd roast you for less."

"But I'm not a man."

"No." His eyes fall to my mouth. "No, you certainly aren't."

My stomach drops.

"We better keep going, or you might not make it back, with that blister." But John doesn't move.

And neither do I.

The heat I'm feeling has nothing to do with being Fire Called. But since he said I could *explode,* maybe I should focus on learning. For now. I tear my eyes away from his and tromp down the path. Now who's lagging? Eventually, we reach the path past the two closest volcanoes, and an interminable, nail-biting length of time later, we emerge on the other side of them.

No spears. No lava spatter. Only one throbbing blister. A huge success in my book.

We're not even clear of the shadow from the volcanoes when John stops. "I'm sure you're wondering why we came out the far side instead of simply exiting the way you entered."

That hadn't occurred to me, actually, but if I hadn't been so distracted by his dimples, it would have. "Right," I say.

"I'm impressed you didn't ask, since you seem to suffer from indefatigable questioning of everything."

"I assumed you'd share when you were ready."

"Most of the newly Fire Called will be training just outside the path you entered. That's how they realized you were there right away."

"Actually, I'd been circling your little city and shouting for hours by the time I found that path."

John's lip quirks. "A long time ago, they had sentries posted on the top of each volcano, but since no one has dared attack us in centuries, we let that practice lapse."

"No one has attacked you in centuries?" I blink.

"That makes us sound pretty bad, doesn't it?" John's brow furrows. "The Ice Called do pick fights, they just don't bring them to our doorstep."

I clear my throat.

"But back to what I was saying. The reason I avoided training you there—"

"Was to spare me the embarrassment of being the only woman?"

He frowns.

"Or maybe the only adult?"

He shakes his head. "I suppose that would have been polite."

"Then why?"

He points. I look sharply to the right, and notice something I didn't expect. A lake.

"Why—"

"The hardest thing for newly Fire Called kid to master is dousing the fire."

"Okay."

He lifts one hand and splays his fingers. A large flame appears just over his palm. He closes his hand and it blinks out. "I imagine you'll master igniting the flame quickly, but it may take some time for you to put it out again."

"Don't all students struggle with that?"

"Every other Fire Called has a master teaching who's much stronger than the student."

What does that mean?

"I'm not entirely certain I can douse the largest fire you could light," he says. "So we'll practice near a failsafe."

Ah. "Safety first," I say.

He chuckles. "Let's go."

Just when I thought our trek was done, we hike another quarter mile to the edge of a small, but beautifully clear blue lake. "Does it have a name?"

"Prism Lake," he says.

"Because of all the colors reflected in the smooth surface," I say. "I love it."

"Alright." He holds his palms out. "The first thing you need to learn about fire is that you must always be its master. You can't ever cede control or relax, not when you're manipulating it. If you do, it'll burn past you."

"Okay." I turn my hands palm up and think about being poked and prodded and shoved. I think about how helpless I felt and anger flares up like before. Two large flames burst to life above my hands.

John shouts, "No!"

Whoops. I'm not sure what to do, now. The flames only grow.

Until they wink out.

"What's the first thing you learn when you ride a horse?" John's eyes are flinty.

"Uh, where the head is and where the tail is?"

"What kind of horse did you ride?" The corner of his

mouth turns up and he casts his eyes skyward. "It's wonderful that you have so much strength, truly. I'm not jealous." He grunts. "Not *very* jealous, anyway. But the first thing you should learn before you take off riding a horse down the road is how to *stop* it. It's not safe to be riding something you can't halt."

"Okay." I'm not entirely certain whether I've ever ridden a horse.

"Likewise, when you begin mastering fire, you must first learn to douse it." He lifts his palms again.

When I lift mine, he shouts, "Ah, ah, not that. I want you to focus on my hands for the time being."

I drop mine to my sides.

A flame appears over each of his hands, a very small flame. His tiny flames didn't impress me before, but now that I'm watching and learning, I wonder whether small flames aren't harder to manage than large ones.

"What now?"

"I want you to focus on *my* flames, and I want you to make them disappear."

Disappear? I inhale slowly, trying to sense his flames. They're barely there, really. This should be simple. I want them to. . . stop.

Only, nothing happens.

"Are you trying?"

I stomp one of my overlarge boots. "Of course I am."

"Maybe imagine that you're dumping water on them," he says.

"Have you ever taught anyone before?" I cock one eyebrow.

"Look, Miss Critical, no one else would train you."

"I'll take that as a no."

He huffs. "Everyone else is scared of you."

"Because I'm a woman, or because of that Inferno thing?"

"Both?"

This time I smile. "Why aren't you afraid?"

The flames over his hands blink out and he steps closer to me. "No idea. I should be."

"But you aren't? At all?" My voice is stupidly breathy, and my face turns downward, forcing me to look up at him through my eyelashes.

"Last week, the Master of Initiates asked me to start taking teaching shifts. I turned him down flat. But when I heard you calling out, shouting and arguing, I couldn't stop my feet. I raced toward you—and then I offered to train you without a second thought."

"You don't know why? Really?" Why do I sound like an idiot teenager?

Actually, I'm not sure how old I am. I might *be* an idiot teenager.

"I can't think of a reasonable reason." His eyes travel from my hair to my eyes, and then down to my lips. "But I feel. . . drawn to you, like we're connected. Does that sound insane?"

I shake my head, since I can't form words, not with him this close.

"You're not married, are you?" His voice is gravelly to my light and airy. "Please tell me you aren't married."

Married? The thought makes me want to laugh, and it makes me want to cry. He cares whether I'm available. He feels the same way I do.

The whole world is upside down. I can't remember my own name, but this feels right. He feels like home to me.

And suddenly, I need to touch him. No, more than that. I want to feel his mouth against mine. I grab the front of his shirt and pull him forward, our lips colliding like an avalanche, like lava spatter, burning through every part of me. His breath and mine entwine when we pause for a breath, and it's like air blown on an open flame.

"I want you." My words are pained, as if being apart from him for long enough to say them hurts. Maybe it does.

"This isn't safe." His eyes flash. "Not until you're proficient in basic sparking and dousing." He stumbles backward until his boots splash against the edge of the water from the lake.

"What's wrong with me?" I ask, mostly rhetorically.

"Whatever it is, you're not alone." He holds his palms out again, not bothering to walk out of the water. Maybe he's too afraid to move closer to me.

That thought makes me smile.

"Focus on these flames." I notice they're much larger this time.

I stare at them, letting the lights dance in my eyes, and reaching for the heat I know they're releasing. "What's their energy source?" I ask.

He shrugs. "I think it's me," he says. "My life force, maybe."

Interesting. Instead of seeking the flames, I reach for John. He's much easier to sense. The bundles of energy that make up John suddenly flash brightly, like a bunch of filaments all twined together. I blink a few times and it's John again.

"Laney? Are you alright?"

I swallow. "I'm fine."

"Think about the flames. . . not burning."

I try, whether he believes me or not, and I try, and then I try more. Finally, in an abundance of frustration, I pinch at the fires, thinking of cutting off their oxygen. They don't blink out, but they smoosh downward, pressing against John's palms.

"Oh." I release the pressure, worried they might burn him. "Are you alright?"

His palms look fine, but the color has drained from his face. "What did you just do?"

I shake my head. "I'm not sure. Was it wrong?"

"I've never seen any Fire Called do anything like that *ever.*"

That doesn't sound good. "I thought maybe if I cut off the air to the fire. . . "

He shakes his head. "You shouldn't be able to control air." He looks at me warily. "Don't mention that to anyone else."

"I won't." No one else has bothered to speak to me anyway, except the woman who just killed herself. I shudder.

"This might be a terrible idea," he says, "but. . . " He steps another foot into the lake. "Why don't you join me here?"

"In the water?" I eye the gorgeous water suspiciously. The only thing worse than boots that slip and slide around on my feet would be *wet* boots that slip and slide on my feet.

"In the water."

I gulp. "Alright." I step in up to my ankle, a foot or two away from him.

"I'm going to show you what happens when fire meets water." He twists his hand around once, then twice, almost as if he's gaining momentum, and then a huge fireball erupts from his palm and slams into the water. It plunges downward, causing an enormous mushroom cloud of steam to blow upward from the lake's surface.

"Water defeats fire."

He frowns. "Not usually. I can sustain a flame and a fire in a downpour. I can push past sustained water attacks to burn down whatever I want in spite of hoses and streams of water."

"But you can't burn the water itself," I say.

"True."

"What did you want me to do?"

"I want you to try and sense the water."

I stumble backward. "Sense the water? What are you implying?"

"I'm not implying anything," he says. "I'm asking, out here with no one else around. Laney, I'm asking whether you might also be Wind or Ice Called."

"You saw me," I say. "I'm clearly Fire Called."

"I know you are." He grimaces. "But there are legends. Stories so old that no one believes them anymore. They speak of an All Called, someone who can manipulate *all* the elements, not just one."

"What's this person supposed to do?"

He shrugs. "I don't remember exactly—only that they test everyone as a child to this day. It seems ludicrous, since we're always Called to the same thing as our mother's father was, but we do it anyway."

"You don't recall a single thing about this mythical person who could manipulate all the elements?"

He sighs. "They're supposed to unite all the tribes. They're supposed to change our way of life forever. They're supposed to. . . I don't know. End the world and restart it, or something equally nonsensical. I remember thinking it was a lot of useless double talk and that it could mean most anything, or nothing at all."

"Did it specify a gender?"

"You know, I assumed it was a male." He grimaces. "But that might be my bias showing."

I snort. He's pretty aware, but we all have biases.

"In my defense, I think everyone assumed it would be a man, since no women have ever been Called to any element."

"Until me."

"You can see why I might wonder whether it could be you—as you're already an anomaly."

It doesn't sound very flattering. "An anomaly."

"Is it really such a stretch that you might be Called to more than one element?"

"I can't even use fire right."

"Laney, I'm not sure what you did with that flame, but it wasn't fire manipulation. It was something else, something that I didn't *feel* at all, and I can sense pretty much every flame, no matter who starts it."

I don't *want* to be All Called. I don't want to be anything at all, but my wants don't seem to factor into any part of my life. "I'm not sure that I can sense fire," I say.

"That's normal at the beginning," John says. "Believe me when I say, you can't Call the Inferno unless you're Fire Called."

"I couldn't do that again if I wanted to," I protest.

"It's in your blood," he says. "You'll get there. Only the Katika family has ever been able to incinerate everything in a perfect circle, sparing those they choose."

"Are there other Katikas?" I ask. "Did Marietta have cousins? Uncles or Aunts?"

His eyes are full of regret. "I'm afraid you're the last of that line. We thought it died with your father."

I gulp. "It did. You were right." My hands tremble just a bit. I hope this isn't a huge miscalculation, but with the minuscule amount that I do know, it feels like an egregious error to lie about anything.

"What?" John tilts his head.

"I can't lie to everyone. I'll go even more insane than it feels like I already am. Truth may be the only thing I really have."

"Truth?"

"I'm not Laney," I say. "She died—she was never kidnapped. Marietta died to make sure that everyone didn't find out that she and her husband made up the story about Laney to force the warriors to choose him so they could start a war."

"If you're not Laney, who are you?"

I'm no one.

I'm nothing.

The look of shock on John's face, his sputtering, it forces me to face my real fear.

I don't belong here—I don't belong anywhere.

I'm an anomaly.

My palms heat, and I rage inside, at the injustice of being attacked for existing. At not knowing who I am, or where I belong, or my purpose in life.

At being utterly alone.

A tremendously large fireball rips out of my palms and plunges into the center of the pristine lake, the water rippling outward in a terrifying wave toward us.

I reach for the water in the lake, all of it, desperate to keep from drowning John and myself.

Surprisingly, it responds, lifting straight up into the air. I push it up, up, up, as far as I can, the contents of the entire lake streaming upward into a huge gelatinous blob. Fish splash out and I shove them back in. The vegetation where the water has vacated looks squashed flat, limp against the muddy lake bottom.

"*Who are you?*" John asks.

Even more than the water from an entire lake hovering suspended over my head, my lack of an answer to that question engulfs me.

What if I never know?

What if I never belong?

What if I'm always alone?

The same dark-haired boy from before flashes through my mind. He's smiling at me, his eyes squinted up, his whole body leaning back as the smile turns into a laugh. He knows me. He loves me. He cares for me. With him, I'm not alone.

But where is he?

For one perfect moment, I hear the echo of the belly laugh that accompanies that beloved face.

I don't even know why that sound fills me with joy and pain, longing and fury, comfort and devastation, but it does. When I reach for it, demanding more, desperate for an explanation, for any kind of context. . . the memory darts away.

Gone.

And with it, my desire for anything, for everything, for life at all, disappears.

I let go.

ANCIENT EGYPT

"No!" I don't want to cry out. The beast might hear me—it might claw me. It might take me. But I'm scared. I can't help it. "Go away!"

Strong arms slide around me, lifting me off the reeds, and cradling me against a familiar chest. The linen's scratchy against my cheek. "Shh," a strong voice says. "You're fine. It was only a dream."

My eyes flutter open, confirming what I already knew. Somehow he heard me, somehow he knew. "Daddy."

He presses a kiss against my head, and all my fear melts away. Nothing can hurt me, not when Dad's close. I'm drifting off again when I hear it—the call of my favorite spotted cuckoo. The one who lives outside my window. "Dots!"

Dad smiles. "It's nearly sunrise, yes."

"Oh good." I stretch and yawn. "That means we can wake up now." I blink and open my eyes. "Why are you here? Where's Aha?"

"She went to visit one of her children," he says. "She'll be back tomorrow night."

That's why Dad heard me—when my nanny is gone, he sleeps in my room instead. "I'm sorry," I whisper.

"For what, cub?"

I lean against his chest. "I wish I didn't have nightmares."

"Nothing matters to me more than you, Sekhmet. Nothing. Don't ever apologize for needing me."

I snuggle against his chest and breathe in his smell—spicy and sweet at the same time.

"Are you sure you don't need more sleep?" He rocks me back and forth.

I poke the side of his face. "I'm sure, Dad."

He groans. "Alright, well, if you're sure." He stands up abruptly, moving away from my bed.

I'm expecting it when he drops me, and I land on my feet.

"You're such a cat," he says. "My very own lion cub." I roar at him with my completely human voice and he chuckles. "Get dressed. I'll tell them to bring our breakfast."

I always try to beat him to the dining room, but I never do when Aha's gone. It takes me *so* long to tie the sash around my dumb tunic—my arms don't bend that way very easily. I'm grumbling when I finally finish. I race down the hall, but when I shove past the heavy doors and burst into the main room, the enormous table's already laden with platters and bowls.

"How?" I ask. "How do you always get things here so fast?"

"Your father cheats," Anat says, her full lips quirked upward. She's standing against the wall, keeping guard as she always does. Her sword is strapped to her back, but I know she rarely needs it. "He has Heka prepare the food before either of you are awake."

My jaw drops open. "Dad wouldn't cheat."

"Yes, Sekhmet." Mother walks into the room, her

flowing gown fluttering behind her. "Your father has never played fair, not a day in his life."

Dad's laugh precedes him as he walks into the breakfast room on her heels. "You'd be bored if I did, Hathor."

I slide into a chair and grab a chunk of bread. "But that means I never had a chance to win."

"You win every day, little one." Shu drags the chair next to me away from the table. "No one with a family like ours is ever allowed to lose."

Mother tosses a chunk of bread to Shu, and he catches it easily. "Listen to your older brother, darling. It's useless crying foul with your father. When you make the rules, you break them with impunity."

"That's enough of that," Dad says. "We have a lot to accomplish today."

"We do?" I ask. "Like what?"

"I'm going to meet with the Nubian delegation," Shu says. "They're complaining again—it's like they'll never learn."

"You will hear them out," Mother says. "The last time they brought a formal complaint was almost twenty years ago. It seems recent to us, but time passes differently for most people."

"Twenty years seems like a long time to me," I say.

"Of course it does. You're not quite eight," Dad says. "But." He smiles. "I think you're ready to try reviving a lotus blossom."

"She's too young to start pushing such things?" Mother asks.

Dad leans toward her, his palms flat on the solid table. "She's ready for this, trust me."

"She may be ready, but that doesn't mean she should be learning about Assimilation yet. What we *can* do and what we *should* do aren't always the same." Mother folds her hands in front of her and glares at Dad.

Anat exhales loudly.

Mother arches an eyebrow. "Do you have something you wish to add to our private family conversation, Anat?"

I'm not sure why, but Mother dislikes Anat.

It can't be her appearance. I love to look at Anat, with her brightly colored clothing and her elegant shape. Her eyes are large and bright, and her lips are always painted a color that matches her dress.

"The first transfer is a memorable and exciting day for an Assimilator," she says. "That's all."

"Which is clearly something I'll never understand. Is that your point?" Mother's lip curls, and she stands up. That's odd because she's only eaten her bread.

"You won't let me leave until I've eaten at least two onions and two leeks," I complain. "Why don't you have to eat any of them?"

Mother rolls her eyes. "I ate earlier, before you were awake."

I should have known Mother's never wrong.

"She did not." Shu snorts next to me. "I suppose Dad's not the only one who breaks the rules."

"I won't be chastened by my infant daughter *or* my adolescent son." Mother glares at both of us and storms out.

"Adolescent?" Shu looks heavenward. "Thirty-nine is adolescent now?"

"Why does Mother hate Anat?" I whisper.

Sometimes other people lie to me. I'm not sure how, but I can always sense when they're not telling me the truth.

But Shu never lies. Occasionally my big brother won't answer, but he never fibs.

"Anat is very beautiful, and she's devoted to our father," Shu says.

"Those are both good things," I say. "Aren't they?"

"They are," Dad says. "But sometimes Hathor sees things differently. She doesn't see her own beauty clearly, so she can feel threatened by the lesser beauty of others."

Dad always makes sense. "So do I have to eat them?" I poke at my leeks. "Heka overcooked them."

"Heka never overcooks anything," Dad says. "He's magical with all food."

"You really ought to hire an actual cook," Shu says, his blue eyes full of laughter. "It's not fair that the strongest Healer in the land is chopping vegetables and baking bread."

"I don't trust anyone else with our food," Dad says. "He doesn't mind."

I Lift the mushy leeks and zip them under the table while they're arguing. Shu will feel what I've done if he's paying attention, but I don't think he'll tell Dad.

"I saw that," Dad says.

"All I do today is lose," I complain. "I want to make the rules so I don't have to follow them either."

When Shu Lifts another blob of leeks from the serving tray and dumps them onto my plate, I slice up two and eat them, one limp, disgusting bite at a time.

"Even I have to follow the rules, my blossom." Dad strokes my hair. "It's just that I can bend some of them."

"When can I bend stuff?" I ask.

"Today will be a good step in the right direction," Anat says.

"That it will," Dad says.

Once I've finished my breakfast, Dad finally stands. "You're ready, my cub?"

I spring to my feet, more than ready.

"Have the crates brought to the east courtyard," Dad says.

Anat salutes and disappears.

"I'll see you later," Shu says. "Your day will be far more exciting than mine. You'll have to tell me all about it."

"Really?" I scrunch up my nose. "Haven't you revived a lotus flower before?"

Shu smiles. "I'm a Lifter," he says. "I can't revive anything."

My excitement whooshes out. "If you can't do it, I don't want to either."

My big brother drops into a crouch, his fingers tilting my chin upward to make sure I'm paying attention. "You're special, Sekhmet. You're different than me—better than I am."

I shake my head. "I don't want to be different than you."

"It's a beautiful thing, you know," he says, "being different."

I swipe at a tear that snakes down my cheek. "But I want us to be the same."

"Dad can do what he's going to teach you. I've been teaching you to Lift, but you can do more than me. More than Dad. More than everyone, actually, and that's something that you should never disparage."

"What does 'disparage' mean?" I ask.

He laughs. "It means you shouldn't ever wish your gifts away. You should hold your head high. You're the daughter of Hathor the All Called, Lady of the West, and Amun-Ra, son of Ma'at, the Great Balancer, the Sun God of Egypt."

"Dad says he's not really a god."

Shu stands up, shaking his head. "You're too big for your own good."

"What does that mean?" I stand up as tall as I can, but my head barely reaches above Shu's hip. "I need to be a lot bigger."

"You're exactly as you should be," Dad says. "Now stop asking questions and let Shu do his job so we can do ours."

"What's *your* job?" I ask. "I never see you doing anything."

Anat snorts against the wall.

Dad offers me his hand and I take it, sliding my tiny fingers against his large ones. He tugs me along kindly, and I trip along after him. I hate wearing sandals, but Mother says a princess shouldn't run everywhere barefoot. Mother says a lot of things, and I try really hard to listen.

Once we've walked out into the early morning sun, we finally stop in front of a large woven mat. On one corner, there's a lotus blossom, but not a very nice one. It's wilted and brown on the edges. "It looks half-dead," I say. "Why did they bring such a yucky one?"

"Because I asked them to," Dad says. "Now sit." He drops onto the mat, right next to the wilted bloom. I collapse next to him with a mighty sigh. "I want you to look at that lotus blossom and imagine what it might have looked like when it was *not* half-dead."

That's simple enough. There are large displays of lotus blossoms placed in my room every day. Sometimes there are also bowls with blossoms floating right on top of the water brought up from the Nile. Since this one has dingy, pinkish-brown petals, I imagine it as a bright pink one, smooth and sleek, no brown spots at all.

"Okay."

"Now, I want you to imagine that you can heal this one, that you can make it bright and fresh again."

I open my eyes. "I'm not a Healer, Dad. I'm a Lifter."

"Yes, thank you, Sekhmet." Dad's exasperation is softened by his half smile. "I'm aware. You're not really healing it. Even a Healer can only heal other humans, anyway."

I frown. "Then—"

He leans so close our noses almost touch. "Hush."

My eyes widen, but I snap my mouth closed.

"Ah, there you are." Dad waves and several men carry

crates into the courtyard and set them down next to us. "That's all I need. You can go."

They bow and disappear.

"What's in the crates?" I crawl toward one, my face peering between the slats. A stinger nearly pops me in the nose, and I scramble backward. "Scorpions!?" I fall onto my bottom. "Why would you ask for a box full of scorpions?"

Dad points at the lotus. "I told you to listen."

Listening is hard.

"What do flowers and scorpions have in common?" Dad asks.

I shake my head. "Nothing."

"That's not true," Dad says. "And that's the point of today's lesson."

I want to say a lot of things, but I clamp my teeth down over my tongue to keep from speaking.

"Nice job, Sekhmet. I know it's hard sometimes to sit back and learn when you really want to be *doing*, but it's important right now."

I bob my head up and down.

He lifts the dead flower, and a petal falls off, dropping with a plop instead of floating to the mat because it's so smooshed and tired. I've never thought about what must eventually happen to the flowers that fill my room each day. I didn't realize they were all dying, like this, and being replaced. The thought makes me sad. I wonder where all those flowers go when they're no longer beautiful. It doesn't seem fair that their time here is over so quickly.

"Do you value lotus blooms?" Dad asks.

Sometimes I wonder whether he can read my thoughts, but I don't ask, I just nod.

"What about scorpions?"

I shake my head. "I hate them."

"You're not alone in that sentiment. More people are injured from scorpion strikes in Thebes than from most any other creature, whether animal, serpent, insect, or arachnid."

"What can we do?"

"Why do you think that people call me the Great Balancer?"

I shrug. "You keep bad things away?"

"The only thing the flower and the scorpion share is that they both have a life force, and it's limited," Dad says. "The energy of life connects all living things. Even dead things have an echo of that power, in fact. The vestiges of the energy that holds us all together lingers, even after death."

"But scorpions take, and flowers bring joy."

"Exactly so," Dad says. "Which makes this all the more elegant of an exercise."

He lifts the lid on the crate and I gasp as not one, but two scorpions scuttle out. "Dad!"

"It's alright, Sekhmet. Do you trust me to keep you safe?"

I nod, but I don't take my eyes off the dirty little creatures. One of them scoots under the edge of the mat, only the curl of his stinger still visible, but the other rushes toward us, his myriad legs moving in disturbing sort of harmony. That's when I see it— the light Dad's talking about. The scorpion's energy, maybe. When I cross my eyes, it kind of *glows*. He doesn't have a lot of light. Dad glows way more, but I can still see a bit of it.

"What do you think I could do to keep the scorpion from harming anyone?" Dad doesn't flinch as it approaches him, closer and closer and closer, its stinger bobbing back and forth threateningly.

Without a word, I reach for the light in that threatening little pest and I tug. When I pull, the light flies out and the lifeless scorpion collapses flat on the mat, its energy extinguished like a flame that has been snuffed.

"You did it!" Dad's smile splits his face, brightening his eyes and bringing joy to my soul. "I'm so proud."

"You are?"

"Now, think about this little flower."

I focus on it. Its light is so much dimmer than the scorpion's, and much less than Dad's. I reach for it, but my finger stops just shy of touching it. I shove a little bit, pushing the light I lifted from the scorpion at the lotus flower.

And it perks up.

It's not perfect, but it's much brighter.

"That energy transfer was sloppy," Dad says. "You kind of sprayed it all over." But he's still smiling.

"I can do better." I shift my attention to the left of Dad, where the smarter scorpion's hiding, its stinger barely exposed. I'm surprised that when I squint, I can see its light, even through the edge of the woven mat. Once I've found it, I pull. It's farther away, but just like before, the light flies to me. I can't see the critter collapse, but I feel that its life is gone.

I hate scorpions. I loathe them, really, yet I feel an unaccountable sadness. This one wasn't threatening me or Dad. It was hiding and afraid.

I stole its life for no reason at all.

"Sekhmet," Dad says, "the flower."

That admonition reminds me that I stole from it to please my dad. Wasting what I stole would be the worst tragedy of all, so I redirect the light I took and funnel it into the center of the lotus blossom. When it revives, it practically glows, even the stamen shimmering in the morning light.

This time, when Dad beams at me, I smile right back.

"That might have been the most effortless initial energy transfer I've ever seen," Anat says softly. "It took me dozens of mice to revive a single lotus blossom my first time."

I didn't even realize she had followed us into the courtyard, but once I look back at her, I realize she's not the only one who did. Behind her, Am-Heh, Ptah, Bastet, Pakhet, Mehen, and Ammit are all staring at me with rapt attention.

"Why is everyone here?" I whisper. "Do you have a big meeting, Dad? Is there a problem?"

Dad laughs, and as though it's some kind of signal, all his lieutenants do as well. Am-Heh's laugh is sharp and bright. Anat's is throaty and sultry. Bastet and Pakhet almost purr. Mehen's sounds like a bark. I've never considered how different each of Dad's warriors is up close. But in spite of their differences, they all pulse with the same golden light, and it calls to me now that I see it. My eyes stop focusing on their faces, their sounds, and their joy, and focus instead on the pulsing light inside of each of them.

It beckons to me.

I could revive every flower in the world with this much power. I could Heal every injured citizen. I could raze the armies that threaten us to the Earth.

There's not much I *couldn't* do with all of that strength —the strength of Dad's strongest followers.

"Sekhmet." Dad circles my wrist with his thumb and forefinger. "It's time to break away from the call."

To what? Ah. I blink. He means that I need to stop looking at their golden glow, and thinking about taking it. "I shouldn't just take it."

He shakes his head. "No, shouldn't, but you could. And that's why they're here, watching in awe. You know that Anat is an Assimilator as well."

"Just like us."

Anat shakes her head. "No, I'm not like you or Ra. I was the most powerful Assimilator in all of Crete when I was born. My trainer wept every time he taught me something new—I was so powerful, such a terrible threat, and so awe-inspiring to him. And, Sekhmet, darling, I'm far, *far* less powerful than Ra. And he in turn, I believe, is less powerful than you."

I don't understand.

"In order to Assimilate the life force from a living being, I must reach out and make physical contact with them," Anat says. "I could only have taken the energy from that scorpion by touching it with my finger."

"But it might sting you." The thought frightens me.

"It certainly would," she says, "so you can see that the power of Assimilation without the requirement of tactile contact is transformational."

"It's the reason the people believe Ra to be a god," Ptah says. "Because he's been blessed with godlike power."

"No other Assimilator has ever possessed the ability to Assimilate life force from a distance," Anat says. "It's the reason I sought him out when I heard of his existence, in the hope he might teach me. When I discovered it wasn't something one could learn, I chose to serve." She inclines her head toward Dad.

"But just because we *can* do something," Dad says, "doesn't mean that we should. So while you *could* Assimilate the life force of everyone in this room, to do so would be an evil act."

I could kill them all, and doing it would be as easy as breathing, and a lot more fun.

That realization—that I *want* to take the energy from everyone around me, that I would enjoy it—hits me like a punch to the stomach, and I curl inward. "I don't want to be evil. I don't want to hurt anyone." I didn't even want to kill that scorpion. The lotus flower's time was past. I shouldn't have stolen from the scorpion to prolong it, even if it is beautiful.

"You are the furthest thing from evil, little one. You and I have been blessed for a reason. We who are stronger have an obligation to protect the weak. We must only Assimilate light in order to bring balance to the world. We only eliminate darkness and evil, like scorpions and people or things that pose a threat to the safety of those weaker than us. We use that light to create beauty and peace instead. Do you understand?"

I lean back until my bottom is resting on the mat again, and I force myself to look at Dad's warriors. "I'm sorry for being greedy and looking at you like you were honeycakes." My gaze flicks from Ptah to Anat, and then to Mehen. "I'll do better."

Anat drops to her knees in front of me. "If you were to reap my soul energy, it would be a joy to serve." She presses her face to the ground in front of me.

Her words make me feel weird, but Dad just smiles.

All of his lieutenants drop to their knees and bow to me in the same way. "The Blessed," they murmur. "A pleasure and a privilege to serve."

I keep waiting for Dad to tell them to stand up, but he never does. Finally, I tap his arm. "Can I go play now?"

"Sure," he says, "but make sure you're cleaned up and presentable by dinnertime."

"Why?" He doesn't usually care how I look. Only Mother really cares.

"I have a surprise for you," he says.

I clap my hands. "Ooh! What is it?" Last time he brought an ostrich, and I got to wrap my arms tightly around its neck and go for a ride. "Is it a dolphin?" I bite my lip and bounce up and down on my toes. Oh, I hope it's a dolphin.

Dad laughs. "It's not a dolphin, or a bird, or any kind of animal. It is a gift that I think you'll like. Your mother brought it back from Nubia." He pauses. "Where did you even hear the word dolphin?"

"Shu told me they're the smartest animals alive, and sleek, and fine, and that they like to jump and play and that they sing," I say.

"Shu needs to stop running his mouth so much."

"It's okay if I can't see any dolphins," I say. "I know they don't live in the Nile because of the crocodiles, and the ocean is far away."

"Now that I know you'd like to see one, I'll work on it, little cub. But tonight, I've got something else planned. Run along, or you'll spoil it."

I shuck off my sandals on the corner of the mat. Anat winks at me when I do. She always understands. I'm stepping off the mat when Dad says, "You're leaving? Just like that?"

I wondered whether he'd forgotten. "How much do you love me?" I ask.

"More than the sun loves the moon," he says.

"Is that all?"

"More than the earth loves the ocean," he says.

"That's it?"

"More than the sky loves the stars," he says.

I blow him a kiss. "I guess that's enough."

"You're the miracle I prayed for, the miracle I waited for, the miracle I'd all but given up on." He blows me a kiss back. "You're all that matters to me in all the world. I'd burn the entire Earth to the ground if you asked."

When I finally run down the steps toward the Nile, and while I splash in the cool water, no part of me, not even a speck, wonders whether my dad loves me. I'm not sure any father has ever loved his little girl like Ra loves Sekhmet.

We may not really be the gods the people think we are, but we truly are Blessed.

❈ 13 ❈

EARTH

"Alora!" Someone slaps my face.

I blink repeatedly before my eyes start working properly. I groan. "Stop hitting me."

"Oh, you're awake." John sighs mightily. "I thought you'd never wake up."

"Jesse said it's hard to wake me." I look at the window, which is still black as pitch. "What time is it?"

"Two in the morning."

"No wonder I wanted to sleep." I yawn. "What's going on?"

"Were you in Erra?" His eyes are bright, nervous even.

I nod. "For a while."

"But not the whole time?"

I shake my head. "I'm pretty sure I had an actual dream. A super weird one, but definitely nothing that I had control over. I was a little kid, not even eight years old."

John's eyes shift to something behind me and he nods.

Beth shuffles inside. "John said your last sleep study showed you didn't go into REM once?"

"That's what Scott said."

175

She extends a piece of paper to me with squiggly lines on it.

"Uh, thanks."

"You were in REM for almost two hours," she says. "I'm not a doctor, but I've never seen anyone be stuck in REM for that long."

I look back at the paper, willing it to make sense. "What does that mean?"

She shrugs. "Did you have any dreams?"

"I sure did."

"Were they helpful?" John asks.

"Not really," I say. "They were bizarre. Jesse was there, only he went by another name and he was like, way older than me. My mother and father were dressed strangely." I can't quite bring myself to tell John that my dad was Ra. I feel like he'd read way too much into that.

"Probably a combination of your concern for Jesse and your fear about the Followers of Amun and Isis." John laughs. "I'm surprised you weren't in Egypt, chatting with Isis."

His joke actually makes me feel better. It does seem absurd to give meaning to my very first dream. From what I've heard, people dream of all kinds of things. It's the brain's playground—of course all the things I've read about ancient Egypt while researching Isis and Amun would work their way into my subconscious. Add that to my understandable desire for a mother and father who love me and will keep me safe and. . . bam. A wacky dream in which I'm Sekhmet, daughter of Ra, Assimilator extraordinaire.

"Since I got almost two hours of REM, does that mean I won't be tired tomorrow?" I think about that. "Er, today?"

Beth shakes her head. "You'll definitely need more sleep."

"So what do we do?" I ask.

"I'm not sure whether the treatment to send you into REM—"

I throw up my hands. "No, no, I don't even want another dream tonight. Maybe I'm better off in Erra. At least I'm training there, learning to use my firepower."

"You are?" John leans forward, his eyes intent. "I'm training you, right?"

He sure is. I can't help thinking about the kiss we shared—way hotter than any kiss we've had here. "Uh, yes, you are."

"And have you learned much?"

Not exactly. "I'm hoping I didn't drown us both," I say. "Can you swim on Erra?"

"How should I know?" His brows draw together. "How could you have drowned us?"

"Nothing, really," I say. "Only, I might have Lifted a lake and accidentally dropped it. On our heads."

"You can Lift there?"

"Should I not be able to Lift there?"

He grimaces. "I mean, no one will know what it is. They'll think you're. . . I don't know what they'll think. Maybe they'll think you're Wind Called?"

I swear under my breath.

"Did someone already ask that?"

"So far, only you," I say. "You said you thought maybe I was All Called."

He exhales. "That's not great. I might kick you out if I really think that."

"Fabulous," I say. "Expelled from the friendly community of spear-throwing, lava-launching, bloodthirsty, fire-exploding lunatics in the middle of crazy lava town." I flop back against my pillow. "Are you sure I didn't get enough sleep already?"

"Do you think you can fall asleep again on your own?"

Beth pats my arm. She's trying to be reassuring, which is cute.

"I'm not sure."

"I can give you a half dose of Ambien. It won't impact whether you enter REM or not, but it should help you drift off again."

Wait. I sit back up. "How's Jesse doing? Aren't you monitoring him, too?"

"He's been in REM twice, both times for roughly thirty minutes. He should cycle back in again soon," she says.

"That's good, right? It's what a normal, healthy human would do?"

Beth nods. "Quite normal."

That's a relief, at least. "Sure, give me the Ambien, I guess." I just hope I don't drop back into Egyptian la-la-land for more whackadoo complete-family fantasies.

When Beth brings me half a pill and a glass of water, I down it quickly. "Thanks." Her smile isn't even forced. "I do hope you get some solid rest."

She ducks back out.

"Are you sure your dream was a dream?" John asks. "And not. . . a memory?"

"Why would you ask that?"

"You said your brother Jesse was there."

"Okay."

"And the sleep guy yesterday said that REM can dislodge memories for people. That's what we were hoping for, after all." John leans against the bed. "What exactly was so strange about it?"

"Are you suggesting that the memories jogged loose might not be from my own childhood? That they might be from *another lifetime?*" Because that sounds whack.

He shrugs. "You're connected to Terra, Erra, etcetera—that's undeniable. The most logical explanation is that you're Isis reborn, as many of the Followers of Isis already assume. Any chance you're reliving your, er, your first childhood?"

I sigh. "John, I did a lot of research over the years into Egypt. Wouldn't you, if you were in an alternate world run by followers of 'Isis' and 'Amun'? When I searched those names the first time, guess what popped up? Egyptology. I became borderline obsessed."

He nods.

"I'm pretty familiar with all the names. I know that Isis was the sister of Osiris and Seth, and that when Seth killed Osiris, Isis saved him and then married him, which is all pretty incestuous for me."

"You do love Jesse. Could *he* be Osiris?"

I laugh. "Ew, no, I don't love him like that. Thank heavens."

"Fine, fine."

"Isis loved Osiris and resurrected him—put him all back together, and they ruled the underworld after that."

"That's what the records say," John agrees.

"In my dream, if you must know, I was Ra's daughter. And my brother Jesse was an older version of himself—muscular, like Terran Jesse, but with smooth, dark skin and the same dark blue eyes. He was just as kind, and he doted on me just as much as he does on Earth."

"Alright."

"You still think this might be a memory?"

John shrugs. "Maybe not, but you have to admit that dreaming you're in Egypt—"

"Thebes, to be precise."

"And that Ra is your father, well, it's pretty on point."

"My mother was Hathor," I say. "And she wasn't at all like a cow, nor was she a goddess."

John frowns. "We know that Ra wasn't a god. He was a very powerful Assimilator."

"Right," I say. "I mean, Kahn told me that. Which is

probably why, in my dream, he *was* a powerful Assimilator."

"Are you sure it wasn't a memory?" John straightens the sheet I'm sitting on top of as much as he can, almost like he's avoiding making eye contact.

"You're saying you think I could be Sekhmet? Ra's beloved daughter?"

He shrugs. "I'm saying we don't know, and until we do, we shouldn't rule anything out. Maybe when you wake up from now on, write down any details you can recall so we can look back at them later."

"I'm telling you," I say. "If my dreams now are memories, the little girl in them would never have imprisoned her dad. I *adored* Ra. I was his biggest fan."

"I liked my dad when I was little, too. And my dad used to love acid wash jeans and tie-dye. Things change." He meets my eyes then, and his own are pained and tired. Not sleepy, but tired, like he's been carrying a heavy load for too long.

Maybe I'm not the only one suffering. "I'm sorry, John. I spend a lot of time feeling sorry for myself, and not enough time thinking about other people who have been through just as much." Except he didn't have a Jesse to support him. He was an only child—and his best friend, his second cousin, blamed him for becoming an orphan and cut him off.

I reach up and brush his hair back so I can see his eyes better, his gorgeous golden eyes. "I'll consider it," I say, "but I really hope that I'm not a reborn version of some Egyptian screw-up."

"I don't know." He smiles at me. "I think that heavy eyeliner and those big collars are kind of hot."

I kiss him then, but the edges of the world around me are softening as the Ambien takes hold. The last thing I remember is that he's holding me, and that I'm safe.

It's a nice feeling.

❧ 14 ☙

ERRA

When my eyes open, I'm surrounded by darkness. . . and submerged in cold water. My lungs burn, my limbs tremble, and even though I know I shouldn't, even though I try to stop it, my body involuntarily tries to draw a breath. As I knew it would, water floods my throat and lungs. I begin to spasm, flailing around desperately, trying somehow to eliminate the lake water I've inhaled. I need to get back to the surface—I need air.

Right now.

But it's so dark that I can barely make out my own hands in front of my face. I can't tell which way is up, which means I don't know which direction to move. I could spend my last bits of energy paddling sideways, or even worse, down. With no air in my body, it's not even trying to float.

Finally, from the depths of my body, I'm able to expel my last bit of air. The tiny, insubstantial bubbles. . . shoot downward. Which means down is up. I flip my body clumsily, already losing my coordination, and paddle along the path the bubbles took.

Except, I'm out of energy.

Bright spots swim across my eyes.

John thought I might be Water Called? Won't he be shocked when I drown down here?

And it's my fault, too.

I'm the one who somehow lifted all the water. . . Lifted it? A memory flits through my brain. Lifting water droplets while a gorgeous blond man stares at me in awe. The more I try to grab hold of that image, the slipperier it grows until it's gone. Just like my energy, my oxygen. . .

And my hope.

The world begins to shake all around me, the water, and the fish, and the plants all vibrating violently.

And then everything goes black.

ANCIENT EGYPT

The streets of Sa'inu are not nearly as busy as those of Memphis or Thebes, but still, I stop counting people when I reach three hundred. It may not be a major hub, but there are lots of merchants and traders bustling to and fro. They're also much more diverse than the people I see around Dad's main palaces. I'm fascinated by the variety in clothing, and the different hues in skin color and hair.

"What are you doing?" Dad asks.

The litter we're riding in is being carried by people, rather than pulled by animals, so it's not as bouncy as those to which I'm accustomed, even though the streets of Sa'inu are much worse than those at home. "Just looking."

"At what?"

"All sorts of things, like that woman. She's carrying a huge cask of beer, and her husband is strolling along beside her, doing nothing." I frown. "Or over there, that child's darting between horses and snatching things that aren't his. His mother isn't paying attention at all. I hope he's not injured." I turn toward Dad. "And why don't the children have any clothing on?"

He laughs. "Not everyone has things as fine as we do, cub, but that doesn't mean they aren't happy. Do you think it's our fine clothes that bring us joy?"

I shake my head.

"Most of our people don't bother dressing their children until they're old enough not to soil themselves. It's not as if young children are concerned with modesty or finery."

"But that girl must be almost my age." I scrunch my nose and point. "And she's still entirely naked."

"The weather is beautifully warm, so she's not cold, and it spares her the trouble of washing and cleaning clothing. If the world was full of people who were all exactly as we are, it would not be such a fine place."

I suppose so.

"What are your favorite things in all the world?" Dad asks.

I tap my lip. "You."

He beams.

"Shu."

"Another good choice."

"Mother, too. And Aha, of course." I sense my nanny, loping along behind the cart in her lioness form. She's never very far away from me when we travel.

"Not our palace?" he asks. "Our clothing? Our fine meals?"

I shrug. "No. Which is why I'm sad that Shu and Mother couldn't come. They packed their trunks—they meant to come."

"Your mother left her entire life after we met and fell in love," he says. "Her people—"

"The Macedonians," I say.

"Right," Dad agrees. "The Macedonians dislike me immensely. They feel I'm their enemy, though I've never been aggressive toward them, and that discord is hard on your mother. She wants to spend time with the people who raised her, the people she loved her entire life before marrying me, but she can't simply travel to see them in the open. When word came early this morning that they'd be waiting to see her just outside the border of my lands, she had to go. You understand?"

"Why didn't we all go?"

Dad smiles. "It's not safe for a tiny cub beyond my borders."

"You'd keep me safe."

"I would," he says, "and I always will, no matter what. But if something I did to keep you safe harmed someone your mother loves, you can see that would hurt her."

I can't really understand what he might be talking about, but a bizarre chanting draws my attention, so I drop it. Dad looks relieved when I don't argue any further. I shift over toward the window to see what is causing the odd noises. Lots of men standing in a line are shouting something. They're far enough away that it's hard to hear, but it sounds like they're saying, "Blot out the eye of Ra the Oppressor. Remove the Abomination."

I lean farther out to make sure I'm hearing them right, and sure enough, that's what they're saying. Why would anyone call Dad an abomination? Why would they want to blot out his eye? Are they Macedonian?

"Why would you say that?" I call out. "Ra blesses you all. He keeps you safe."

"Ra's a blight on the fine land of Egypt. He enslaves Nubia and Persia." The man in front points at our cart and sneers. "Men! Look! Here passes the Thief of Souls!"

They move quickly toward us.

"Sekhmet," Dad says. "Come away from the window and sit by me."

In the split second before I turn away, the men freeze and tremble. I obey Dad, but I'm bothered by it. Everyone loves Dad—they call him a god. He brings balance and peace. "Why are those men saying terrible things?"

Dad smiles. "Have you ever stubbed your toe?"

"Of course." I wince at the memory.

"It hurts, doesn't it?"

I nod.

"Some people have conflated my blessed power with divine power. No matter how many times I have insisted that I am but a man, they persist in calling me a god."

"Because you balance things. Like the Earth moves in the sky, as the stars move around us, you bring predictability and prosperity to your people."

"But I'm not a god, and the downside to people's belief is that, although they are grateful when things are good, when they stub their toe, they want to blame someone for that pain."

"We're not talking about stubbing toes, are we?"

He shakes his head. "There hasn't been enough rain here."

"You should send the Earth and Ice Called to help."

Dad smiles. "They have been in great demand across all our lands. Because Sa'inu is close to the Nile Delta for irrigation, and to the Mediterranean Sea for fish, their need has not been as dire."

"So why are the men angry?"

"If they don't have irrigation rights, if they rely on flooding for their crops, then they're suffering while others are surviving. If they cannot afford fish, they may even be hungry."

"And they blame you for that?"

"I do the best I can, but I can't do all things."

"Why can't we tell them that?"

"When people are angry," Dad says, "it's hard for them to listen. I allow them the freedom to speak their feelings, but if they move from feelings into action. . . " The threat hangs in the air between us.

"Because they might hurt others, and that's not fair."

"Ma'at," Dad says. "Exactly so. There must be harmony and balance in all things, even in hardship, even in trial."

"But you won't let them starve, right?"

"We have arrived, Most Divine." Anat's voice is smooth, calm, and undisturbed. She must have seen the men too, but she's smiling when she opens the door to our cart. That reassures me. Surely if they had done something—moved from words to action—if Dad's lieutenants had to take action, she wouldn't be peaceful and happy. "They're ready for you."

"Who's ready?" I ask. "You still haven't told me why we've come all this way."

"You may not remember this," Dad says. "But several months ago, you mentioned something. Something you wanted to see."

I pause and listen. The sounds of the people have faded. The sounds I can hear now are strange. The wind rustling the clothing of the attendants and soldiers accompanying us, and a strange, small sort of rushing sound that keeps repeating. I shrug. "I don't remember."

"You asked me about dolphins." A grin has stolen its way onto Dad's face, his eyes lit with merriment. He waves his hand toward the open door where Anat stands.

"Wait, we came to Sa'inu to see. . . dolphins?" I leap to my feet. "Do they really dance in the water? What does their song sound like?"

"You're about to find out, my cub."

I leap to the ground, pausing only because Anat grabs my arm. "Patience, little one."

She must not remember being eight years old. I hate patience. It's the word they always fling at me when they want to tell me to stop.

It takes Dad forever to climb out of the cart and arrange his robes properly. The air gusts here in great, sweeping rushes, like a Wind Called initiate is practicing forms. Badly.

"Now?" My eyes scan the great mass of water as it rolls into the sandy ground and then rolls gently back again.

Dad takes my hand, and we walk toward the water's edge. Although I have to take two steps for each of his, I wish we could go faster—I cannot wait! But finally, we do reach the edge of the sea where a dozen people wait for us.

"Do I go into the water?"

Dad looks at a tall man standing at the front of the group of people. The tall man nods. "Yes, you may walk into it."

I shuck off my shoes and splash up to my ankles, the small waves bumping into my calves. Up to my knees. Up to my waist, the fabric of my tunic belling out and tangling around my legs. The water isn't too cold, but it's not warm either. The sand puffs up under my feet when I kick it, and then settles back down. The waves moving back and forth hardly seem to bother it at all. A tiny fish darts past my ankle. "Whoa."

Another flies past, and I take care not to step on any.

"The sea is full of life," I say.

"It is," Dad says. "And now it's time for you to meet some of it." He points behind me.

And when I turn, a beautiful grayish fish leaps out of the water in bounding arcs, crashing back into the surface of the water, only to jump out again. Then more appear, following the first. Some of them are almost all grey, with white bellies. Some have several colors, including brown and tan, and some have lots of white speckles. "They all look so different!"

"Would you like to touch one?" Dad holds out his arms and I leap into them. To my delight, he flips his shoes off and wades all the way into the water, carrying me forward with him. His eyes light up. "If you're interested, you could even ride one."

"Ride one?" I can hardly breathe. "Are you serious?"

Dad nods.

"Wait." I glance at the people standing next to us. "Are these *real* dolphins? Or are they Reapers?"

"I think, since they eat other fish, technically, they're Renders," Dad says.

A little of my excitement dissipates, knowing that they aren't truly wild animals. But even so, humans who can transform into dolphins are still dolphins.

"You're so demanding," Dad says. "Many of those dolphins are 'true' dolphins, but I'm certainly not going to let you try to ride one of those. You can barely swim."

I put one hand on my hip like Mom does when she's annoyed. "Barely swim? I've been swimming in the Nile for three years."

"The Nile doesn't have waves."

"It has a strong current, and these waves are super small." I kick at the water, but it's hard to reach it when Dad's holding me. "I'll be fine."

"You will be fine," Dad says. Because he trusts the people who will be taking care of me.

A moment later, when I'm treading water and a dark grey dolphin with a white nose and underbelly swims up alongside me, sliding its dorsal fin under my hands, I grasp it, just as Dad told me to. . . and it sails through the water.

I barely even remember that it's not really a wild animal. We move so fast it feels like we're flying, the salty spray pelting my eyes. But too soon, it drags me back into the shallow water and spins around, dislodging my hands, before darting back out to the deeper section. I stumble a bit, my head dipping under the water momentarily, but I right myself quickly and turn to wave goodbye.

Dad's dropped off next to me a few heartbeats after I straighten, and he stands up slowly, his robes bunched all around his knees, the brilliant red ruby of his amulet sparkling even more with the light reflecting off the water below. Dad introduces me to several different dolphins next —the males much larger than the females—and even a few babies. "They grow fast," Dad says. "Much faster than humans."

"I wish I was a dolphin," I say, "instead of a dumb old lion."

The tall man next to me laughs.

"Who is that?" I whisper.

"He's the alpha of the dolphin pod."

He'll ensure that all the other Reapers and any wild dolphins behave as they ought—he'll see that I'm safe. It's a little less exhilarating, knowing that nothing scary even *could* happen, but I suppose that's Dad's job, to keep things around me from being dangerous. Every time Dad tries to hustle me back to the cart where his lieutenants are waiting with dry wraps and new clothing, another dolphin comes by and splashes. Under Dad's direction, I'm able to take as many rides as I'd like, hug them, tap their fins, pet them, and some of them even spray me with warm water.

But the coolest part is when one of them pees.

It's bright yellowish green! "Fish must have really weird guts," I say. "To make that color of urine."

Dad just rolls his eyes, but he thought it was pretty neat, too. He certainly stared at it long enough. By the time we're back in the cart, on the way to the smallish palace Dad says we have in Sa'inu, I'm exhausted. More than ready for a bath, dinner, and bedtime. "That was probably your best surprise yet," I admit.

"Really?" he asks. "Better than the ostrich?"

I nod vigorously. "Better than the pond full of water lilies. Better than the big balloon in the sky."

"You liked it better than the floating balloons the Fire Called made for your birthday?" Dad's eyes widen.

I shrug. "I love animals *and* I love water."

"Most Divine," Anat says, leaning her head through the window and jogging to keep pace with the cart.

"Yes?"

"The local priest has a few difficult cases he was hoping you'd adjudicate?"

Dad sighs. Since he can see the measure of each person, he's often asked to help the priests make difficult decisions. "Alright."

Anat smiles, her full lips parting to reveal perfect, pearly white teeth. Her kohl-lined eyes sparkle. "He will be pleased. Many thanks."

"Can I watch?" I ask. "I'm getting really good at *seeing*."

"You are," Dad says. "But I'm sure you're tired—"

"Not too tired to learn." Learning is Dad's weakness. If I can convince him that something will teach me more than I know, he almost always relents.

"She's awfully young." Anat's face is no longer visible, but her voice drifts through the open window.

I would be annoyed, except that Dad never listens to anyone else's opinion. He makes up his own mind. If anything, he's more likely to let me—oh. Maybe she knows that, too.

"Fine," Dad says. "You can watch, but only if you tell me what you see before I make any rulings, and tell me what you would do."

When we reach our palace, which isn't so small after all, and is perched at the highest point of Sa'inu, with a view of the sea below, I patiently allow Aha to bathe and dress me. I even let her fuss with my hair. "Your hair grows thicker every day," she says.

"You tell me that at least once a week," I say.

Aha's laugh always sounds a bit like a roar, probably

because she has a tendency to slip back into her lioness form whenever she's not consciously trying to remain human. Mother chose her to watch me the second she came to pick me up in my crib and there was a lioness cub where a baby should have been. Apparently Renders manifest early, and it's critical to have an alpha around to prevent a child from shifting into an animal form and never changing back.

"There," she finally says. "You're presentable."

My hair's twisted into complicated knots that still tug at my scalp, and my shoes pinch, but if I complain, Aha could tell him I'm too tired, and Dad might change his mind. "Thank you."

She pats my cheek. "There, now. Be on your way."

Ptah is waiting outside the door for me. "You look lovely, Sekhmet," he says, "but you're missing something." He Lifts a small lotus blossom from a vase nearby and tucks it into the side of my hair. "Now you're ready."

He's probably Dad's nicest lieutenant, other than maybe Anat. I still can't figure out why people call him Ptah the Fierce. He's almost the opposite of fierce.

Then again, they call Anat the Leveler of Sinai. I've been there, and it wasn't leveled, so. . .

I follow Ptah into the main chamber of the palace. It's a long room with a raised throne on the far wall, and a long gallery that ends with an open ledge providing a view of a cliff overlooking the ocean. A refreshing breeze blows through the room, thanks in part to the open-air end point, but the breeze is a little too cool for me to believe it. I look around until I spot the Wind and Ice Called servants responsible. I wave and smile at Donatu and Erratus by way of thanks, and then jog down the length of the room to sit in the smallish throne set next to Dad's.

"We're ready to begin." Dad's using what I call his 'God of the Sun' voice. It's so different from the way he speaks to me that the first time I heard it, I burst into tears. I'm used to it now, but I feel sorry for anyone hearing it for the first time. He's wearing a beautiful, richly dyed, crimson robe that exactly matches the color of the stones set into his wide, gold hammered neck collar. The stones sparkle, as usual.

"Most Divine." Am-Heh drags a woman inside and releases her. She immediately drops into a deep bow. "This woman has been accused of murdering her own infant child."

I can't believe it's true. She looks so nice.

"Look within," Dad whispers. "Tell me what you see."

"The weight of a soul should be lighter than a feather, if the soul is in harmony," Dad says in his sepulchral voice.

I cross my eyes and then uncross them, but nothing happens. "I'm trying," I say. "I need a minute."

"The more distractions, the harder it is to truly see. Focus only on the woman." Dad raises his voice. "Am-Heh, step aside. Bastet, you as well."

Am-Heh opens his mouth as if to argue.

"Do you think me incapable of protecting myself from this woman?" Dad's tone is wry.

They both move.

I stare at the woman. I close my eyes and then open them again. This time, I see it. Her mind and heart are full of light, but I can't see quite what kind. I want to ask Dad to bring her closer, but he would probably say I'm not ready. I rub at my eyes, and then I focus again.

This time, it unfurls before me. A pulsing, quivering mass of light. One small, dark strand pulses at the center. "I don't think she could have murdered her own child." My voice trembles, which is a little embarrassing, but a lot of people are watching.

"Why?" Dad's face is impassive, but the corner of his mouth twitches. I think he agrees with me.

"She's too light and bright. She's done something wrong, something she's ashamed of, but it's not as bad as killing someone, much less her own child."

"What has she done?" Dad asks.

I shrug. "How should I know?"

"Where is the darkness located?"

I rub my eyes again. "It's inside of her, deep, deep down, from her heart, down into her core."

Dad beams this time. "You're right. It's deep inside her, so it's a violation of a trust that is central to her life. It's in her core, which means it's intimate."

I have no idea what he's talking about.

"She's been unfaithful to her husband, cub. That's likely the reason she hasn't been able to prove her innocence, her fear of revealing that infidelity, but she's not a murderer." Dad waves his hand. "The ways of Sinai are strong in this region, but we don't enforce laws of chastity. That darkness in her soul exists because of her own guilt. She doesn't love her husband, or the darkness would be much, much more significant. Tell the priest to offer her a divorce and to keep looking for whoever harmed the child. She should be consoled in this time of tragedy, not punished."

Am-Heh is much gentler when he takes her arm this time.

But he's unaccountably rough with the man he drags in next. The man's hair is pulled back into a tight topknot over his head, and his eyes shoot daggers at Am-Heh. I'm surprised to see that. Perhaps because he's Dad's general, most people are terrified of Am-Heh. I've even heard people call him the 'devourer of millions.' They say he lives in a lake of fire—which is silly. He's Fire Called, but he doesn't *live* in a fire lake.

He wrenches his arm out of Am-Heh's grip. "I'm sorry if I seem angry, Most Divine, but I've been manhandled and abused, and like that woman you just vindicated, I've done nothing wrong." The man's eyes flash. His fists wave erratically. "The lies about me were concocted by my neighbors, who are jealous that I've been prospering while they struggle."

"Of what crime does he stand accused?" Dad asks.

"He has been brought before the priest on accusations that he abuses his children and his wife."

"Abuses?" Dad's eyebrows rise.

Anat shrugs.

"What do you see?" Dad asks in a low voice, so low that only I can hear.

It's easier this time. Am-Heh and Anat are already standing several feet away from the angry man, and I've already managed to see the light in someone else. I close my eyes, and open them. Then I cross my eyes and uncross them, and the ball of light lifts from his head and heart, like last time, unfurling slowly.

Only, it's hard to see the individual strands, it pulses with so much darkness. I sink back into my seat and shake my head.

"What do you see, cub?"

My hands clench, fur starting to sprout along the backs of them. I inhale deeply through my nose and exhale through my mouth as Aha taught me to do when I want to avoid the change. The lion only takes over when I'm afraid, and I can't show fear, not in front of all these people. I must be strong. Dad says that looking strong is often more important than *being* strong. When you look weak, people will attack. If they're afraid of you, they won't.

I wonder whether this man has taken that principle and pushed it out of balance. Ma'at allows someone to be strong, and that helps them to instill respect in others. Healthy fear, that's what Mother calls it. But this man has used that fear to harm others, not to keep himself and his family safe, I'm positive of it. There's so little light, that his

energy looks more like coils of snakes, twisting and strik-
ing, than actual heart energy. "He's guilty," I whisper. "He
did that and more."

The man's head whips toward me, and I'm positive he
heard my accusation, even though I whispered.

Dad leans toward me. "What do you think he did?"

I shake my head. "I don't know. But whatever it is, it
was really, really bad."

"Bad enough that he deserves to die? Or can he simply
pay restitution?"

I gulp. Ma'at says we can teach people, that we can train
them to improve. Through hard work, through consistency,
and through teaching a better way, most bad things can be
turned into something good. Death is reserved only for
those who are beyond redemption. "He deserves to die, and
he will not be accepted into the world beyond. His heart is
very heavy."

I think about the scorpion whose energy I stole many
months ago. It was light and bright. I don't like them, but it
did the things it was made to do. This man is not bright.
He has done things that a human should never do. He
harmed those he should protect—that kind of behavior
must not be tolerated. "I think you should do it."

A gasp from Anat is all the warning I get before I turn
and see a dagger hurtling my way.

No one has ever tried to kill me before. Or at least, not
that I know of. I should have stopped it by Binding it in
place, or by Lifting it out of the air. But I'm too shocked to
do anything other than stare dumbly.

It's less than an inch away from my throat when it
freezes in mid-air, courtesy of Mehen Binding it in place,
judging by the blinding light shining from his aqua eyes. I
notice that Am-Heh's holding a sword to the throat of the
topknot man. Things are happening so quickly, it's hard to
keep up.

Mehen drops to his knees and presses his face flat against Dad's feet, his grey goatee brushing the polished floor. "Forgive me. I was too slow, and Sekhmet almost suffered harm thanks to my lack of diligence. I request that you punish me immediately."

Dad's hand reaches out into the air above his bodyguard's head. "Mehen the Loyal, the Serpent of Ra, the Protector of the Sun, rise."

He stays bent double on the ground.

"Mehen," Dad says in a much softer tone. "I've allowed you to age too far. That's my fault. I've been waiting for the right offering, you see, and I think we have one. The frailty of the human body is no more your fault than the rising or setting of the sun. These things are eternal in nature and outside of our control."

Dad's guard sits up then. "You must not reward me for my failure."

"Failure?" I ask. "I'm alive. You stopped the knife."

Mehen gulps. "It got far too close."

"I'm rewarding you as I punish a very heavy-hearted man. My daughter saw something tonight that is difficult to see, and difficult to accept and process once you have. She saw the darkness and depravity of a heart laden down with wickedness and evil actions."

I sit up straighter. "So you saw it too?"

"I did, cub." He raises his voice so loud that it rings from the rafters. "Bring him closer."

Am-Heh shoves him forward, not being very careful with his blade. Blood streams down the bad man's neck and onto the front of his tunic. But the bad man's still not repentant. He sneers at me, at Dad, and at Mehen. It only reinforces my belief that he can't be taught—to be taught you must be willing to listen.

"I'm not afraid of you," the man says, "or your attack dogs."

"The most evil among us have the most to fear," Dad says. "I'm not sure what misery awaits after you die." Dad stands up. "But I have no doubt it will be in perfect balance with the pain you caused in this life. I won't do you the honor of reading your name. I hereby declare you guilty of crimes against your family, your neighbors, and this throne, and I sentence you to death."

The man's eyes widen, the whites showing on all sides.

"And now, I'm going to use your filthy, contaminated life force for something good." Dad points his index and middle fingers at the man, and I watch with awe as he *pulls* the life energy out of him, slowly, so very slowly. The man wheezes and chokes, struggling against Am-Heh pointlessly. He flails around furiously at first, but as time passes, his struggles lessen.

I've seen Dad remove someone's life force in a split second. He's doing this slowly to punish the man.

I don't blame him.

Dad's still pulling, but now he's gesturing with his other hand for Mehen to turn toward him. "It's time for something good to come from something terrible." He directs the energy into Mehen, and I watch in awe as Dad shapes the dark power into light and Mehen reverse ages in front of my eyes. His grey hair darkens back to a deep russet color, the lines in his hands and face recede and his dark brown skin becomes perfectly smooth and unmarked. The stray hairs on his arms and the rough spots on his hands lessen and disappear. His shoulders straighten, and his bowed legs turn back the way they should—hale, straight, and strong. By the time the man dangling in the air has gone utterly still, his eyes glassy, Mehen seems to positively glow, his strange aqua eyes startling against his deep, polished brown skin.

Dad drops both hands and steps back to his throne. "Have you learned anything yet, cub?"

I nod. "But I'm tired."

My dad's arms tug me onto his lap, squeeze me tightly, and rock me back and forth. "Then you should go to sleep." He motions toward the back of the room. A great, tawny lion leaps toward us. She rumbles loudly, and bats at the base of Dad's throne. "Aha will guide you back to your room and sleep beside you until morning."

"I'll go with them as well," Anat says.

Dad nods, and I'm finally able to leave the scrutiny of all the people watching. As soon as we've left the main room, Anat swings me up in her arms. I rest my head against her shoulder, the familiar scent of jasmine rolling over me. She helps me change while Aha paces back and forth, and then Anat places me on my mat of woven reeds and sings me a lullaby.

Aha curls up next to me, the rise and fall of her breath steady. Anat closes the door softly just as Aha drops off to sleep. Even with the cool breeze and the familiar smell of lotus blossoms, I can't stop thinking about what I saw.

What I caused.

It's Ma'at to take the bad and transform it into something good. When death overtakes us, our bodies fertilize the new growth. Time and seasons help to provide balance to our lives and the earth itself. There's harmony and justice in the cycle of life, but it still makes me sad. Dad took something from one person and gave it to another. It was beautiful in many ways.

But it also felt. . . *wrong,* like the man's darkness somehow infected us. Normally, the rhythmic sounds of Aha's breathing would comfort me, but not tonight. Tonight, I keep hearing the chant of those men in the streets over and over. The chant that only this morning I thought was so baseless and unfounded.

Look! Here passes the Thief of Souls!

❧ 16 ❧

ERRA

Pain radiates outward from my chest. It's like I've been stabbed, right above my stomach with something hard and hot. Except I can't breathe, and my body isn't listening to me. Strangely, the world around me looks *wrong,* as if it's made of webs. Cables and ropes of shining light are everywhere, instead of water and earth and rocks and sky.

"Wake up!"

Pressure—terrible, awful pressure—hits my chest, right where it hurts. I want to close my eyes and never open them again. I want the pain to disappear.

As if my thoughts could possibly control something like that, the pain just. . . evaporates.

It comes back to me then, where I am. I'm lying on the edge of the cursed lake where John dragged me, and he's shouting and banging on my chest. Silly guy—what will that accomplish? I'm not even real. I'm made of webs and fibers and cables of energy. I'm sure my lungs are full of water, but that water isn't real.

With that thought, I drag in a labored breath, and then another.

John stops shouting, and in fact, he stops moving entirely. "Are you alright?"

I drag in another breath and cough—water that I thought wasn't real pouring out of my mouth and all over the already-soaked ground. John shifts closer and helps me to sit up. I cough again and again, each time expelling more water.

Why did I think it wasn't real? My thoughts are as fluffy and insubstantial as the clouds floating overhead.

"I thought you were dead," John whispers.

"So did I," I croak.

"How did you pick up the lake like that?" John backs up enough to look down at my face. "I've seen a lot of Ice and Wind and even Earth Called men do extraordinary things, but nothing that could compare to what you did. Your eyes were shining like lanterns."

Lanterns? "I don't know how or why I did what I did."

"Are you really not Laney?" John asks.

I shake my head. "That woman wasn't my mother. She lied to everyone." I cough again.

John's face drains of color. "Why?"

"Apparently she and her husband lost their daughter, and rather than accept it and move on, they buried her quietly and pretended she was taken by the Ice Called."

"I don't understand." John frowns.

"She said it was so that the Fire Called would go to war again." None of this makes sense to me. "She felt like, if the truth got out, well, she chose to kill herself rather than face your dumb circle with that lie."

"They'd have executed her," John says. "I'd rather die of blood loss than be burned in a fire. I suppose I don't even blame her."

"Will you go to war again, now that she's not around to stop you?"

"Absolutely," he says. "That's one of the reasons the Circle wanted her gone. She kept blocking their attempts."

"Why?" I wring the water out of my wet hair, finding a worm wriggling in it in the process. Blerg. I suppress a shudder.

"Why what?"

"I don't understand why you want to go to war. You don't value peace? What about happiness?"

He tilts his head. "I told you that Fire Called must learn to control our power. . . or we explode."

"Okay."

"It's like that, kind of. We live for war—it's in our blood. Without it, without proving ourselves, without burning, what are we?"

"Do *you* feel that way?"

He runs his hand through his shaggy hair. "Sometimes."

"What does that mean?"

He stands up. "I've always had a need to win, and a corresponding desire to defeat anyone who opposes me. I suppose it burns inside of all of us." He pauses. "You don't feel it?"

Maybe. I'm not sure what I feel.

"Who are you, then, if you're not Laney?"

"I wish I knew."

"But you don't feel anything pulling you toward the water?" He looks almost. . . hopeful.

"Sorry."

"What about the ground beneath us?" He lifts both eyebrows.

"Still no. Just normal old Fire Called, here."

"What you did wasn't normal." He drops down to a cross-legged position in front of me. "Can you do it again?"

"Lift the lake and drown us?" I scrunch up my nose. "Pass."

"No," he says. "Not that, specifically, but I don't know. Move something without touching it, maybe?"

I shrug. "I've never tried. Other than, you know, the water."

"I wonder if that's what you did before, pressing my flames down into my own palm."

Could he be right?

He plucks a blade of grass and shakes the water off of it. "Here." He holds it out in front of him, and then places it on his open palm. "See if you can pick this up."

I stare at it, and then I try to move it.

Nothing.

"This is a waste of time," I say.

"Well, we've gotten nowhere with containing your fire abilities. I should at least try to teach you to douse before we head back. Plus, that'll give us some time to dry out a bit."

I swear. "My boots." They're gone.

He looks around us, as if they'll magically appear.

"They were so big, they must've come off when we were underwater."

"Which means they're on the bottom of the lake."

Probably. And now I get to walk all the way back along the cobblestone path barefoot. Today gets better and better. "Alright. Just tell me again how you douse a fire."

This morning he was excited. He had, well, fire in his face. Now he looks almost dejected. In spite of the setbacks, he does exactly as I ask, holding out his right hand, palm turned upward. He splays his fingers again, which seems to be some kind of command or trigger, and a flame bursts to life, floating in the air in front of him.

"Alright, Lan—" He presses his lips together. "Whoever you are." He frowns. "What should I call you?"

"Should we tell the other warriors that I'm not Laney?"

"Probably not," he says. "It's only because you have an

identity and you're a known quantity that they've allowed you to stay. If they oust you—and we're preparing for battle against Ice, most likely—where will you go? You can't go to the Ice Called. One whiff of your abilities and you'd be out on your ear, or worse, executed. If you went to Earth. . . they might accept you." The fire over his hand winks out. "Would you want to do that? They're a little boring, but they're good people. Obsessed with plants and crops and earthworms and trees and chickens, and I don't know what all weird stuff, but they're mostly harmless."

"What about Wind?" I'm curious now, after his description, what the rest of the world is like.

He shrugs. "They're the least predictable. They might love you, or they might hate you, and even if they do feel one way or another, they might change their minds tomorrow. No one can pin them down—some of them literally float from place to place. It's the one thing I envy about those who are Wind Called—the strongest among them can fly."

I turn my face skyward, as if one of them might come zooming over any second unannounced, which is likely ridiculous. If it did happen, though, I'd really hate to miss it.

"They mostly live in the mountaintops far north of here, between Earth and Ice," he says. "They may be unpredictable, but they're not bloodthirsty. With their portability, they choose locations that keep them safe and isolated."

Makes sense, I guess. I probably would, too. "Alright, well, I think for now, act like I haven't told you the truth. I'll keep pretending to be Laney, and maybe we can say I was kidnapped by Wind if they press for details. Then I can say I can't recall where I was—it was always changing. Sounds like Fire won't pursue them anyway, if it's like chasing smoke."

"You're pretty smart for someone who knows nothing."

He stands up, backs a few feet away from me, and then the flame bursts to life over his right palm again. "Let's apply some of that intelligence to this. I'd love it if you were at least safe in your own skin."

Me too. "Okay, when your fire blinks out, what do you think about to make that happen?" I scramble to my feet so we're not at different levels.

"Right now, I'm feeding it. I don't have to think about dousing it, since it's not burning independently. I simply release the push, for lack of a better word, and it gutters."

I cup my hands in front of me and imagine a flame roaring to life.

"That cupping thing is something the Ice Called do," John says. "You—"

But a tiny ball of fire pops into existence right in front of my nose. "Look at you! You're so cute!"

John throws his hands up in the air. "Maybe it's all different for you because you're a woman."

"Tell me how to put it out again."

"Stop feeding it."

So I do, and it blinks out. "Oh, no. Now I miss it."

"You can't miss a fire. It's not alive—it has no personality."

"Maybe your fire doesn't. Mine was adorable."

"Please." He sighs as if I'm the most trying person he's ever met. "Now, this time, I'll make the flame, and I want you to extinguish it."

"But it's not burning anything," I say. "How am I supposed to put out *your* magically fueled fire?"

John steps closer, peering at me around his flame. "You cut it off."

"That's what I was doing before," I complain. "When you said I was smooshing it toward your hands."

"Try that again," he says.

I stare at the flame and imagine cutting off the air

around it. I push and push and push and it flickers, and then compresses somehow, pushing downward against his palm.

"It happened again," he says. "Your eyes lit up. That's what you did before." The fire blinks out and he snags the jagged leaf from some kind of weed. "Do the same thing, but instead of doing it to my fire, do it to this."

I think about smooshing it. . . and the weedy leaf floats up above his hand, suspended in air just like the lake water was before. And when I hold up my hands, even in the broad daylight, I can see that they're bathed in light. . . from my eyes.

John swears.

And I lose it, the leaf fluttering to the ground.

"You may not be the All Called, but you're certainly something," he says. "And we need to figure out what."

The pounding of hooves against lava rock behind us has us both turning around. Mounted riders—at least a dozen of them. And they have spears. Of course they do.

John steps in front of me and holds up his hands.

"Rochester? What happened to you? Decide to go for a swim?" The man at the front laughs as he approaches at a trot, wearing the same red robes he had on before. I think his name was. . . Marcus? His eyebrows rise when his gaze shifts to me. "You both did, I see."

Right behind him is the mohawk guy who was going to kill me, Robert.

I'm only missing the white-robed old guy to have my favorite people all in one place.

John scowls. "What do you want?"

Marcus yanks his large roan to a halt in front of John. "I could ask you the same thing. First you offer to train this freak of nature, and then you choose to do it out here— away from everyone else. Why?"

"I don't answer to you," John says, "and you didn't come

racing out here so you could yell at me for breaking no rules and doing nothing wrong."

Marcus glares. "I have news. Elbion sent us to find you." He tosses his head. "And her."

"What news?"

Robert slides off his horse, his mohawk stiff, even in the wind buffeting us. His grin is practically feral. "The All Called exists."

"Oh please," John says. "You can't possibly believe in that old story."

If I hadn't just spent the morning with him, I'd never know he was nervous. But it's clear in the stiff way he's holding his hands. The tight set of his shoulders. His forced smirk.

At least no one else seems to notice.

"Apparently it's not a story," Marcus says, still perched on his horse. It probably suits him to look down on everyone else. "There are reports from our allies in Ice *and* Wind that he's been to see both. He's Ice Called, and he's Wind Called, and he's born of neither. They say that he's approaching Earth right now."

"If it's true, why would he visit everyone but us?" John asks.

I don't offer my thoughts, but if there was a tribe that was known for incinerating people first and asking questions later, I might not reach out to them until I had the support of everyone else already lined up.

"No one knows what he's planning for sure," Marcus says, "but the messengers insist that he's not conquering anyone."

"You're sure it's a man?"

Robert glares at me. "Of course it's a man. There aren't any women who are Ice or Wind or Earth Called." He spits on the ground, as if to say that I'm a freak by anyone's standards.

"Why does Elbion want Laney?"

Marcus glances at me, and then shakes his head. "He wants to offer her to the All Called, as a peace offering. Seems to think that with him being a man, and an oddity himself, maybe he'll appreciate her—the first woman who's Fire Called."

"He sent you out here to bring her back so he can offer her up as some kind of sacrificial lamb?" John's tone is mocking, but there's a hint of fury underneath it.

"That's why he wants her," Marcus says. "It's not why he wants you to return."

"I'm the other prong of his plan?" John's tone is bitter.

"Offer a treat with one hand." Robert glances at me.

"Threaten with a hammer in the other," Marcus says.

"I don't understand," I say. I mean, I get that they're saying they want to send me to some unknown man as a peace offering, which is disturbing enough, but what do they mean, a hammer?

"Elbion wants me to lead the Fire Called army if it comes to that." John crosses his arms.

"No one can match you for sheer firepower," Robert says.

John doesn't look surprised by that pronouncement. "And if I decline?"

"Is that what you're doing?" Marcus grabs the pommel of his saddle as his horse shifts, probably sensing its rider's agitation.

"Not yet," John says.

"Why would you?" Marcus frowns. "It's an honor."

"We aren't even at war," John says. "I'll wait to express an opinion once I've heard all the news, like any member of the Circle."

"The Circle has already called for the army," Marcus says.

"On what authority? There's no General anointed, nor

can there be for at least three days after the death of the Head."

"Elbion declared a state of emergency." Robert waves, and four other men dismount.

"And he wants you and the girl to report to him immediately." Marcus exchanges a glance with Robert.

"I don't answer to *Elbion*," John says, "emergency or not."

"Oh." Marcus' smile is pure evil. "Did I forget to tell you that we voted while you were out here playing with your freaky little girlfriend? He's our new General."

"You can't vote without the full Circle present." I can't see John's face, but fury is now the primary note in his tone.

"In light of the potential threat of the All Called, we had no choice." Marcus shrugs. "Don't force my hand here —hand the girl over and come back peacefully. I'd hate it if things turned unnecessarily ugly, and Elbion would be devastated if you couldn't lead his men to victory."

"I won't let you drag her back," John says. "And I certainly won't agree to lead the fight for a war I haven't voted to ratify."

"You'll refuse a direct order from your General?" Robert's eyes widen.

"I don't acknowledge Elbion as my General," John says.

"Pass the little princess over." Marcus looks past John and directly at me. "She's not *bad* looking, but if I'm being honest, I don't see the appeal."

I'm about done with this guy.

And I'm sick of hiding behind John.

I focus on the person I hate the most, the freckle-faced, smooth-tongued one called Marcus. I pretend he's a particularly disgusting blade of grass, or maybe a worm, and I shove him out of his saddle. Watching him tumble to the ground, his hands thrown out to break his fall, his face a rictus of terror, makes me feel much better. There was a flash of light from my eyes, but between the brightness of the afternoon sun, and the way all the soldiers are focused on John, I doubt any of them noticed.

Unfortunately, Marcus doesn't stay down for long. He leaps to his feet and throws his spear, right at John's head.

I don't have time to think. I simply hurl both my hands up in front of my face and incinerate it. One second it's a solid wooden spear spinning toward John, and the next it's a cloud of ashes fluttering to the ground.

The men stumble backward, their eyes wide. "What's wrong with her?" Robert asks.

"She *is* the Inferno," John says. "What did you expect?" He tilts his head nonchalantly. "Did you think I was protecting her?" He shakes his head. "I was trying to protect you from her. I wouldn't piss her off if I were you."

Marcus is still staring at the place where his spear disappeared, half-dazed. "I—"

"We should head back," Robert says.

Some part of that must've clicked for Marcus, because his head snaps up. "Not without the girl. I won't fail to accomplish the first task the General assigned me."

I spread my legs out and lift my hands again. I may not know who I am, but I know what I *don't* want, and that's to become some kind of property that is offered as a gift to a conquering warrior who calls himself the All Called.

"I don't acknowledge his usurpation of power," John says. "In fact, I decry it."

Robert blinks. "You're disputing his elevation?"

The old man? Why would they be worried about John when he's fighting an old man? Didn't they just say he was the strongest Fire Called warrior?

"You know he'll choose daggers." Marcus' smile is far too predatory for my liking.

"He can choose the weapon when we fight, it's true," John says, "but he's grown slow. I won't lose this time."

This time? What's going on?

"You have until tomorrow at sunrise to prepare." Marcus swings back into his saddle and then he spits on the ground at our feet. "I hope she's worth your life."

"This isn't about her," John says.

"Keep telling yourself that." Marcus wheels his horse around, clumps of dirt flying up from his hooves he kicks it into action. "Maybe you'll even believe it by the time you die tomorrow."

❦ 17 ❦

ERRA

By the time the sun begins to set, I've finally figured out how to douse a fire.

John breathes a heavy sigh of relief as we set off down the long road back to town. He walks next to me along the side of the road where I'll occasionally step on a poky stick or a nettle, but at least the rocks don't slice my feet up. "At least, no matter what happens, I don't have to worry that you'll burn yourself to death, or burn down an entire house full of children by accident."

"Like I'd do that on purpose?" I lift one eyebrow.

"That's not what I worry about."

"Oh?" I ask. "What do you worry about?"

"I totally thought you might fry Marcus earlier," he says.

"You'd cry, would you?"

"Oh, no. I'd celebrate," he says. "That guy's the worst."

I snort. "How nervous should I be about my only friend fighting the old guy tomorrow?"

"Your only friend?"

My foot lands on a nettle and I whimper.

John glares at me. "Just take my boots already."

I don't even slow down. "Changing the subject isn't very promising. Is it really that bad?"

"Look, I don't know why Elbion wanted you hauled back, or whether that claim was an excuse put forth by Marcus to piss me off, but I doubt Elbion has anything good planned for you. I know it was a joke, but I'm worried that I am your only friend."

"You don't think the All Called is a threat worthy of an emergency vote?"

He shrugs. "It's an old story, right? People don't really believe it, but then, as far as we knew, women could never be Called, and here you are."

"No one has suggested that perhaps I'm not really a woman." At least that's something.

John coughs. "We did all see you wearing nothing but ashes."

My cheeks heat up, and I cross my arms over my chest. "Why did you challenge Elbion? I'm capable of defending myself."

I want to be annoyed when he laughs, but his eyes are so warm, and he's done so much to teach and defend me when he had no reason to do it. I can't summon an ounce of anger. "Rude."

"Were you going to take on the entire circle of Fire Called Warriors before or after you picked up a lake full of water and dumped it on your own head?" He shakes his head. "You're extraordinary, and there's no denying that. Once you're in command of your abilities, you might be able to overpower even me. But right now, you're as likely to incinerate a kitchen table as you are to light a candle. You won't be able to defend yourself until you're in control of what you do and when you do it."

He's right, of course. I just hate feeling so helpless and, well, dopey. "I don't even know my own name."

"Maybe we can guess it on the way back," he says. "Perhaps Elbion was onto something with this, 'how does this
sound?' thing."

"Really?" Instead of coming out skeptical and mocking,
my one word question sounds pathetically hopeful. "Okay,
fine."

"Mary."

I think about it. Nothing. "I don't think so."

"Rita."

I giggle. "Rita?"

"No? Sarah."

I shake my head. "Definitely not. Or at least, I don't
think so."

"Laura?"

Laura. I gulp. That actually sounds familiar. "That
might be close."

"Laura?" He smiles. "I like it. Laura."

So do I. It's better than nothing, anyway. "So tell me
how this thing goes tomorrow. What exactly do you have
to do?"

John kicks a rock and it flies off to the left to smash
into the upcoming volcano. "Tell you what. Since we're
about to pass through the volcanoes, and there's no way for
you to tiptoe along the grassy area and keep from injuring
your feet, why don't we make a deal? I'll tell you whatever
you want to know about the duel I have to fight in the
morning, if you agree to take my boots."

"They're way too big."

"That didn't stop you last time."

"I'm not fighting someone to the death tomorrow." I
expect him to laugh at that.

He doesn't.

I stop and put my hands on my hips. "This isn't to the
death, right?"

He shrugs. "Not necessarily."

"What does that mean?"

He leans down and unties one big black combat boot and tugs it off. He extends it toward me.

"Fine," I grumble. "You're the most stubborn person I know."

"Says the girl who literally knows no one but me."

"I knew Marietta for five minutes before she died." After my joke falls unbelievably flat, all I can think about is how John might be dead tomorrow too, to save me as well. "Can I fight in your place?"

John hands me his other boot.

"Oh, come on. You can answer one or two things while I'm putting them on."

He shakes his head.

I lace up the second boot as tightly as I can, but my feet feel like tiny rocks bouncing around in a cup. I stand up. "Alright. It's your turn."

"It's not strictly to the death," John says. "But for it to end sooner, one of us would have to relent. I'd need to renounce my protection of you, which was the reason for my defiance in the first place, or he'd have to step down from his position as General, which is the basis for which he could order me to return you. Got it?"

"And will he do that?"

John shakes his head. "Not a chance."

"Then give me up," I say. "I may not be able to defend myself perfectly, but I can't watch you die for me."

He holds his hand to his heart. "Such faith. It's really confidence building, you know." He picks his way carefully across the rocks, but he doesn't seem to be leaving streaks of blood behind him, so that's something.

"Alright, then tell me how it works."

"I challenged him, so we both have until the next

morning to prepare, and as the challengee, he picks the weapon: fire, blades, hand-to-hand, or projectiles."

I'm not sure I could feel sicker if I tried. "He won't pick fire," I say. "Right?"

John snorts. "Not a chance."

"So, blades?"

"Elbion has always had a real affinity with them. His dad did, too. They say he began throwing butter knives as a toddler."

Fabulous. "What can I do to help?"

"Nothing." We've finally reached the inside of the volca-noes, and I can barely see the path, thanks to the height of the walls around us and the setting sun. "I know you feel guilty that I did this for you, but try to keep in mind that I'm actually fairly capable."

"You're also the only friend I have, remember?" I ask. "I don't want to lose you."

He takes my hand. "Trust that you won't." He doesn't release my hand as we walk down the path.

I'm glad of it. For the first time since I woke up in the middle of nowhere with no idea who I am, I'm not terrified and lost and alone. John's not just doing the right thing—enforcing justice. I think he actually likes me.

"What? No more questions?" He glances at me side-ways, his entire face cast in shadow.

"How will we make it back home without any sunlight?"

"You mean, if the path wasn't completely straight, and assuming that if we stumbled off it, we wouldn't feel the corn and wheat fields and shuffle our way back?"

I try to tug my hand out of his.

He squeezes my fingers more tightly. "Or, if we weren't about to have moonlight to guide us?" A ball of fire springs up in front of us, floating along a few feet ahead, moving as we move. Thanks to that flame, I can see that the mocking tone of his voice is playful from the sparkle in his eyes.

"I guess that's what I mean."

He stops. "I'll make you a promise."

My heart pounds in my chest. "What kind of promise?"

"I'll promise you that I won't lie to you, about anything, and that I'll keep you safe to the best of my ability."

"What do I promise you?"

"That you'll stop worrying."

My eyelids flutter. His eyes are so golden, and in the firelight, they look like twin flames. "That doesn't seem very comparable."

"It is to me." He shrugs. "It might sound pathetic, but since that moment I saw you alone, enduring the hateful pokes and prods and jabs of people who are afraid of anyone and anything different, I haven't been able to think of anything else."

"Anything but how mean they were?" My voice comes out as a whisper. I try again. "Is that what you mean?" Still stupidly breathy. What's wrong with me?

"I haven't been able to think about anything but you." Dozens of tiny flames spring up all around us, lighting the night like stationary fireflies. "I haven't been able to think about anything but keeping you safe, and teaching you to control your powers, and. . . "

I swallow slowly, never looking away from the chiseled curve of his jaw, the stubble on his cheek, the intensity in his gaze, and the full curve of his lips. "And what?"

"And this." The flames flare up brighter, and his head shifts downward slowly, inch by inch.

His hand releases mine, but only to circle my waist and lift me up a hair. And then his mouth presses against mine, and suddenly the floating flames around us aren't the only things on fire. His mouth sears me all the way down to my curling toes.

His hands loosen on my waist, which warns me of

what's coming. He begins to straighten, the pressure of his mouth against mine lessening.

But I'm not ready to let him go.

"I've thought about you too," I whisper against his mouth.

And he groans, his hands moving from my waist to my jaw and tangling in my hair. "Yes." His lips claim mine again, and I wish we could stay right here and never cross into tomorrow. Except we can't, and at sunrise, he's going to be fighting someone.

For me.

For my freedom.

I lean into the kiss for another moment, and then one more, darting my tongue against the perfect line of his teeth once, and pressing my palm against the hard line of his chest, before breaking the contact and stepping backward. "You need to sleep. We need to get you back so you can rest."

His eyes flare. "Home. Yes." He captures my mouth again, and a thrill races through me head to toe. Home. His home, not the empty house of a dead woman with whom I shared nothing. I'll be staying the night with John. Like this.

No! Not like this! He needs rest. He needs sleep. He needs to be at his quickest and best. I slide my hand up against his face, gently rubbing my fingers across the black bristles of his cheek. "We can't, John."

His eyes are unfocused, his lips parted. "Why not?" He bites his lip, his beautiful white teeth drawing my gaze like a moth to a flame. It's an apropos comparison, because if he's not prepared, we could both fail to survive.

"You made me a promise," I whisper. "To keep me safe."

He swallows. "I did. That's right." Then he shudders and takes a step back, his gaze never leaving my face. "Have you heard of the fire tetrahedron?"

I must have misheard him. "What?"

"There are four things a fire requires. First, a chemical reaction to get the whole thing moving. Then heat, fuel, and oxygen. If you take one of those things away, the fire collapses."

My brain complains at being forced to process things again. Or maybe it's my heart that's upset. "I thought we were done playing school for the day."

John steps closer. "I've never had trouble creating a flame." A fireball bursts into existence above his hand. "I've always understood, innately, what it needs. Heat, check. Oxygen, which is all around us, check. And fuel, which comes from me or an external source."

I'm still not sure what he's saying, but I could probably listen to him all night.

"You're right that tonight, we need to prepare for tomorrow." He steps closer still, his lips only a few inches from my ears. "Since I'm Fire Called, I thought I was the one who created the chemical reaction, but I was wrong."

I lift my eyebrows. "You were?"

His smile is practically wicked. "I didn't understand what a chemical reaction was until a moment ago. And now that I've felt it." He shakes his head. "Once we put this duel behind us, I'm not going to douse this fire." He presses a finger to my lips, and a shiver ricochets through my entire body.

Just as quickly, he drops his hand and walks the rest of the way to his house. When we reach it, he shows me to a spare room and turns to leave. "What? No kiss goodnight?" I can't believe I asked.

He smiles. "I can't."

"Why not?" Please don't let him be engaged or something.

"I already explained." He leans a little closer, and my hands itch to reach for him. "You're like a pile of kindling and I'm a Fire Called initiate—from the moment of that first spark. . . I won't be able to stop."

It's really, really hard to close the door, and it takes me a long time to go to sleep.

⚜ 18 ⚜

EARTH

John's slumped sideways in his chair, sleeping, when I wake up. Poor guy probably didn't get much decent rest all night—and on Erra, he's about to fight everyone he knows on my behalf. He should have brought another bed in here, if he insists on staying so close. It's an unbelievably sweet gesture, but now I feel guilty. I stare for a moment at his face, so calm, so innocent, and still charming, even in this state. I slide out of bed, disconnecting the sticky circles and diodes and whatnot from all over my body.

Luckily, nothing starts beeping, but I half expect Beth to come running in here, alarmed.

When she doesn't, I tiptoe away.

Except I forgot one little wire, and I feel it tug as I move. I spin around and see a large rectangular metal box tipping sideways, but I Lift it back up before it makes any noise. The flash of light from my eyes quickly blinks out, but I worry that will wake John instead of the crash I prevented.

Thankfully, it doesn't, and I exhale quietly with relief and tiptoe out of the room.

Beth's sitting in a hard wooden chair in the hall, her cheek propped on top of her palm, snoring softly a few inches away from a computer screen with a split feed. It's obvious which feed is mine—since it's now a bunch of flat lines and the screen for it is flashing red.

The other readings show a sharp spike from—I lean toward the screen and examine the boxes—ten minutes or so ago. What does a sharp spike mean? Oh, no. Beth's been asleep, and Jesse's *leaking*. . . A sharp spike in anything can't be good. I race into his room.

He's tugging on a lead, trying to work out how to free himself.

That sharp spike must have been what happens when you wake up. My shoulders droop and my body relaxes after an unnecessary surge of adrenaline. "You're fine. Thank goodness."

Jesse's eyes lift to meet mine, and I realize that he's not fine. His lips are almost blue. His skin is white as a sheet—and it's usually almost olive. He's been sitting in here, awake, for ten minutes and he still hasn't removed a single monitor? Why not? I race to his side just as he collapses against me.

"What's wrong?"

He opens his mouth and then falls backward, his body shaking uncontrollably.

No.

I close my eyes to try and think. No, no, no, no. Not again. I can't let this happen again. Not to Jesse. Not to me. So he has a hole—so what? I can fix that; there must be a way.

When I open my eyes again, he looks the same—seizing and flailing in my arms—but he's also different. There's a light inside of him I can see, and it's dimming.

I scream. "Martin! Oliver! John! Kahn! Anyone! I need help!" I reach outward, casting about wildly with my amazing, powerful, epic senses. I could Lift this entire stupid barn up into the air. I could pull up every tree by the roots, including the ancient elm and the monstrous old pecans.

And none of that matters!

Why can't I do more?

Tears stream down my face. "I need more time," I say. "You can't die. I'm not ready. I still need you."

His body stills, and I panic. I push past the barn, past the farm, past the road and the fences, as far out as I can sense anything, and I *pull*. Everything around me trembles then, not like the vibrations on Terra or on Erra. No, this is different. It feels like I'm ripping the world apart.

And I realize that I'd do it, if it would save him.

But when I look down, that light is all but gone, and shaking the world won't make a bit of difference. I pull back inward rapidly, panicked, desperate. And then suddenly, it's there. Energy. Light. I'm not sure where it came from, but it's close. I shove it inside of Jesse, pushing, shaping, and reforming.

And it works.

Jesse blinks. His cheeks flood with color. His breathing resumes. When I press my ear to his chest, I hear his heartbeat, strong and steady.

Sobs wrack my body.

The door behind me is flung open, but I don't bother checking which useless idiot finally showed up. I don't care —all I care about is that it's okay. Jesse's still with me. I haven't lost him.

I won't lose him.

"Alora?" Martin's eyes are wide. "What's wrong?"

I release Jesse and he scrambles up to a sitting position, tearing the stickers and wires off quickly. "We're both fine," he says.

"Why did you shout?"

John pushes past him next, and quickly shifts sideways,

his feet sliding across the floor without any other movement. Kahn's eyes light up the room as he walks through.

"Don't ever Lift me again." John scowls at Kahn.

"Then don't block the door like a greedy hog." Kahn crosses the room in three strides, searching me head to toe, and then moving on to Jesse. "You seem alright."

"Jesse was. . . " I shrug. "I thought he was sick." He was dying. I should tell them that he was dying, but if I do, how will they respond? How will *Jesse* respond?

"He was what?" Martin's not invading my space, but I can tell he's itching to delve Jesse.

I stand up. "Go ahead. Check him out."

"I'm fine," Jesse says. "Really."

"It won't hurt to make sure," Martin says. "It's no bother, really."

Kahn and I back toward the wall with our eyes still on Jesse, the backs of my knees knocking against the armchair. I stumble a bit, but Kahn catches me. "You alright?" His concerned look grates. I should be paying attention, sensing my surroundings easily, but I'm too distracted.

And guilty.

Where did that light come from? The light that I found at the last minute?

It's uncomfortably close to what Sekhmet was learning to do in my oddball dreams. And they're not screwy and inconsistent like I hear dreams are. They're terribly. . . realistic. And I've now had two. But they must be dreams. It's just that they're my first two ever, that's all.

I'm not All Called.

I'm not a Render.

I'm not Isis reborn.

I'm not an Assimilator.

And I'm definitely not Sekhmet, beloved daughter of Ra.

The whole notion is too ridiculous to countenance.

Besides, if that's true, if my dreams are real, then Ra's not the villain everyone says. He balances things. Why would anyone want to imprison him for that? For eliminating the threat of that awful, terrible villain? It was the right thing to do.

Martin straightens, the tension in his lips troubling. "It's still there."

"What is?" My heart accelerates.

"The leak," he says, "but he's fine otherwise. Actually, if anything, he seems stronger than before. He seems. . . " He shrugs. "Full of life and energy. What made you scream again?"

"Jesse was shaking," I say. "Like, twitching."

John pats my arm. "People do that when they're dreaming. Haven't you ever had a dog? They run in their sleep."

"No, I've never had a dog." I've never had anything or anyone except Jesse. I won't feel bad about saving him. Not after what's been done to us. I won't. Even if I killed a few scorpions. Even if I withered a tree.

Even if I'm worried about what it says about me, that I *could* shove light into Jesse.

"How about some breakfast?" Martin asks. "That makes everyone feel better, right?"

My stomach growls loudly, and Jesse laughs. "That's the Alora I know. Always hungry."

"Now that you're Lifting, you'll be starving all the time, too." I wait for John to walk out first, and then I follow him out.

Beth's still asleep, but she's shifted a bit, her head leaning against the computer monitor. "Hey Beth," I say. "Wake up. We'll get you some breakfast and you can sleep for real."

She doesn't move.

"That's strange," John says. "You were yelling really loudly, and she said she always works nights. She shouldn't be *this* tired." He shakes her shoulder, and she falls over sideways, collapsing to the floor.

Martin crouches over her immediately, his hands cradling her head. I freeze, my heart pounding in my chest. She was right outside the door. Other than maybe John, no one was closer. And when I pulled my senses back in, that light was just *there*. It was close. It couldn't be. . .

I gulp.

"Beth's gone," Martin says. "Her heart stopped, but everything else seems totally fine."

"Can we restart it?" John asks. "Maybe you could—"

"No," he says. "There's nothing we can do. If it could have been restarted, I'd have done that already."

I close my eyes. "She didn't deserve this."

John wraps an arm around my shoulders. "We didn't cause this. She's an older woman, and she had a heart attack. It happens, and the world is an especially scary place right now."

"Did she take any medicine?" Jesse asks. "Maybe when we took her—"

"Surely she'd have said something." John runs his hands through his hair. "Right?"

"What do we do now?" Jesse looks how I feel—guilty and stricken.

"We can't just. . . dump her somewhere," I say. I've killed plenty of people on Terra—and they blinked out of existence on Earth afterward in their respective lives. I saw plenty of dead bodies on Terra. I even killed Jesse's attackers here on Earth, but I've never been face-to-face with a dead person.

And I'm really, really hoping that I'm not responsible. "Let's check her purse," I say. "Maybe she did have some kind of heart condition?"

But there's nothing in her purse that indicates she was unwell.

"We need to notify her family," I say, "and somehow transport the body. . . away from here."

"You can't leave this farm," Kahn says. "Not unless you're planning on calling Duncan to ask for his help, anyway."

"Which we aren't doing," John says firmly.

"Hold on." My voice is a little too high and squeaky, so I clear my throat. "We can't just—"

John squeezes my shoulders even more tightly, his eyes intent on mine. "I know how you feel about this, Alora. Trust me, I do. But we've got plenty of things to worry about. Beth was a very nice woman, and you could have ordered her around, or threatened her, or held a figurative gun to her head, and you didn't do that. Even with our stakes, you reassured her, you treated her like a human, and she chose to help us. I believe that. But you can't start taking responsibility for everything lousy that happens in the world. No one can bear up under those kinds of standards."

"Did her sleep study voodoo actually help?" Kahn asks. "Not to be insensitive, but I haven't heard whether you actually entered REM or whether you learned anything in Erra or recovered any memories."

I frown. "So, about that." Everyone looks at me. "Does anyone know how challenges work on Erra?"

"Challenges?" John groans and drops his arm. "Why are you asking?"

"Someone named Elbion seized power, and you didn't take it very well. You might have said you're 'decrying' his claim or something? You're fighting him in the morning. Should we be worried about that?"

"Is there anything you can do about it?" John leans against the wall and exhales.

"Probably not," I say. "But maybe I could, I don't know, encourage you to run away?"

"Would you remember that we decided that?" John's expression is pretty grim.

"We could do what we did last time," I whisper.

Kahn ignores that I'm whispering. Or maybe he's intentionally pretending I didn't. "What did you do last time?"

"Never mind all that," John says. "I'm sure I'll be fine."

"The guy there, Marcus someone, seemed to think you would be in trouble. He said Elbion will choose knives, and I got the distinct impression that you're not great with them."

"We'll think about it. Right now, you need to eat." John drags me around the corner. "I know you're stressed, and distraught, and overwhelmed. But let's eat first, and then we'll make a plan."

"I could really go for some breakfast tacos right now," John says.

"Oh, me too." My saliva glands kick into overdrive just thinking about bacon and eggs and cheese.

"I'll go get tacos if any places are open today," John says. "There's a taco place right around the corner. Assuming it's serving, I'll be back in ten minutes. If it's not, probably five."

"I can get them," Thomas says. "If you'll give me the keys." The Thomas I know was my acrobatics partner. He seemed like. . . well, like a kid. On Terra, we were both young—goofy and full of hopes and dreams. He's a few years older than I am, though, and here, on Earth? He looks so different. Earth Martin looks almost exactly the same, but Thomas is almost a hipster in his tight jeans and thick-framed glasses.

"Alright," John says. "Let me draw you a map to the closest place since you all ditched your cell phones."

While he's drawing a map, I collect orders. Eight people, and we're ordering fifty tacos. We'd be ordering way more, except only three of us are Lifters. Healers don't require nearly as much fuel.

"Do you have a second?" Jesse asks.

"Sure." I walk toward the front of the barn, doing my best not to obsess over what we'll do about Beth. It feels like the only thing I can think about. "What's up?"

"Did you have any dreams last night?" His eyes are pathetically hopeful, which only reminds me how desperate we are for answers.

"Two," I say. "Both super strange."

"What about?" He plops down on a barstool.

I sit next to him and tell him all about the first one—the lotus flower and scorpions—and my family in ancient Egypt.

"I was there?" He beams.

I nod. "Older. A little more confident, maybe, but it was definitely you."

"Even in the first real dreams you have, you can't escape me." Jesse picks up one of the wacky almond bags of M&Ms we bought at the grocery store off the counter, rips the bag open, squeezes one out, and tosses it up in the air.

He catches it in his mouth.

"Whoa," I say. "Hey!" My eyes well with tears. It's something small, and Jesse did this on Terra too, tossing food into the air. Even so, it's the reassurance that I need. He may be damaged. He may be broken, but he's still my Jesse. I swipe at my eyes quickly. I don't think he notices, since he's shaking more M&Ms into his hand.

"These are pretty good."

"You've always loved them," I say.

He meets my eye. "We talked about your odd dreams pretty often, didn't we?" Jesse asks.

I nod.

"Is there any chance that the Egyptian stuff. . . isn't a dream? Like Terra wasn't really a dream?"

My breath catches.

"I mean, I know you're the one who's experiencing it, so I trust your judgment, but could it be a memory?"

"Meaning, you think I *am* this Sekhmet person? I am Ra's daughter?"

"It sounds insane," he says. "I know that. But everything in our lives is pretty bonkers."

"Bonkers?" My eyebrows lift.

"The reason I thought maybe it might be a memory is that. . ." He bites his lip.

"What?"

"I think I remembered a few things last night."

"You did? Like what?" Hope explodes inside of me. If he's regaining memories from his time on Earth, then that means he's all there. He's not just an empty shell or a reflection of the real Jesse, but he's all of himself. Broken, maybe, or damaged, but not destroyed.

"I guess you'll be able to tell me whether this happened. Or, I hope you will."

"Okay," I say. "Go ahead."

"So here's my dream." He cringes. "It's not very flattering."

"The likelihood it's true just went up," I say. "Tell me."

"You and I had moved in with a really loud woman, Aunt Trina?"

My heart expands in my chest to three times its usual size. "Yeah."

"She had dark, dark hair, and deep brown eyes. She used the word 'bonkers' all the time."

Eventually, she used it to describe me. "That's where you got it from," I say.

He nods. "She said anything odd reported in the news was 'bonkers.' She said the woman next door was 'bonkers.' As was the newest requirement that someone had to be home to meet the school bus."

I remember her being furious about that. She had to work. She couldn't be there every day at three to meet her eight- and six-year-old niece and nephew. We were plenty old enough to stay out of trouble for a few hours. After a lot of complaining, one of the neighbors offered to meet the bus and then drop us off at her house afterward.

"For a bit, I kind of blurred through a few things. Her complaining, her yelling on the phone, and her smoking on the back porch."

I close my eyes. I hated that part of our lives so much, but at least it's something. We endured it together, and he's getting it back. The tears well up again. "It's real, J."

"Here's the part that was the clearest." He tosses a few more M&Ms up, catching each one.

Right, he said something wasn't very flattering. "What?"

"That very first week, one of the things Aunt Trina complained about was how the darn aphids had killed one of her rosebushes and were moving on to her favorite one."

Oh, oh man. Now I know exactly what he remembered. "Yeah?"

"We wanted her to like us so badly. She was so frustrated that we were there."

"She hated us," I say. "Like, if the bus driver would have kidnapped us, she'd have never looked back."

"I liked the bus driver," Jesse says. "Miss Debra."

"Yes! She always wore crazy hats."

Jesse chuckles. "I don't remember all of them, but the day I dreamed about, she was wearing a huge, broad-brimmed straw hat—"

"Covered with silk flowers, with a huge plush bee!"

Jesse laughs, and it's like a clean winter snowfall, like that first bite of watermelon in the summer, or the moment you finally find a four leaf clover after looking all afternoon. It's something mundane that you know exists, but it's inexplicably magical. "That day, we got off the bus, and you and I decided to eliminate those evil aphids."

"We plucked them off," I say. "Every single one we could find, smooshing them between our fingers."

"They weren't crunchy or hard to kill, and they were too dumb to run or crawl away," Jesse says. "We were pretty proud of ourselves. We meant to show Aunt Trina that night, but she was in such a bad mood that we snuck away and went to bed."

"We figured we'd tell her the next morning," I say. "Because you wanted to ask her if you could join the math club, and we thought our efforts might earn you permission."

"Only, the next morning, there were just as many as ever." He sighs. "We told her what we'd done and she laughed and called us—"

"Bonkers." I forgot how much she used that word.

"After school that day, we tried to figure out a better solution, because of the math club thing. We hunted far and wide, and we found that half empty bug spray can in the bushes. No idea how old it was."

"You read the directions from the back out loud since my reading wasn't so great, and it said that Off Bug Repellent was bad for wood surfaces," I say. "I figured that meant it was no good for roses. After all, rose bushes turn into wood."

"And I argued that only trees were wood, and that living trees aren't even wood and humans are living and it doesn't hurt us."

"I went and sat down and started to cry," I say.

"And I called you a big baby." He frowns. "Sorry about that, and also for spraying that entire rosebush and everything near it."

It wasn't actually that funny, but I can't help my laugh. "We were idiots."

"I was the idiot—you vetoed it. And you were right. *Everything* died. Like, dead, dead, dead. By the next morning, even the ground cover and the bushes next to it were brown and crackly."

"You might not remember this, but even the next plant she bought for that spot died." I'm still laughing, but Jesse's not.

"We didn't know she had bought aphid dust—she insisted we confess, and before I could tell her what I'd done, you said it was you. You said I tried to stop you, and that you couldn't read and you were *so* sure it would work."

"If you'd admitted it was you, there was no way you'd have gotten to do the math club," I say.

"That was probably the most ashamed I've ever been," he says. "When I watched her spank you and shriek at you for something that I did."

"It wasn't really that bad," I say. "She made a lot of noise, and she wasn't very nice, but she stunk at beating people."

Jesse's smile is wry. "A poor consolation for my bruised sense of chivalry, but I vowed that day that I would never, ever let anyone hurt you again, certainly not me."

"And you never have." I place my hand over his, trying really hard not to think of that night—the night he died trying to save me.

"It really happened, then?" Jesse asks. "That was an actual memory?"

I nod.

He closes his eyes and smiles.

I'm not sure exactly what it means that he *can* remember things that happened here, but it's the best news I've had since that awful night. It's the first time anything has really gone right for me. The first bright spot in my life, and if he'd died a few moments ago, I never would have even known he had that memory. Which only makes me feel worse about Beth—because if it was a memory, then my dreams might be memories, and that light I snatched—it really might have been hers. I might have sacrificed someone who did nothing wrong to keep Jesse close. "I need to tell you something."

"Yeah?"

"So the other dream I had, I was Sekhmet in that one too. A little bit older? But kind of like the scorpion and lotus flower, I watched Ra transfer life energy from a man. . . to another man. It reverse aged the one who *got* the power, and. . . "

"What?"

"The other guy died after Ra stole his light, just like when I killed those scorpions."

"Whoa. So, in this dream, Ra's an Assimilator, right?"

I nod. "But unlike most Assims, apparently, he doesn't have to touch something to transfer its power. He can snatch it from afar."

"Like, how far?"

I shrug. "Not sure. But definitely a room away."

"Wow, that's crazy. And you're saying that Sekhmet can do that too, right?"

I nod.

"And you think you might be her? That your dreams might also be memories?" Jesse's eyes are so earnest, so pure, that I almost chicken out. But I need someone to know. I need to be accountable.

"Actually," I say. "I lied before. When I went into your room this morning—"

There's a knock at the door.

"Did you lock it?" I ask no one in particular.

"Oh man, I'm excited to try these tacos," Jesse says.

Try the tacos. It shouldn't gut me, that he doesn't even remember how much he loved them, but it does. One memory returned, a million still lost. "I hope Thomas got salsa. That's always your favorite part." I hop off the barstool and walk across the room to open the door.

"And avocados," John says from across the room. "That's the key to a good taco."

I swing the door open, my mouth salivating involuntarily.

"Alora."

It's definitely not Thomas.

"Uh-oh," Jesse says. "Was the taco place closed?"

I back up slowly, unable to look away.

"Alora, say something," Duncan says.

"What are you doing here, Dad?"

19

EARTH

I'm going to kill Kahn.

How *could* he have lied to me like that? And I trusted him. Apparently the buzzy feeling he gets when he's around me, if he really does get that, wasn't enough to keep him from betraying me to advance his own position.

"You need to leave," I say.

Duncan lifts his hands up defensively, palms out.

"It's not Thomas?" John walks up next to me. The second he sees Duncan's face, he lifts his hands and shoots flames straight at my dad.

An invisible wall diverts the flames, which go shooting right into the doorway, setting the molding on fire.

"Ouch," someone shouts.

I throw up my hands. "Stop," I say. "We don't even know what he wants, and it feels like. . . " I reach out with my senses. Thomas is outside, but I don't sense anyone else within the barn property. The only other people I sense are two large people driving past in a car at a brisk pace.

"What was that for?" Thomas pokes his head around

the corner, his eyes widening with alarm. He drops a big brown bag and swears loudly.

"Were you injured?" I raise my voice to make sure he isn't too distracted to listen.

"Singed a bit, but I'll be fine soon. We heal even faster on Earth than we did on Terra, you know."

"Then everyone calm down." I look over my shoulder and pin Kahn with a glare. "You have some major explaining to do."

Before Kahn can do any more than throw his hands up in the air, Oliver steps around him. "I know, and I'm sorry."

"Wait, you're the one who told Duncan where we are?" I can hardly believe my ears. Kahn kept his word? But why would Oliver betray me?

"It's not really his fault," Duncan says. "I applied pressure—"

"Am I the only person who's glad he's here?" Jesse asks.

Duncan freezes mid-word and blinks several times. "Jesse?"

My older brother beams. "I'm so happy to see you, Dad. I've been telling Alora—"

Duncan sprints across the room and throws his arms around my brother. "But you were Wasting. And you di—" He chokes.

"I died on Earth," Jesse manages to croak. "That's all true, but Alora's the Warden, remember? She pulled me out before my filaments unraveled, and here we are."

Duncan turns toward Oliver. "Did you delve him? Is he alright? Why didn't you tell me he was alive?"

"I'll be the one asking questions, thanks," I say. "And you'll be answering."

My father, the one I don't recall even seeing on Earth since he gave me up for adoption as a very young child, frowns. "But—"

I hold up my finger. "You came alone. For that reason,

I'll hear you out. Well, that *and* Jesse has been, like, pining to see you again. He has actual memories of time spent with you on Terra—memories that aren't offset by the way you abandoned us here. Yet."

"Yet? He's remembering his time on Earth?"

"Ah, ah, ah. I'm asking the questions. Remember?"

He clamps his lips together, but I can tell he's dying to ask a million things. Well, too bad. You ditch your kids, you lose the chance to pretend you're invested in their health or happiness.

"Why did you come?" I sit down and cross one leg over the other. I'm not going to let him think I'm nervous, or expecting an attack any second.

"You need my help right now," Duncan says. "And I believe you're Isis reborn. I believe we'll all need your help very, very soon."

"Isis reborn?" I roll my eyes. "Please."

"She was an Assimilator, one of the strongest and wisest who ever lived," he says. "She created Terra to begin with in order to afford us the chance to prevent the strong from exploiting and dominating the weak."

"Why in the world, if she created Terra, would she be reborn. . . as me?"

Duncan grabs a stool and drags it across the room, ignoring John's death glare, Kahn's irritation, and Oliver's terror. He perches on top of it as though he and I are the only people in the room. "Let's consider what we know. Isis created the prison by convincing women everywhere, or at least, a substantial number of them, to sacrifice their powers in order to bind everyone on Earth and confine the misery to established worlds—mitigating the power even there."

"Okay, so you're saying she struck a bargain, a rather garbage one for women if you ask me, which no one ever does, that muzzled powers in Terra, and eliminated them here. Maybe she didn't know about the major flaw—that people could be Woken with severe trauma on Earth. Or maybe she screwed up and that's why it's possible. I still have no reason to believe that this person was reborn, or that if she was, I might be her embodiment. Wouldn't I know it, if I were?"

"I think we'll discover that you're an Assimilator," Duncan says, with a completely straight face. "The first one that Earth has seen in millennia."

I suppress the terrible unease that worms its way up my spine. "Why would you think that?" I Lift him and slam him against the far wall, right next to the flatscreen. I stalk across the room until I'm standing next to him. "I'm a Lifter, but so far, that's all I can do."

"You'll eventually find that you can do more." He doesn't even look nervous.

"Try to break my Binding," I whisper. "Pit your strength against mine."

He gives a pitiful shove, like a puppy pouncing on a butterfly.

"You can do better than that. Convince me you're the ally I need."

The shove is more forceful this time, but I laugh it off. "I'm a Lifter," I say, "not an Assim. You're wrong about that one."

"You absorbed the energy of Terra," Duncan says. "And you used that energy to fuel your return to Earth with all those thousands and thousands of souls."

I turn around and spear Kahn with a glare. "You told him. I didn't explain that to Oliver."

"I asked Kahn if he knew how you did it," Oliver says. "And then I explained it to Duncan. You can fault Kahn for sharing information with an ally, but not for betraying you to your own father."

The second I shift my glare to him, he looks away. "Why? Why betray me?"

"Isis has my little sister," he says. "She got into some trouble."

Duncan chuckles. "Trouble?"

"What?" I ask.

"She used her 'gift' to kill a dozen people," Duncan says.

"Rapists and murderers," Oliver mutters.

"They were all tried and acquitted," Duncan says. "It took us months to figure out who was killing them, since there was no pattern—except they were all acquitted in the same court. Where a stenographer who was one of us decided to take things into her own hands, literally."

Okay, wow. "You were going to kill her if he didn't tell you where I was?" Our dad really is a lowlife.

"She was already sentenced to the death penalty for committing twelve premeditated murders," Duncan says. "This all happened through the American justice system. We didn't even interfere, other than providing convincing evidence a jury might understand. But when Oliver disappeared on the same night as Kahn. . . I reached out to her. I mentioned there might be a chance of her escaping in all the chaos, if her brother were able to do me a favor."

"But how could you reach Oliver?" I shake my head. "They all got rid of their cell phones."

"I turned mine off," Oliver says, "but I left last night to check for messages. My sister was due to be put to death next week. We have an appeal pending, but with the world the way it is. . . " He sighs. "I couldn't completely check out."

And his sister conveyed the deal, and here we are.

"You could be an Assim *and* a telekinetic," Duncan says.

"What about Fire Called?" I ask. "Could I be a Lifter, Fire Called, *and* an Assim?"

He frowns. "I'm not sure. Who knows what creating

the prison might do. But I can't think of anyone other than Isis who could have saved Jesse—who might have been able to bring him over from Terra to Earth successfully. You must have used some of the energy from unwinding Terra to do it."

"For the record," I say, "I didn't do anything to unwind Terra. It was already coming apart." At least, I want to believe Devlin's claim that it was. Certainly ripping Jesse out accelerated the whole process.

"There's no evidence that Terra was unraveling," Duncan says. "In fact—"

"My father insists there was. He said my mother Wasted on Erra and *then* died on Earth." John's leaning against the counter casually, as if he's not absolutely livid, but his lips are compressed and his eyes are flinty. I've rarely seen him this angry.

"Devlin Rochester?" Duncan laughs. "Oh, that's rich. Ra's strongest supporter is spreading the story that the prison containing him was already doomed?"

"Dad's never been a huge fan of Ra," John says. "And I'm not sure why everyone loves Isis. Everything happened so long ago that none of us know what really took place. But he has been insistent that Terra was a sinking ship for a long time—the reason he left Isis was that no one would *listen*. You keep asking Alora to hear you out, but what you really want is for her to obey."

"You're as bad as your dad," Duncan says. "Who, by the way, is now taking orders from some kind of zombie acolyte of Ra. What will it take for you to see things clearly? If we can't rebuild the prison—"

"Whoa." I hold up my hand. "You're here to convince me to try to rebuild the prison?"

Duncan nods.

"So one half of Isis, the half that has taken over the US government, wants me dead. Yes?"

He grits his teeth.

"But the half that you lead, is that right? You're in charge?"

He looks pained, but he nods. "Mostly in charge."

"What does that mean?" John asks.

"I'm one of a half dozen leaders who work together to rule the fragment of Isis that isn't controlling the US government. They listen to me, so sure. You can consider that I'm running that half."

"Your people want me to figure out how to recreate Terra, and then send all the people I just freed back there."

"You're acting like they're being punished," he says. "But that's not the case. Everyone was better when our powers were restricted here."

"You were Awake, though, no?" I lift both eyebrows.

"Inadvertently," he says. "Think about it. Amun and Isis are roughly the same size, but Amun has actively attacked and recruited members, whereas we have grown only from people who found their actions so reprehensible that they had no choice but to fight against them."

"Bravo," I say. "I'm sure the moral high ground is a lovely place to stand. Probably has a great view and peaceful dreams. But from where I stand, you guys are split down the middle, which means there are really three groups—and no one has any clear or convincing answers for me."

"On the contrary, once Terra has been restored—"

"You have someone who can teach me how to recreate Terra? An Assim who can show me what to do?"

He sighs. "No."

I release him and suppress a smile when he collapses to the floor. His legs probably went to sleep while he dangled up there. Serves him right. "So what's your big plan, then? Maybe you have an old Assimilator 101 textbook?"

"Wait," Jesse says. "Are you saying that neither the

Followers of Amun nor the Followers of Isis have *ever* located a single Assimilator? So as far as you know, they might not even exist?" He glances around the room for confirmation, and I follow his gaze.

No one argues with him.

"Our theory," Duncan says, "is that they're rare—less than a thousandth of one percent of the population, and even of those, only perhaps one in a thousand has enough power to do anything significant." Duncan shifts to his knees and then climbs back to his feet.

"But you have theories, no more?" Jesse asks. "You haven't Woken even one?"

"Correct," Duncan says.

"Great." I'm sick of all these guesses and hopes and plans.

"If you believe Devlin has one of Ra's lieutenants," John says, "then there is someone we could ask for information."

"Sure," Duncan says. "And we might get some—but it might not help us if he or she succeeds in killing Alora before we can implement it."

"Do you really have so little faith in your own abilities?" John shoves himself up from the barstool and walks toward Duncan.

"What does that mean?" Duncan's shoulders square up and his hands wiggle, as if he's preparing for something.

"Stand down, you two," I say. "I think what John's saying is that, if we set up a meeting, perhaps your followers, the Isis contingent that isn't plotting my immediate demise, could run security."

"Besides," John says. "It's not like this lieutenant could overpower Alora. He or she may be ancient and rather skilled, but they're going to be a Lifter, right? And no Lifters we've ever seen can match Alora."

"What makes you sure of that?" Kahn frowns. "Do you have a cell phone, too?"

"Of course I do, idiot. I've got several," John says. "How do you think we called you?"

"So you have been in communication with your father," Kahn says.

"No," John says. "But Alora's Fire Called on Erra, which means she's Fire Called here too. . . and she can't use that power at all. She needs to be Woken here for that too, apparently. That means the prison walls are still doing their job, wherever they're in place."

"Which means that if someone woke up, it's because they were freed with the unraveling of Terra," Duncan says. "And that's only other Lifters."

"But how could anyone who served Ra, like actual Ra from thousands of years ago, possibly still be alive?" Martin's utterly calm, and seemingly unconcerned. I almost forgot my found family was even here, they've been so quiet. He crosses the room and presses a taco into my hand. "We can keep talking, but you need to eat."

"We all do," Jesse says. "Plus, cold tacos are not good."

The old Jesse would have said 'no bueno,' but otherwise, it's exactly what he would have said before, and it reminds me of what matters most. "There are too many things we don't know anything about—and almost all of them could be answered by the same person." I take a bite of my taco as I think things through. Any way I process it, we're stuck with the same problem: we don't know enough.

And there's only one real solution for that. "John?" I ask.

"Yeah?"

"Call your dad. We need to set up a meeting."

20

EARTH

Of course, the very instant John dials the number, I have second thoughts. Maybe trusting Devlin is a huge mistake. Meeting with Ra's lieutenant, held in some kind of bizarre stasis for thousands of years, is definitely insane. I mean, let's say I'm *not* really Sekhmet and I'm not remembering my past life. Then what I'm doing is possibly suicidal.

If I *am* Isis, this ancient lieutenant will surely try to kill me.

And if they *are* memories, and I *am* Sekhmet, I still somehow have control over the prison where Ra is being held, and where this guy was held until very recently. So it's likely that something happened between my memories and the creation of that prison, and any servant of Ra will still be mad at me.

There's also the small issue of me not wanting to be a reborn version of anyone. Not that I've been given a choice in any of this at any point.

"Hey, Dad. It's me."

Jesse hands me a second taco while we stand in silence. "I can't eat this right now," I hiss.

"You'd better," he says. "They'll be gross when they're totally cold, and you need food."

"Yes, of course she knows I'm calling you. She asked me to set up a meeting—if one of Ra's representatives really is awake, as you thought."

Another pause.

"When?" John looks at me. "Maybe today?"

I shake my head.

"Er, I mean, tomorrow. We're very busy today." He cringes, and then tosses his hands up in the air, holding the phone between his shoulder and his ear.

"I need some time to prepare," I hiss around a mouthful of eggs and potatoes.

"Yes, tomorrow late morning would work. But we need to find a neutral location, somewhere that Alora feels safe."

John listens. I suppose I could have called him myself. Or part of me wishes he were on speakerphone, but then again, there are a lot of people in this room, including Duncan. And I never want to talk to Devlin Rochester. Whether he intentionally harmed me or not, I still blame him for almost everything bad that's happened to me. If I heard his voice, I'd only want to jump through the phone and strangle him.

"Yes, I know the area, but how can we trust that you won't bring an army? You're not exactly known for keeping your word." John's got almost as many issues with his dad as I do.

Another short wait. Jesse tosses me another taco. I pull a face and he ignores it, pointing at his mouth and then patting his belly.

"I suppose you're right. We'll have to trust each other." John rolls his eyes. "Alright, eleven a.m., tomorrow. Brazos Bend State Park, no more than eight people from either side." John hangs up.

"Eight people?" Duncan asks. "How did you come up with that figure?"

"You," John says, "me, Kahn, Alora, Jesse, Martin, Thomas, and one of your people."

Duncan laughs. "Uh, no. How about Alora, me, and six of my best people."

"I'll decide who comes," I say. "But for now, we have a lot of things to take care of."

"Like what?" Duncan asks.

"That poor dead woman for one," Jesse says, "and then there's the matter of Oliver's betrayal, and preparation for tomorrow. Obviously we need to scope this place out."

"A dead body?" Duncan blinks. "Who died?"

Before I have to come up with some explanation, Martin jumps in to tell him about Beth.

Oliver's trying to sneak out the back door when Kahn Lifts him and shoves him into a chair. "Not a good plan," he says. "Your sister may be free now, but I'd hate to see you take her empty cell."

"Actually, that would be fine with me." John scowls.

Oliver gulps.

"What's done is done," I say.

"He's my friend," John says, "but I agree with Kahn. We can't simply ignore that Oliver betrayed us, even if Duncan turns out to be an asset. It should have been your choice to make. If we can't trust people, at a bare minimum, they have to be neutralized."

That sounds dangerously close to 'eliminated.' "What's he guilty of, exactly?" I ask. "I was contemplating meeting with Duncan anyway, and as it turns out, he seems to be genuine in his offer of help."

"Oliver knew who you were," Kahn says. "He was willing to risk the lives of countless people by putting you at risk, to save the life of one person who had done something very bad. All because he loved her."

Which sounds dangerously close to what I would do, and possibly have already done, for Jesse. "No harm, no foul," I insist. "Sometimes in life, things don't go smoothly, and other times, when they do, it's pointless to inflict punishment for the sake of justice." I wave my hand at Kahn and Oliver. "Let him go, and he can choose whether to stay with me and serve, or whether to leave and find his sister."

When Kahn releases him, Oliver falls at my feet, pressing his head to the rug. It's disturbingly similar to the way Ra's bodyguard prostrated himself after what he perceived as his failure and it makes me even more uncomfortable with this entire thing. "Stand up." I try not to sound annoyed, but I don't succeed.

"I've been on a lot of hikes at Brazos Bend," Roland says. "I only moved to Dallas last year—before that I lived in Rosenberg for more than twenty years. The wildlife's abundant, and there are lots of big trees. The conservatory's in the center of the park, and I'm assuming they'll get there by Park Road. It's really the only way in. Except there's a little bee place on Lake View Road. We could travel there and hike in the back way."

I hate hiking. "There's a trail?"

He shakes his head. "No, but with a compass, it wouldn't be hard to stay on course. It's not like it's very far or there are wild mountain lions roaming."

Just a lot of walking through uneven ground in the woods. Ugh. "Well, I guess Roland, you can take point on our plan, and coordinate with John, who knows his dad better than the rest of us."

"I might know Devlin as well as his son, and from a different angle," Duncan says. "And I doubt any of you would know what to do with the poor deceased woman. I can take care of that—notifying her family and disposing of the body."

His offer only reminds me of how efficient they were at cleaning the crime scene after Jesse was killed. "Sounds fine," I say. "And you can weigh in on Roland's and John's approach if you want. I'll take Roland, since he knows the area, Martin, to have a second Healer on hand, Kahn, John, and you. Add me into the mix, and that brings us to six. You can pick your two most trustworthy people to bring along."

"What about me?" Jesse asks.

My mouth turns to cotton just thinking about taking Jesse with me into a battle zone again. "I need someone to stay here and make sure—"

"You want me to sit in the car?" Jesse asks.

He's making movie references. "Whoa, are all your memories back?"

"Actually, I'm not even sure what that means. The phrase just came to me." He frowns.

I can't help being a little gleeful, knowing that some of the Jesse I know is surfacing, whether from returning memories or simply some kind of healing process. "Please don't make me face this and worry about you at the same time, J."

"It's you and me against the world. It always has been."

My heart breaks hearing that, and I can't argue. "Fine. You can take Martin's place since Roland can Heal most things well enough until we're able to meet up with the others again."

Duncan and Roland and John start arguing immediately, and I can't handle any more. I walk toward the door.

"Where are you going?" Jesse asks.

"I need to train," I say. "Kahn?"

His smile's not forced, not even a little bit. "Sure."

"I think more than training, you need to do something fun." Jesse bumps my shoulder with his upper arm. "When's the last time you did anything you *wanted* to do?"

"I'm meeting with a zombie warrior tomorrow," I say. "And you think I should play a game of cards?"

"You can't remember," Jesse says slowly, accusatorially. "I mean, clearly I can't remember the last fun thing I did. But I figured you'd be able to come up with *something*."

I sigh. "You were working on some kind of coding thing I didn't understand, the night before I went in to my dishwashing job and got sacked, so I read a book. I stayed up way too late because the book was ridiculously good and super long."

"And you enjoyed it?" Jesse asks.

"I did," I say. "A lot."

"You should read another book, then," he says.

I laugh. "That first book was one I grabbed for free—something about a secret race of people known as Evians—but the next six books cost money. Ironically, even though I could now Lift a school bus in the air with my mind, I still don't have any money."

Jesse frowns. "I'm sure someone here can buy you—"

"Or," Thomas says. "Maybe you can both win."

"What?" Jesse asks.

"Remember back on Terra, how much fun we had practicing for our routine?" Thomas grabs a broom that's leaning against the wall. "You could train and we can reenact our routine at the same time." He tosses the broom to me.

Instead of Lifting it, I catch it with my palm. The impact actually stings a bit—and the rush of adrenaline is just what I need. "Yes. Good idea."

Ten minutes later, I've assembled a rather ridiculous looking high wire, made of baling twine that's Bound in place, and a rickety paint ladder so that Thomas can climb up on his own power.

"Your strength is already beyond what anyone else can

do," Kahn says. "What you really need to work on is your control, and your focus."

Thomas is climbing up already. "What does that mean?" I ask.

"You stumble and knock things over too often," Kahn says. "That tells me that while you have the ability to sense the world around you, and you likely did it naturally on Terra, you haven't really grown accustomed to doing it here. You need to maintain that awareness as second nature, like knowing the guns held blanks, and at the same time, be able to act quickly and manage more than one thing at once."

"So you want her juggling while balancing a vase on her nose and also singing the ABCs?" Jesse asks. "This should be fun."

I don't really end up looking like some kind of freak show, exactly, but Kahn does have me juggling heavy equipment from the back pasture while also sparring with Thomas and answering questions Jesse shoots my way. It's embarrassing, and it's exhilarating, and it's fun.

"Whoa," Kahn says.

"What?" I turn back toward him.

"Look at your foot."

My right foot isn't balanced on the baling twine—it's pressing against nothing but air. Smooth, hard, supportive air that I Bound in place without thinking. "Huh."

"You're doing it. Paying attention to the world around you while using your power." Kahn points at Thomas, who's coming at me with his stick. "Now, carry on."

We practice until a white van shows up, rolling slowly down the driveway.

It's here to pick up Beth. "Maybe we'd better take a break and see how the plans are coming." I swing down from the baling twine tightrope by hopping from one Bound spot to another. And then I stand, transfixed, as they load her, in a pristine white bag, into the van. I know it's not Jesse—he's standing right next to me—but I can't help thinking of that day when I opened that bag and saw my brother's frozen face.

Is it my fault that someone is about to be doing the same thing with her?

"You look sick." Jesse walks over next to me. "Are you alright? Maybe you ought to release all that stuff." He gestures at the heavy equipment I'm still circling around idly in the air.

Right. I lower the tractor and its various attachments to the ground, settling them back in the tall weeds I Lifted them from. "I'm fine."

Thomas and Kahn head toward the house, presumably to give us some space.

"You were trying to tell me something earlier," Jesse says, "right as Dad arrived. You were saying something about when you came into my room? Or maybe it was about your dream? I can't remember."

"Oh," I say. "Um, so the thing is." I don't want to tell him now. I'm not sure what I was thinking. If I tell Jesse what I think I might have done. . . how will he react? Will he be mad? Disappointed?

But most of all. . . What if I ever have to do it again?

I never thought I could lie to Jesse, but I really can't lie to myself. No matter how guilty I may feel, if I had to do it over again, knowingly, aware of what I was doing, I'd still sacrifice Beth's life for Jesse. She did nothing wrong. She was helping us, and I'd watch her die if it meant saving my brother.

Which probably means I'm a monster.

Jesse can't know that—he can't. I can't survive him hating me.

"What's the thing?"

My mind scrambles around for anything else to share.

Anything else that I might have made such a big deal out of. "Do you remember how after the Ascension, I told you about the ground, or well, the whole world vibrating in Terra?"

"You trashed the ring," he says. "Yeah, I remember."

"That's the first time I recall anything being strange about my reality."

His brow wrinkles. "Okay."

"And it happened on Erra, too. I can Lift there, only no one can Lift there so they don't know what I'm doing. Actually, I don't know what I'm doing either. It's weird. I lifted an entire lake, and then dropped it on me and John."

"You did what?"

"Obviously I'm not so great with the control and understanding of my limits there. The point is, when I thought I was drowning, I totally saw the whole earth sort of vibrate. Just like it did on Terra, and when I was coming back from the near-drowning, I saw everything as cables and ropes of energy."

"Do you think Erra's unstable? Or is it just that you can see that it's not *real* because of who you are?"

"I wish I knew. The problem with all this is that no one really has any answers."

"Dad might, if you'd listen to them."

"He's not my dad."

Jesse flinches.

"I know you love him, but I've never thought of him as my dad," I say.

"You did call him that, once."

"You'd used the word so much, that I guess I did too. It didn't mean the same thing to me as it did to you."

I hate seeing the hurt look on my brother's face.

"I didn't know him on Earth, and I didn't know him on Terra."

"But you didn't know me on Terra either," Jesse says, "and you and I always got along."

"You weren't tasked with the duty of taking care of me in the first place." I shrug. "Maybe it's not rational and maybe it's not fair. Or maybe my feelings on Earth spilled over into Terra without me knowing it, but he's never felt like my dad."

Someone clears his throat, probably Kahn, ready to grill me again about being more aware. I should have noticed that someone walked up behind us. I turn around, ready for a reprimand and a lecture on safety.

"We made some sandwiches." Duncan offers Jesse a plate and turns around again to leave.

Which means he probably heard me saying he never felt like my dad.

"Actually, I thought I might go get something to drink." Jesse hands me the plate. "Why don't you stay, and I'll be right back."

When Duncan starts to follow Jesse back inside, my brother points. "You stay. Someone should be with her, just in case anyone else shows up."

Could he be any more obvious? It's not like Duncan and I will magically bond once we chat for a moment. I grab a sandwich and take a bite to avoid having to say anything. I might apologize to avoid an awkward interchange, and that would just be one more lie to deal with.

"You forgave Oliver."

That's totally not what I expected him to bring up. "Uh, well. I don't trust him, but I don't see the point in casting non-enemies away. Or punishing people for doing what they think they must." There's no way I'm telling him that I couldn't very well eviscerate Oliver for doing what I would totally do for Jesse in a heartbeat.

"But if someone had wronged you, not intentionally

maybe, but in a moment of weakness, would you forgive that?"

The hypothetical annoys me. "Spit it out, Duncan. Are you asking whether I'm still angry you shoved me and Jesse off on someone who never loved us?"

His eyes widen and his jaw muscles work overtime.

"No? Just say what you want to say. I don't have the mental energy for any extra puzzles right now."

"You had a friend—someone named Henry."

My heart sinks. "Yeah. What does he want now?"

"He's never been the most decisive person in the world, and his mother is a bit of a battle axe. She runs that family like a drill sergeant."

"Why should I care about that?" I ask. "I trusted him— I thought he was a friend, and actually he knew about Terra, about everything. And when I went to him for help." I can't even look at Duncan, and my body trembles.

"You've never done the wrong thing and wished you could undo it?"

Beth. Beth. Beth. But I wouldn't undo it, that's the difference. I didn't know quite what I was doing—it was an accident. But if I had known, I'd have done it anyway.

I think.

"What do you want me to do about Henry?"

"Isis has split into two branches. One of them, as you know, is running the US government. My side was more focused on finding you and keeping the first group from killing you."

"You think I'll restore Terra."

"I know you will," Duncan says. "I have faith in you, faith I don't think you even have in yourself yet."

"But what does that have to do with Henry?" Like everything, he's handling this all wrong.

"You said I can bring some men along, people to help us when you go to meet Devlin." His tone makes it clear he thinks that's a huge mistake—he could have been saying 'when you go to jump off that cliff to your death.'

"You want to bring Henry?"

"He wants to come," Duncan says. "He knows he messed up, but he wants to make things right. He wants to keep you safe."

"Last time I asked him to help, he told me his mom turned me in and refused to lift a finger on my behalf."

"His parents sided with the group that controls the government. They want you dead, but Henry fell out with them. He's on our side. For the first time ever, that boy is showing some real backbone. He did that for you."

"Or his parents told him to try and lure me in so they can whack me."

Duncan laughs. "He's showing backbone, but the boy can't lie. He's a wreck, not because he betrayed his parents —because he betrayed you."

"Fine. If you want him to be one of the men you bring, I don't care."

Duncan beams at me, clearly shocked I relented.

I finally take a second bite of my sandwich, sensing the emotional turmoil has past.

I'm wrong, of course. Seconds later, his entire face falls. "I am sorry I abandoned you, you know."

An apology he's only making because he heard me tell Jesse he's not my dad. "It's fine," I say around a mouthful of chicken salad.

"It's not fine. I let you down."

"Mom took me. If you'd followed, it only would have drawn attention to the fact that we were alive. You were trying to protect us." As I say it, I realize that while I do believe the words, I think he was wrong. He was a powerful Lifter from an established family. He had money and connections—and he let someone else raise me. He let my powerless mother walk away. . . because it was easier for him to pursue his ambition. He became who he was on Terra more easily without the anvil of a Lifter daughter dragging him down.

"I wasn't talking about that." He Lifts a large wooden spool and a bucket from a pile of junk near the outbuilding and sets them down next to me.

I'm not sure what else I can do, so I sit and take another sandwich. "But on Earth, you were trying to protect Jesse. Believe me, I support that."

"I know that was wrong, but can I at least explain *why* I did that?"

I don't even know how our mother died. I haven't heard any part of his story here—why they both abandoned us. "I guess." I shift on the bucket. I should have picked the spool. It looks flatter.

"My father, your grandfather, was a dentist."

Weird start.

"He worked hard, and we were really comfortable while I was growing up. And of course, as you would expect, he employed the latest and greatest techniques on all his children." He chuckles. "I have four sisters."

I have aunts, and possibly cousins. I hadn't even contemplated that possibility.

"Anyway, one of the things he did was use silver fillings on each of our molars that had a deep recessed area, to prevent any cavities from forming."

I'm totally lost.

"Silver fillings were all the rage at the time, and so was the practice of filling in teeth as a preventative measure. What they didn't realize was that the silver expanded and contracted over time and with variable temperatures. So over an extended period, it usually resulted in a fracture to the tooth. Either that, or a cavity would form down inside the filling as space opened up. Both alternatives were bad. It would have been much better for him to teach us good dental hygiene and ensure that we followed through instead of trying to save us from ourselves with those preventative fillings."

Ah.

"When your brother was born, defecting to join Amun was all the rage. Lots of our friends changed allegiances—which meant that everyone knew our identity and our powers. Because your maternal grandfather had been a very strong Lifter, and I was as well, we knew there was every chance that Jesse would be impressively powerful."

I see where this is going.

"Some friends of ours had a little boy about five years before we had Jesse. He was only four years old when a defector family gave up their information to Amun. Their young son was kidnapped and forcibly Awoken. They never recovered him. Our friends were distraught, as you might imagine. As a result of that, nearly everyone we knew who stayed loyal to Isis decided that it would be wise to hide our children. Your mother couldn't bear the idea of parting with Jesse, and then when you came along, with either of you."

"Then why did you?"

"They only stole boys, you understand, since the girls couldn't be Woken. We knew we should hide Jesse right away, but we put it off for too long—when we did try to separate the two of you to keep Jesse safe, you had bonded too deeply."

"I heard that part," I say. "That we both refused to eat."

"Your mother blamed herself. She stole that extra time with Jesse, and in doing so, we lost you both."

"Well, don't worry. Judging from what I've seen, I got the better end of that deal."

Bright red spots appear on Duncan's face. "You can hit me with any rage or anger you feel, but don't disparage your mother. She was an amazing woman, and she spent the rest of her life watching you both from afar and attacking anyone who might wish you harm. That's what killed her, actually. She found out you were being traced by Amun and she took action. Without powers, she didn't stand a chance against the men she accosted."

I'd feel a lot more sorrow, probably, but I've already mourned the loss of the only version of my mother I ever knew.

"Look, you may not believe this, but I have to at least say it. Whether you're Isis reborn or not, and I happen to think that you are, to me, you're still my little girl. I will protect you to my dying breath. When we go to that park tomorrow, I don't want you worrying about watching your back around me."

His story might not have forged the connection between us that Duncan was hoping for—he still doesn't feel like a father to me—in fact, the only person I've really felt feelings of fatherly affection toward is probably Martin.

Or maybe Ra, in my bizarre dreams.

If they really are memories, maybe that's why I struggle with Ra.

After having had not one, but two fathers who cared for me, how could I ever accept anyone who would wrap me in a papyrus basket and leave me on a riverbank?

But at least Duncan accomplished what he set out to do: I won't need to worry about whether he'll betray me tomorrow. I may not love him, but I'm not afraid of him anymore either.

Mostly, I pity him. It must suck to regret almost every choice you've made.

I really, really hope I never end up like that.

Her familiar voice is angry. Very, very angry. "You may be able to convince people that the sun is the moon and up is down. You may be able to drain every scrap of life from me and turn it into a beetle you can squash under your shoe, but you can't force me to forgive you, and you can't make me love you, not anymore. Not now that I know the truth."

Something's wrong. Why does Mother sound so angry? Who's she yelling at?

Dad?

Why?

I crawl out from under my blanket and work my way past the woven mat. By the time my feet hit the stone floor, I've shifted and my paw pads make no sound. I creep slowly toward the doorway, careful not to wake Aha. It's hard to sneak past her, but I've gotten much better in the past few years.

"You *do* love me. I don't need to *make you* do anything. You're just confused. Isis lies. You know this."

Something slams against the wall, but I'm not sure what.

I bump the door with my nose, pushing the door open far enough that I can peer out.

Mother's holding Dad against the wall with her palm flat against his chest. "Don't mistake me, Ra. Love and hate were never opposites. I'm not saying I feel nothing for you. I'm saying that your *lies* have turned my love to hate, and that will never change."

If I weren't in my lion form, I'd have cried out by now, or at least whimpered. I'm glad of this feline body to remind me to stay silent.

"You can't take her with you."

Mother drops her hand and backs up as though he burned her. "Have you heard a word I said?" She hisses. "I don't want anything to do with her. She's an abomination. You ensured that."

Dad scowls. "Those are the lies she tells. Listen to yourself. What kind of mother believes anything like that about her own daughter? If I didn't love you so much, and if it wouldn't destroy her, I'd rip your throat out for even repeating such a monstrous slander."

"You're pure evil," Mother says. "Isis was right. I can't believe it took me so long to see it."

"If you leave," Dad says, "don't expect me to welcome you back."

Mother's laugh has no joy in it. "Delusional." She waves her hand and air rushes past her, lifting her off her feet and shuttling her down the hallway like a falcon in flight. Only, with her magic, she doesn't even need to shift.

"Mraow," I say, suddenly frustrated that I can't speak in this form.

Dad freezes and turns slowly toward me. "Sekhmet, cub. How long have you been there?"

I blink at him. Lions don't cry either. Maybe that's a blessing.

He crouches down next to me and gathers me against

him. My head rests against his chest, my whiskers brushing his face, and deep inside, I begin to rumble. Mother left. She said I'm an abomination. Is it true? What did she mean? I shift then, my limbs transforming magically back to human limbs. Luckily, whatever clothes I'm wearing when I shift are still there when I return.

But the tears I would have shed also manifest, and suddenly I'm soaking Dad's beautiful golden robes. "Why?"

Dad lifts my chin so I'm looking at his eyes. "Your mother's angry with me, and she said many things she didn't mean."

"She said I'm a monster," I say. "She said she hates me."

"I just found out she's been visiting Isis when she goes to see her family." Dad sighs. "Isis is many things, and one of those things is clever and silver-tongued."

"What does that mean, silver-tongued?" I stick out my tongue. What little I can see of it is pink.

Dad chuckles. "How could anyone think you're anything other than a delight? A joy? A ray of sunshine in this depraved world?"

"Why would she say that if it's not true?" I choke back more tears. "She has to love me—she's my mother."

"Sekhmet?" Shu's standing at the end of the hall, his face searching for me.

"I'm here," I whisper.

Even though he's at the other end of the house, he hears me, and he races toward us. "Mother left."

"You didn't go with her?" Dad's eyes are hard and angry when they look at Shu.

"I've been accompanying her on her trips because she made me—she said otherwise you'd insist on sending someone else to keep an eye on her. That doesn't mean I bought into the nonsense Isis peddles."

Anat races around the corner. "Most Divine! The Macedonians are assembling forces in the far east."

Dad groans. "Shu." He stands up and looks my older brother in the eye. "Can you talk to her?"

They stare at each other for a very long time.

Finally Dad hands me to Shu, like I'm a baby. I wiggle in his arms. "I'm not a child. I'm ten years old."

Shu laughs, and it's the first right thing I've heard since I woke.

Dad leans close and places a hand on Shu's arm. "If you don't think you can handle this, I'll send Am-Het and Ammit and Anat, and I'll stay with her."

Shu lifts one eyebrow. "I'm aware you're flawed, Father. I see your faults, but I don't believe the lie that cracked Mother's faith." He glances down at me and smiles. "You can go and defend our borders, and I'll repair the damage here. Have you considered why, knowing your flaws for what they are, I stay?"

Dad nods. "For her."

"For her. Anat told me what Mother said before she flew out of here. I could kill her for that alone." Shu's eyes flash and his hands tighten underneath my legs and around my shoulders. "I may yet."

"Good," Dad says, as if he agrees. But before he ducks out of sight around the corner, I see him swipe at his cheeks. He may be angry with Mother, but his heart is broken, too.

"You saw it?" Shu asks.

"He's hurting," I say. "He needs us."

"I'm more worried about you."

"You shouldn't be. I'm fine." I sense the moment Dad is gone from the palace grounds. And then I leap out of Shu's arms, shifting to a lion midair, and landing on all fours. Then I let out the largest and longest roar I've ever made. The fur on my back stands up, and my claws unsheathe, and I roar again.

"You look fine." Shu smirks. "But, even with as 'fine' as

you are, I imagine you're still hungry. I hear all that shifting leaves Renders ravenous."

I grumble a bit in my throat.

"As cute as you look—"

I growl.

"Sorry. As formidable as you look—" He pauses.

I bob my head.

"It kind of puts me off my bread and figs when someone next to me is tearing into a raw rack of lamb." He stares at me.

I don't want to change back. He's going to want to talk to me. He's going to ask me questions and I'll have to answer them.

Abomination.

I shudder.

"Come on, Sekhmet. You're going to have to talk to me sometime. It may as well be now."

I shake my head.

"Alright, I hear you. Believe me, I do. I'd better summon Dad, though. It seems I can't handle this for him."

My eyes widen. He can't call Dad back. Not when there are enemies gathering to attack. What might happen to our citizens in the east? How will he keep them safe? What if, without Dad, Ammit's harmed? Or Am-Heh? Or Anat? What if something happens to their soldiers?

It would be my fault.

I huff. I rumble and claw long rivets into the wall of the hallway.

But finally, I shift. I look ridiculous, sitting on the floor of the palace hallway in my nightshirt.

"Are you planning to go to breakfast like that?" Shu asks. "Or did you want to run and change into some more appropriate clothing?"

As if the words summoned her, Aha opens the door in

human form. She waves me inside. "I'll bring her to the breakfast room in ten minutes."

She must have heard what Mother said too, because she keeps her human form the entire time, not even shifting to lick my hair free of tangles. Which is really too bad—she's terrible with a comb.

"It's not true," she says.

I ignore her. I don't want to talk about it.

Shu is waiting on me, clearly wanting to speak all the words too. "I have a lot of training to do today," I say. "I don't think I can spend much time in here."

He doesn't argue. He watches as I gobble all my food, even my disgusting leeks and onions.

It doesn't occur to me until I've already eaten them that I didn't have to do it. For the first time in my life, no one would yell at me for scraping them into the scrap basket. Because. . .

Mother's gone.

She yelled a lot.

She fussed all the time.

She raged, sometimes, and oh, it was glorious. The wind would whip her hair, plants would grow riotously up the walls, and ice would form over all the flat surfaces. But eventually she'd calm down. She'd light the torches, and she and Dad would kiss and laugh and sometimes, they'd dance.

She sang to me.

She taught me two languages.

She showed me how to douse a fire. She taught me how to make flames shimmer and grow and then disappear in a puff. She showed me how to tie my sash. She helped me pick out my first coronet, and she placed it on my head only a few months ago.

Abomination.

She hates me so much, she left us.

And she's never coming back.

There are a lot of things I want to ask, a lot of things I want to know, a lot of fears clawing at me from all sides.

But I can't articulate any of them. Or at least, even if I could, I'm not sure I can handle the answers.

"Why?" It's the only word I can form.

Shu stands up and circles the table. He picks me up like a baby again, only this time I don't care. Something inside of me snaps open and I'm sobbing again. Pathetically, like I'm not a warrior. Like I'm not Dad's fierce little cub.

For a moment, I'm actually relieved Dad's not here to witness this. How ashamed he'd be. He fixes problems effortlessly. He fights armies. He vanquishes foes, and feeds our people, and adjudicates disputes. He improves the barren places and cultivates the creatures that inhabit them, large and small.

And I'm so pathetic that a few words from Mother eradicate me.

"I can't answer the why," Shu says softly. "I heard the same things as Mother, but I didn't believe them."

"What things?" My eyes are wide, hopeful. Let them not be as awful as I fear.

Shu presses a kiss to my forehead and carries me into Dad's library. He sets me on one of the large inlaid wooden benches that line the front wall. "I need you to listen to me, Met, carefully. Can you do that?"

I frown. I've already heard too much today.

"Isis convinced Mother that Dad had magically altered you, that you weren't Blessed. That's why Mother thinks you're. . . not her daughter."

The words strike at my heart. I know what he was going to say instead of 'not her daughter,' because I heard her say it. *Abomination*. "She thinks I'm a monster." My voice is small. Why does it sound so small? I wish I could roar as a human. I hate that all we can do is cry and sob and yell and screech. Why can't we roar? It's so bracing.

Shu hugs me to his chest. "You're not a monster."

"How do you know?" I ask. "Aha tells me that I'm different every day. Anat says I'm a miracle."

"See? You should listen to them."

I pull away from him and lean against the wall so I can see his face. He can lie with his words, but he can't lie to me with his eyes. I'll know it. "Different. Miracle. Monster. They're all words for 'not normal.'"

"Have you ever seen a fig that grew doubled?" Shu asks.

"What?"

He pulls one out of his pocket. Instead of a single fig node, like every fig fruit I've ever seen, there are two figs joined at the top, that share the same stem. "You can see for yourself." He tosses it up in the air and I snatch it away by reflex.

It feels exactly like every other fig I've ever touched.

"Go ahead," he says. "Take a bite."

I do.

"How does it taste?"

I shrug. "The same as always."

"So it's delicious?"

I roll my eyes. "I prefer dates, remember?"

"Well, miss sass, I couldn't find a doubled date, and I love figs."

He does. He always has. "What are you saying, Shu?"

"The world is a beautiful and varied place. Do you know what dictates whether someone's a monster, Met?"

I shake my head, and to my dismay, a tear rolls down my cheek.

Shu wipes it away and frown-smiles, where his eyes say, 'I'm so sorry,' and his mouth turns both up and down at the same time. He feels sorry for me.

I can't take it. I can't. I don't want people to stick around so they can teach me out of being bad. I don't want to be the one who needs help and intervention. "I don't want to be a doubled fig." Another stupid tear escapes and I wish I could set something on fire. I wish I could rend something with my teeth. I wish. . . I wish. . . all the things a monster wants. That's what I want to do. To destroy, to rage, to shred something, anything, beyond repair.

Shu sets his hand on my arm. "Our actions are what make us into monsters or what make us into something wonderful. Nothing else. You're a blessing in my life, and you were a blessing in Mother's. Sometimes people get so confused, they get so angry, that they can't see things right. That's what happened."

I can't meet his eye.

"Met, look at me."

I wish he'd stop using my nickname. I can't tell him no when he calls me that.

"Sekhmet, look at your big brother right now."

I finally look up, and I startle.

His face is inches from mine. His eyes aren't sad. They aren't angry. They're sparkling and happy. "My life is blessed because you're in it. Anat's life is blessed by you. That's why she calls you a miracle. Everyone who knows you, everyone who's not blinded by hatred and fury, they see the truth. You're not a monster. You're not an *abomination.*"

Great sobs tear through me when he uses that word.

Shu Lifts me and rocks me back and forth, pulling me against himself again. His arms wrap around me. "Never forget that you're a blessing. Promise me that."

"Okay." I hiccup.

"You may not believe me today," he says, "and you may not believe me tomorrow."

He's right.

"But I want you to know that I stayed for *you.* Mother is furious that I didn't leave with her. How dare her nearly powerless son, the disappointment who can only Lift, and not even that powerfully, choose to stay with Father instead of following her?" He shakes his head. "Our actions determine what we are, so if there's a monster here, it's Hathor. I'll tell you that today. And tomorrow, and every single day, until you believe me. The same way that I believe in you."

I feel a lot better by the time Dad returns from battle late that night. He tiptoes over to my bed, his eyes worried. "I'm awake," I say. "I couldn't sleep until I knew you were safe."

He drops to one knee and brushes my hair back from my face. "I'll always be safe, and I'll always keep you safe."

"I know."

"Shu says he convinced you." Dad stares expectantly.

"Uh-huh."

The left side of Dad's mouth tucks upward. "So he tried really hard."

I nod.

"Well, listen to *me*, then. I can do something he can't."

"You can do a few things he can't."

"That's true," Dad says. "But I'm talking about something you and I share, the ability to look upon someone's true heart. I've seen plenty of monsters in my time, believe me. And when I look at you, I see nothing but pure, blindingly beautiful light."

I know, beyond any worms of doubt, that Dad loves me. But that might make it hard for him to see clearly. And the one soul I can't see, the one heart I can't weigh. . . is my own.

I finally drift off to sleep, but in spite of everyone's best efforts, a tiny part of me still wonders: what did Mother see that no one else does? And is it possible that she's right?

22

ERRA

The sun hasn't yet crested the horizon, but I'm awake, dressed, and ready to go when John's door opens and he emerges.

"Whoa," John says. "You're up early."

"Sunrise," I say. "Isn't that what Marcus said?"

"I figured you'd sleep in while I took care of this."

"*Took care of this?*" I ask. "I'm not going to hide inside your house while you go out and fight for my freedom."

"What if you thought of it as me fighting to prevent the tyrannical rule of Elbion?" John says. "Then maybe it wouldn't annoy you."

"Why do you care whether I go with you?" I glance down at my dingy and dirty clothes. They didn't look great before I drowned in them, and then walked home barefoot. The addition of a pair of John's way too large boots with three pairs of socks underneath isn't helping, but I wasn't impressive to look at before. "If it's about how I look, you could go find—"

John invades my personal space. "It's nothing to do with your appearance, which there's nothing at all wrong with." His eyes drop to my lips.

"Why not, then?" I can't quite prevent my half smile, watching him want me.

"It won't be easy to watch," John says, "and frankly, I'm not sure how everyone else will react to your presence. Marcus wasn't very forthcoming with the reasons Elbion demanded your return. Before all that went down, my plan was to bring you back once you could douse and spark and a few other basics and show everyone that you're safe to have around. Since that wasn't possible, I'm a little nervous. I'd rather eliminate the problem, come get you, and proceed with my plan from there."

"I'm not a sculpture that will shatter at the smallest blow," I say. "You might need me."

"You can't let anything go, can you?" John's eyes flash. "Fine. I don't want you to come because I'm worried that you'll do something rash that will put you at risk."

"What do you mean, rash?" My palms heat and I'm desperate to set something ablaze.

"It means that if you do something today like you did yesterday, even a fraction of the nonsense you pulled with the lake or knocking Marcus to the ground, or incinerating his spear, the Fire Called will see you as a threat, and they'll likely do everything they can to eliminate you."

I swallow. "But you might need me."

His hand slides around my neck and tugs me roughly upward, his fingers caressing and guiding the back of my head. John's lips press against mine firmly, possessively. His hand slides forward, cupping my face, and he releases my mouth to say, "I'd rather endanger myself than you."

"I don't remember anything about my life right up until the moment I was dumped outside this stupid volcano-encircled camp." I kiss him quickly, biting his lip as I pull away. "I couldn't sleep last night for thoughts of you." I step backward and fist my hands at my sides. "But if you try to hide me away, if you can't allow me to *be there* for the pivotal moments in my own life. . . I'll never forgive that."

John's nostrils flare, but he nods. "So be it." He spins around on his booted heel and opens the door.

I follow him out.

I'm not sure what I was expecting, but definitely not this.

We have to unceremoniously shove our way through hundreds of people crowding the main road to the large columned building at the base of the largest volcano.

"Where are we going?" I should have asked before.

"Any challenges between Circle Warriors take place at the top of the steps to the Tribunal Building."

I was nearly stabbed with a spear at the base of those same steps two days ago. "Can't wait to get back there."

John rolls his eyes.

"But what are all these people here for?" I ask. "They won't possibly be able to see from here."

John points at where people are setting up ladders along the edges of the streets.

"There's no way all these people can climb up those."

He laughs. "No, but a few can, and they'll announce the action for the others."

By the time we finally shove and bump and elbow our way to the front of the road, the sun is well and truly up. "Are you late?" I ask.

He laughs. "They didn't clear a path for me, so they can wait." The press of bodies disappears on the very first step, where we're approaching from the far left corner of the tribunal building.

"They don't follow us up?"

John shakes his head. "It's not safe."

"I'm not staying down there."

"What a shock." His smirk reassures me. He can't be that nervous if he's smirking with such confidence.

"They'll let me up here?"

"That's why I'm here in the first place," he says. "They wanted you *right* here. So let's hope I win, because if I die, it was literally for nothing at all, since you've given them just what they asked for by following me."

By the time we reach the top, we can see them. Two dozen warriors stand in a loose semicircle in front of the enormous white-columned building. Their robes range widely in color—purple, yellow, orange, green, grey, red, black, blue, and in the very center, one man in a white robe. Elbion's hair is just as bright as I remember, but his face isn't quite as lined. He looks younger than I recalled, and for the first time, I panic.

What if John dies? The very thought shreds my heart.

And then selfishly, I wonder what will happen to me if he does.

There are too many things I don't understand, too many variables I can't control. Who's the All Called? Why am I here? Who am I really?

Somehow, with John nearby, I don't worry about everything nearly as much. The prospect of losing him focuses me on all the things about my life that I don't know and can't control.

I'm vulnerable.

I don't just hope he does well—I'm desperate for it. "John."

His blue-robed shoulders freeze, and he glances over his shoulder.

"Please, please disembowel that awful old man."

He barks a laugh. "I'll do my very best."

He points to a spot on the edge of the steps. "You'll have to stop here. Maybe even go down a step or two so you're not putting yourself in the line of the fight, and don't do anything rash. Please?"

I nod.

And then I watch, heart in my throat, as he walks across the white marble tile to the center of the semicircle.

Elbion doesn't waste any time asserting his dominance. "John Rochester, so named by the light itself, do you challenge my position as General, voted on unanimously by all other Warriors of the Circle?"

"Perhaps this can still be amicably resolved," John says. "I didn't realize that you had grown so old you were senile. See, 'unanimous' is a word that means 'every single one.' And if I wasn't present to vote, you didn't have all twenty-four warriors. So you're not General after all."

Elbion scowls.

"Which means I don't challenge your position as General." John spits at Elbion's feet. "I'm saying that you never received that position in the first place. Thankfully you're too old to keep what you've stolen. So yes, I'm here to fight you." John turns around and faces the gathered audience. "But I'm actually here for them. To allow something like this to go unchallenged—an unabashed power grab—would do all of you a huge disservice. Our job is to serve all the Fire Called, not our own interests."

"Moving speech," Elbion says. "As the challenged, I select the weapon."

John shrugs. "True."

"I select blades," he says.

John unsheathes a long, narrow sword. "Understood."

Elbion pulls two long, curved black daggers from his belt. "Then we begin."

A bizarre clapping and chanting starts with the warriors behind them, but it's quickly picked up by the audience. John and Elbion circle, moving away from the warriors and toward the edge of the audience.

John strikes out first, slicing the edge of Elbion's robe with the end of his sword. The next few swipes come from John as well, and one of them slices more than white robes.

In fact, the left shoulder of Elbion's robe is now stained red.

Thank goodness—John was right. No reason to worry.

Except, something shifts, and Elbion's attacks speed up instead of slowing down. And then, Elbion throws one of his knives—and it arcs in a parabolic path, nearly hitting John, and flying back around to his hand.

My jaw actually drops open.

The audience begins to chant. I can't figure out quite what they're saying. Something about. . . white. . . stripe?

John dances back from another lunge and wipes his brow with his sleeve, and Elbion tosses his blade again. At the very last second, John blocks it with his sword, but it only bumps it out slightly, and the dumb thing continues on its path around. Elbion dances sideways and catches it again.

That's when I realize what they're saying.

White strike.

I gather that Elbion, in spite of John's seemingly promising start, is the favored winner. I move up one step, only a single stair level below the fighting. I wish I could wade in and help, but I hold my position, my stomach tied in knots.

When John lunges for Elbion this time, his sword erupts in flames. I stumble backward, barely catching myself without rolling backward down the steps. He manages to singe the bottom right edge of Elbion's robe, but no more. I suppose when your opponent can douse a fire, a flaming sword is more for show than anything else.

A few people do chant 'wall of fire,' which I think might be in support of John, but not many.

Elbion works John toward the far edge of the front platform, throwing his dagger on the right and blocking with his left. It takes all my resolve not to climb up the last stair and. . . do. . . I don't know what. This is agonizing, just watching.

And then John stumbles—dropping to his knees on the first step—the same step I'm standing on, but on the opposite side of the platform.

Elbion sees his opening and throws his right dagger, and then his left. John avoids the first, but the second grazes his ribs. Luckily, that contact sends it clattering down the side of the steps. Instead of looking upset, John stands up with a triumphant smile. He hops up to the top level again and I wonder whether his fall wasn't a ruse to lure Elbion out.

His attack with one dagger and block with the other method has been moving John around the fighting area handily, leaving John on the defensive at all times. But now Elbion has but one blade. Will he strike or defend?

He can no longer do both.

Thank goodness. I breathe a sigh of relief. John lunges forward, sensing his victory is imminent. He lands a glancing blow on Elbion's left thigh. He moves more slowly on his left leg, a vulnerability John has clearly also noticed. John presses his advantage on the left again.

Elbion tosses his dagger the other direction to block.

Barely.

John whirls toward him again, but he's slower this time and Elbion blocks. I worry that he's slowing because of his injury—the one he took to part Elbion from his first dagger. But again, John recovers and advances, wiping sweat from his brow and preparing to attack again. But his arm looks almost sluggish, like the sword has grown heavier.

I squint, wondering what I'm missing. The injury John took from the dagger is small. The dark patch against John's deep blue robes is no more than the size of an apple. His blood loss shouldn't be. . .

Unless.

John shifts his grip so he's using two hands to hold his sword. He swings again, but this time it's way too wide.

Elbion's smiling, and it makes my blood run cold.

"What did you do?" I shout.

John's head wrenches toward me and he shakes it.

"I'm sorry," Elbion says. "Are you addressing me?" He's not even looking at John anymore.

But I am.

John sinks to his knees, dropping his sword. His hands press desperately against the wound in his side.

"You poisoned him," I say.

Elbion snorts. "That's a baseless accusation. Some wounds just take a longer time to make their impact upon a person." He steps toward John, and kicks him, sending him flying backward. "Looks like it was a slow leak."

"Liar." I step up to the top level, and look out at the audience. "Is that who you want leading you? Someone who lies, who cheats, and who poisons his companions?"

"This *woman* doesn't know what she's saying," Elbion says. "Women aren't supposed to be Fire Called, and it has addled her brain. She's delirious."

"I am Fire Called." I raise my voice. "I'm the first Fire Called woman, apparently. But that doesn't mean I'm delirious, or hysterical, or anything else. In fact, he's trying to use your own prejudice to redirect your attention away from the truth." I point. "Someone grab that dagger, but be careful to hold it by the handle."

No one listens to me—no one takes a single step toward the dagger, where it glistens in the sun on the third to last step.

"Seize her," Elbion says. "I've defeated her misguided champion."

Three of the warriors behind him start toward me. "Are you all too afraid to question them?" I glance at John, who's now slumped facedown on the hard stone floor, his dark hair shining in the early morning light.

A memory slips through my mind, of another man with dark hair, lying on the ground, blood pooling around him. My heart shattering in a million pieces. A monster laughing in the background—NO!

"If none of you will grab that dagger, I'll do it myself. I'm not afraid of him. I'm not afraid of any of them."

I sprint across the platform, pausing a little as I near John. Maybe he needs my help more immediately. Perhaps I'm focused on the wrong thing.

"Now," Elbion says.

The three men who were headed for me are only a few feet away, and they all raise their hands toward me. Flames billow my direction, and I stop, right next to John. Even if I would have been willing to ignore their threat to me, John can't protect himself right now. I brace my legs and think about what he taught me.

And I douse their flames. All of them at once, cutting them off from the source, removing one of their basic requirements.

Elbion blinks. "Again. Now."

The men shake their hands, as if it was uncomfortable to have their fires extinguished. I hope it was. They fling them toward me again, shooting fire at me another time. This time it's even easier. I shake my head, and they simply blink out.

The audience behind me begins to murmur.

"Grab the dagger," I shout. "Please."

A tall girl in a red jacket jumps up the steps, reaching for it.

But a flaming arrow hits her in the chest and she collapses. I'm so shocked, I don't know what to do right away. By the time I realize I need to douse her, her front is already badly burned. Which might not matter—her hands fly up to the arrow, clutching it at the base, and she slumps sideways, her face falling against the stone steps.

A woman in the audience cries out, but no one does a single thing to help her.

What kind of leader fires on his own people?

"Someone else," I say. "Someone grab it! We have to stop him."

Elbion barks a new command. "Grab my dagger before she can steal it."

Two more warriors break off the end of the semicircle's edge and trot down the stairs. They've almost reached it—murderers of youth, supporters of lies—when something inside me snaps. John may not have wanted anyone to see what I can do, but I can't think of any other way. I focus on that dagger, about to be recovered by the enemy, and I *pull*. It flies up in the air and sails toward me.

At the last minute, I have an idea. Instead of bringing it to myself, I step aside and send it hurtling toward its owner. "What's going on?" I glance around as though I have no idea what's happening and pray that in the bright daylight no one will notice my eyes.

The dagger lodges itself in the center of Elbion's chest with a dull thunk. His entire body shudders.

One of his warriors takes it upon himself to flame me again.

As if that might work. I douse it without another thought and crouch down next to John. When I shift him sideways, his face is pale, his lips nearly blue, but he's breathing. Barely. "I need a healer."

Of course no one listens.

Several of the warriors have rushed to Elbion's side. They're whispering.

I ignore them.

"I need a healer!" I stand up and look at the audience. "Where can I find one?"

"The General is dead!" Marcus stands up in his red robes and turns toward the crowd. "Elbion has been killed."

I stand up too, sick of not knowing basic things, like how to find a healer. Elbion may have gotten a full dose of his own wretched poison, but John only had a bit, and he's still alive. "He died from the poison on his own blade. It was justice."

"Justice?" Marcus sneers. "You killed him. I don't know how, but you sent that dagger back at him."

"I did?" I laugh. "If I could do that, why would I have been begging everyone for help? Why wouldn't I have done that from the beginning?"

Marcus frowns.

"I'm Fire Called and a woman," I say. "I can't explain how or why, but I'm only here to try and support a loyal servant of the Circle of Warriors. John Rochester needs medical help urgently."

"Wrong," Marcus says. "He lost and he will die for it. The only people who could possibly heal him are the Earth Called and they'd never help one of our warriors. Now that he's gone, we can start in on what's most urgent—contacting the All Called and taking you as a tribute."

A tribute? "I refuse."

"You can't refuse," Marcus says. "I understand why you might think you can, but you haven't heard the whole story yet. The All Called has been searching the tribes in search of a woman who's special. A woman who has been Called by one of the elements. He says he's looking for his *bride.*"

"No," I say.

"No?" Marcus glances over his shoulder and shakes his head. "Take her."

I glance down at John's pale face again, his dark hair stark against the white marble. Another dark head, dying, flashes before my eyes, and I'm flooded with rage. Whether it's for John or the other man, I don't know. Maybe it's on behalf of both.

Or maybe it's the idea that I've been dropped here with no idea who I am, and now they're planning on trussing me and delivering me to some random man to be his wife. I think about the feeling of John's lips against mine. About the way I felt safe with him by my side.

It was an illusion, of course—no one can keep me safe.

Except me.

A dozen men advance toward me, all with weapons raised. Bows with flaming arrows. Flame stroked swords. Daggers. Even an axe.

"What exactly do you plan to do if I resist?" I ask. "Slice me up and deliver me as a burnt offering?"

A few of the men frown, but they don't stop moving.

"I'm not a pig to be roasted and presented with an apple in my mouth." I raise my voice. "I'm not a sacrificial lamb. I'm a person. I won't allow you to force me into anything. Ever."

They're only a few feet away now, and I can feel the heat from the flames licking their weapons.

The fury grows inside of me, and then when the closest one drops his weapon and reaches to grab me, all my rage explodes. It's not the calm, controlled fire of the first day I woke up inside this ring of volcanoes. It's not contained. It's not small.

It's like an ocean beside that stream. That first outburst was a single star to the vast expanse of the night sky. The flames billow out from my entire body, incinerating everything they touch.

Except John.

And when they reach the base of the stairs, they disappear.

But when the fury inside of me is done burning, every single Warrior of the Circle is gone, dark black blotches on the pristine marble floors the only evidence they were ever here.

At least this time, my clothing remains intact.

I'm done pretending to be someone or something I'm not. I focus on John's body, far too heavy for me to carry on my own, and I push it upward, light spilling out of my eyes too brightly to be ignored, and I walk down a step, tugging him along behind me. I brace myself for hostility and threats and danger.

I'm utterly unprepared for what happens.

Every single person standing in the street bows down and presses their face to the ground.

"Hello? What's going on?"

They bow, but they don't answer my questions. It's almost like they've checked out of their bodies or something.

"I still need a healer. I know you may not like me, but if I'm going to save the last Circle Warrior you have, I'll need some directions, at least." And I wouldn't turn down boots that fit and maybe a horse.

Finally a few people near the front sit up.

"Are you all going to ignore me forever?" It's better than flaming me, or throwing spears, but it's not ideal.

A tall woman near the front stands up and turns to face everyone else. "Behold, the General!"

The cheering that erupts after her proclamation is *insane*.

I blink a few times to make sure I'm not missing anything, like projectiles or fireballs headed my way. Since none of that appears to be happening, I wave them down until they settle a bit. "Can anyone find me a horse and tell me how to get to the camp for the Earth Called?"

The same woman who announced me as the General smiles at me. "Of course, General. Whatever you need."

23

ERRA

I have no idea what anyone thinks about the fact that I literally melted their former leaders into dark spots on the front porch of their esteemed warrior building. No one yells at me. No one casts aspersions or freaks out. They don't even seem to be too concerned that I'm dragging John around behind me, through the air, like a kite on a string. Or that light spills out of my eyes, bathing them in a bizarre golden light.

Maybe they're all so scared or awed that they don't dare bring it up.

I would worry more about it if I weren't so worried that John would die before I got him help. As it is, when they bring me a black horse with a large white blaze and flaring nostrils, I swing up into the saddle, pausing for a moment when a memory floats through my mind of riding a horse at full tilt without a saddle. Like every other time, when I try to focus on the memory, when I try to gain any kind of context, it shoots away like a terrified minnow, leaving me grasping at nothing but mud and vegetation.

So for now, I don't argue with them over using a saddle.

"Which way do I go?"

"I'll guide you." A man with a beaky nose swings up into the saddle of another horse—a paint. "We all will."

Another mounted rider, this one a woman, swings around the corner on a bay, and four more follow quickly on her heels. I haven't seen any horses in Volcano City up until this point, and I'd love to know where they were keeping them—and how the streets are so pristine if they do keep horses here—but there's no time to ask right now.

Plus, I don't have the energy to argue. "Thanks," I say, hoping the beak-nosed man won't waste time.

Their actions may not make sense to me, and they may even creep me out a little with their bizarre deference and cryptic responses, but none of them even glance twice at John, floating along behind us.

Our horses are another matter.

Mine flips out royally the second I ask him to move and John's body follows. He rears back, and I almost fall off. I decide to shove John a bit further back, though it makes me nervous to have him so far away from me, but that seems to worry my energetic mount a bit less.

"Perhaps we should ride in the front and far behind," Beak Nose suggests. "Your mode of transportation for Warrior Rochester appears to upset the horses."

My mode of transportation? I snort. "Yes. Let's do that."

Once we clear the part of the path that passes through the volcanoes, the dozen people who have joined me ride like the wind, slowing up intermittently only to let me know we ought to allow our horses a break. Their speed improves my opinion of them quite a bit. And luckily, we're only in the saddle an hour or so before we reach a thick, tall field of wheat, encircled by a tall, thick hedge with shiny, dark green leaves. "This is new," I say.

"We're on the edge of the Earth Settlement," Beak Nose says.

We drop back to a walk to allow our horses a chance to take a real breather, and I decide I should try to discover a little bit about them, my newly converted supporters. "What's your name?"

"Theodore," the beak man says. "And this is my wife, Olivia." He points to the short woman riding next to him. She's much, much better looking than he is—which tells me he's either rich, funny, or very, very powerful.

"And why is everyone calling me 'General' now?"

Theodore and Olivia glance at each other. "You destroyed the entire Circle alone."

That was as clear as mud. I'm a terrible murderer, and that qualifies me to. . . oh. My fake-mother told me they select their Generals based on their skill on the battlefield. They were my opponents and I eradicated them. Therefore, I'm capable of leading them to great glory, or so they're probably thinking. It's a little. . . brutal, but it's also simple. The people didn't help me, because they don't respond to appeals for aid or empathy.

The Fire Called don't help the weak—they eliminate them.

Which makes John an even rarer find among them. He stepped in to spare me, and then risked his own reputation and life to protect me, something apparently not a single one of them would do. I'm even more desperately resolved to reach the Earth Called leaders and beg them to do whatever it takes to reverse the effects of the poison. I turn around in my saddle and focus on his floating body. His chest still rises and falls, even if only barely.

"Are we close?" Please say yes.

"It's just around the corner," Olivia points to a tremendously large grove of trees. "Where the treeline ends a mile or two ahead."

"And what are the Earth Called like?" I ask.

"Strange," Theodore says. "They love all things that

grow and they spend all their time with plants and trees and vines."

"Which makes sense," I say. "Since they're Earth Called."

"It's more than that," Olivia says. "The women are the same. Men, children, they're all obsessed with anything that grows. They have whole fields of tulips. They cut them and stare at them, once they've died, and then they replant and do it again. They give cut, dead flowers to one another as a sign of affection, killing the things they swear to love."

"And they commune with trees and plants," Theodore says. "They'll walk around among fields and plants, for no reason other than to breathe and to think."

They're right. That is bizarre.

"It's said that the strongest among them can grow a seed all the way to a mature tree in a week or less." Theodore shrugs. "They're all delighted with their skill, as though it's the best gift given, but trees grow without them just fine with a little more time, so I'm not sure why it's such a blessing."

"They can make barren earth bear fruit," Olivia says. "And make an existing tree produce twice or three times the normal yield. They have large, perfect peaches all year round. I do envy them that."

"Sure, it's a great gift if you love to eat." Theodore laughs. "Which is why they're all so large."

"But if you harm one of their plants, they'll never forgive you," Olivia says. "Don't forget that."

The sides on my beast of a horse are no longer heaving. I check out the other horses—sweaty, but not miserable. "Think we could manage a trot, at least?"

No one really encourages me, but they don't argue either, so off we go. Just as Olivia said, a mile up the road, the treeline simply gives way to a profusion of blooming bushes, and I can finally see a tremendously tall wall made of massive wooden beams.

I'd be lying if I didn't admit it's a little intimidating, but I can't allow anything to stop me. John risked everything for me. My poor, exhausted mount balks at riding up to the closed gate, so I dismount and hand my reins to Theodore. "You wait here."

He doesn't argue. My followers may be supportive, but they're certainly not fierce or committed to my cause. I try not to worry about their lack of passion and fervor. It takes me a lot longer to hike to the gate on foot than I initially believed it would, and the wall looks even more horrifyingly tall when I'm standing at the base of it. I focus on what matters, and reach up to the one smooth spot in the entire wall—the door. I bang on it as hard as I can, and then I wait. Impatiently. Bouncing from one foot to the next.

When no one comes, I decide to try a little harder. I pick up a large stone from the hedgerow and wham it against the door hard enough to leave a ding.

Still nothing.

Fine.

I step back a few paces, and I use my mind to fling that same stone against the door as hard as I can. It hits so hard that it lodges in the wood. I pick up another and hurl it too, and then another.

By the time the twelfth stone has struck their massive door, the hinges creak.

I quickly set John's body down on the ground next to me.

The door opens slowly, and the head that pokes around the edge is shaggy—thick red hair, thick red beard, bright blue eyes. "What do you want?"

"I'm here to request your healing services. My friend needs them desperately."

"Who are you?" His eyes scan me, and then look past me to John's prone form.

"I'm Laura of the Fire Called." Seems best to keep things simple.

His gaze travels back farther still, to our heaving mounts and the dozen sweaty-faced riders waiting on me. "Must be someone important."

"This is John Rochester, one of our Warriors of the Circle."

The red-headed man frowns. "We won't heal him." He shoves the door closed and it clicks, some kind of latch catching behind him.

"I beg you to reconsider! He'll die if you don't help him."

A deep chuckle behind the door raises my hackles. "That's always the case when people come here, miss. He's a Fire Called warrior. All they do is destroy things—trust me. He won't be missed, and you'll be better off without him. With time, you'll see that."

A familiar fury rises inside of me. What kind of person has the ability to heal someone and opts out? How could he deny my request, when neither John nor I have done anything to harm them? "If you refuse to heal him, immediately, there will be a price."

"What's that?" His voice is low and gravelly.

"Heal him, and I'll help you with anything you might need. I am a pretty useful person."

"No."

"Then I'll burn down your beautiful forest."

The hinges groan again, and his head pops back out. "You're a woman. You mean your companions will burn it?"

I shake my head. "I'm Fire Called. I'll do it myself."

He laughs and closes the door again.

John's color is worse than ever, and his breathing is

almost nonexistent. I'm out of time. "I'm warning you for the last time. Save my friend, or pay the consequence."

His laughter grows quieter as he walks away from the gate.

I don't even feel guilty when I turn toward the thick forest we just passed and extend my hands. After my practice with John, sparking a flame is easy, and I'm plenty mad enough to feed it. Once it reaches the trees, I don't even have to do much else.

Heat, fuel, and oxygen. If you take one of those things away, the fire collapses.

John taught me that only yesterday—and here I am, forced to use his lesson so that uncaring people—greedy, selfish people—will do what they should have done all along.

The right thing.

Mere moments after I begin incinerating their stupid forest, the gate behind me springs open again, two dozen or so men—how I can sense them, I'm not entirely sure, jogging toward me, shouting and yelling.

A spear zings toward me. I can't see it, but like the men, I can also *feel* it. So I reach out with my bizarre ability and freeze it in place, and then I slowly turn it around so the sharp end is directed at the hurlers. And then I drop my hands and turn toward them too.

The fire blazes along now without my encouragement—after all, it has heat, fuel, and oxygen. All the things it needs to thrive.

"I'm your only hope at saving that forest," I say. "The forest I never would have touched if you had agreed to help my friend. Feel like healing him now? Or should I let it burn, like you meant to let him die?" I shove the spear back at them, intentionally planting it in the rich, dark soil at the feet of the red-headed gatekeeper.

"We'll heal him," he says, "if you stop the fire." But he doesn't look very happy about it.

That's okay. I don't need him to be happy. I just need John's life to be spared.

I douse the flames. "Just remember how easily I can restart it."

When I look upon the barren, ash-covered desolation I created, I probably ought to feel guilt, but I don't. Maybe the Fire Called aren't wrong. Maybe I *am* a fitting General for a nation of destroyers. Because I smile at what I've done—it worked. They're taking us inside.

And if it saves John's life, I won't ever regret it.

❧ 24 ❧

EARTH

I made it for years and years trusting no one but my brother Jesse. Now I'm surrounded by people who call themselves my 'friends,' but none of them have much common ground.

Thomas, Roland, Rosalinde, and Martin took care of me in Terra when I had no one else, but we lived on the fringes of Terran society, scraping by on the unwanted leftovers citizens cast aside. Meanwhile, my biological father Duncan made plans to improve the world while ladling soup from a silver tureen brought to him by a dozen servants. He's leading an even bigger group here on Earth.

John grew up among the Followers of Amun, and his father is one of the leaders of that rival organization, the one that has been at odds with Duncan's people for thousands of years. And I can't forget Kahn—the man to whom I'm bizarrely drawn—who has major issues with John, his second cousin, for inadvertently causing the death of his parents.

Then there's Oliver, a guy who has now managed to betray both his friend John and his new ally Kahn in his haste to reveal my whereabouts and spare his sister.

I have no idea why I thought they'd be able to work together to formulate a plan to take me safely to the George Observatory. I should've known that when I finally woke up, exhausted and terrified, they'd be fighting.

"Obviously we aren't going to hike in to the meeting from a shop full of loony bee fanatics," Duncan says.

"I'm telling you, we can simply drive there and walk right up to it," John says. "The last thing Amun wants to do is upset Alora or betray her, whatever you may think."

"It's better to be safe than dead," Roland says. "And no one will expect us to come from SweetNes."

"Please tell me that's not the name," Duncan says. "Sweetness?"

Roland scowls. "Actually, it's a play on words. It's Sweet as one word, and then N-E-S—"

"Is he kidding?" John shakes his head. "When Duncan and I agree that something is a terrible idea, you know it must be really bad."

"That's about enough of this," I say. "What a wonderful example of why straight-up democracies don't work."

"How about we each present our plan," Martin says, "and then you can decide which one we use?"

"We can save ourselves some time," Duncan says, "and—"

"Ah, ah," I say. "I'll hear Roland and Martin out, thank you very much. You may have grown too accustomed to being the arbiter of everything."

My dad snaps his mouth shut without any further argument. It's a strange thought, that if I'd been raised differently, I'd likely follow all his commands, like Jesse does—"Wait, where's Jesse?"

John glances around, and so does Kahn, as if he was *just* right here and they've lost him.

"No one knows?" I try to remain calm. It's not like he's a wandering toddler. Maybe he's in the bathroom, or he went for a walk. "Okay. Well, I'd like to make sure he's here and safe, and then we'll select an approach."

Luckily we don't have to look for him for very long.

He's still asleep.

My heart skips a beat when I see him there, eyes closed, his lashes too dark against the skin of his face, his mouth peaceful. . . because he's sleeping way too late. I walk toward him slowly, refusing to acknowledge that we might need Martin or Oliver or the other Healers. "J?"

He doesn't react.

"J?" I try speaking louder. Then I touch his arm.

He jolts awake. "What's wrong?" His eyes focus on me, and then shift past me. "Why's everyone crowded into the doorway?"

I flip my head around and glare at them. They go—but part of me wants to call Martin back again. I don't because Jesse would hate it, but I wish I could. "How ya feeling?"

He rubs his eyes and yawns. "Fine. How are you?"

I shrug. "You know, just planning a trip to meet an undead member of the evil Ra's posse. Same old, same old."

"Pretty regular life we lead, right?" Jesse swings out of bed. "I ought to take a shower."

"Right," I say, "but if you need anything, or if you don't feel right, you'll let me know."

"Knock it off," he says. "I'm fine, I keep telling you."

At least this time, when I leave his room, no one's dead in the hallway. I listen patiently to all the men argue back and forth about what our best option is. Rosalinde catches my attention and rolls her eyes a time or two. I wish we had more time—I wish I wasn't worried about, well, about everything and I could spend some time talking to her, getting to know the Earth/Terra combination of the Terran girl I grew up with. I miss having time to talk. To read. To bake. I even miss washing dishes. It was familiar, it gave me a sense of accomplishment, and I never wondered whether it might corrupt me.

I never had to contemplate that I might be some kind of monster myself.

It seems like total madness, the possibility that *I* might be some Egyptian goddess reborn, but even now, an hour after waking, when I think about Hathor leaving, it revives the dull ache in my chest. And between possibly killing Beth here in Houston, and murdering two dozen people on Erra by melting them into goo—I'm beginning to really fit the profile of the monster Hathor named her daughter, Sekhmet.

Right now, however, I need to ruminate over my origins less and focus more on our immediate plan. If I don't corner this old Egyptian dude, I may never figure out how to fix Jesse.

They've all gone silent, and they're staring at me. I must have missed something. "What?" I ask.

"If we don't leave soon," Kahn says reasonably, "we won't be on time."

"I think he can wait a few minutes," Duncan says with a half smile. "If this isn't just an Amun trap, this guy's already been waiting for thousands of years."

"I'm ready to choose a plan." Mostly because Roland has annoyed me the least, and his plan makes sense. Plus, I like honey. "We head for the bee place and walk a mile or whatever over to the meeting point. Then Duncan and Kahn can do a preliminary sweep, making sure they don't sense anything unacceptable, and Jesse and John will stay with me to Lift or burn anything hostile that the others don't manage to eliminate."

"Who's going?" Duncan asks.

"I can sense your people outside," I say. "All three of them, and even if I only take Roland, John, Kahn, me, and

Jesse, there's not room for more than three. Unless you're staying here, they can't all come."

To be honest, the thought of seeing Henry again makes me a nervous wreck.

"He'll stay here," Duncan's voice is soft, barely loud enough for me to hear. But I know exactly who he means.

"To do what?" I ask.

"He wants to apologize to you later," Duncan says. "And if your people need protection while we're gone, he'll provide it."

"Who are we talking about?" Jesse asks.

"Henry's out there," Kahn says. "Can't you sense him?"

My brother's eyes widen. "Yes. I can now, but who are the others?" Jesse asks. "Or maybe I should say *what* are they?"

"What are they?" Duncan frowns. "That's not a polite—"

Jesse rolls his eyes. "What abilities do they possess? Because the man with the broad shoulders keeps sniffing the air like he's uncomfortable as a human, and the other guy keeps rocking up on his toes, like standing in one place is a foreign concept to him."

I try to suppress a giggle.

"The sniffing guy is a Render who can shift into a lynx," Duncan says.

"A lynx? Aren't they like big house cats?" Jesse asks. "Were the lion and the tiger both taking naps? Is that why we got the B team?"

"We aren't going to be in danger," John insists. "So all of this is irrelevant."

"Preparation is never a mistake." Duncan scowls. "But the type of beast doesn't matter much in comparison to the—"

Instead of intervening yet again, I jog toward the door

and push my way outside, unwilling to keep standing here like an idiot while Henry stands outside.

The sniffy guy and the tall, bouncy man freeze. And then they bow, practically folding themselves in half. "Your Most Divine."

Really? "Stand up," I say. "Please tell me who you are, and don't ever call me divine or anything like that ever again. Got it?"

Henry gulps loudly. "If I can't bow, what should I do?"

"We're running a little late," I say. "I'll be taking formal apologies and oaths of fealty later."

Henry nods. Like he has no idea I'm kidding.

I hug him, in spite of myself. The last few days have been a whirlwind in a teakettle and anything familiar right now, even imperfect things, are welcome. He smells just as he always has. "Thanks."

"For what?" His whisper against my ear makes me shiver.

"Duncan says you defied your parents. . . for me."

"Oh, that." He releases me. "Too little too late, but I'm hoping to make it up to you. I promise I'll never do anything like that again."

I actually believe him.

"My name is Linus, Most—" The sniffy man coughs. "I'm an alpha Render who can shift into the form of a lynx."

Duncan wasn't kidding. I was kind of hoping he was. "And you?" I ask the third Isis person.

The eerily thin man smiles. "I'm Horace, and I'm Wind Called."

I try not to let my bafflement show on my face. How in the world will someone who's Wind Called help us? I may never understand—

The thin man twists his finger and zips upward, presumably riding a wind gust straight up into the sky above. Then he plunges almost straight back down, slowing at the last second. "I'm helpful when someone wants to move fast without being stopped."

So he's my escape hatch, should I need one.

"We came in a Tahoe that seats eight, just as Duncan requested," Linus says.

A few moments later, Henry has gone inside to wait with Oliver, Thomas, Rosalinde, and Martin. I'm actually relieved we're leaving someone with some power here to protect them if it comes to that.

We all climb into the Tahoe. Jesse grabs the seat in the very back and I slide in next to him. John and Kahn elbow each other in their attempt to snag the seat next to me. Jesse rolls his eyes. "You should put a stop to that nonsense."

"I've tried," I say. "Believe me."

In the end, John scores the seat, but I'm so annoyed I don't even care.

Luckily this park isn't very far away. I can survive most anything for half an hour. Duncan doesn't waste any time getting on the road. For all his bluster about how old the Egyptian guy is and how he can wait, it appears he's not anxious to be late either. Or perhaps, like me, he can't wait to get it over with. The men start breaking down details of our plan and reviewing them, but my part amounts to walking from the bee shop to the conservatory and not dying or being kidnapped by Amun's Followers.

"I had another dream last night," Jesse says quietly.

"You did?" I'm delighted to talk about something other than the upcoming ordeal. I'm not sure whether I'll get the answers I want, or even if I do, whether I can believe them.

"It might be a memory, but I kind of hope it's not."

"Tell me," I say.

"You were really young. We'd been with Aunt Trina for two years, maybe? When school ended, we didn't ride the bus, because there was some meeting you had to go to with someone right after school. Aunt Trina was there, and she was angry. She and I had to sit outside for a really long time. She didn't say much, but she did ask me whether you'd always made up stupid stories."

I remember this.

"I told her you didn't make up any stories at all. She got mad at me too, and she told me there was no way that you lived on another world where you were on the run, hiding with a circus, and where you had magical powers."

I swallow, wishing he'd had a different memory.

"Then you came out, and Aunt Trina went into the room. You had been crying—your eyes were puffy and your cheeks were wet. You asked me whether Aunt Trina was mad, and. . ."

I look down at my hands, folded on my lap.

"I yelled at you. I told you that you needed to stop telling people, because they would never understand. I told you that I was the only person you could talk to, and that you were ruining everything."

I can't talk about this.

"Alora, did that really happen?"

I shrug.

"Did it? Did I tell you that you couldn't share your stories with anyone? That you were ruining our lives?"

I finally turn to face him. "You were right." My voice is so small. "At first I only told people once we knew them really well, and they always thought I was making it up, but since they knew me, they laughed it off, usually. But then as I got older, I got sick of people I cared about laughing at me for it. I started telling people the very second I met them. I figured I'd let them know who I was and what I thought, and then I'd find out right away whether they would make fun of me, before their opinion mattered."

"And they all laughed."

"Of course they did. You know how ridiculous I sounded. You were giving me sensible advice, and you were teaching me a life lesson. If I'd learned it better, we might not be where we are."

"But I was telling you to live a lie, and I essentially made sure you had no friends."

"I didn't need friends," I say. "I had you."

Jesse punches the seat in front of him.

"What's wrong?" Kahn turns around.

"I'm learning that I was a better person on Terra," Jesse says. "The more I remember, the less impressed I am with my own decisions."

That twists my heart. "You were barely older than I was, but you were big enough to see the ramifications of what I was doing—what I was sharing. People couldn't accept it, and that shrink started insisting on seeing me every week. If you hadn't told me to lie, they probably would have put me in restraints or something. I learned a lesson I needed to learn: to trust no one but you."

"But that's the wrong lesson," Jesse says. "Tell her."

"You do need people to support you," John says.

"All people need social connection," Kahn says, "but you need more than most, given what's being asked of you."

I don't bother arguing. What's the point?

"We're here," Roland points.

It's about the cutest little shop I've ever seen. Bees and honeycombs are painted on everything. When I reach my senses outward, I sense four people inside the storefront—after all, it is midday on a Thursday—and even though the world has turned upside down, the sign in the front window reads, "Open for Buzzness."

"I really hope we don't cause them any trouble," I say as we all climb out in the small parking lot.

"How about while Roland scouts around," Duncan says, "I go inside and buy a trunkful of honey products."

"I do love honey," I say. "See if they have any of the flavored kind."

"Honey sticks are the best," Jesse says.

"I'll grab some of those too," Duncan says.

"Hey, I meant to ask," John says. "I'm assuming by my ongoing life here on Earth that all is well, but what happened on Erra last night?"

It's been so crazy on Earth that no one has even asked for an update on Erra. I'm glad no one's asking me more about Egypt—I don't want to share anything about how, if I really am Sekhmet, my mother left us because I'm such an evil creature. "You totally lost the challenge," I say.

Kahn's head whips around at light speed. "What?"

"Elbion cheated, using poisoned daggers, but I ended up incinerating Elbion and all your friends into dark puddles of goo before the poison killed you."

John blinks. "Poisoned? I lost?"

"I commandeered some horses after that and we rode as fast as we could to the Earth Called settlement."

"They hate Fire Called warriors," John says. "We haven't been very good neighbors."

"I figured that out," I say. "But they're treating you anyway."

"Why?" John asks.

"I might have burned down half their stupid forest and told them I'd level everything around their entire settlement, including their walls, if they didn't heal you."

Kahn's face is entirely blank. John's either shocked or horrified, or maybe both.

"It worked," I say. "I mean, you're still alive."

"They'll turn on you the second they can," John says. "I'd warn you to be careful there, but it's not like you'd remember it."

"It's extremely frustrating," I agree. "I mean, I have all this power no one understands, myself included."

"It's going to be an obnoxious hike." Roland crashes through some bushes at the edge of the big field behind SweetNes. "But it's only a mile, and I don't see any signs that make me nervous."

"I don't sense anyone in that direction at all," I say. "At least not in the somewhat near vicinity."

"I'm telling you, it's not a trap," John says. "Dad's a zealot, but in this instance I think that will work in our favor."

The door jingles and Duncan walks out carrying two enormous brown bags. "They said it's fine if we park here for as long as we want. Unsurprisingly, business hasn't been too brisk the past few days."

"Let's get that in the car," Jesse says. "Unless you think we should take some kind of tribute gift to this old guy."

Duncan rolls his eyes. "What I've been worried about is, even if Devlin's not planning anything nefarious, what happens when this old Egyptian guy, if he exists, confirms that Alora's Isis reborn?"

If any part of my dreams are true, Dad's about to be in for a rude awakening. That doesn't mean that the old Egyptian guy won't try to kill me—somehow Ra did end up in that prison. "Only one way to know," I say. And my fear about Jesse's ongoing health outweighs my concern for myself if the old guy hates me.

Duncan loads the honey in the trunk and returns with headsets for all of us. "These will allow us to coordinate our efforts, even as we spread out." When he hands me mine, he pauses. "Are you sure you wouldn't rather delay?" He glances at the heavy forest in front of us. "I could easily bring many, many more people in on this to make sure you're safe."

I'm usually all for putting things off—I've never been someone who tackles things head on, not since we were kids and my honesty wrecked everything over and over.

But when have more weapons improved a situation?

Jesse's leaning against a tree, as if standing is wearing him down. In the end, that makes up my mind for me. He's the priority.

"I want answers." I start walking. "We go now."

"Please let this not be a trap," Duncan mutters, but thanks to the earpiece, I hear him loud and clear.

"You missed the latest update," Jesse says, "but Alora apparently melted the entire Circle of Warriors on Erra last night. I think if Devlin double crosses us, he may discover that he's bitten off more than he can chew."

"Time for us to spread out," Duncan says. "Kahn, you and Linus will sweep west, and Horace and I will take the east side."

They move away quickly, disappearing almost the second we pass all the apiaries, bees buzzing in and out noisily. Thanks to the earpieces, my anxiety isn't as high as it would be since we're still all synced.

"Alora, have you ever hit a wall?" Kahn asks in a tiny voice in my ear. "Like, Lifted so much that you can't Lift anything else?"

"What?" I ask. "On Terra? You know I did. I passed out after the Ascension."

His voice isn't even staticky. Duncan may not be a perfect father, but at least his tech is good. "Your powers, like ours, were dampened on Terra. I meant here, on Earth."

I think about it. "I haven't used my powers here much."

"You were juggling a tractor, a rototiller, and some other huge chunk of metal yesterday while dancing around on top of a rope you Bound in the air," John says. "You're telling me that didn't wear you out at all?"

I shake my head and realize only John, Roland, and Jesse can see me. "Not even close."

"What happened when you were tapped out on Terra?"

Jesse asks. "That time you passed out?"

"The same thing happened on Erra too," I say. "The world around me starts to shake, to vibrate."

"Wait," Kahn says. "You said you pulled energy from Terra to get everyone back to Earth."

"I think the vibrations were because I finally realized I could literally consume the entire construct—for the first time, I saw it as it really was, insubstantial, a resource to be utilized."

"Isis was one of the world's most powerful Assimilators," Duncan says. "She could consume the energy of things she touched and convert that energy into powerful magic. The very same way you are talking about now, as far as I know."

I doubt it was like me siphoning the construct of Terra —I bet Isis saw golden light in the center of living things, just like I do in my dreams. But I'm not about to start arguing with him and open that can of squirmy worms.

"They say that's how she created Terra to begin with— she accepted donations of magic from her followers, especially women, and used those to form the walls and everything else."

'Accepted donations of magic' sounds. . . bizarre. It sounds too good to be true, honestly. I'll have to reconsider that one later. No matter how you look at it, I don't think the pull of energy from the scorpions or the bad man could be termed a 'donation.' Then again, I know so little, Duncan could very well be right.

"We are really, really late." John glances at his watch.

I wipe my forehead. "If you're thinking I'm about to start running, you're out of luck. It's stupidly hot for the first week of October, and this is my maximum speed. I may not be dressed for the part of reborn energy stealing Egyptian goddess, but I'm not going to show up there like a dirty bum either."

"Actually, the hike is less than a mile," Roland says. "So we're already almost there." He points.

Sure enough, I can make out, just ahead, a white dome between the trees. "That's it? That big, ugly canister-looking place?"

Roland laughs. "It's an observatory. What did you expect?"

"I don't think you're understanding how our life went," I say. "I've never been to an observatory in my life. What do you do there, exactly? Observe things?"

Kahn snorts. "It's for watching the stars, which is presumably why they suggested it now, in the middle of the day. No bystanders during the daytime."

"I'm in place on the east side, just in front of the road," Duncan says. "I see a black suburban, and I sense eight people near the front of the largest dome, as they promised."

I sense them too, gathered closely around one individual.

"We're in place on the west side," Kahn says. "Ready for Alora to move when she's up to it."

"Seeing as we're already late, no sense delaying," I say.

In spite of my senses confirming that everything is as it should be, I'm nervous. Jesse takes my hand, and I squeeze it tightly. "It'll be alright," he says. "Whatever happens up there, never forget that you're a blessing to me."

The world tilts a bit and I nearly fall over.

Never forget that you're a blessing. Promise me that.

That's what Shu said to Sekhmet in Egypt.

Now Jesse's telling me the same thing here, and I'm wondering: am I cracking up? What are my dreams, really? Some kind of prophetic warning? Memories? Or are they a delusion—some combination of things I've heard or studied, my fears, and my deepest, most hidden dreams?

I think it's finally time to find out.

25

EARTH

I release Jesse's hand on the way up the hill to the main conservatory building. It's not that I don't need the support. It's not even that I worry I'll look like a little kid, holding my brother's hand.

No, it's that, Houston is at least eighty degrees and muggy, even now, and our hands are starting to sweat.

Ah, the glamorous life I lead.

A million possible scenarios run through my head as I travel the last hundred yards. But when I crest the rise, the first person I see is Devlin Rochester, beaming at me as though we're long-lost friends.

"Alora," he says. "I'm so pleased you came."

I know John has been working hard to forgive him, now that he knows Devlin didn't abandon his mother. I know that he had reasons, and that he thought he was doing the right thing in Waking Jesse, and later, in Waking me.

I don't care about any of that.

He chased orphans. His people caused my parents to abandon us in the first place with their attacks. And then, instead of looking for another way, a better way, he forged ahead, unconcerned about the collateral damage. In my book, he'll never be more than a necessary evil.

I can't bear to greet him. I don't slam him up against the side of the dome and make him beg for forgiveness. That's about as polite as I can manage to be. "I'm not here to see you, Devlin. I do hope I haven't wasted my time."

"Not at all," he says. "I assure you."

And he steps aside—revealing a tall, broad-shouldered man with dark, deep brown skin, and startlingly bright aqua eyes.

"I'd like to introduce you to—"

"The Serpent of Ra," I say. "The Protector of the Sun, Mehen the Loyal."

Mehen's mouth drops open and his arms fly wide when he sees me, and he sprints down the hill toward me.

That's when my friends completely lose it.

John's hands flatten, palms up, and he releases two enormous fireballs, flying through the air directly at Mehen. Duncan and Horace, as well as Kahn and Linus, sprint toward him from the treeline.

Luckily, Mehen knows how to deal with fire—he was best friends with Am-Heh, and however strong John is, I'm pretty sure he can't compare to the Devourer of Millions. He wraps himself in Bound air until the fireballs have flown past, and then sprints toward me with redoubled effort.

John screams with fury beside me, and Jesse runs ahead of me, his hands held outward. He Lifts Mehen off his feet, his eyes flaring bright blue.

"Shu?"

I'm close enough to him now to hear the surprise in his tone.

John spins his fingers again in a way I've come to recognize.

"Stop!" I shout.

Everyone, including Jesse, Mehen, Duncan, and even John, freezes.

Mehen looks from Jesse to me and back again. "Most Divine, I cannot express how delighted I am to find you alive and well." He's speaking ancient Egyptian, but of course *I* understand every word.

Jesse, on the other hand, has no idea what he's saying.

"What does that mean?" Kahn asks. "Is he cursing you? Threatening you? He looks. . . giddy."

I laugh, when what I really want to do is cry. "He's speaking Egyptian, and he *is* delighted."

"Why?" Duncan asks. "He's *happy* to see you? I don't understand. Amun Ra and his followers always hated Isis."

Mehen's head snaps to the side at that word. "Isis?" he asks. "Is she here? What is he saying?"

I consider sending Devlin and Mehen packing—not even explaining to my friends or to my brother what this means. But as much as I'd like to run, I'm not sure this is something I can really escape.

"Set him down," I say.

Jesse complies, but keeps Mehen's arms Bound at his side.

"Free him, too." I don't have the heart to explain that there's no chance Mehen couldn't have broken free—he was only standing there politely because of who Jesse *is*. And who *I* am.

I almost wish I were delusional.

"Mehen," I say in ancient Egyptian. "I hope you're in good health?"

"Quite," he says. "Your father has kept us all quite safe and healthy while we slept, and now that I'm free, I will work at your side to prepare the world for his return."

Oh, geez. Here's where it gets complicated.

"So the thing is," I say in ancient Egyptian, "I'm not quite sure whether I want to prepare for his return."

"Most Divine, Sekhmet, daughter of Ra, God of the Sun, how could you *not* be moving mountains to bring him back? He would do exactly that for you."

I actually believe that. "The thing is, I don't remember a lot yet. Only bits and pieces." I clear my throat. "But you're absolutely positive that I am. . . Sekhmet?"

Mehen blinks as if he can't quite make sense of what I'm asking. "Of course, Most Divine. I would never fail to recognize any child of the Most Divine Father of All."

"What's he saying?" Devlin asks. "We have the hardest time communicating with him."

"Lucky that Alora speaks every language," Jesse says.

"But what is he saying?" Duncan scowls at Devlin, as if he stole his question.

I lick my lips, wondering if there's any way to avoid it. . . but I can't think of one, so I finally spit it out. "He's asking me about my plans," I say.

"That's promising," Devlin says. "I think we'd all like to know the same thing."

"He wants me to help him free Ra," I say. "Of course."

"That's never going to happen," Duncan says.

"Why wouldn't she help dismantle the prison?" Devlin says. "It's crumbling, it's unsafe, and its time is past."

"He expects me to help him because of who I am." I gulp and look around the circle of people gathered. I know everyone here, except for the six men who accompanied Devlin. Men, all of them, since only a few women have any powers at all, and they're all new to their telekinetic abilities. Maybe it's time the past is left in the past as we move ahead. Maybe Devlin's right and we can create a fairer world for everyone.

"He attacked you." John glares at him, his hands still held up threateningly.

Mehen may not understand English, but he comprehends the nonverbal messages just fine. "I would never harm you, Most Divine. You must tell them that. I've sworn my eternal loyalty and devotion to you. Your father made me vow to protect you before even himself."

Of course he did.

"What did he say?" Kahn asks.

"He's telling me that he would never hurt me, and that he's pledged his eternal devotion to me." I can't keep the frustration out of my voice, and my lips twist. All my friends, all my supporters. . . they're all about to hate me.

Except Devlin. He'll probably kiss my feet.

"Why would he do that?" John frowns. "Do you believe him?"

"I do," I say. "Because he's confirmed something that's been worrying me now for several days."

"What?" Jesse asks, but I think he already knows.

"I'm not Isis reborn, like Duncan has been hoping," I say. "I'm Sekhmet, the daughter of Ra."

"Oh, I think you're a little more than that." Devlin beams. "No need to be modest now. Sekhmet is the *Heir* of Ra, stronger and more powerful than he is in every way."

Oh, bloody hell.

26

EARTH

"They are not a peaceful people, your followers, are they?" Mehen asks.

My followers? I struggle not to laugh.

They barely listen to me on a good day.

He's right that they're all arguing—Duncan and Devlin are shouting about Isis and Terra and what should be done. Kahn and John are arguing about Mehen and whether he's evil or here to help. Jesse's alternating between interjecting points in support of both. And Roland and Duncan's two men are chatting awkwardly near the circle of men Devlin brought.

I wonder when that powder keg will explode and exactly how much damage it will do.

"I think they mean well. The problem is that there are too many things we don't understand."

"Like what?" Mehen asks. "Perhaps I can offer assistance."

I wish. "Well, for starters, can Terra even be rebuilt?"

His eyes widen and his mouth dangles open.

"I had to siphon the power away. . . " I haven't told many people about what precipitated my destruction of

Terra. "I understand that it had already begun to break down, but when Jesse died on Earth, I couldn't bear it. He was Wasting on Terra."

Mehen looks confused.

"How much do you understand about how Terra operates?"

"It's a prison," he says. "It ties all humans into a cell that they won't try to break away from, because they don't even know it's there. And on Earth, where their real bodies live, they have no idea what powers they possess or who they really are."

So he has a decent understanding. "But you weren't there?"

"Not exactly," he says. "Ra knew Isis was planning something. She had made many attempts. He had his own contingencies in place. The first wave of people trapped were the telekinetics, which includes me, and so I don't know exactly what happened afterward. I simply know that Ra had made provisions for his lieutenants to be. . . preserved outside of any containment efforts so that we could one day come forth again. Something, some small detail, went wrong and we were trapped anyway—our powers held in the walls somehow, and our bodies preserved outside them. As the last one to be trapped himself, Ra was able to prepare a way to keep us alive in this state."

Weird.

"So you don't really know anything about what I can and can't do?"

"Why would you care to rebuild Terra, after you've gone to such great lengths to destroy it?"

"I didn't want to destroy it," I say. "Or at least, I'm not sure whether I had any opinion one way or another, but Jesse was dying."

"Who is this Jesse?" Mehen's mouth tightens, like he's not sure he really wants to know. "Is it your lover?"

"Eww." I shudder. "No. He's my brother."

His shoulders drop. "You have another brother?"

He knows him as Shu. Duh. "It's Shu's name, for this life."

"He was not trapped as I was?" Mehen frowns. "You're saying that, like you, Shu was reborn?"

I nod.

"That's unexpected," he says. "My understanding was that only one person could be reborn, and it was the Warden of the prison. To be honest, we expected to face Isis again as the prison crumbled."

You and everyone else alive, apparently.

"I thought I would be meeting my greatest foe."

"Nope," I say. "Just little old me."

"It's excellent news," Mehen says. "You just need to do what you did to Terra to Erra, and then to Rra, and then to Ā, and then Ra will help guide us in how to ensure this never happens again."

Except I'm not sure I trust Ra. Why would I be the Warden if I do? Why would Isis have given *me* the key? Why does everyone think he's a villain?

After all my recent dreams, I *want* to trust him. I *want* to free him. I wish I knew answers to all the things. It feels like I'm still casting around in the dark. "I'm not sure I can figure out how to disassemble the prison world, at least, not until I know how it was made. That's why I want to know how to rebuild it," I lie.

"The only person I know who could tell you that is trapped inside the prison."

"You mean Amun-Ra?"

Mehen shakes his head. "You should know, he's not a big fan of the use of the word Amun in front of it."

"He's not?" I don't get it. "His followers call themselves the Followers of Amun."

"They probably dropped the Ra over the years, which is unfortunate. Amun was your grandfather," Mehen says. "Ra does not love him well, but as he seized his power from him initially, he simply merged the names to ease that transition."

That sounds ominous, but it's also a rabbit hole. I need to focus. "But you are saying that Ra is the only one who can answer my questions."

Mehen shrugs. "Isis could as well, but if you're holding the key to unlocking Terra, my guess is that she's dead."

He's guessing. Isis is gone. And Mehen's idea is that I should just ask good old Dad, who happens to be trapped in the deepest of all the prisons. Which I should really consider freeing him from. . .

No problem.

I had pinned so many hopes on getting the answers I need today, and it seems that, although I'm not in any great peril from Mehen, I've only dug up more questions.

"You said Shu died?" Mehen's forehead is furrowed. "That cannot be. Who would dare harm a child of Ra?"

It's hard, but I suppress my laughter. Many, many people have tried to harm us, and I doubt that will stop anytime soon. "Well, you see, your precious Followers of Amun—"

"Alora?" John's tone is urgent—he's distressed.

"Yeah?"

He glances at Mehen respectfully, his head bowed a bit. "I'm so sorry to interrupt, but I think there's something wrong with Jesse."

My heart stutters. "What?"

"He sat down, which we didn't think anything of at first, but then I noticed his head was kind of resting against his chest. When we tried to wake him up. . . he's not responding."

I fly to my feet, Mehen leaping up as well. "What's wrong?"

"My brother—Shu—he's not well."

"What's wrong?"

"It's hard to explain." I follow John down the hill to the tree where I left them. Jesse's slumped against the tree, with Roland at his side.

"What is it?" I ask. "Is it the hole?"

Roland shrugs. "He's fading. I don't know how else to explain it. I suspect it may be thanks to the amount of energy he used today—he Lifted Mehen, if you recall, and held him for an extended period of time. I noticed he looked weak afterward, but I thought he'd recover."

I drop to my knees and press my hand to Jesse's head. It's far too cool.

"Why is he unwell?" Mehen asks. "You have a Healer, no?"

"I do," I say. "But he died here on Earth, and the way it works is that after someone dies on Earth, they kind of get hot and sick on Terra. . .and a few days later, they die there too."

"But the real body is here on Earth," Mehen says. "Right?"

I need *answers,* not more questions. "Look, I can try and explain this later, but right now, I need a miracle."

"You need to use your gift to restore his energy," Mehen says. "If he is alive, you can rejuvenate him until you can find the answers."

I turn toward him slowly. "You mean, I can Assimilate energy from one thing and pass it on to him?"

He nods. "Of course."

"But I can't," I say. "Not without being Woken. I've only unbound Terra—Erra's intact, so I can't use my Fire Called powers here on Earth because of that, which means I can't use my Assimilator powers either."

Mehen shakes his head. "That can't be right. You're the key to the entire prison. Are you telling me you've never Assimilated any energy here on Earth?"

"Not in this lifetime," I say. But as I hear the words, I realize that they aren't true. It's how I saved him before. Which means I am responsible for Beth's death. "Or maybe. . ."

"Maybe?" Mehen smiles. "So you admit that it's possible?"

"How can you be so sure?" I ask.

"The Warden of a prison is not bound by its walls." His aqua eyes are calm, assured, supportive.

"I can't just take energy from someone here and give it to Jesse."

"Why not?" Mehen lifts one eyebrow.

"It's wrong," I say. "It's stealing."

"Explain what you need to them. One of them will offer to be of service."

I'm flabbergasted. "You're telling me to ask them if one of them will, what, give up his or her life to save Jesse?"

"Yes," Mehen says. "But let me be the first to offer myself." He bows then. "It would be my life's greatest honor to give my own life force to save a child of Ra."

Is he kidding?

"What's he doing?" Devlin asks.

It's time—for me to come clean or decide to keep hiding.

I don't really have a choice. Even if they hate me. Even if they call me a monster. This is my only hope—for one of them to offer up their power to Jesse. If they don't—

I can't even think about that. I can't lose him. I didn't give Beth a chance, but I won't do that again. Ever. "I'm Sekhmet reborn, daughter of Ra. And one of the things I can do is Assimilate power from. . . well, from other living things, and use that power to do, well, to do most anything."

"You think you can save Jesse with it?" Devlin asks.

I nod. "I do."

"Martin said he felt like he had a leak," Roland says. "Like his soul is losing energy for some reason. It makes sense that refueling might at least buy you more time."

"But how long will it last?" Kahn asks. "If one of us is willing to donate part of our life force to him, is it like funneling gasoline into a tank with a hole in the bottom?"

"Probably," I say. "Only it might be even worse than that. I don't know what I'm doing. If I do this, I'm worried that whoever I pull power from will die."

"I'll do it," Devlin says. "I'm not saying that to be a martyr. I took his life wrongly, and you told me the night that you eradicated Terra that it wasn't a sacrifice. You were right. It wasn't. But this would be—my life for his, or at least to buy you time to heal him and right my wrong. It's something I have a right to give—my own life—and it's just that I do it."

I'm shocked that he's offering, but I can't turn him down. Not with Jesse so faint and pale.

"How do you know you can do this?" John asks. "You couldn't Call fire. Why do you think you can transfer Dad's power to Jesse?"

I was hoping to avoid this, but. . . "I may have done it already," I confess.

Kahn frowns. "What does that mean?"

"It was inadvertent," I say. "I swear it."

"What was?" Duncan asks.

"That morning you heard me cry out?"

"Yesterday?" Roland asks.

I nod. "When I found Jesse, he was much like this, only worse. He was dying. I knew it, and I was. . . desperate. I had dreamt of being Sekhmet, I had seen how she, how I, could transfer power, and in the last moment, when he was about to disappear forever, I felt light near me. I felt energy pulsing close to me, and I took it and gave it to Jesse."

"Beth." Kahn looks as sick as I feel.

"But you're not doing that this time," Devlin says. "You're not taking from someone else. I'm offering myself. You didn't know then what you were doing or whether it would work, but you know this time. Buy some more time, and do it with a clear conscience."

My gaze shifts to John. I can't help it. I need to know what he thinks. His eyes are trained downward, his fists clenched at his sides.

"John," I say.

His eyes shift upward and meet mine. And he smiles. "Do it. It's my dad's one shot at redemption."

My hand trembles as I cup Jesse's cheek. I close my eyes and reopen them, focusing on Devlin. He looks. . . serene. Like he's contemplating eternity. Like he's finally accomplished what he came here to do.

It's easy, like singing along with a pop song on the radio, like drinking a strawberry lemonade in the heat of summer, like that first breath after a long swim.

The golden light inside of him pulses, bidding me to take it. There are a few dark strands, but not nearly as many as I expected. Far fewer, even, than I saw on Terra. It would be so easy to reach for that energy as my father took from that dark man, and to use it for something I desperately want.

And like that night when I nearly left Devlin on Terra to die, I ache to do it.

But I can't.

Because it's not right for me to steal from another soul. It's not. I stole from Beth, but it was an accident, and I still can barely stand the memory.

I might do it anyway, except that everyone knows now.

Duncan, whom Jesse loves. Kahn, whom he admires. John, with whom he's becoming friends.

If I kill Devlin, *Jesse* will know I did it, and he'll never forgive me. Which means that the next time this happens, and I'm terribly worried it will happen again and again and again, I'll have to take someone else. And someone else. And someone else. And even if I'm okay with it, even if I don't miss the bright, golden parts of my soul, Jesse will grow to hate me for it.

And that would be the only thing worse than losing him to death.

So I focus instead on the trees around me, dozens and dozens of large trees, and I feel the sparks of light inside each of them, and I siphon that instead. It's not what Jesse needs. It's not as bright or as strong as what pulses inside of Devlin, and on top of that, I don't know what I'm doing. But I pull it, watching the leaves on the trees blacken and drop, and I spin the energy into a long, thin golden thread and funnel it into my brother. I hope it will hold him here until I can figure out a better way.

Jesse's color brightens a bit, but he doesn't wake up.

"You can do it," Devlin says. "I'm ready."

I shake my head. "I can't. Jesse would never understand."

"I killed him. He'll accept it," Devlin insists.

"Look at the trees." Mehen points and the others finally notice.

"You chose them instead," John says. A single tear rolls down his cheek, and I know that I made the right decision. It wasn't only Jesse who would look at me differently.

"He's not awake," Duncan says. "It's going to take a lot more trees than you just killed, I think, to save him."

"I also don't know what I'm doing," I say. "I think the transfer of energy from a tree to a human is different—I have no idea how to make it work. Human to human is simpler."

"You used energy from Terra to save him before," John says. "Could you do that again?"

The last time, I was panicked on Terra—as desperate to save Jesse from the Wasting as I was on Earth to bring him back. It was a tiny tap against a stack of dominoes, ready to go down. When I'm on Erra, I don't even recall that Jesse exists.

"I can certainly try," I say.

"Anything she does there will accelerate the destruction of the prison," Duncan says. "It's out of the question."

"Even when your son's life hangs in the balance?" I ask.

Duncan's eyes are haunted, but he doesn't waver. "Jesse wouldn't want to unleash millions of monsters on the world just to save himself."

But they're already here. It's just a matter of them having access to their abilities on Earth. "It's not that simple," I say. "For all we know, Erra's coming down no matter what I do."

"That's true," John says.

"Terra was already unraveling," Devlin says.

"And I'm not at all sure what benefit it serves at this point," Roland says. "I mean, the Lifters and the Healers are already here, which means there's a dramatic imbalance in terms of power structure."

"Which he's fine with," John says, "because it favors him."

"It's not like that," Duncan says. "Other than the Assimilators, we're the smallest group. Even so, it has caused untold havoc. Nations are in upheaval. Amun and Isis are openly fighting. People don't know what to do, and no one feels safe. That will only worsen if Erra unravels as well."

"Or perhaps the equilibrium will again be found," Devlin says. "Perhaps the need for Terra is past us."

"Oh please," Kahn says. "We need to restrain villains even more today than ever before."

"These people need a leader," Mehen says softly. "I can't understand them, but they argue amongst themselves like children. All groups, like a family, require someone to make the final decision."

"I'm going to try," I say loudly. "I'm going to send myself a message and see whether I can figure out how to wake myself up in Erra so that I know what's at stake. Then, once I can see what it's like there, once I can *see* Erra itself, I can decide what to do."

"The Followers of Amun stand with you." Devlin crosses both arms across his chest, his hands in fists, and bows.

Mehen smiles. "He says that he speaks for the followers of Ra, and that we support your decision?"

I nod.

"He's correct. I will support any decision that you make, as would your father."

"Even if I never release him?" I lift my eyebrows.

"Even then," Mehen says.

As someone who was raised in America—a place with freebie offers and fine print everywhere—I don't entirely trust his vow, but it's nice to hear. Certainly my earthly father doesn't support any decision I make. But Mehen's right. Once I've made up my mind, the arguing stops.

Now if only I felt better about my plan.

✵ 27 ✵

ERRA

"Laura?"

The voice is familiar, tugging me into awareness. I rub my eyes and sit up in a hard, beautifully carved wooden chair, shifting from side to side. My backside is sore, but my lower back throbs.

"Where are we?" he whispers.

A large room, clearly, with a big window that looks out over a beautiful orchard. Butterflies flutter from one delicate pink blossom to another on a tree outside, and bees buzz too. At the base of the trees, flowers bloom riotously. I've never seen so many living things in bloom at the same time in my life.

Or, what I can recall of my life.

John's lying back against a thick stack of pillows on a bed in a small cottage among the Earth Called settlement nearest the wall to their border.

"I had to bring you here," I say. "Elbion. . . "

"I lost." John closes his eyes and sinks deeper against the pillows. Vines cover the posts of the bed, blooming with bright yellow flowers. Tendrils creep toward him, a few even twining in his hair. When I glance at the foot of the bed, the same vines have begun to spread toward his legs. "Why didn't he kill me?"

I'm not sure what I should tell him, so I stick to the truth. "He poisoned you—it wasn't fair."

John's eyes narrow. "Why didn't I die?"

I cringe a bit. "I might have been furious and. . . stepped in to defend you."

He coughs and tries to sit up.

I press him back against the pillows. "Do you know how hard I worked to get you here? Don't ruin it all now."

"The other warriors didn't side with Elbion?" The hope in his eyes pulls at my heartstrings.

"So, that's the bad part," I say. "They all did."

He opens his mouth and closes it again. Baffled, clearly.

"I know they were your friends, and that you had known them all a long time, but they were all trying to kill you. And frankly, they were trying to take me, too."

"What happened?" His words are soft, and I can't tell what emotion is the strongest.

"I—I didn't want to do anything. I asked for help, I begged the people gathered around. I told them you had been poisoned."

"Fire Called don't mind cheating," John says. "They only support the strongest warrior, the most cunning, no matter how he wins."

"I guess that's why they're following me now," I say. "Because I killed every last useless Circle Warrior. You were the only one with any integrity, and unlike the other Fire Called, I value honesty and compassion and loyalty. All the things you've shown me."

John swallows and meets my eyes, his such a bright gold that they practically glow.

A bird whistles from near the rafters.

John looks upward, past my face. "Is that a *tree* inside

the room?" The enormous branches spread across the top of his bed like a canopy.

"The Earth Called tending to you is named Vernon," I say. "He's the nicest one I've met yet, which isn't saying much. He refused to answer most of my questions, but he did say that the vines and plants, including that tree, are what's healing you—apparently the Earth Called magic grounds them to all things that live and grow, including humans. It's just stronger when they're able to utilize nature to remove contaminants."

John closes his eyes. "So the vines and the tree are. . . healing me?"

I shrug. "They're supposed to be. How do you feel?"

His eyes cut toward me. "I'm upset."

I don't know him that well yet, but I understand this, at least. He's embarrassed he lost, and he's angry with me for killing his friends. I knew he would be, but I've tried not to think about it. I've hoped that he'd forgive me since I saved him. I sit on the edge of his bed, brushing the creeping vines out of the way. "If he had been honorable, I think you'd have defeated him."

John still won't meet my eyes.

"Get better," I whisper. "Be mad at me if you need to— never talk to me again, that's alright—but heal."

His head turns slowly. "You think I'm mad at you?" His voice is rough and low.

"For killing your friends?" I bite my lip.

"My friends?" The bark of his laugh is angry. "They were close-minded, hot-headed, and selfish. None of them were a loss." His hand balls into a fist and then he relaxes it slowly and reaches for me, stopping short of taking mine.

I close the distance between us and interlace our fingers. "Why are you upset, then?"

"I couldn't keep you safe. I failed you, and I'm only here because you saved me."

What an idiot. "You taught me how to douse. You stood up for me when no one else did, not a single warrior in that settlement. I may not know you well yet, but you matter to me, John. I couldn't let you die. You're the only one I care about in this whole world."

"Even though I couldn't keep you safe?"

My laugh isn't forced or full of anger or self-loathing. It rises up like a bird winging into the branches overhead. "The Fire Called may not believe this, but I value intentions. I value actions and bravery. I couldn't be more impressed with what you did for me if you'd saved me flat out. I actually think it's more impressive that you went there, knowing that Elbion cheats, knowing he might defeat you."

His eyes drop to my mouth, and I know just what he wants. It's what I need as well. I release his hand and lean toward him. He struggles to sit up all the way, and somewhere in the middle, our mouths meet at last.

He tastes like honeysuckle and sunshine. And home.

I'm not sure how long my lips move against his mouth, but it's not long enough. I shift so he can lie back again—the last thing we need is to slow his healing—and a vine snakes its way up my right arm, wrapping around my wrist. "These plants are miraculous," I say, "and freaking creepy." I reach over with my left hand to tug it off and brush my forearm. With even that slight pressure, pain shoots up my arm like a brand. "Ouch."

"What's wrong?" The dreamy look in John's eyes evaporates as he searches me for injury. "Your arm?"

I sit back and pull up my sleeve. Letters are carved into my arm. I squint to try and focus on them. At first they make no sense. "Is this a language you know?"

John tilts his head to get a better look, and then shakes it. "Sorry."

"When could this have happened?" I think back. The

Earth Called finally relented and agreed to heal him. I told my people to wait outside, and then I helped get John situated. I fell asleep on the chair, and woke up here.

"I'm the wrong person to ask. The last thing I remember is stupid Elbion, advancing on me with his boomerang daggers."

His *I'm a loser* face is back. I hate it. But when I glance back at my arm, the words seem to have shifted, or at least, something has changed, because I can read them now.

Catch the memory. Jesse needs you.

It's the same name I recalled the day after I showed up here—it's my brother, I'm sure of that. But will the name mean anything to John? "Do you know any Jesses?" I ask.

"Who?" John shrugs. "Are you asking about a boy or a girl? Did they say they were a friend of mine? What did they do?"

I scratch the edge around the slices on my arms—they itch. They're half healed, as though the magic of this place is working on me and John both. Maybe that's why the vine was so eager to climb my arm. It's a little creepy. I'm grateful, but it's weird too. "Well, I'll add another bizarre thing to the list of things that make no sense about my life."

"You said we're here, in the southernmost settlement of the Earth Called?" John winces. "Because according to the warriors you killed, this is where the All Called is coming, if we believe he exists. It's where they wanted to send you."

I hadn't even thought about that—I was too focused on saving John's life. "What's he supposed to do again?"

"Either unite or destroy the tribes, depending on whom you believe."

"Let me guess. The Fire Called were pulling for destroy."

John laughs, but it turns into a cough and he clutches his side.

"Does it still hurt?" I stand up, nervous that I've made things worse by squishing him.

He shakes his head. "It's fine. When I coughed it was a little tender, but don't worry about me. We need to get out of here as quickly as possible, or you'll be stuck right in the middle of what I was fighting to spare you from." He shifts in his bed, swinging his feet out toward the floor.

I grab his arm. "John, no. Not yet. Vernon said it will take at least two days for you to be fully healed."

"I'll settle for half-healed. It's a huge improvement from dead." His jaw's set, his eyes flinty. "I insist we get out of here right now."

I can't argue with him without seeing that defeated look in his eyes again. It's a conundrum. Do I do what's right for his male ego, or for his injured body?

The door swings open, and I sigh. Maybe Vernon will be able to convince him to wait. I turn around with a sigh. "Will you tell him—"

My request dies on my tongue—the men entering are not here to help. Two of them are holding Theodore and Olivia, each with a knife pressed to their throats.

"We'd like to encourage you to behave," a small man with deep brown eyes and long dark hair pulled back into a ponytail says. He's standing in front of the others, clearly their leader. His deep brown tunic is ringed with golden embroidery in geometric shapes around the neck and sleeves. "As you probably know, Earth Called are not an angry people. We find all kinds of violence abhorrent, but it seems to be the only language you speak."

"I'm not threatening anyone." I try to catch Olivia and Theodore's gaze, but they're staring at one another.

From the corner of my eye, I notice John's hands, a tiny twist, but I know what he's doing.

"No," I say sharply.

One of the Earth Called men clearly saw the same thing—
he hurls a dagger at John's head. I barely stop it in time, and it
hovers in the air a few inches from John's shocked face. His
pupils dilate and then focus on the blade, and his breathing
accelerates. He's not strong enough for this, not yet.

"What do you want us to do?" I slowly turn the dagger
back around, my eyes spilling light that brightens the shady
room, even in broad daylight. "I'm not usually prone to
violence either, but you saw what happened when you
refused my very reasonable request earlier."

The man holding Theodore presses his dagger harder
against his throat, a line of red appearing. A drop of blood
trickles down his neck.

My lip curls in reaction. "I have been polite each step of
the way, until you forced me to behave otherwise."

The leader says, "We did as you asked. Now that he's no
longer dying, we want you to leave."

"We were about to vacate anyway," John says. "This
uncharacteristic show of violence was unnecessary." His
smile may be forced, but it's also triumphant. Unfortunately, the second his bare feet reach the tile floor, he
slumps, leaning against the bed for support.

He's clearly not ready to do anything on his own.
"What's the rush?" I ask. "No one mentioned the urgency
to me last night. In fact, Vernon was somewhat insistent
that this would be a two-day process."

"If you must know, there are armies gathering outside
our walls, and we believe you're the cause. We don't have
two days to spare."

Armies? From where? What do they want?

It must be because of this stupid All Called.

The Circle of Warriors thought he was coming this way,
and they seemed to think he would want me, the only
female-called of anything. I suppress a shudder.

"Will John survive without further healing?" I ask. "Or will our departure undo the work you've already done?"

"Can our trees be saved?" The leader's nostrils flare.

I stand up. "I think you're asking yourself the wrong question." I yank the daggers away from Theodore and Olivia's throats and shove them up against the throats of the men who were previously holding them. They scramble away from the warriors and toward the wall behind me. "What I did to those trees?" I press the daggers harder. "I was just getting started." My lip curls. I'm sick of being threatened. Heartily tired of being afraid.

John touches my arm. "It's okay, Laura," he says. "We can go."

I shake my head. "They'll heal you first, as they promised." I force the dagger that was dangling in mid-air against their leader's chest, just over his heart. "If you expedite his healing, I'll leave the second it's complete." I force a smile. "Perhaps that's a suitable compromise."

The leader gulps, but he waves his hand, clearly signaling the rest of the men not to move. "Do as she asks," he says. "With this many of us, we should be able to speed it up and get them gone."

I'm nervous to allow him nearer to John, but if I don't, I can't verify what he's saying. I lower the daggers, floating them through the air to hang by my side. Olivia and Theodore inch away from me—slowly, as unobtrusively as they can manage, but it's clear that they're uneasy about my ability as well. The leader is nearly to John's side when he pauses. "If we heal him, you'll go?"

I nod tightly. "Harm him and you'll wish very much that you hadn't."

A dagger glints at the man's side, and I realize he hasn't used his—which means he still has it. I focus on the eight remaining blades in the room—and I tug them all up and toward me. I ignore the shouts, grunts, and whimpers. If they're going to speed John's healing, they don't need them. I hang them all ominously just out of reach, near the top of the window. "You'll get them back when you're done."

"You're a terrifying woman," Theodore says softly, as the men work, vines and blooms and tendrils sprouting on all sides of the bed.

"I'm sorry if I scared you—"

Olivia beams at me. "You mistake him, General. It is a pleasure to serve someone so fierce."

Uh. "Thanks."

I'm not sure how long we stand guard, but not more than an hour. My legs grow weary, and my shoulders ache. The injury on my arm throbs and itches at the same time. I slide my sleeve up slowly, finally able to ponder the possible meanings of the words.

Catch the memory. That almost sounds like something I might say to myself—vague memories keep slipping away when I reach for them. The dark-haired man in a pool of blood. Riding a horse without a saddle. A gorgeous blond man smiling at me, while I float water droplets around us both. But whenever I try to focus on any of them, they evaporate.

Jesse needs you. What does my brother need from me? Where is he? Does he have something to do with my arrival here or my powers? I want to catch the memory of Jesse— of who and where he is and how he needs me, but I can't! And possibly more worrisome, I can't think of a single way the words could have been carved into my arm. . . unless I did it myself.

The leader finally drops his hands—I can barely see John for all the leaves and blossoms—and exhales deeply. "Finished."

"He's healed?" I look past him to where John's asleep. "He's not awake."

"In the next few moments, he'll wake up." He practically spits the words out—not that I blame him. I've basically forced this, again.

"I'm sorry," I say. "This isn't how I wanted to do things."

"You always have a choice." His eyes flash.

I actually respect his anger. I'd be ticked in his place, I'm sure. "As promised, we'll leave the second he wakes."

"I have an additional request," he says.

I lift my eyebrows.

"If you're being honest about your claims, that you never wanted to threaten us—"

"I am." I fold my arms over my chest, and as a show of good faith, I return the daggers to the men, tucking them neatly into their belt loops and sheaths.

His eyes widen. "Yes, well, then we ask that you will turn your army around and march home immediately. Wars, even wars in which we aren't involved, take a heavy toll."

I blink. I must have misunderstood him. "*My* army?"

His brow furrows.

"I only came with a few other people." I gesture at Olivia and Theodore. "These two and perhaps another six."

Olivia clears her throat.

Oh, no. What now?

"We might have sent the others for reinforcements," she admits, "when you burned their forest. We thought it might help keep you safe inside, if they knew you weren't alone."

I can't really be angry—they were protecting their leader, which as I understand it, isn't common among the Fire Called. Maybe their desire to fight and attack and burn overcame their reticence to do anything loyal or selfless. Even so, it feels like they were trying to help. "I didn't realize they were even here. Of course we'll turn around immediately."

John sneezes and a butterfly wings away from his head.

This is a bizarre place, the Earth Called settlement. "Laura?"

I step past the leader and crouch near John. His cheeks are full of color, his eyes bright. He shoves stems and plants and branches out of the way and sits up. He stretches his arms out, groaning a little as he does, and then he yawns so wide it nearly cracks his jaw. "How long have I been asleep?"

I shrug. "An hour?"

He nods. "I feel much better. Completely well, in fact."

Something in my heart eases at that pronouncement— as if I didn't quite trust the men to do the right thing, even with daggers literally hanging over their heads and a figurative fire pressed to their feet. "Thank you," I say.

The Earth Called are already filing out.

"Here." Theodore hands John his boots, which were in the corner of the room. "Apparently we're in a hurry to get out of here."

"Don't have to tell me twice." John slides his boots over his feet and laces them up.

Earth Called soldiers line the road when we leave. They don't salute or smile, but they don't attack us either. The enormous exterior wall looms up ahead, making it simple to figure out which direction to go. I was so exhausted last night that I didn't pay much attention to where we entered. I didn't realize we were quite so close to the front all this time. With all the flowers and trees and butterflies, it felt like we were way out in the country.

"Thank you," I say as we reach the front gate.

The Earth Called soldiers don't even acknowledge I've spoken. Their disgust for us couldn't be more plain, but I don't entirely blame them. If there was something I could do to take back the devastation I wreaked on their beautiful forest, I would do it. Sadly, that's not among my bizarre powers.

"I won't miss their hospitality," John mutters.

"You haven't been the recipient of it," one soldier says, not meeting our eyes.

He's not wrong. Instead of waiting for them to open the massive gate, I focus on the edge of it and wrench it open myself. "Until next time, gentlemen." The light shining from my eyes makes their horror even more apparent, which only fuels my sick sense of perverse glee as we walk through the gap into the courtyard outside.

The leader who hated us so much was correct. Three enormous banners wave in the wind—one with a dark red flame to my left, near the blackened forest. Soldiers stand twenty men wide, shoulder to shoulder, but I can't tell how many rows there are. At least several dozen.

Directly ahead of me, there's a man seated on top of a tall white horse, holding a tall flag of light blue that whips furiously in the wind. It moves so quickly, in fact, that I can't make out any embellishment or emblem. Soldiers stand behind the flagbearer, but only ten wide. "Is that Ice?"

John's words are clipped. "Wind."

He points to the right where soldiers stand at least fifty across, their heads all covered in bizarre, shining helmets. Their flag is the only one that doesn't move—and I realize it's coated in something—frozen in place. It's bright white. "Ice." They hold spears that shimmer in the same unworldly way.

My heart hammers against my chest. This can't be good. "Any chance they'll let us turn around and head home?"

John scoffs. "Doubtful."

A man approaches us from the column of fire soldiers leading two horses, one white, one black. It's someone I recognize from my original ride here. I can't recall his name, but he's smiling with what looks an awful lot like anticipation. "Your mount, General." He passes me the black horse—the same horse I rode before, I think, judging from the white blaze on his nose. The soldier offers the reins for the white one to John.

John swings up onto his horse immediately, wheeling him around and preparing to join the Fire Called troops.

"Wait," I say.

"You should mount," he says. The soldier who brought our horses is already jogging back, and my black horse is tugging on the reins, eager to return with him.

"If I ride from here to there," I say. "If I join the army, what kind of signal does that send?"

John frowns. "I'm not sure what you're asking. It sends the signal that you're Fire Called, and that man called you General, just like Theodore and Olivia do. So I'm pretty sure that any way you look at it, you're stuck with us."

"I promised the Earth Called that I'd try to avoid a war." I turn toward the Ice army and a chill runs down my spine. The Wind army is somewhat less intimidating, but I gather they'll be harder to pin down. "And even if it weren't for that promise, I don't want to fight anyone."

John stands straighter. "You say that now, but wait until the battle starts. You'll be glorious—like you were made for this. We could defeat them all, right here. We could finally rule all the elements."

Theodore and Olivia are just as excited. Both of them are practically bouncing on their toes. "Go stand with the army," I say. "All of you."

John's face falls. "I'll stay with you."

"No," I say. "You'll go where your General orders." Because if he's here, he'll push for something I don't want. He may be the most reasonable of the Fire Called, but I can see his ambition, burning just below the surface. I can't be influenced by it.

A muscle in John's jaw twitches.

"Go!"

Olivia and Theodore jump and then run toward the Fire Called. I let go of my horse and slap the butt of John's. I doubt he could have stopped his mount from running back if he tried. Thankfully, although he glares at me, he doesn't appear to be desperate to wheel back in my direction.

I probably should have kept my horse. As I walk toward the center of the cleared area in front of the Earth Called's main entrance, I feel very small. Very alone. Very unsure. At least atop a horse I could have moved away quickly. I'd look more. . . imposing.

But that's not what I need right now. To have any hope of defusing this situation, I must lower the intensity. The Earth Called did as I asked. I have to try to do as they requested.

"Where are your leaders?" I shout, once I'm sure they can hear me. "I'd like to speak to them."

A single man walks away from the Wind Called column, walking as I am, not atop a horse. He doesn't appear to be armed either, though it's difficult to tell from here. A mounted rider follows behind him, clearly carrying a bow and a quiver of arrows.

Another mounted rider leaves from the column of Ice soldiers, a spear strapped diagonally to his back, the side of it very nearly brushing the flank of his grey horse. The mounted soldiers could reach my side quickly, but they keep their horses to a walk, seemingly taking their cues from the walking man.

Hoofbeats behind me warn that someone from Fire Called approaches as well, and not slowly. I'm unsurprised to discover, when I turn around, that John has come to a stop behind me. "I can't let you face this alone, but I promise I'll wait for your orders."

It's as good as I'm going to get.

The only other man without a horse has finally drawn

close enough that I can make out his face—and it's the man from my memory, the stunningly beautiful man above whom I'm holding all the water droplets.

That can't be right.

I rub my eyes and open them again, but it's still the same person, and he's smiling broadly at me. He picks up his pace, jogging now, instead of running.

Behind me, John snarls. When I glance back, he's holding his hands out, clearly ready to attack.

"Wait," I say, holding my hands up. They're all moving too fast.

The man stops, and the Ice and Wind soldiers behind him halt as well.

"Do I know you?"

"He's the All Called," the Wind soldier shouts. "He knows no one and everyone."

That makes no sense. "I'm not asking you. I'm asking him." I stare at him pointedly. "I woke up a few days ago outside Volcano City, and I don't even remember my name. So I'm asking again. Do you know me?"

The man starts walking again, slowly this time, his hands resting at his sides. "I appeared in the same way. I also don't recall my name." He smiles again. "Clearly we're connected in some way."

It pulses then, as though it was always there, but I didn't feel it until he pointed it out, a warm, bright, energy between us. It draws me toward him, and I stumble forward one step, and then another. A dopey smile tugs at my lips, and I can't figure out why. "You don't know your name either?"

Catch the memory.

I stop and grab my head with my hands. What's going on? I don't know this man. No one knows us. Yet here we are, stumbling down a path we didn't choose, being poked

and pushed and prodded by enemies in a war we didn't
start.

"Stop!" I shout.

To my surprise, he listens, as do the other soldiers.

"Why are you here?" I glance around, staring pointedly
at the Ice and Wind soldiers. "What do you want?"

"I seek only to join these warring tribes in peace," the
blond man says. "It's my purpose, my only desire."

"What does that mean?" John asks. "*Join* us?"

"For as long as you've kept records, the different groups
have been at war," he says. "My purpose is to end that war."

"By bringing two armies carrying spears and arrows?"
I ask.

The man steps toward me again, closing the small space
between us. "It's hard to bring a man into hostile territory
without anything to defend himself. I tried, but I failed."
He stops again, this time no more than an arm's breadth
from me. The Wind and Ice soldiers are only a few feet
beyond him, and I can hear John's horse just beyond my
back.

Not that any of them matter. The entire world has
narrowed to only me and him.

"I didn't even call an army," I say. "I came here only to
beg for healing for my. . . friend John." I'm not sure what to
call him, but there's no room in my head for any titles or
labels right now. And I'm strangely reticent to discuss what
John means to me with this man. "But my army has come
to defend me from the threat you pose."

"I may not know my own name," the blond man says,
his full lips drawing my complete attention. "I may not
know where I came from, or the extent of my abilities." He
takes one more step, so close to me now that I could lean
forward and kiss him. "But I am absolutely positive about
one thing."

"What?" When I gulp down a breath, I smell him—the

metallic tang of a flame, the sharp spice of a spruce, the seaspray of the ocean waves, and the delicate floral scent of snowdrops.

"There is no world in which you and I are enemies." His eyes are the lightest ice blue I've ever seen. He's surrounded by a bizarre golden glow, as though he's an. . . an angel. He's only lacking wings.

An image of a winged human with a golden circle around its head flashes through my brain. I want to shake my head, or maybe whack it with the palm of my hand a few times. An angel? How do I know what that is? *Who am I?* I'm tired of all of this.

As much as I'm drawn to this man, my heart reacting, heat pooling deep inside my belly, as much as I want to drag him toward me and press my lips against his, that's not what we need. He may not be my enemy, but I don't trust that he's my friend either.

And if he's as clueless as I am, he can't do much to help.

"We want to return to Volcano City," I say. "Will you grant us permission?"

"Of course," he says.

Ice shouts, "But if they return—"

Wind growls, "That's not a good idea—"

The blond man waves his hand through the air, and both the Ice and the Wind soldiers fall quiet. "They rarely agree with me, but they always listen when I issue an order. If that's really what you wish, you and all the Fire Called may leave. We're not here to start a war." His eyes are open and earnest, and suddenly my anger seems irrational.

"What would you want instead?" I can hardly believe the words, even as I say them. "If you were able to make a request of me?"

He shrugs. "The fighting is destroying this land and its people. It helps no one. Think of what we could accomplish if the Wind, Ice, Fire, and Earth Called all worked together. That's my request, that your people will hear me out. That they'll consider what I propose: an end to the fighting amongst them."

"And who would lead this happy, contented people?" John asks.

The blond man shrugs. "Someone they can all agree upon."

"Like you?" John asks. "Or you and *your new bride?*"

Before the blond man can respond, the gate behind us creaks open and a new rider emerges, moving quickly toward us on top of a dark bay.

"Oh, good," John mutters.

No one speaks while we wait. The rider doesn't check his horse until he's nearly upon us, dirt and grass spraying on all sides as he stops a scant few feet from where I stand.

"You're all represented," the blond man says. "Fire." He nods at John. "Ice." He eyes the spear-wielding warrior. "Wind." The thin man with the arrows. "And now, Earth. Welcome."

"You're the All Called?" the short man who threatened me and ultimately healed John asks.

The blond man shrugs. "I am able to manipulate all four elements. The leaders of Wind and Ice call me the All Called."

"My name is Philip," the Earth leader says. "I welcome you to Erra."

"Do you?" the blond man asks. "Thank you."

"What exactly do you want?" John asks. "Saying you want peace and unity between us and that *someone* will rule is pretty vague."

"Selecting a ruler's not the priority," the man says. "Reconciling your differences matters more." He glances from Wind to Ice and back to me. "We spent days discussing the injustices, the past wrongs between Ice and Wind."

Judging by the twisted angle of Wind's lips, he's still harboring some pent-up issues.

"So you're offering to mediate for us?" Philip asks. "Is that why you're here?"

The blond perks up. "Yes, that's why I'm here. I'd like to mediate between your tribes and find a common ground."

"There is no common ground between Ice and Fire," John says. "Literally. Some of them even live on floating islands of ice, as you may have noticed. We'd melt their towns into oblivion simply by existing."

"Without their islands in the ocean, where would Ice be safe?" Philip asks. "Are they planning to move inland? Because there's no room for them here."

"We wouldn't want to live here." The leader of Ice sneers. "Your entire village stinks of manure."

"All life begins with death," Philip says. "But—"

A moment later, everyone's shouting. When I look past John, I notice that the fire armies are creeping steadily nearer. The soldiers' rows aren't as sharp or pristine, either, as if they're being drawn toward us involuntarily.

I spin around—Ice's ranks are moving, too. And Wind. . . I gape. They're gone. Where did they go?

Motion above my head draws my eye and I look up. Soldiers whip through the air.

The first arrow hits a Fire Called solider near the front of their formation. His shout is sharp and desperate. He falls to the ground, his dark hair spilling across the green ground, blood welling up from the arrow hole. I don't know him, but the image is close to one I've seen over and over on repeat. A memory I wish I could forget.

A man with dark hair dying. My heart shattering into a million pieces.

As if the rage around me, the old wounds, the anger over the injustices of the past throws that memory into sharp relief, I focus. . . and I snatch it from my mind. It tries to slide away. The dark-haired man I've been seeing over and over *is* Jesse—my brother. But what happened and why? Where is he now? What happened to us? I refuse to let that snatch of memory go, the worst moment of my life. The moment that Jesse died. I cling to it as though it's all that matters.

The blond man is speaking to me. John's shouting, and Philip's swearing, and the Wind solider has an arrow nocked, and even so, I block it all out.

Jesse is gone. His death punctures my heart and I can't breathe thinking of life without him, but I don't have any context. I don't know what our life was like, or what brought us there.

I must know, no matter how much it hurts!

I crawl toward my memories of him, forcing myself to examine that one moment, the only image I recall perfectly.

I don't want to see it.

I can't bear it to be true.

It didn't happen.

He's not dead.

But I know that he is!

I force myself to look, to focus on it, and to shift his body until I see his face.

Pain splits me in two, and I clutch at my head. *Jesse*. He was murdered. My brother, my best friend, the only person I trust. He was ripped from me—or was he?

Like an axe has cleaved my brain in half.

Like fire incinerates my insides.

Like ice has frozen my heart to a dead, black lump.

Like my entire soul has been pulverized in a blender, I *remember*.

As my memories snap into place—as the knowledge of who I am invades my every cell, I know what I must do.

Kahn's eyes are desperate as he throws an ice wall up in front of John, and incinerates a barrage of arrows flying toward the Earth soldiers who are now pouring through their gate.

"You can't save them," I say. "They don't want to be saved."

Kahn's eyes meet mine. "You *know* who I am."

My eyes well with tears, and I nod. "You're a friend. You've always been a friend. But I need more than that right now. I'm afraid you won't forgive me later, but if you're here—if your efforts are accomplishing nothing, then Devlin was right. The prison's already collapsing."

"Who are we to each other?" Kahn reaches for me, his hands circling my waist. "Can you tell me that, at least? You're the first thing I've seen in this place that has brought me peace. The first thing that feels *right*."

I want to sink into his arms. I want to ignore the world that's burning down and icing up all around us, but I can't. I may not know most of the people here, but I know John.

And I'm finally aware of how little time is left to save Jesse.

Which means I need to do what I did last time. It's time for the elementals to escape the bars of this place. Perhaps their memories on Earth will anchor them— perhaps they'll be able to let go of their rage and find compassion in their hearts.

"Are you—are we in love?" Kahn's voice is rough, filled with need.

I bite my lip and look into his eyes. "I think we were once," I say.

"But not anymore?" So forlorn. His words tear at me— but there's not much sorrow left in my body. It's all wrung out.

"Not in this time, maybe," I say. "I'm beginning to think

that this, this *thing* between us. . . it may come from another lifetime."

"I loved you then," Kahn says. "As I'll love you in every lifetime."

A tear rolls down my cheek. Something about what he's saying makes perfect sense. But I can't do anything about it, not right now. "Keep them from harming one another as long as you can," I say. "I'll try and hurry."

He brushes a kiss against my cheek and steps back, squaring his shoulders. His eyes light up, and I realize that, like me, he can Lift here.

I watch him for a moment, dumbstruck at the skill he possesses, wielding all four elements and his telekinetic powers in harmony.

With my help, I realize, we might be able to fight them back. We might force them to listen.

But that won't help Jesse.

So I focus on the ground beneath my feet, willing it to reveal the truth to me: that it's not real. It's hard, and my head already pounds, but when I cross my eyes and uncross them, finally, it works. The grass, the walls behind us, the horse on which John sits, it's nothing but pure energy.

Like last time, I shape a doorway, and I prepare to walk through it.

Kahn's eyes widen, and I know he can see it too. Before he can follow me, I press a kiss to my fingers and blow it to him. Then I slam the door in his face.

❦ 28 ❧

RRA

Something's wrong. I'm not on Earth, not even close. My feet—no, my *paws*—pound against the rocky ground. I'm running—away from something? Toward it? *Where am I?*

A growl next to me causes me to stumble and I plow into the ground face first, rocks grinding against my closed eyes and the fur of my face. Fur? A giant roar tears its way free in my throat, and the growling next to me shifts farther away.

I blink and force myself to a seated position, my head swiveling. A pack of wolves circle me, baring their teeth.

What am I doing in the mountains, surrounded by wolves?

I wanted to get to Earth.

The fur along their backs stands straight up, growling coming from all their throats. Renders, of course.

Which means I went the wrong way.

If I had a voice, I'd swear. Instead, I'm stuck thinking furious thoughts as the wolves run around me, circling steadily closer, their jaws snapping.

My tail lashes back and forth. My muscles bunch and relax. I can't stay here, but with this idiotic pack of wolves circling, snapping, leaping, and diving, I can't think.

They all need to STOP!

The thought is so intense, so clear, and so forceful that it almost hurts as it leaves my brain.

And the wolves stumble back, whimpering and whining. They slink away from me, glancing back reproachfully.

LEAVE AND DON'T RETURN.

The message is easier to send that time, and it works. Instead of slowly giving me space, they yip and run. Grey and white, black and brown, and pure white wolves all turn tail and flee. I roar again, this time with fury, and intense glee.

They obey!

Earth. I need to get to Earth. I can't stay here, frightening and bullying wolves, no matter how satisfying it feels. I need to stay on task, but it's hard with my brain wrapped in the mind of an animal. I wonder whether I can even squint in this form, but I do, the rocks and scraggly bushes and even small creatures, like a lizard, all coming into sharp relief. I never thought my eyesight as a human was lacking, but now I know the truth.

I was almost blind.

The lizard has forty-six small freckles on its back.

The rocks have tiny fissures, small wrinkles, and infinitesimal holes that my human eyes could never see.

The light plays on the water of the stream down below in a way that's almost staggeringly beautiful.

But it's not real.

I cling to that thought, as though it's my raft in a stormy sea. I can't get stuck here. I can't be lost again, I absolutely cannot. Jesse needs me. So I close and open my eyes, and then I cross and uncross them. And finally, the ropy filaments that comprise everything here come into view, and I force another door open.

And I step through.

❧ 29 ❧

Ā

his is not Earth either.

I'm clearly not nearly as good at any of this as I thought.

It's so dark here that I can't see my hands—but at least they're hands again—in front of my face. I touch my nose to be sure that I'm me.

But where am I?

"Hello?"

Movement in the dark sends a chill running up my spine.

I should not have made any noise, not here, not in the dark. Not when I don't know where I am or why.

Something's coming closer. I hear a soft scraping. It's still a hundred yards away, but it's moving steadily. My heart's trying to claw its way up my throat. I've always hated the dark.

Until it hits me where I must be. I was in Rra, and now, if I'm not on Earth, there's only one other place I could be: Ā.

I twist my wrist and a fireball flames to life above it.

I'm not alone.

Dozens of creatures are creeping toward me on their hands and knees, humanoid in shape, but their eyes are not adjusted to the light. They swivel toward me, their eyeballs almost entirely white, milky and clouded.

They don't recoil from the light. They don't cry out in pain or fear, either. No, they crawl faster. Some scuttle forward on their hands and knees. Some drag themselves with only their hands, and some struggle to their feet, jerking along toward me like animated puppets.

I want to be strong, but I can't help it.

I scream.

Loud, long, and full of terror.

The noise only intensifies their efforts, and I realize when I spin around, that several of them have nearly reached me. They're wearing clothing—but it's no more than rags.

They're bony, and some of them are misshapen. The one closest to me has only a handful of hairs sprouting from the top of—her?—head.

I scrabble backward, the heel of my foot connecting with something that squishes.

My stomach threatens to revolt. I Bind air above my head and claw my way upward, barely evading the grasp of the skeletal woman in front of me. I keep climbing, climbing, climbing until I'm sure none of them could possibly reach me . . . unless they can fly.

Only once they stop struggling do I pause and survey what now lies beneath me.

I increase the size of my fireball, and finally they cover their milky-white eyes.

Twenty. Thirty. Fifty. A hundred of the disgusting creatures.

I stop counting.

Every time I think I've counted them all, more crawl into view. None of them have spoken a word, as I dangle above them in the air. I'm equal parts horrified, disgusted, and terrified.

"Sekhmet?" the voice is raspy, wobbly, and weak.

I lower my fireball until I can make out who spoke.

"Who's asking?"

One of the nightmarish creatures lowers her hand, revealing a mouth still full of teeth and nearly a full head of hair. Her body is gaunt, but not nearly as emaciated as the others. "Is it really you?" Her voice is steadier, but just as weak as before.

"Who are you?" She doesn't resemble anyone I've ever known. Not that I've known many Assimilators. I freeze. Other than Ra, I've known exactly one, that I can recall. "Anat?"

Her lips peel away from her teeth in a way I'm terribly afraid is supposed to be a smile. "It is you. Most Divine! Praise be that you yet live."

What has happened to her? "What—how—"

"Isis trapped us," Anat whispers, the other figures around her slumping to the ground. "But Ra spared us. Our bodies don't die the same way that others do—we were wrapped on Earth as undead, preserved in tombs and pyramids."

The mummies? If I had eaten anything here recently, I'd probably be retching. Then it hits me—what that means. "You've been suffering in here. . . " I can barely make myself think the words, much less speak them. She's been trapped inside here for *thousands of years*? With nothing but these. . . disgusting creatures?

"It wasn't as bad," she says, "before Ra went to sleep."

My fireball dips. "Ra's here?" I glance around, suddenly ill at the thought of the Ra I remember as a blackened, wizened, crawling *thing*.

"Your father yet lives," Anat rasps, "but he's nothing like

us." Her mouth breaks into that horrific smile again. "He's glorious. He's Divine."

Uh-huh. "Where is he?"

"Are you here to save us?" Her eyes light up then, the first flash of color I've seen.

I gulp. "I—I'm not sure."

She nods. "As you will it, so shall it be." She gestures toward the other zombie Assims. "Stop crowding her. Move back. You're frightening her, you disgusting slugs."

To my shock, they actually shift away from the place I recently evacuated. My heart slows a bit in my chest. "Where's my father?"

I should be terrified at the thought of confronting Ra—after all, he's the bogeyman the Followers of Isis rallied to depose. He's the reason this entire prison was constructed, as I understand it, and yet. . . I thrill at the thought of seeing him. I shouldn't, but I find that I *yearn* to find him. Almost as much as I burn to save Jesse.

"He's there." Anat points above me.

My head turns upward and I send my flame higher, higher, toward steps in the corner of the room that wind up, up, up. At the top of the steps, there's a dark wooden door with a large iron handle.

"May Ma'at carry you," Anat whispers. Then her head drops again to the floor, as if even this short conversation has sapped her to the point of ruin. I look around the room, and I cross and uncross my eyes. I see a rocky outcropping on the edge of the area my light reaches. It juts out from the wall and serves no purpose. I reach for it, parsing out the ropes of energy, and slicing one off. Then I toss it, guiding its fall, shoving it at Anat like I might toss a treat to a dog.

Her head snaps up and her lips part in rapture. She inhales the energy filaments, her pupils dilating and her eyes brightening to the violet hue I remember. Her body transforms then, filling out, her limbs rounding, her perfect breasts returning, and her rags transforming into a beautiful silk gown. "Ah!" Her groan is full of joy and pain, and I can't tell whether I hurt or aided her, until she turns her face toward me. "Most Divine!" She shudders and stands up straight, her hair flowing once again down her back in a familiar black waterfall.

The look on her face is one of total adulation, and frankly, it creeps me out.

As if they can't help themselves, the creatures, the other Assims, move toward her as they moved toward me—clearly sensing the extra energy.

"No," she says, a tiny pulse leaving her.

They freeze, each of them inhaling as she inhaled, each of them improving in some odd way, and I realize that to satiate them, she shared a tiny bit of what I gave her with the rest. A grey streak appears in her hair, near her temple, and crows' feet crease at the corners of her eyes, but she's still just as full of joy as before.

And the slugs, as she called them, all improve as well. Some now sport a full head of hair. Some sit upright. Some have full, fleshy hands, or bright green eyes. The random, inconsistent improvements only serve to make them more hideous to look at, to me anyway.

I shudder and Bind air in front of me, moving along hand over hand until I reach the middle section of the stairs. I'm about to release my Bindings when I realize there are corpses—or at least, squishy forms, littering the stairs as well.

This time I do vomit, the contents of my stomach slapping onto the ground far below. Creatures move toward it, and I gag all over again. Instead of walking up the stairs from the middle of the stairwell, I continue to Bind air and climb upward, hand over hand until I reach the door. Luckily, there aren't any slugs blocking it. I release my bindings, finally, and step onto the smooth stone in front of the entrance to where Ra sleeps.

When my fingers touch the handle, it flashes brightly, golden light filling the room for a brief second.

The slugs cry out in pleasure, and I cringe, but the door opens, the hinges creaking mightily. I step inside. Unlike the antechamber, this room is small, the ceilings only ten or fifteen feet high.

A beautiful, brightly colored rug covers the floor. Shimmery, sheer curtains flutter in the window. A cool breeze blows through the room, drawing my attention to the focal point—a vast canopy bed with golden drapes and swaths of embroidered fabric covering it on all sides.

My feet move slowly across the plush carpet. My hands tremble at my sides. Every time I close my eyes, I see slugs who used to be human. Balding, emaciated zombies who are desperate for energy, for power, and for life. I brace myself to see some form of that here, where Ra sleeps.

When I'm only steps from the edge of the bed, I pause.

Anat said he's better, but how does she know? It doesn't look like anyone has been in this room in a very, very long time. As I think those words, a bright ray of sunlight streams through the window, casting dust motes and glittery bits of whatnot into sharp relief.

Someone draws a deep breath in front of me, and a combination of fear and anticipation glues my feet to the spot.

"Sekhmet?" His voice isn't raspy. It's not weak. It *is,* however, unsure.

"Dad?" my voice sounds just as it did in every dream. Small, light, and uncertain.

"You've come." The bed groans as he rises from it, and for the first time in thousands of years, I see my father.

His shoulders are broad. His hair is dark and silky, and it flows over his shoulders. His eyes are the same exact shade of hazel as mine—not quite green, not quite golden, not really brown. He's wearing the same robes he wore in every one of my dreams. His skin is a burnished gold, and his teeth, when he smiles at me, are as big and white as I remember.

"Dad!" I fling myself through the air, and he catches me in his powerful arms, hugging me tightly.

Tears stream freely down my cheeks.

"It's alright. Everything will be okay." His hand makes soothing circles on my back.

"The Assims outside are—" A shiver runs up my spine.

He pulls back enough that I can see his face, his strong nose, his perfectly shaped jaw. "Unfortunately I haven't been able to keep them healthy and strong. I wasn't sure when you'd come."

"You've been keeping them alive?"

His nostrils flare slightly as he breathes me in. "I've missed you, darling. I have been doing what I can, but my reserves are running desperately low."

"Your reserves?"

His brows draw together. "My reservoirs, you know." He taps the thick golden chain that circles his neck, inlaid with a dozen red stones, glowing softly.

I shake my head. "I'm afraid I only began to remember things a few days ago. There's still so much I don't know, I don't recall."

His lips compress. "That's fine. I can teach you whatever you need."

"But my memories. . . " I say. "I didn't even know you were my father until—"

"Ah." He frowns for a moment, almost as if this disappoints him deeply. Then he inhales and exhales slowly. "Never mind. It can all be restored," he says. "It will be."

"That's why I'm here, sort of," I say.

He releases me and walks across the room to a plain,

wood carved bench. He pats the spot next to him. "Tell me what I can do."

"Jesse's dying." The words come out as more of a sob than a sentence, and tears run freely down my face.

He takes my face in his hands, and my heart contracts as it never has before. This man, he's my father, in a way Duncan and my adoptive dad never were. I know in my bones that he loves me. He would do anything for me.

"Who's Jesse?" he asks—no judgment, no reproach, only curiosity.

I keep forgetting. "Shu," I say.

His eyebrows shoot up. "He's alive?"

"He was reborn with me."

His eyes get a faraway look, as if he's processing this new information. "He was."

I nod. "He's been my only real family. He's kept me safe, and happy, and alive."

"But you said he's dying," he says.

My throat closes off, and I can't form words. I choke back my tears. I can't get help if I don't explain. "He died on Earth," I admit. "The Followers of Amun, well, their leader, a man named Devlin Rochester, killed him to Wake me—to free my powers from Terra."

Ra closes his eyes. "They didn't."

"They knew I was the Warden," I say. "They didn't know what it meant or who I was, not until Mehen awoke, anyway."

"Mehen?" His eyes light up. "He's with you?"

I nod.

"Excellent. Keep him close. He'll do whatever it takes to keep you safe."

"Why am I the Warden?" I ask.

Ra's face falls. "I can't answer that for you. You'll have to remember it yourself."

I groan. "You can't tell me anything? Why not?"

"I can't tell you that," he whispers, "because I don't know." The pain on his face is stark, and I realize what it means: I betrayed him.

And he loves me still.

He forgives me for whatever I did—possibly locking him up in this ghastly prison—but he can't tell me why I did it.

Because he has always loved me, and he's not sure why I did what I did.

Which means. . . I really am the monster.

I swallow and try to focus. "Jesse died on Earth, but I couldn't bear it. He was still present in Terra," I say, "the prison world for those with telekinetic and healing powers."

"Okay," Ra says.

"I burned the place down and dragged him back to Earth," I admit. "But he wasn't quite right. The Healers say it's like he has a. . . hole. . . in his soul or something. Like he's bleeding energy all over."

Ra's shoulders slump. "That's a hard one." He shakes his head. "I'm afraid I can't tell you quite what to do without seeing him myself."

"I can't bring him here," I say.

"I understand."

"Is there anything you can do?"

"You're an Assim, darling, the most powerful alive." He lifts my chin a hair, gently. "You can keep feeding him power until we find a solution."

"I can't." The words feel ripped from somewhere deep inside.

"Why not?"

"I have to get the energy from somewhere," I say, "and. . ."

"Ah, the age-old question. What makes your desire worthy of the sacrifice of others?"

I nod.

He shrugs. "Find an injustice and use that to right the wrong that was done to you."

"Siphon a prisoner on death row?"

Ra laughs. "I don't entirely understand what you're suggesting, but yes. Locate someone unworthy, they never seem to be in short supply, and take the energy from them. Give it to your brother until you find a more permanent solution."

"Is there a permanent solution?" I hold my breath, terrified of the answer.

"There's always a solution," Ra says. "To every problem."

Thank goodness. "Okay."

"I'm sorry I can't help more," he says. "I'm afraid a hole in someone's soul isn't a problem I've encountered yet."

My laugh sounds a little demented. "You and me both."

He laughs too, but something about it brings me back to joy.

"Are you angry with me?" I can't quite make myself look at him when I ask.

"Because you betrayed me?" His voice is soft.

I nod.

"Of course not," he says.

I look at him then, and I realize that he's utterly sincere.

"How could anyone ever stay angry with the one person they love more than anyone else?" His smile is sad. "I must have let you down, and I'm sorry. I wish I could go back and change whatever I did. . . " He shifts closer to me on the bench. "If you remember nothing else, remember this, Sekhmet. You didn't betray me—you would never do that. Whatever happened, it happened because I failed you."

"You can't know that."

His enormous thumbs brush my tears away. "I do know

it." He straightens. "Just as I know you can't stay here. You came for help, and now you need to go back to fix him. Save Shu. Prepare, and seek for answers. Only then can you decide how to proceed."

I wait for him to ask me to free him.

He doesn't.

I gulp. "What if I can't find anyone—what if—"

"What do lions eat, cub?" he asks.

It's such a bizarre conversational shift that it takes me a moment to process the question. "Meat. Animals."

"Could a lion survive on leeks or onions or bread?" His expression is so honest, so open.

I shake my head.

"What about a wolf? Could it survive on dandelions?"

I laugh.

"A rabbit would be fine, however," he says.

"What's the point?" I feel it coming.

"Not all beings are created equal. Ma'at provides balance, yes, but balance does not mean homogeneity. Do you see?"

"Not really."

"You can't expect a lion to survive on milk or bread or grass. Lions must eat meat. You feel guilt in your heart, you always have, for your ability. My guess is that you've known the unworthy—if you don't remember how to weigh the human soul yet, you soon will—but you've been unwilling to eat the meat you need, the energy that sustains you."

How could he possibly know that? My surprise must show on my face.

He laughs. "Thousands of years and a new lifetime, and you haven't changed a bit."

I had the same issues as a child. I recall feeling sorrow for the scorpions, and I hated scorpions.

"Don't deny yourself what Ma'at dictates you require.

You're a rare blessing, you are divine, even if that idea bothers you."

It does.

His hand cups my jaw. "Don't starve, cub, and don't starve your brother. It would destroy your very soul."

That sounds dead right.

"But if you struggle too much. . . If you can't bring yourself to eat meat. . . " He leans back against the wall, his head resting against the stone as if he's profoundly tired. "If you find my reservoirs on Earth, you have my permission to use them."

I glance down at the dimly lit red stones in his necklace. "You need them yourself."

His smile is weak. "Haven't you figured this out yet? I'll give anything that I have for you. Now. Forever. Always."

I believe him.

"I'm not totally sure how to get back to Earth," I say. "I came here through Erra and Rra, but I really need to get back to Jesse."

"How do you usually go from the prison world to Earth?"

"I go to sleep."

Dad's smile warms my heart. "One of my favorite things has always been watching you sleep." He opens his arms to me, and I step into them. He pulls my head against his chest, and whispers against my hair. "Sleep now, little one."

I do.

❋ 30 ❋

EARTH

When I wake up, I'm lying next to Jesse in one of the bedrooms in the barn. I'm not sure who put me here, but someone knows me well enough to know I wouldn't want to be far from him.

"You're awake?" Kahn's slumped in an armchair in the corner. I'm not sure he could ever look bad, but bags under his eyes and rumpled clothes aren't his best look.

"You're still alive. That's good."

His brow furrows. "Was I in danger of *not* being alive?"

"You're on Erra," I say.

He straightens up, his head tilting. "But I was on Terra."

"You're also on Erra," I insist. "You're the 'All Called' there."

"Is Alora awake?" John flies through the door, his face relaxing when he sees me. "You are."

"I'm fine," I say. "But you two are going at it on Erra right now."

John frowns. "Kahn's not on Erra."

This is actually kind of fun. "He's the All Called." I sit up, careful not to jostle Jesse. "He can use fire, ice, wind, and earth. Though I doubt earth is helping him much right now. It's more of a slow-growing power from what I've seen."

"You can't be on more than one prison world," John says. "Except for the Warden, I suppose."

"I think it depends," I say. "Anyone with the powers that prison world represents will be caught."

"You're saying that if someone is blessed with more than one ability," John says.

"Or cursed," Kahn says.

"That they'll be stuck in both places?" John looks as if someone hit him in the face with a two-by-four.

"I think." I say, "that like me, Kahn was dropped there as soon as Terra collapsed."

"Like winning the lotto," Kahn jokes. "Money in the bank."

"Actually, there's a war going on over there," I say. "Things are bad. Fire's attacking Ice. Wind's attacking Fire. Earth and Ice are lobbing spears and rocks."

"What am I doing about it?" Kahn asks.

"Trying to stop it," I say. "But they aren't listening to us."

"Erra sounds like a mess," Jesse whispers.

We all freeze. I shift so I can see his face. "J!"

His smile's half-hearted, but it's enough. It must be good news—that he's awake.

"I'm glad," he whispers. "That I got to see you one last time."

No. No, no, no. I grab his shoulders. "You can't die, J. I won't allow it."

His eyes flutter closed. "I can't stay here, Alora. I'm a funnel to nowhere. You can't keep shoving magic inside me forever."

"I can." The resolve builds inside of me. "In fact, Ra told me about a reservoir that I can use. He said once I have that—"

"I'm sorry," John says. "Did you just say 'Ra' told you?"

I forgot they were there. "Uh, yeah. So I tried to leave Erra and come here, like I left Terra and came back to Earth before I sort of siphoned it and brought everyone back."

"Ra stopped you?" Kahn's voice is all astonishment.

"Not exactly," I say. "I sort of went the wrong way." I catch them up on how I passed through Rra and then wound up in Ā. "He is my dad," I say. "Yours too, J, and he loves us."

"Debatable," Kahn says.

"We can debate whether he's a good person," I say. "But he loves me, beyond a doubt."

Kahn's eyebrows rise and his lips compress, but he doesn't argue. He does, however, stand up and begin pacing. The room's so small that he looks a little like a ping pong ball stuck in a pinball machine.

"You need to let me go." Jesse doesn't open his eyes, like he's barely strong enough to form the words.

"I can't," I say. "I won't."

"Actually," John's voice is somber when he says, "my dad offered his life for yours. He was very willing—he wants to set things right."

It's small, but Jesse shakes his head. "No."

I knew he'd say that. "Fine," I say. "Fine. You want to die? Okay."

His face relaxes, peaceful for a moment. Is he that tired?

"But first, help me make one last decision." It can't be about him. It must be about the good of everyone who's trapped. "Erra's a disaster right now. Armies have gathered. Longstanding fury and anger have come to a head, and the people who can Call the four elements are murdering one another."

My brother's eyes open, full of concern.

"I have no idea how many will die. A lot. And as you know, they'll die here shortly after they die there. It includes John and Kahn, both of whom are on the front lines."

"What can you do, though?" Jesse asks. "If you go back, will they listen to you?"

"The last time I asked for a small favor there, I had to burn down hundreds of trees to make them listen. They don't care much for women's opinions."

"Maybe let them die," Jesse's voice is grim.

"Or if she brings them back here," John says, "it might prevent that kind of thing. Think about it. When they join up with their memories from Earth, they'll realize that Erra's a prison. They'll see that justice, and equity, and peace are valuable."

I'm not entirely certain that's what people here on Earth believe.

"I think the prison really might be past its time," John says. "It's not a coincidence that tensions are rising to a fever pitch. It's the confirmation Alora needs to feel comfortable dismantling it."

It sounds like Devlin's words coming from his son's mouth.

"He might be right," Jesse whispers.

I need to tell him. I should confess that the reason I want to dismantle Erra is that he needs power from it. But if I confess that, he'll go all noble on me. He'll insist I shore it up on principle.

"Have you ever made cookies?" Kahn asks.

John throws his hands up in the air. "Is he kidding right now?"

I'm kind of wondering the same thing. It's a strange time to be jonesing for treats.

"Bear with me." Kahn ignores John and looks at me. "Have you?"

I shrug. "A few times. I'm not very good at it, to be honest."

"Did you figure out how to make them from eating them?"

I roll my eyes. "I'm not a moron."

"When I was eight, I made my first batch of cookies," Kahn says. "I had eaten a lot, so I figured I could make them." He wrinkles his nose. "They were disgusting, of course. I didn't realize that you can't simply eat something a lot and divine how to make it yourself. You need someone to teach you, or give you a really clear recipe."

Jesse turns his head—he's listening now too.

"That's the problem with Terra—you can't rebuild it, because you don't have the recipe or a teacher."

John smacks his head. "Now I know what to get her for Christmas. I've been agonizing. I mean, what do you get the girlfriend who has everything? Maybe a guidebook with recipes for magical prison creation!"

My nervous laughter might not be helping, but I appreciate John's attempt.

"What do you mean?" Jesse asks.

"Last time she dismantled Terra, she was flying blind," Kahn says. "But if she goes to Erra this time and she takes her time, if she pays attention to how the prison's made, what power goes where. . . If she isn't in a rush because she's waited so long that the walls are caving in. . . "

"You *want* me to dismantle Erra?" I pin Kahn down, staring at his face to try and uncover his real feelings.

He smiles at me gently, and then he looks at Jesse pointedly.

And that's when I realize. He doesn't want the prison to come down. He's always been opposed to that.

There is no world in which we are enemies.

What he said on Erra, with no idea who I was, it was still true. He meant it. He's always on my side, even if it goes against his principles. He's given me the justification I need to save my brother. If only Jesse will agree that it's the right move.

"What do you think?" I ask.

"Yes," Jesse says. "I think if you're going to learn, so that you can repair whatever's broken, then you should do it now. Maybe bringing the people here will be the right move, but if the world dips into chaos like Erra is drowning in, then you'll have the tools you need to try and figure out how to fix the damage."

It's all the encouragement I need.

"Sekhmet?" Mehen's beautiful brown face appears in the doorway, his aqua eyes searching for me. "You're awake?"

I meet his gaze. "I saw Ra."

His face lights up as he steps into the doorway fully. Someone gave him modern clothing, and it's bizarre in the extreme to see this man, who speaks only ancient Egyptian, dressed in Gap khakis and a Tommy Bahama polo shirt. "He's well?"

"As well as he can be, trapped in a prison." I think about the slugs and shudder. "He's better than everyone else. I saw Anat, too."

"What's he saying?" Kahn asks.

Mehen turns to look at Kahn, and then stiffens. His eyes fill with rage, and he Lifts Kahn and flings him against the wall. Kahn's head makes a terrible cracking sound when it strikes the drywall.

"Whoa! Hey!" Then I remember to switch to Egyptian. "What are you doing?"

Jesse struggles to sit up.

I press him back gently. "It's okay. Mehen will listen to me." I hope.

"Mehen, release him, now."

Kahn's struggling to breathe.

"Now!"

Mehen looks back at me. "Your memories are not yet complete. This is Apophis, Ra's second greatest enemy, the thief of all light."

I'm so frigging confused. "What?"

"He will kill you," Mehen insists. "You must let me rid the world of him before he comes into his full power."

Kahn's face is turning purple, his feet kicking feebly at the wall. *There is no world in which we are enemies.* Mehen would know who he is, and the threat he poses to me, to Ra, to the world, but I believe his words in my bones.

"Release him right now," I say. "I command it."

Mehen obeys, but never takes his eyes off of Kahn. "You snake. You have wormed your way into her faith, but you will strike at her heart, I know it."

Okay. Mehen may not be quite as stable as I thought. "I've known Kahn in three places, now. I swear, he's on my side."

I holler for Martin. He and Thomas rush into the room and carry Kahn out to delve him in a room with more space.

Mehen steps back so that he can keep an eye on the doorway while still addressing me. "Most Divine, I know it's hard to be where you are. Information comes at you from all sides, but I beseech you, do not trust this one. I apologize most profusely that I did not pay enough atten-tion to your companions before now. I'd have noticed immediately if I had been fully on guard against your truest enemies. I thought he had been vanquished."

I groan. "I don't have time for this right now. I want your vow that unless you actually see Kahn attacking me, you won't harm him."

The Adam's apple in Mehen's throat works up and down, but finally he nods. "I do so promise."

I exhale with relief. "Kahn was just telling me that I ought to dismantle Erra and use the extra power to save

Shu. Do you still think he's a criminal mastermind, plotting my future demise?"

His eyes narrow with suspicion, but doesn't argue further.

Good enough for me.

"J, I'm going to go. You alright?"

He doesn't respond—unconscious again. I hate that I didn't get to tell him goodbye, just in case something goes wrong.

But nothing will.

Because I won't let it.

I press a kiss to his cheek and straighten.

John wraps his arms around me and whispers in my ear. "Be careful, please."

I smile. "I will."

"Don't forget to bring me back." He presses his lips to mine, and I thrill to his touch, even with the world upside down, even with my brother circling the drain. "If you don't have room to bring everyone, I'd say leave the guy who keeps causing people like Mehen to have conniption fits."

I snort.

"What was that about anyway?"

I keep forgetting that no one else can understand a word Mehen says. "He thinks Kahn is some kind of ancient Egyptian god, the enemy of Ra—and therefore of me."

John frowns. "If anyone would know. . . "

I had the same thought, but I can't give John any ammunition there. He's hardly impartial. "Drop it, please."

"I don't actually want anyone to hurt Kahn, you know."

"You don't?"

"If he gets whacked, I'll always wonder."

"About what?"

"Whether I could have beaten him fair and square." He smiles.

I slug him on the arm, but one of the things I adore

about John is how he always turns everything into a joke. No matter how dire things are, he'll try and make me smile.

"I wasn't kidding about this: be careful, and come back." When he kisses me this time, he's not smiling. He convinces me with his mouth and his hands that he means what he says. "I'll miss you."

"You're courting this one?" Mehen's unimpressed.

I laugh. "Another thing I don't need is relationship advice."

"At least Ra would prefer him to *Apophis*." He practically spits his name for Kahn.

And that's my cue. I sit in the chair by Jesse, and I close my eyes, feeling for the pathway that takes me to Erra. It's harder to find than the Terra one was. I'm still fumbling around when I hear a crash.

I open my eyes. John's sitting down on the floor next to me, and Mehen's trying to squeeze into the space between my chair and the bed. He's far too big for the space, and he knocked the lamp to the ground. "It's hard enough for me to find the pathway," I say.

"Sorry." Mehen's eyes are full of contrition.

I chuckle. Men. "Try to be quiet."

He nods.

I close my eyes again, and this time. . . it works.

When I appear in Erra, things are not going well. No one appears to have noticed that I've returned to the exact spot I left, somewhere on the Earth Called side of the vast courtyard outside of their settlement. Ice has created a series of barricades and has people huddled behind each. Every time they hurl a spear over their ice block walls, one of the soldiers waves his hands up and down and creates another spear.

Limitless weapons. Fabulous.

Not that the spears do much when thrown at Fire. The Fire Called soldiers melt them immediately. But against

Earth. . . I can't watch. The trees and vines they Call to block the spears take far too long to grow. They're the largest group, from what I can tell, but the least equipped to handle war.

Wind's warriors swoop and swirl, firing arrows at everyone indiscriminately. Kahn's still in the middle, trying to block anyone and everyone. I'd like to help him, but I have a more urgent need right now. I glance around for my target—a dying man. The arrow pierced his heart cleanly, and he's fading fast. Instead of watching him twitch, I isolate his light, and I siphon it. Power surges in my chest alarmingly.

That was bad.

I'm not sure that's quite what Kahn had in mind. I've got extra energy, but I'm not sure whether it's enough, especially once I travel back to Earth. I glance around for something inconsequential, but large. A wagon sits just behind the Ice front line with a trebuchet resting on it. Perfect. I squint at it until the filaments of energy appear, and I tug.

Nothing happens. They're definitely firmly fixed, every stray thread tucked in tight. No squirming or flailing like on Terra. Nevertheless, I need it. And Ice will only use it to destroy. So I dig deep down, and I focus, and I plunge my hypothetical claws into the wagon, yanking as hard as I can.

It bows at first, but then the filaments unspool, and I siphon them quickly.

It's enough, I'm sure of it. I focus on opening the door the right way this time. When I crack it open, it almost feels like a breeze blows through Erra—and Kahn's head whips sideways. When he sees me, he smiles beautifully. And an arrow hits him in the throat.

No! I need to get back and fix Jesse. I didn't mean to collapse Erra unless I had no other choice.

Kahn collapses on the ground, spasming. I sprint

toward him, my feet barely touching the bloodstained grass. By the time I reach his side, he's coughing, but blood spews from his damaged throat instead.

I swear under my breath and cross my eyes so I can see his inner light. It's still radiant, of course, immaculate. I gather him, just as I gathered the souls in Terra, and I plummet back to Earth.

Just like before, he flies alongside me, a beautiful, shining vision. This time, he doesn't peel off like before. He slams into Earth just as I do, his body not far from mine.

I stretch and straighten. Jesse's even paler than before, as if talking to me, saying goodbye, tapped his last reserves. I leap to my feet, startling both Mehen and John.

"How long was I gone?"

"An hour?" John shrugs. "Maybe?"

"An eternity and a moment," Mehen says.

That guy is odd.

I cross my eyes and uncross them and Jesse's light pulses in front of me, as pristine and beautiful as Kahn's. I hope Kahn's alright—hopefully Martin and Thomas are close by if he's not. I can't spare a moment to confirm. I spread my hands above Jesse's heart, above that pulsing, shining light, and I shape the power I stole and funnel it into him, trying to make a deep, thick circle of energy at the bottom of his soul, plugging any holes that might exist.

Then I collapse backward, nearly knocking John over. His arm wraps around my waist, steadying me.

Jesse springs upward in the bed. "Alora!" He beams at me. "What's going on?"

Clearly he's fine.

He swings his feet out of bed and stands. "What's going on? The crazy Egyptian guy came back with us?"

"Do you recall the conversation we had not long ago?"

He blinks, his eyebrows drawing together. "I was dying, but now I'm not."

"Not anymore."

"Please tell me no one sacrificed themselves for me."

I shake my head. "No one at all." The first guy was beyond saving, and the other donor was a wagon. I think even Jesse couldn't disapprove of that. "I need to check on Kahn real quick."

"What happened to him?" John asks, trotting along after me.

Jesse and Mehen are right on our heels. I'm beginning to feel a bit like I'm fostering some eager puppies. "It's a long story. I'll explain when I'm not worried that he's injured."

But Kahn's laughing at something Thomas said in the main room. He smiles at me when I enter, and that smile broadens when he sees Jesse up and walking around.

"So the wagon worked," Kahn asks.

He knows. "You saw me?"

"The second you returned," he says. "But I wasn't expecting you to open that door, and the wind was unexpected."

"What wind?" John asks.

"I'm just glad you're alright," I say.

"Totally fine. And hey, looks like Erra is alright, too." Kahn tosses his head at John.

I return the smile. A happy resolution all around.

Or, at least, until John falls on the floor and begins to seize.

"This happened before." Devlin's voice is grim. I hate that he's here, in my safe place. Part of me still wishes I'd killed him—either time I had the chance.

But he's right. I know what's wrong. Erra isn't fine. Whether it was the wagon siphon, or bringing Kahn back, I'll never know.

"It did."

"You won't have time to be leisurely this time either," Kahn says.

I shake my head. And then I sit on the sofa and imagine the pathway to Erra. I've traveled it far, far less than the one to Terra, but I find it on the first try, and I shoot toward it immediately.

Luckily, John's close.

Unfortunately, he's not the only one in trouble. Warriors all around me are unraveling, the filaments of their bodies and souls fraying in front of my eyes. I genuinely want to study the construct, but I don't have time. This world is far, far larger than Terra. I know that, consciously, but it's one thing knowing something, and another dealing with it.

I reach outward, siphoning energy from the ground, the grass, the rocks, the ice spears, and also gathering souls. Dark souls, salt and pepper souls, and shining white souls. Unsurprisingly, many of the souls of the Fire Called are a mixture of dark and light. The Wind Called, plunging from the sky, are nearly all bright. But these are only strange things I note as I gather, siphon, gather and siphon.

Until I can't possibly contain another speck of power, or another single buzzing light.

I plunge back to Earth, and just as with Terra, the pressure builds. I'm nearly there when I feel my own body begin to shudder under the strain. My own filaments writhe, my arms spasming, my legs separating into beams of energy, and then the lights begin to veer away, lessening the pressure on me with each departure.

I want to know whether John's alright—I desperately want to return to my body on Earth. . . but I can't. There are too many souls waiting for me on Erra, and I have no idea how far the decay has spread. So instead of checking on John, I brake and reverse, returning as quickly as I arrived.

I arrive in another place this time. A giant iceberg, floating in the middle of an ocean of tumultuous waves. Mothers and children shriek while fathers block the waves, steadying the iceberg in every way they can. I reach out, sensing the angry motion of the waves is created from the breakdown of the prison structure, and I suck them up greedily.

The iceberg is next, and as it disappears, I gather frightened children, protective mothers, and combative fathers. Each of them blinks out the same way, flowing into the buzzing, blinky pile of souls frenetically circling me. This time I stop a little shy of where I did last time—I can't do this over and over if I nearly disintegrate on every return trip.

Dozens of icebergs, a few mountaintop eyries, and even a half dozen burrows full of mushroom-growing Earth Called later, and I've completely lost count of the number of souls I've ferried back to Earth.

My filaments throb, my insubstantial limbs quake. But more lights blink and flicker, so I return. Again and again and again.

Until finally, when I travel back to Erra, there's only a single Volcano adjacent city left. The souls gathered around it have run, have hid, and have fought against my services. Their lights are dim, many, many dark strands for every light one, but I'm no longer sure that I can aptly judge the weight of a man's or woman's soul with only one facet to examine, only one side of their soul visible. So instead of leaving them, or absorbing the energy without ferrying those souls, I gather them in as well, and I make my final trip back, so tired I can barely stay on the familiar path.

When I finally release the last Erran prisoner, I sink into my body with great relief, and I groan, long and loud.

"Alora?"

I rub at my eyes and focus on the person speaking. It's Jesse.

I beam at him. "Yes, I'm done, finally." But when I look past him, we're not in the barn. We're not in a place that I recognize in any way. I'm on a bed in an enormous room, hooked up to beeping monitors, and a bag is connected with a clear tube to my arm, dripping and dripping and dripping.

"Where are we?"

Jesse presses a button, then turns to face me fully, his smile so broad it makes his eyes squinty. "I'm so relieved you're finally awake."

"Maybe instead of where we are, I should ask how long I was asleep."

"Three days," Jesse says. "And Isis has been busy."

"Wait, Isis the person? Or the group?"

He snorts. "Not the person, so I suppose it could be worse."

"Okay, start at the beginning and go slowly." I tug the diodes off my chest, and the machine next to me freaks out. I wonder how badly it's going to complain when I yank this stupid tube out of my arm.

"You needed fluids," Jesse says. "I told them it was alright."

"Never mind all that. Are you alright?"

Jesse nods. "I am, but Isis and Amun. . . they kind of swept the influx of a few hundred thousand telekinetics under the proverbial rug. But there was no way to contain this, Alora."

Seven million plus elementals? I guess not.

"Isis began seizing control of governments, so I believe Devlin when he says that Amun had no choice."

I flop back against the pillows. "It's as bad here as it was on Erra, isn't it?"

Jesse's voice is not reassuring. "Maybe worse."

If you enjoyed Adrift (and want more!) don't worry! Book 3, Awoken, is available on preorder right now. It's set to release on July 15, but I might get it out early if summer goes as planned. ;) There will be four books total, but Capsized won't be out until September.

If you have time to leave me a review, they help SO MUCH! On any and all platforms! (Goodreads, BookBub, and your bookseller of choice!)

If you want to chat with me or other fans of my work, check out my facebook reader group here: https://www.facebook.com/groups/750807222376182

SAMPLE CHAPTER OF MARKED

I'm a big fat coward.

I've known this about myself definitively since one month before my sixth birthday. The night I lost my dad.

Case in point: I'm just shy of seventeen. I've been in love with the same guy for almost three years. Even though I see Wesley a few times a week, I haven't said a word. But tonight I have the perfect opportunity to do what I've always feared to try. Tonight, to celebrate our upcoming Path selections, all the teens in Port Gibson play a stupid, risky game.

Spin the Bottle.

I glance around as I walk toward the campfire in front of me. Only thirty-five kids turned seventeen in the past year, so of course I know them all. My best girl friend, Gemette, waves me over. I try to squash my disappointment at not seeing Wesley. When I played this scene in my brain earlier, I was sitting by him.

"You gonna scowl at the fire all night, Ruby?" Gemette pats a gloved hand on the slab of granite underneath her.

"You couldn't have saved us one of those seats?" I point

at the smooth, flat stumps on the other side of the fire. I sit down and shift around, trying to find a flat spot.

"I think what you meant to say was, 'Thanks, Gemette. You're the best.'"

Her straight black hair reflects the campfire flames when she tosses it back over her shoulder. It's against the Council's rules for hair to cover your forehead. Gotta make it easy to see anyone who might be Marked. Except tonight, no one's following the rules. Everyone's wearing their hair down, and Gemette's silky locks frame her face beautifully. I envy her sleek hair almost as much as I covet her curves.

"My bum's already hurting on this," I mutter.

"If you weighed more than eighty-five pounds soaking wet, it wouldn't bother you so much."

Instead of curves, I've got twig arms and a non-existent backside. I shift on the huge slab, trying to find a position that doesn't hurt. I arch one eyebrow, not that she can see it in the dark. "I weigh ninety-two pounds, thank you very much."

Gemette snorts. "That proves my point, you bony butt."

She leans toward the fire and picks up the glass bottle lying on its side. She tosses it a few inches up into the air before catching it again.

"Be careful with that." That bottle's the only reason I'm sitting here, sour-faced, stomach churning.

Slowly the remaining seats around the fire fill up. Wesley shows up last. There aren't any seats left, but before I can convince Gemette to squish over, he grabs a bucket. He turns it upside down and takes a seat a few feet away from everyone else. I guess that's fitting. His dad's the Mayor of Port Gibson and a Counsellor on the Centi-Council, so Wesley's in charge by default tonight. He'll probably take over for his dad one day, which isn't as glamorous as it sounds since less than two thousand people live here.

He looks around the fire, and his gaze stops on me. He bobs his head in my direction, and I shoot him a smile. I'm glad he can't hear the thundering of my heart.

Although we're all huddled around a campfire, and I've known most of the kids here for years, we maintain carefully measured space between us. Tercera dictates our habits even when we're rebelling. Which we're only doing because it's a tradition.

Maybe Tercera's made cowards of us all.

"Are we starting?" Tom's sitting to my left. His parents are both in Agriculture and he's Pathing there, too. He has broad shoulders and tan skin from working outside most of the day. Gemette likes him, and it's easy to see why. Of course, he's nothing to Wesley.

I glance across the fire in time to see Wesley stand up. He straightens the collar of his coat slowly and methodically, like his dad always does before a town hall meeting. Wesley loves doing impressions, and he's usually convincingly good at them.

"I'd like to take this opportunity to welcome you all to the Last Supper." His voice mimics his father's, and he touches his chin with his right hand in the same way his dad always rubs his beard. Wesley himself is tall and lean with long black hair that he's wearing down, for once. It falls in his eyes in a way I've never seen before, and I feel a little rush. I want to touch it.

Wesley smirks. "I know you may be less than impressed with the culinary offerings for our gathering, but as I always say, Tradition has Value." He cracks a grin then, and everyone laughs. "Seriously though." He drops the impression and returns to his normal voice, which I like way better anyway. "I know the food sucks, but this whole thing started with a bunch of teenagers who were sick of rules and ready to throw caution to the wind for a night."

I look down at the three or four dozen nondescript metal cans with the tops peeled back, resting on coals. Another few dozen are open but sitting away from the fire. Presumably they contain fruit or something else we won't want to eat hot.

Wesley leans over and snags the first can, his gloves keeping him safe from the heat. "I hope you'll all forgive me, but this was what we could find."

"This is a pretty crummy tradition." Lina reaches down and grabs a can with mittened hands. Her dark brown hair falls in a long, thick braid down her back, like it has every single time I've seen her.

"Traditions matter, even the silly ones. They help pull us together as a community, which is valuable when fear of Tercera yanks communities apart. We're stronger when we aren't alone. Thinking every man should look out for himself hurts all of us." Wesley takes his first bite right before Lina. I grab a can of baked beans.

The food really is as bad as it looks, but at least it's not spoiled.

Wesley talks while we eat.

"As you already know, we come from a variety of backgrounds. Before the Marking, Port Gibson housed approximately the same number of people, but not a single person who lived here before the Marking survived. We cleaned out the homes, burned some to the ground and rebuilt, circled the city with a wall, and made it our own. The Unmarked who live here are Christian, Muslim, atheist, black, white, Hispanic, Russian, German and Japanese. I could keep going, but I don't need to. Before the Marking, these differences divided humanity. Now, we know that what truly matters is what we all share. We embrace the traditions that bring us all together, because we're more alike than we are unalike."

I swallow the last spoonful of baked beans from my can and set it down on the ground by my feet. I'm almost the last one to finish eating, but several half-full cans are scattered around the campfire. A few people grab a can of fruit. I prefer the stuff my Aunt and I process and can ourselves, so I don't bother.

I rub my hands together briskly. Even in mittens, my fingers feel stiff. It's usually not too cold in Mississippi, even in January, but a late freeze has everyone bundled up. The Last Supper's supposed to be a chance to rebel, but I'm grateful that everyone's as covered as possible. It means I won't look as cowardly for keeping my mittens on. My aunt is Port Gibson's head of the Science Path, so I know all about how Tercera congregates first in the skin cells, even before the Mark has shown up on the forehead in some cases.

The wind moans as it blows through the trees, and we all huddle around the meager fire. Even though the flames have died down to coals in most places, it burns hot. My face roasts while my back freezes. The bottle lies stationary on the weathered flagstones by the fire where Gemette set it, light glinting off of the dingy glass at strange angles.

The quiet conversations die off and the nervous laughter ends. Eyes dart to and fro among the thirty something teenagers gathered.

"So." Evan's voice cracks, and he clears his throat. "Who goes first?"

"Thanks for volunteering," Wesley says.

I suspect no one else asked for just this reason. All eyes turn toward poor, gangly, redheaded Evan.

Evan gawks momentarily. Even though he and I work in Sanitation together, I don't know him well. I haven't been there long enough to guess whether he feels lucky or put upon. He sighs, and then leans forward and tweaks the bottle. It twists sharp and fast and skitters to the right, spinning furiously.

I really hope the bottle doesn't stop on me, and I doubt I'm alone in that thought. Evan's funny in a self-deprecating way, but he isn't smart, and he definitely isn't hot. I bite my lip, worried about what I'll do if it does stop on me.

It slows quickly and finally stops pointing to my left. I sigh in relief, which I belatedly hope no one heard.

Tom gasps, and then in a raspy voice says, "No way. I mean, you're nice and all Evan, but I'm not . . . I don't . . ."

"Yeah, me either. Chill, man." Evan laughs. "So, does it pass to the next person over?" Evan raises his eyebrows and glances at me.

I want to protest, but my throat closes off and I look down at my feet instead.

Evan stands up. "So Ruby . . ."

He may not have saved me a seat, but Wesley jumps in to save me now, thank goodness. "That's not how it works. If you get someone of the same gender, and neither of you . . . well, then your turn passes to him or her. Which means you sit down Evan, and you spin next, Tom."

"Who made these rules?" Evan grumbles as he sits.

Gemette smiles. "They make sense, Evan. I mean, it's not spin the bottle and pick best out of three. Your way, you'd basically pick someone in the circle who's close and kiss whoever you want."

Evan shrugs and glances at me again with a smile. "Sounds pretty okay, actually."

Tom snorts. "I don't hear Ruby complaining about Wesley's rules. I'd say that's your answer, man."

I look back down at my shoes, but not before I see Tom's wink. Jerk. Evan must feel idiotic, and I definitely want to sink into the ground.

I bite my lip again, this time a little harder. Tom's an

obviously good-looking guy, but I have no interest in kissing him. I hope his wink was a joke about Evan and not some kind of message.

Cold air blows past me as Tom leans forward to spin the bottle, his body no longer blocking the wind. One thing jumps out at me as he reaches for the glass bottle. In spite of the cold, Tom isn't wearing gloves. He must've taken them off at some point. He's either a daredevil or an idiot. I'm not sure which.

Tom spins the bottle less forcefully than Evan and rocks back and forth as the bottle circles round and round. His eyes focus intently on the spinning glass as if he can somehow control where it stops. I wonder who he's hoping for and look around the circle for clues. Andrea seems particularly bright-eyed. My eyes continue to wander. One gorgeous, deep blue pair of eyes in the circle stares right back at me. Wesley. I've looked at him a lot over the past few years, but this feels different somehow. A spark zooms through me, and I quickly stare at my feet.

No luck for Andrea tonight, or Gemette. The bottle comes to rest on Andrea's best friend, Annelise, instead. She and I were in Science together a long time ago. Her dark brown hair hangs loose, framing high cheekbones and expressive chocolate eyes. She frowns. Tonight doesn't seem to be going right for anyone so far.

"Now what?" Annelise's voice shakes. "We just kiss, right here in front of everyone?"

"No, of course not," Gemette snaps.

"Who made you the boss?" Evan frowns. Judging by his sulky tone, he's still mad about losing his turn earlier.

"Unfortunately, I'm the boss," Wesley says, "and she's right." He points to a dilapidated shed at the top of the hill. "You two go up there."

"Romantic." Tom rolls his eyes as he stands up. He rubs his bare palms on his pants. Gross. At least I know I'm not the only nervous one here. Tom and Annelise trudge a path through clumps of frozen brown grass toward the rundown tool shed.

What a special memory for their first kiss.

Gemette sighs and I pat her gloved hand with my own. I'd feel worse for her, but Gemette likes every decent looking guy in town, including a few boys a year younger than us. She'll recover from missing out on a special moment with Tom.

I glance again toward Andrea, an acquaintance from my time in Agriculture. She and Tom trained together for years. She may have liked him as long as I've liked Wesley. She looks into the fire while her foot digs a messy hole in the soil. I wonder how I'll feel if Wesley spins and gets Andrea. Or worse, Gemette. I'll have to sit here and twiddle my thumbs while I know he's in there kissing a friend. My stomach lurches. Coming tonight was a stupid idea. I clearly didn't think this through.

No one speaks to distract me from my anxiety. The shed isn't far. We could easily eavesdrop on them if the wind would shriek a little less.

"How long does this take?" Evan asks.

"Who the heck knows?" Gemette points at the bottle. "Impatient for another crack at it?"

Kids around us chuckle.

After another few awkward moments, Gemette grabs the bottle and gives it a twist. "No reason we have to wait on them."

"Sure," Wesley says. "Whoever it lands on can go next."

"Wait," Evan asks, "whoever it lands on goes next as in it's their turn to spin? Or goes next as in Gemette's going to kiss them?"

The bottle stops before anyone can respond, pointing directly at Wesley. His perfectly shaped brows draw together under disheveled black hair. Gorgeous hair. His lips form a perfect "o". His bright blue eyes meet mine again.

My heart races and the baked beans sit like a lump in my belly. I shouldn't have come. Of course Wesley will want to kiss her. Gemette's gorgeous, curvy, and smart. Ugh. Am I going to have to sit here while my best friend kisses the guy I like twenty feet away? This is all my fault. If I'd only told Gemette, she'd beg off.

I bite down a little harder on my lip and taste blood this time. I really need to kick this particular habit, especially with kissing in my future. Maybe. Hopefully. I'm such an idiot.

Wesley clears his throat. "I think I'm going to sit this game out. I'm more of a moderator than a participant."

"No," I blurt out. "You can't. You're here, you're seventeen, you have to participate." What am I doing? Why am I shoving him at my friend? But if I don't make him play, I'm flushing my chance to kiss him down the toilet. I want to cry.

"Well, then I guess it's my turn to spin." His deep voice sounds completely different than any of the other kids here tonight. My stomach ties in knots when I hear him speak, which is ridiculous because I've heard his voice a million times.

I glance at Gemette. She looks disappointed and I want to cry with relief, but I don't blame her. He could've kissed her but didn't pursue it. I imagine most any girl here would be disappointed. He glances up and his eyes lock with mine again. Caught. I start to shiver and try to stop it. This look is different somehow from any before, like something shifted. Wesley clears his throat, looks down at the bottle, gracefully reaches over, and snaps it between his fingers.

It spins evenly, not moving to the right or the left. It spins on and on, and I wonder if it'll ever stop. It slows, whirling a little less with each rotation, the butterflies in my stomach swooping and swirling with each pass.

Until it finally stops. On me.

My eyes snap up reflexively, wide with shock. Wesley doesn't even seem surprised. He simply stands and inclines his head toward the shed.

"Isn't it still..." I clear my throat. "Umm, occupied?"

"We can wait over there." He gestures at the hill to the right of the shed. One side of his mouth lifts in a smile and I feel an answering grin form on my lips. Which makes me think about what we're about to do with our lips.

Swarms and swarms of butterflies flutter in my chest.

"Sure," I say.

I stand up and without even thinking, I wipe my palms on my jeans. They aren't even sweaty and what's more, I'm wearing mittens! I really hope no one noticed. Okay, more specifically, I hope Wesley didn't notice. Gemette holds something out to me when I stand. I can't tell what it is from feel alone thanks to my thick mittens, and in the dark I have to squint to make it out at all. A tube of something. "What—"

"Lip gloss," she whispers. "A gift from my mom. I was going to use it, but looks like you need it more, you lucky, lip-biting brat." She winks.

I'm glad Wesley's still across the fire from me and that it's dark. Maybe he somehow miraculously missed both the palm wipe and her wink.

I walk as slowly as I can toward the old shed, partially to avoid tripping, but also so I won't look overeager. I try to hide my face while I apply the fruit-scented lip-gloss so that Wesley won't notice. It's dark, but I don't want him to be put off by dry, scratchy lips, or worse, dried blood. Gemette's a good friend. I feel guilty for overreacting earlier when I thought she might kiss Wesley. Not super guilty, but you know, a little.

Neither of us speaks a word, but I feel the eyes of the other teens follow us toward the shed. We're only a few crunching steps away when the swinging door flies open and Tom and Annelise barrel out. I jump when it bangs shut behind them.

Tom looks as ruffled as I feel, his eyes darting back and forth. He ducks his head and reaches down to take Annelise's hand. They walk out and away from the fire and the rest of Port Gibson's teens. I can't tell where they're headed, but somewhere far away from here.

"Did you know almost a third of the couples in town trace their start to the Last Supper?" Wesley asks.

"No way."

He shrugs. "We've only been an Unmarked town for seven years, so it's even more impressive. Not all of them are matched up from a bottle spin, but I think the game helps people realize how they feel."

A thrill rushes through me. Does Wesley feel the same as me?

My hand reaches for the door handle and collides en route with his. I'm wearing mittens, of course, and he's wearing shiny, brown gloves, but a thrill runs through me when we touch, even through layers. He doesn't move his hand away, but instead draws my hand in his and pushes the door handle back in one fluid movement. My heart skips a beat and time stops. When the door's completely open, he slowly releases my hand. I lower my eyes and step over the threshold into the rundown little building.

Although there's clearly no power, and consequently neither heat nor an overhead light, the walls at least cut the wind. It's at once both warmer and quieter. Two tall candles burn softly on a pile of rusted metal boxes in the corner. Someone prepared this dump, I realize. I wonder whether it was Wesley. The flames provide enough light that I can see his face. His dark brows are an even more startling contrast to his dark blue eyes than usual, accentuated by his hair falling in his face.

"So," I say. "Here we are."

Wesley looks at me from less than a foot away. The shed's small and crammed full of moldering farm implements. The air around us practically hums, but that isn't new. It's always like the moments right before a lightning storm when he's near. Supercharged almost, like the electrons around my body might fly off at his slightest touch. The difference is that here, away from the town's work projects, away from my family and his, it feels like anything really could happen.

Wesley's so close I can smell him, the same citrusy, woodsy smell I've secretly savored for years. It's even stronger tonight, like he put on more of whatever it is he usually wears. I breathe deep, and all the memories of him re-imprint on my brain. Scrubbing, sanding, painting, digging, cleaning, hammering. Projects his dad made him attend, but I suffered through to be near him. When I'm with him, I belong somewhere for the first time in a decade.

When we become adults next week, Wesley's mandatory attendance at work projects ends. Wesley steps into his role as an administrator, and I'll become part of Port Gibson's janitorial crew. It's now or never if I want to make any kind of permanent place with Wesley.

I never thought I'd be close to him like this, and I know I may never be again. I lean toward him and tilt my face upward, eyes closed, ready for what comes next. Maybe I'm even a touch impatient. I have waited for this for years.

Except I keep waiting, and then I wait some more.

Not a single thing happens. The trouble with being ridiculously small is that Wesley, who's on the tall side anyway, towers over me. Even with my face angled up, his lips are pretty far away. I can barely make out his expression, but it looks guarded.

Maybe he doesn't know how to do it?

No way. Wesley must know. I mean, it's not hard, right? You just push your lips onto the other person's mouth. Why isn't he doing anything? This is the moment. THE moment!

Until it passes. And then another moment falls on top of it, and another. All passing. Even the butterflies in my stomach get bored and go look for flowers elsewhere.

I'm not sure exactly how much time has elapsed, but the seconds drag, heavy with my growing frustration. Soon, someone will bang on the door. "You've been in there forever," they'll say. "Make room for the next couple."

I want to smack them in their eager faces.

I know I don't have much time, and I want to say something, anything. I need to tell him how I feel, say the words, take a gamble. But like it always does, my tongue shuts down. My throat closes off. The words stick inside my throat. Why am I such a coward? Our perfect moment withers and dies. Tears well up in my eyes, and I can't breathe.

Wesley isn't similarly affected. He steps back and says, "We don't have to do this, Ruby. It's not safe at all. I don't know why my dad even lets these dinners happen."

"Why'd you spin the bottle in the first place?" I hear the desperation in my voice, but the words pour out in spite of myself. "I know you, and you know me. How's it dangerous for us?"

He takes another step back, his expression registering surprise. "People get Marked, Ruby. It still happens. Every few weeks, in fact. Maybe I'm Marked. You don't know. It happens, even here, even with all our rules. It may take years to die once you're Marked, but it's inevitable."

I roll my eyes. "Well I'm not Marked, if that's what you're worried about." I point at my forehead. "See? Clear."

"We shouldn't be taking these risks." Wesley scowls. "Not now, not right before our real lives begin. This whole thing's supposed to be a time to say goodbye to being a kid, not act like an idiotic five-year-old, breaking rules for no reason."

Our real lives? Maybe he never thought it felt right, the time we spent, the way we are together. Maybe I never belonged with him at all. "Why'd you even come, then? Why follow me in here if you're not going to kiss me?"

Was he hoping for someone else? Was he stuck with me and looking for any excuse to bolt? Am I Evan in this scenario?

I look up, but I'm too close. The hair cascading over his face obscures my view. I want to touch his hair; I want to kiss him; I want to tell him I love him, and that I always have. My fingers and toes and everything connecting them zings in spite of the bitter cold, in spite of the indifference of his words. Energy spins round and round in my body, a closed circuit with nowhere to go.

"Look, Ruby, I don't know what to say . . . but the thing is . . ." He sounds torn, confused.

Suddenly, I don't want to hear "the thing," whatever it is. I've been talking to Wesley for years, talking and talking, and working alongside him, but I don't want to talk to him anymore. I know what I want and I'll never have a better chance to play things off as part of a game, if he feels like I now suspect he does. The notion of an excuse appeals to my cowardly heart. I can't speak the words, but I won't stand here and do nothing, not anymore, because he's the real life I've longed for.

I stop thinking and step toward him instead. He tries to step back and slams up against the back wall. I quickly take one more step and use my gloved hand to pull his head down to mine. I push my lips against his. In my haste, I push too hard and pull a little too fast. Our teeth smack into each other and my tooth knocks against my own lip, splitting it wide open again.

It's the opposite of magical.

I look up at Wesley instinctively. He has blood on his mouth, but whether it's his, or mine, I can't tell. And if it's not awful enough already, Wesley stiffens from head to toe like I mauled him, like I forced him into something torturous.

A tear rolls down my cheek and I inhale deeply. I won't cry over this. I can't, because there's no way I can play it all off as a game if I bawl my eyes out. I turn away from him. If I can't stop the tears, at least he doesn't need to see them. When did this go so wrong? I should be calm, cool, in control. I need to laugh it all off and tell him friends can't be expected to kiss well. Whoops.

Except my heart won't listen to the screaming from my head. I'm not calm. I'm the opposite of cool. I've lost all control.

He grabs my shoulder and tugs me around. I turn, but my eyes stay glued to the ground, too ashamed to meet his gaze.

"Ruby, look at me."

He puts two gloved fingers under my chin and lifts. His head comes down then, but slowly, too slowly. My heart stops pumping and I worry it might never beat again. His lips brush mine gently, then with more pressure. I ignore the discomfort of my torn lip and lean into him, connected to him in a way I can't explain. I need more air, but I want less, because that means more space between us. If this never ends, maybe it'll erase the moments that preceded it.

Suddenly, he lets me go and steps back. Emptiness fills the space where he stood. I reel again, sucking air in and blowing my breath back out to steady myself.

When I raise my eyes, our gazes lock. All my sorrow from before is gone, replaced with a feeling like I'm flying, soaring, floating on top of the world. His sapphire blue eyes reflect candlelight back at me. He's breathing as deeply as I am; he's as affected as me. I can't look away from his strong, almost hawkish nose, his square jaw, his flashing eyes and thick black lashes. I continue to stare as Wesley reaches up and brushes his unkempt hair away from his eyes.

I almost faint.

Such a simple movement. Small in the grand scheme of things, but also vast, earth shattering, all encompassing. My dreams crumble. My world spins out of control. He moves his hair off his forehead, and suddenly things make sense. His reticence to touch me, his skittishness, but also his quick recovery. Once he knew it was too late, he didn't hesitate to kiss me.

Because we'd already touched.

A tiny rash mars his otherwise perfect forehead. Before the world died, it wouldn't have mattered. Before the Marking, no one would have cared about a few bumps. It would be harmless: acne, a bug bite, or a reaction to hair product. It shouldn't matter that his forehead has a blemish. It shouldn't terrify me, but it does. Because that small rash means Wesley is Marked, and in under three years, he's going to die terribly.

And now, so am I.

You can grab Marked right now. (The four book series is already complete!)

ACKNOWLEDGMENTS

My cover artist is not only an artist, she's a friend. I could not love Lara more. We've had a wild ride over the past year, but I love her so much for bringing my hare-brained ideas to life.

My kids are so supportive, even when they wish I didn't write and was a good mom instead. LOL! I'm mostly kidding, but I really do appreciate them and their good natured help around the house when I'm on a deadline.

My editor Carrie: I love you, you wizard. You get no notice, you get rushed every time, and you still deliver. Thank you for saving me from myself.

And Carla Stuckey is always willing to pitch in with the kids, OR beta-read and copy edit and everything else in between. You are my anchor in many ways.

And Whitney who is my sun, moon, and stars, my biggest thanks go to you. My husband helps run my reader group with memes. He watches the kids (and even takes them to the beach!) while I'm writing. He never complains, and he cheerleads me alllll the time when I whine and complain and cry and get all angsty and think the book is horrible. (Apparently it happens on every single book!)

But my 'last but not least' thank you goes to my readers! You guys do not understand how much I love you and how much you mean to me. YOU ARE THE BEST. Thank you for being the REASON I write. <3

ABOUT THE AUTHOR

Bridget loves her husband (every day) and all five of her kids (most days). She's a lawyer, but does as little legal work as possible. She has three quarter horse geldings, a Holsteiner (jumping) horse, and she spends too much time riding and not enough time writing. (Or too much time writing and not enough time riding, depending on your perspective!)

She has more chickens than she'll admit to having, two lions head rabbits, a cat, two dogs (one bouncy and one yappy). She makes cookies waaaaay too often and believes they should be their own food group. In a (possibly misguided) attempt at balancing the scales, she kickboxes daily.

So if you don't like her books, her kids, her horses, her chickens, or her cookies, maybe don't tell her in person.

Bridget is active on social media, and has a facebook group she comments in often. Please feel free to join her there: https://www.facebook.com/groups/750807222376182

The Finding Home Series:

Finding Faith (1)

Finding Cupid (2)

Finding Spring (3)

Finding Liberty (4)

Finding Holly (5)

Finding Home (6)

Finding Balance (7)

Finding Peace (8)

The Finding Home Series Boxset Books 1-3

The Finding Home Series Boxset Books 4-6

Children's Picture Book

Yuck! What's for Dinner?